Saudade
The Life and Death of Queen Maria Glória of Lusitania

Studies in Austrian Literature, Culture, and Thought

Translation Series

General Editors:

Jorun B. Johns
Richard H. Lawson

Gloria Kaiser

Saudade
The Life and Death of Queen
Maria Glória of Lusitania

Translated and with
an Afterword by
Lowell A. Bangerter

ARIADNE PRESS
Riverside, California

Acknowledgments

The author would especially like to thank:

Österreichisches Staatsarchiv, Vienna; The Library of Congress, Washington, D.C.
Haus- Hof- und Staatsarchiv, Vienna; *Biblioteca Nacional,* Rio de Janeiro
Biblioteca Nacional, Lisbon; *Biblioteca Garrett,* Porto; *Biblioteca Público,* Evora

The Pedro Gastão de Orléans e Bragança Family in Petrópolis,
Her Majesty, Maria de Orléans e Bragança in Rio de Janeiro,
Dom Carlos Tasso de Sachsen-Coburg e Bragança, Baden bei Wien.

Ariadne Press would like to express its appreciation to the Bundeskanzleramt –
Sektion Kunst, Vienna for assistance in publishing this book.

Translated from the German
Saudade. Leben und Sterben der Königin Maria-Glória von Lusitanien. 1819-1853
© 2003 Seifert Verlag, Wien

Cover Design:
Art Director, Designer: George McGinnis
Photos: With kind permission of Palácio Nacional de Ajuda

Copyright ©2005
by Ariadne Press
270 Goins Court
Riverside, CA 92507

All rights reserved.
No part of this publication may be reproduced or transmitted
in any form or by any means without formal permission.
Printed in the United States of America.
ISBN 1-57241-135-X
(trade paperback original)

.KUNST

CONTENTS

PROLOGUE • 5

CHAPTER I • 21
Maria Glória on November 14, 1853 • 28
"Lisbon, where the Tejo mixes with salty Neptune"

Maria Glória, Childhood in Rio de Janeiro • 33
"So that the splendor of the house branches out"

Graça • 56
"She is ready to accompany me at once"

Journey from Rio de Janeiro to Europe, 1831 • 58
"On such a long journey, with the pain of farewell but without joy"

CHAPTER II • 71
Maria Glória in Brest and London, 1831 • 72
"And destiny abducted her into a different world"

Maria Glória and Graça in Paris until 1833 • 82
"The world still lay wrapped in the light of dawn"

CHAPTER III • 112
Graça in Brest and in Porto, 1833-1835 • 113
"Tell us where the angry sea took you"

CHAPTER IV • 148
Graça and Abrão in Porto, 1835 and 1836 • 149
"The search for the stream guided me"

Maria Glória in Lisbon, 1833 and 1834 • 161
"Who could cleverly escape from the danger that lay in the machinations?"

Maria Glória, September 1834 • 172
"The years flee away, the summertime will soon be gone"

Maria Glória, Second Marriage
The Revolts Begin, 1836 • 193
"My flesh is transformed into hardened ground"

CHAPTER V • 220
Graça and Abrão in Porto, 1839 • 220
"For those mulberries that have decided in favor of love grow better"

Maria Glória, 1836-1845 • 226
"Bend down a bit, your Majesty, and show me the tender face where old age is already written"

Franz Liszt's Visit to Lisbon, August 1845 • 261
"He conquers sensual pleasure and craving"

Maria Glória 1845-1849 • 273
"Then my bones turned to stone"

Maria Glória 1849-1852 • 298
"Just because we accomplish nothing against deceitful guile with human judgment"

Graça, to November 1853
Maria Glória, to November 1853 • 309
"The torch bowed toward the ground and disappeared on the horizon"

AFTERWORD • 321

TRANSLATOR'S AFTERWORD • 328

CHRONOLOGY • 333

PROLOGUE

It is the hour when saudade *calls to us, and we are going to begin a journey through a landscape, through a landscape of the soul, and while doing so, we will lose no time with measurement, calculation, or reckoning. We are going to move out, follow the convolutions, and let ourselves be drawn until we have passed through centuries, two centuries, and have arrived at the point where a turn of the head suffices to look from one end of the world to the other. It is the westernmost land of Europe where we alight, Portugal, and from there we journey across the Atlantic Ocean. We let ourselves be carried by the language of Portugal, from Portugal to Brazil, and here as there we listen to the people, follow the music, the melody of their words. Some of our companions begin to translate, as though they could transfer words, glances, and embraces based on the standards of one landscape into the other, from one century into the other.*

We do not let the dictionary distract us or expel us from this landscape where we have just appeared, where we are going to make ourselves at home for a number of decades, for just as long as a human life lasts, for as long as a human life lasted back then, around 1820.

We have thrown our nets out a long way to draw the events onto land. We are sitting near the most westerly point in Europe, in Sintra, where the weather conditions change by the hour, where the snowflakes and ice crystals are chased across the dunes with the morning mists, where the blossoms of the paradise flowers wilt in the midday heat, and in the afternoon hours the hummingbirds flee before the force of the tropical rain. In the place where the sun still casts fiery images across the tiered forests only moments before it withdraws, and then, finally, night appears, the true mistress of this place. She calls upon ocean and forest and dunes to make the most of the hours of darkness, to whirl, to roar, and to moan. Mistress Night riles the animals and rouses their laments in whimpers and cries; she brushes her hands across blossoms, she opens and closes their calyxes; she shakes them off, and in passing she even com-

mands the wind to bed the petals down gently, on a stone, or in the sand. And it hovers in these mists, in the ice crystals, in the sheets of rain, and in the night: saudade. It will be our companion when we try to order the events.

Saudade, *a word that crosses only Lusitanian lips; we know that it is not unfamiliar to anyone, only, in other landscapes it usually wears a lighter cloak - yearning. Its Portuguese sister lies buried deeply within us; centuries have formed that island where* saudade *lives,* saudade *for a body, for contact, for congeniality of temperament,* saudade *for that spot of earth from which we have grown, for our homeland.*

Two blossoms from the Greco-Roman heritage have taken root in the Lusitanian disposition. Within it breathes the lost paradise, the wish to regain something, to see something again, and the pain caused by what is absent, the unattainable, the pain caused by want. Both blossoms are nourished by love for that pain, for that torment, a love that is intensified to the point of subjection. Saudade *bears Saturn and Mercury within its folds, joy and sadness, sweetness and bitterness.*

We could never live without saudade; *we need the memories that are full of sorrow, memories that we water with our tears so that they produce more and more blossoms.*

We also know of the strength that saudade *gives to us; our souls are kneaded and milled by it, and from generation to generation it has given us powers whose existence others do not suspect. We can order ourselves to go upward, downward, even away from this world.*

So let us go back, let us remember.

History, the inexorable master builder, often riles the waves into surf and casts the people who are in it onto the place where they are necessary in order to fulfill the destiny of a land, of a nation.

That is what happened in the year 1807.

The Portuguese king, João VI of Bragança, together with his family, his retainers, and his officials, fled from Napoleon. The sea power England granted the Portuguese ships protection and escort when they sailed into the Atlantic. In return, the English had reserved to themselves the right to install their officials in the customs offices in Lisbon and thus to share in the earnings of Portugal's trade. With that, the centuries-old conflict between the cultures of England and France took on an additional dimension. King João VI preferred to turn the administration of Portugal over to the English rather than bowing to the French.

Portugal, although a small country in Europe, was at that time an enormous empire in the world! Scattered over the entire globe, it possessed abundant colonial lands that would have been a refuge for the fleeing Portuguese royal family and its retinue. King João VI decided in favor of the largest, the richest colonial land, Brazil. An emigration program for several thousand Portuguese was organized, and after a crossing that lasted several months the project was actually completed, and the Portuguese royal court, the entire Portuguese government apparatus, was moved to Rio de Janeiro.

In 1807 Latin America was still viewed as a dark continent, and all that people knew about Brazil was that the blood-red hardwood, the precious stones, and the spices came from there. But Brazil was also regarded as the "Land of the Negroes and the monkeys," and actually, for Europeans all of Latin America was far away and interesting only for adventurers.

Thus Napoleon had not only roared across the European political landscape and brought everything that had been firmly established into turmoil, but his influence went far beyond Europe. For through the flight of the Portuguese king, Latin America and Brazil attained a different value in Europe. Was it possible to live in the European manner in Latin America? Could Brazil become an immigration land? For Europe those were new perspectives, and in the meantime Rio de Janeiro developed into an imperial city. Business began to flourish. Social life began to thrive. The theater, processions, and festivals attracted the people. All of Rio de Janeiro vibrated with color. Although daily life proceeded according to Euro-

pean conventions, the slaves, who assisted their masters and ladies in every way, fulfilling every wish and every desire, made possible a life of affluence, pleasure, and idleness. They lived lives that corresponded completely with the tropics, and in the tropics everything exceeds all normal bounds: hate, revenge, love, pleasure, the flowers, the fruits, the darkness of the jungle, the blue of the sky, the poison of the animals, and the force of the rain.

Thousands of European immigrants followed the Portuguese court. They came from the Netherlands, from Russia, from Germany, and entire colonies, among them many artists, came from France. Rio de Janeiro became more and more colorful, and both the city and the entire country of Brazil awakened. They became aware of themselves: an enormous land, as large as all of Europe, and yet subjugated and forced to colonial obedience. Initial critical voices made themselves heard. Why shouldn't they be able to govern themselves? Why should they continue to tolerate the idea that sugar cane, latex, precious stones, and wood could only be sold to Lisbon, and moreover at prices that were established by the motherland, by the colonial power, i.e., by Portugal. After the Portuguese king came to live in Rio de Janeiro, the Brazilians had to deal more and more with the English, for the English sat in Lisbon and managed Portugal as governors. With that the screw of exploitation had been tightened even more firmly, with Portugal dependent on England and Brazil dependent on Portugal and England.

After ten years, when Napoleon had been banished for a long time, and following the Vienna Congress, the old, comfortable order prevailed in Europe again and the Portuguese king began to put his house in order. He was happy in Rio de Janeiro. In Brazil he enjoyed all of the amenities of a colonial ruler, but he should have gone back to Lisbon long ago to send the English back home. On the other hand, it was not advisable for him to leave Brazil without installing a regent. During those ten years Brazil had become accustomed to having the government work take place within the country, and the Brazilians would never again have permitted themselves to be ruled by delegated colonial officials.

So it was a political necessity that his son Pedro be installed as regent, and in order that an alliance with a major European power might be secured at the same time, he was to be married. The choice was Austria; Chancellor Metternich and Emperor Franz I were not just agreeable, they were overjoyed. Marrying a daughter off to Brazil also meant sending an expedition of scientists and artists to Latin America, and with the results of that expedition Austria would enter the front ranks of Europe in all areas of science.

Leopoldina of Habsburg, Austria, and Pedro of Bragança, Portugal, were brought together in November of 1817 in Rio de Janeiro. The two royal scions were totally different, in temperament and education. The twenty-year-old Leopoldina was disciplined and reserved. Pedro, with his nineteen years, was exuberant and unbridled in both his outbursts of rage and his joyful raptures.

As a Habsburg, Leopoldina had been strictly trained. She came from an intact family in which life proceeded according to adamant rules, and she was extremely well prepared for her role as wife of the prince regent. Pedro, on the other hand, spoke only a little French and his Portuguese was vulgar. Hardly any of his teachers had been able to make him stay with the books. He was a bold rider, and he knew how to work with his hands. Above all, he had an artistic nature; he composed music. Passages that he wrote still remain in the Brazilian anthem even today.

During their marriage, which lasted for not quite ten years, Leopoldina did significant remedial education work with Pedro. She took care of correspondence and diplomatic reports for him, and she selected his closest advisors. Just how enduring and positive Leopoldina's influence on Pedro's character was can be seen in the last years of his life. Deliberately, persistently, and objectively, he finished his life's work and secured the Portuguese throne for his daughter Maria Glória.

But in the year 1817, when Leopoldina and Pedro were brought together, he was still totally the product of the Bragança family. As a nine-year-old child Pedro had moved with his family from Lisbon to Rio de Janeiro, and he had not known an orderly family life. Among the family members was his grandmother, Queen Maria I of Portugal. After the early death of her husband she had withdrawn into religious mania. Her cry, "The devil has gotten into me," was soon mimicked by the servants in Rio de Janeiro. Pedro's mother, Dona Carlota, a very proud Spanish woman, had never forgiven the marriage brokers for the fact that she, of all people, had been married off to the gluttonous Portuguese king, João. She was a nymphomaniac, and in Rio de Janeiro she became so involved in political intrigues against her husband, the king, that he turned her out of the palace and banished her to a city apartment in Rio de Janeiro. Pedro had loose contact with his sisters, but he lived in constant conflict with his brother Miguel, for Miguel was loyally devoted to their mother, to Dona Carlota. Pedro, on the other hand, was on his father's, on Dom João's side.

Thus for Pedro constant family conflict was normal. They had also granted him the freedoms of the "young gentlemen" at an early age, and as a thirteen and fourteen-year-old he was already experiencing colonial immorality in all its dimensions. He bought himself as many female slaves as he wanted for his sexual adventures. He organized riding tournaments that he was permitted to win. He associated with European families in which baseless snobbism prevailed. Back then in Rio it was considered chic to have velvet and brocade delivered from Europe. They decorated their living space with it, and when the tropical humidity caused mildew to grow on the fabrics and the plush furniture, they sent the drapes and the armchairs to Paris by ship for cleaning.

Leopoldina, Dona Leopoldina, was the first to stop this excessive nonsense in Boa Vista, in the house where the Braganças lived. That seedy building never earned the designation: palace. She had the vermin-infested tapestries removed and had the walls whitewashed. While Leopoldina maintained the household, there were no carpets and plush furniture in Boa Vista. Rather, they lived as one must live in the tropics: with stone on the floors, with wooden furniture set with wooden latticework for ventilation, with windows lacking curtains.

Dona Leopoldina also stopped wearing bodices and velvet dresses in the tropical temperatures, and she stopped having herself carried to church in a sedan chair as the ladies of Rio's high society did. Dona Leopoldina received even high officials in a comfortable linen dress, beneath which she wore no corset; and she rode by herself. Several times a week she rode the long distance from São Cristóvão to her favorite church, the Church of Saint Glória.

In spite of their totally antithetical education, training, and way of life, this arranged marriage of Leopoldina and Pedro became, at least in the early years, a good marriage. Six children were born. First came Maria Glória in the year 1819. Then João Carlos, who died in 1822, at the age of two, during their flight from the revolutionaries. With that, the curse that a Franciscan monk had uttered against the Bragança family in 1740, after he had been refused alms, was fulfilled once more with terrible consistency: no firstborn son would remain alive.

Eventually the other daughters, Januária, Paula Mariana, and Francisca, came into the world, and finally, in the year 1825, the heir to the throne, Pedro.

Obviously, a woman like Dona Leopoldina, who was so disciplined and restrained, could not bridle her husband Pedro's temperament, and after several affairs he involved himself in an alliance with his mistress, Domitila de Castro Canto, an alliance that cast him into such dependency that he was only able to free himself from it after the death of Dona Leopoldina.

In ten years Leopoldina and Pedro were drawn at breakneck speed through the political events in Brazil. Rebellious representatives of the people constantly stirred up revolutions against the prince regent Pedro. The northern, at that time wealthy, regions of Bahia and Pernambuco wanted to break away and, in so doing, initiate a territorial splintering of the enormous country. The gem regions Minas Gerais and Goias were also striving for independence and sovereignty. In the most important harbor city of São Paulo lived many liberals who were influenced by the Freemasons and no longer wanted to bow to a monarchist administration, but demanded their own constitution and special status for their city. For that reason, Pedro crisscrossed the country with his soldiers to win the trust of the Brazilians, and he was successful everywhere. With his charisma he was even able to convince the proud citizens of São Paulo. The territorial greatness of this immeasurably rich land could never be allowed to destroy itself. Brazil could never be permitted to divide itself up into small states. The only guarantee for warding off all the political intrigues that were being stirred up by the Portuguese motherland was the maintenance of the monarchical administration, and especially the presence of Pedro and Leopoldina in Brazil.

In September of 1822 both the private and political events in the lives of Pedro and Leopoldina reached their climax. Pedro, the prince regent, was in São Paulo with his soldiers, a day's ride distant from Rio de Janeiro. For the weeks of his absence Leopoldina had been installed as regent, and during those very days the revolts and unrest in the capital city became so critical that Leopoldina immediately called the state council into session. There was nothing further to negotiate. The subjugation by Portugal had to end, and Dona Leopoldina signed the resolution: As of September 2, 1822 Brazil was an independent state, an autonomous empire.

The mantle of history had floated past Leopoldina and she had seized it. For a Habsburg daughter who had been trained to be obedient, she had committed a reckless act, for an independent Brazil was only possible on the basis of a constitution. And in Austria, in the year 1822, they were still far removed from the principle, "...that the rights of all people are the same."

In October of 1822, Pedro and Leopoldina swore their oaths as emperor and empress of Brazil based on the country's first constitution, an enormous provocation for Europe, for Pedro, like Napoleon, was regarded as an emperor who had been chosen by the people and was not installed "by the grace of God."

Emperor Franz I reacted to this disobedience, to this highhandedness of his daughter, with silence. For two years Leopoldina *received no letter, no message from her father. It was an especially severe sanction. Normally mail from Europe to Rio de Janeiro took five or six months, and Leopoldina trembled in anticipation of every letter from her siblings, from her father. She often rode to the harbor herself to meet the English mail ship, and when she was left without news from her family, she was usually thrown into despair and melancholy for days.*

The fact that her father denied her a few lines for two years meant that they had resigned themselves to it in Vienna: Leopoldina would never return. She would remain in Brazil until the end of her life; she would have to.

In Vienna they had quickly taken note of that fact. After all, they had also gotten over the fate of Marie Antoinette. Leopoldina only gradually understood the sacrifice with which she had burdened herself. With her courage to place her signature on the declaration of independence, she had avoided bloodshed and additional revolutions. At the age of twenty-five she was honored by the Brazilians as "our mother - nossa mãe*," but she would never see Europe or her family again.* Saudade *began to work on Leopoldina's soul; Leopoldina threw herself into her duties. She undertook daylong rides into the environs of Rio. She took refuge in prayer. She wrote letters of many pages to her sister Marie Louise. And slowly, month by month,* saudade *became the companion of her soul, a companion whose pain was no longer foreign to her but enabled her to draw strength from the unknown depths of her soul, enough strength that she could order herself to do things. Leopoldina felt and knew as years went by, that she could order herself both to endure and to let go. The person Leopoldina, her character, had taken on an additional color, and she also wrote to Vienna, a year before her death, as a twenty-nine-year-old: "...with regard to me, honored Papa, you can be sure that I will always remain a Brazilian with all my heart."*

Pedro had experienced, had assimilated the September days of the year 1822 in a much different way. Five days after Leopoldina had written her signature, that news reached him on the Ipiranga

River near São Paulo, and completely true to his nature, with a theatrical gesture he tore the cords from his Portuguese uniform and shouted the famous words: "Independence or death!"

With that, destiny had carried Leopoldina and Pedro to the climax of their political work, and for days everything strange that they previously had not overcome, that they not outlived in each other during all the years, was almost forgotten.

But this surge of nearness only lasted for a few hours, only for a day or two. Then Pedro was again thrown into his saudade for a Brazilian woman, for a passion-filled woman who thought and felt as he did, for a female human being in whom he found himself again. In the September days of 1822, Pedro became acquainted with the woman Domitila, whom he brought to Rio de Janeiro as his mistress, and who gradually destroyed the family life of Pedro and Leopoldina, then Leopoldina herself, and finally Pedro's political work.

They were elevated to the greatest heights in their political efforts, and cast down into the deepest humiliations and into familial catastrophe. Fate had weighed well; it had demanded tribute, for neither of them, Pedro nor Leopoldina, was destined for a life that rippled indifferently along.

Now that the two mortals had fulfilled their task, history, the master builder, withdrew the breaking surf.

For Brazil, a new era began in 1822; colonial bondage had finally ended. "I'm a Brazilian" was the fashionable greeting at the time. Brazilian identity was able to develop, and these political realities had to be lived, exemplified.

Pedro, Leopoldina's youngest son, became Pedro II, Emperor of Brazil, and during the five decades of his regency until 1889, he led the young, independent state to self-awareness, progress, and stability.

Portugal, on the other hand, had grown one enormous colony

poorer, and that meant not only economic losses and financial dependency. Above all it meant the loss of respect in the world, in Europe, and it also meant that the Portuguese surrendered to saudade *and that the country began to wither.*

Portugal had negotiated to obtain the firstborn daughter, Maria Glória as queen. She was to be raised as the symbol for a new, young Portugal and be sent to Lisbon after her fourteenth birthday.

When Dona Leopoldina died in December of 1826, she was not quite thirty years old, and the five children remained behind as semiorphans: Maria Glória at eight years old, Januária was five years old, Paula Mariana four, Francisca three, and Pedro, the heir to the throne, was one year old. For the firstborn daughter and for the heir to the throne the educational goals were established. Of their three sisters, Paula Mariana died at the age of ten, while Januária was married off to Sicily and Francisca to France.

For the little girls and for little Pedro the loss of Dona Leopoldina was certainly a shock. Their mother, her talk, her songs, and her smell were suddenly no longer present. But Januária, Francisca, and Paula Mariana were quickly turned over to a governess, the kind Dona Dadama, and the pain at the absence of their mother could be pushed aside in the rigidly organized daily routine.

Little Pedro received the wise José Bonifácio de Andrade for his teacher, a man of more than sixty years who had greatly adored Leopoldina. "A minha princesa," he had written to her, and in letters Leopoldina had called Bonifácio "the hothead with the white hair." Thus little Pedro found in Bonifácio not only the best teacher, but Bonifácio brought to realization in this boy the educational principles that Dona Leopoldina had written down for her son during the last days of her life: "...so that our son Pedro might receive the same degree of strictness as of love; instill within him my loathing toward everything warlike and destructive. Any humiliation is minor compared to the agonies of a war..."

For Maria Glória the death of her mother was a salient turning point. With her eight years she had long since become mature enough to guess the extent of the catastrophe that Dona Leopoldina's death caused. As the oldest of the siblings she felt responsible for them, and she often instinctively slipped into the role of mother, especially when she wanted to protect her sisters or her little brother from all too strict educational measures. At the same time, she was separated from her siblings by her own daily schedule. She received a new governess. Her history lessons were different than they had previously been. It was no longer Brazil, but Portugal, that became the focus of her studies.

At the same time, she sensed and registered the changes in Boa Vista. For two years her father did not find a second wife. According to the family rules, a noblewoman, a princess had to be found, and such a person existed only in Europe, and from each European noble house the ambassadors brought a "No." When a "Yes" finally came from the house of Leuchtenberg-Beauharnais, and the seventeen-year-old Amelia moved to Rio de Janeiro as Dona Amelia, everyone was relieved. Amelia had been educated in the best manner. She was extremely beautiful, but she was only seven years older than Maria Glória. Was she to be a friend or a mother to the firstborn daughter?

Ambitiously Dona Amelia had made up her mind to become empress, "even if it was in the jungle." But she was only briefly empress in Brazil, for soon after her arrival the political situation began to turn against her husband, Dom Pedro. He had been too late in sending his mistress away from Rio de Janeiro. Above all, after the death of Leopoldina it had become known how she had suffered at his side.

"For four years now I have found myself in a state of terrible slavery because of a seductive monster. I also have to explain that I had to incur debts. I ask you to take care of having my debts paid," was what Dona Leopoldina wrote to her sister Marie Louise in Europe a few days before her death.

The Brazilians, who had cheered their emperor in the year 1822, now, in 1830, showed him their contempt. The entire Bragança family, even the children, experienced ridicule and scorn.

At the age of twelve, Maria Glória noticed everything. With her mother apparently everything calculable, everything that was secure had gone away. She became quieter and more obedient, and for her it still seemed unimaginable, or at least very far away, that she would ever leave Rio de Janeiro, that she would ever live anywhere but in the tropics. They had pounded books full of knowledge about the land of her destiny into her head, but Portugal was infinitely far away for her.

What kind of a country was Portugal? In what kind of a country was she to be placed?

This western region of Europe was tried and formed by history like hardly any other. Again and again Portuguese culture was harried, but all of the actions only hardened the culture and the language and in so doing defined it even more clearly.

First it was ruled by the Romans. They called the Roman province on the Iberian Peninsula Lusitania. Then Arabian Muslims took possession of it. After almost three hundred years it was liberated from Islam by the noble house of Castile-Leon, and around 1500, through the voyages of discovery and conquest, it was drawn into the focal point of European interest under Manuel von Avis (Emanuel I). The Portuguese world empire seemed endless. They had settled in Latin America, in Brazil. In China they had established the first European settlement, Macao, and the Portuguese flag waved over both East and West Africa.

The Portuguese felt a self-awareness that they had never known before. That development can be seen in the Emanuelistic architectural style, with its decorative elements, the intricately entwined pillars, seashells, and exotic plants. In this heyday of architecture and literature, with Luís de Camões the new self-awareness intensified almost to an awareness of a divine mission. Were they a chosen people? With the young King Sebastian, in 1578 they wanted to expand their empire; they wanted to expand Portugal to Morocco. For years the people from all walks of life employed money and work to equip the young hero and his soldiers in the best possible fashion.

But the victory over Morocco did not come. Moreover, their hero Sebastian vanished. For the Portuguese, all that remained was the wish, the belief that he would return, the belief in the return of the heyday of the Portuguese world empire, and that wish, that saudade *intensified into an additional, unmistakable Portuguese character trait, Sebastianism.*

During this period of emergence, the pride of the Portuguese was inseparably tied to their devotion to the Catholic religion. That fact is exemplified in the life of the Jesuit father António Vieira. In 1620, as an eight-year-old child he had come with his parents from Lisbon to Salvador, Brazil, and at the age of fifteen, when his heart was stirred up by the storms and passions of puberty, he pleaded with the Mother of God for reason, for ratio. *He asked the Heavens to transform his emotional turmoil into patience and perseverance in his studies and into the gift of formulation, and he felt that his prayer was heard. For soon afterward he withdrew from his family union, entered the Jesuit school in Salvador, and was noted there for his especially sharp power of reason. In a short time he developed into a preacher who was equally admired and feared.*

From 1640 to 1680 Vieira traveled from Salvador to Lisbon three times under unimaginably strained conditions. He became a diplomat in the service of the Portuguese king. His vision was the unification of Europe under the guidance of Portuguese culture and language. Vieira took the liberty of castigating Portuguese exploitation of slaves from the pulpit. He demanded that the expelled Jews be brought back, and only Coimbra's Inquisition silenced this free spirit by banishing him to Rome for several years. There he formulated and polished his defense statement.

At that time, Queen Christina of Sweden, who had converted to the Catholic faith, was also living in Rome. She was fascinated by Vieira's charismatic, almost demonic personality, and she won him as her preacher and confidant. In the letters that Vieira wrote to Christina we can see the tension-laden relationship between two unusual people.

With his polished formulations and fastidiously placed words,

Vieira influenced the Portuguese language quite significantly. He is regarded as the "imperador da lingua portuguesa [emperor of the Portuguese language]." Even today his sermons are read as aids for living; they are discussed and interpreted. António Vieira is an example of the self-aware cosmopolitanism that was experienced around 1680 in the Lusitanian cultural sphere.

The phase of this self-awareness endured only briefly in the history of Portugal, for Portugal was again soon placed step by step in the status that it was always in: the westernmost province of Europe, a region on the edge, occasionally even jointly governed by the Spaniards.

Under Napoleon, Portugal became the bone of contention between France and England. As we know, England emerged as the victor. All of the goods from the colonial lands first had to be delivered to the homeport of Lisbon. The English were there, and they determined the prices and conditions for resale. What a disgrace for Portugal, for a land that had viewed itself as a world empire. What humiliation for a country that had, through its courage, through its firmness in the Catholic faith, prevented the Muslims from spreading across all of Europe. Europe did not give Portugal credit for having pushed the Muslims from the European continent with its resistance.

It is for this land, for Portugal, that Maria Glória is destined. It is there that she must carry out her life's work, and she does not have to do that unaccompanied. Graça, the slave girl, experiences for her the part of Portugal that remains closed to Maria Glória. Graça experiences things from the bottom to the top, and when they see each other again in Sintra, the two women pour out their lives.

We have thrown out our net from the westernmost point of Europe to Brazil, and we are going to draw the years from 1820 to 1853 on shore. We are going to follow the saudade. Many a fragment does not join itself immediately and seamlessly to the next. Then we will wait for the next wave of the narrative. It will illuminate what was previously said until it fits. Each fragment is a whole *in its own right, and at the same time a part of the whole, and not until the end will we feel how much was kept secret. Then we will withdraw to the island of* saudade, *knowing that there nothing and nobody dies. There they are in good hands, the characters, the events, important ones, unimportant ones, bitter and sweet ones, all of which wear the color of farewell. No power can reach out to take that island. There we are always taken in, and when we almost drown in our tears, when pain chokes us or a disappointment throws us to the ground,* saudade *catches us, rocks us, and gives us our peace of mind again.*

Let us draw in the net and follow the stories -

CHAPTER I

*Just what tremendous act of Providence
was it that brought you on this journey now,
to dare to travel on seas ne'er plied before
to realms that lay on some far distant shore?*

They say Vieira exceeds Mercury in speed and sharpness when proclaiming his opinion: *"...they reported to me that you fell. They tried every means to inform me of it. The guard murmured it casually while he shoved my morning soup into the cell, and they told me directly, in that they drilled a sentence into the messenger who delivers the rolls of paper to me. And they chose the most obtrusive way to communicate important things to me about you, Christina: Brother Francesco included a plea for your recovery in the liturgy! Christina! Even if you drive the soldiers of the pope's guard clear across Rome to me in a torchlight procession, I shall not come, not let myself be interrupted in my work, in formulating, in polishing the words that should free me from my punishment. Do not forget that Grand Inquisitor António da Silva forbade me, the preacher, to speak, on pain of death. Actually I would not be permitted to write either, especially not my defense statement, but then the writing ban seemed too bold to my judges in Coimbra after all. It is better to give the persecuted man the sheets of paper, so that no word, no thought from me is lost to my persecutors. They could ruminate on what was thought about, prepared in writing, and with a few linguistic flicks of the wrist give it out as their speech, those narrow-minded men, whose minds are soggy from too much olive oil and the excess of wine. Christina, time is driving me, and I do not have half a day, not even an hour for conversation, for discussion. Do not moan that you must now drag yourself painfully from your bed to the chair. You should rid yourself of that haste and rashness that threw you down the steps, and once and for all you should recognize that our conversations remain interrupted, broken off. We talked with mind and soul and body, we spoke in all dialects and with all of our extremities and understood each other's words and expressions. I sensed nothing of the virginity mania of the Queen of Sweden. At the age of twenty-eight you ordered yourself to live in celibacy, but with your conversion to Catholicism the passion within you did not dwindle. They say you are hot and dry. But your body does not always obey you. Does it refuse to obey you in order not to release you from the martyrdom of self-punishment? Christina, I reproach you! Do you let carelessness into your soul? When you fast, do you think only about your intestines and not about the abyss within you that you have to starve out?*

"*My reproach goes one more step further: With your letter you reach into the innermost part of me, you reach for my language, tear a piece out of it, a word itself - you write of* saudade!

"*Do not take this jewel of a word into your mouth. Saudade, that is the fragile element in the soul of the Lusitanians, the dark thing, the heavy thing in our Lusitanian veins. No matter how much you move from French into Latin and on into Greek and Hebrew, our* saudade *will remain closed to you. It is our longing for a dream that has already corroded our nature for centuries: as the westernmost province of Europe, not to be regarded also as the most unimportant province. Just who were, who are we? What were, what are we regarded as in Europe? Dictated for a long time by Islam, and later by the Spaniards, then sent to Asia by the Dutch to conquer the Spice Islands for them.*

"*When King Manoel looked into the ocean from Sintra 170 years ago, in November of 1500, and longed feverishly for Cabral,* saudade *had filled his soul and his spirit so completely that he stayed on that mountain for three times seven days. He perceived neither the wind, nor the sun, nor the darkness. No sleep, no exhaustion drew him down, until he finally saw the blue and white sails of Cabral's ships. Cabral conquered an additional empire for us Lusitanians, Brazil! Did the* saudade *now grow less? No, it increased. It ran down the entire country, clear to Minho in the north, and in the south into the valleys of Alentejo and on to the coast of Algarve.*

"*It is also* saudade *that drives me back, back to where all people suffer from the same wound in their heart. With the language it has* wandered across continents, and I have inhaled the air of both, Portugal and Brazil. So as soon as I have finished writing the pages of my defense speech, I shall run to the nearest ship, tear the monk's habit from my body, and in sailor's clothes work with ropes and sails until blood seeps from my fingers and hands and the salt of the ocean eats into the wounds. And when, after three or four months, the scabs turn into scars, the bay of Bahia will be visible, and the saudade will have lost all the bitterness that it absorbed abroad. It will have become a relief, and I will be able to cast it over me with my habit.

"Christina, now I want to level one final reproach at you: You think that with worship and discussion you do enough for the formation and maturation of spirit and soul. You are in error! I find the attributes of 'duty' and 'obligation' missing when I observe your conduct here in Rome. To become matted in intrigues, to give up the power of the 'Queen of Sweden' and then later to want to buy the office of the 'Queen of Naples' with jewels. How petty and disgusting, what a waste of strength and time!

"Enough! For one who has been forbidden to speak, with this letter I have opened my mouth far enough. I send you my blessing and a chaste embrace, António. Rome, on the sixteenth of May 1669."

The words of this letter unreel in Maria Glória to the beat of her riding. For her Portuguese lesson, Father ordered Master Queiroz to read the sermons of António Vieira with her.

"Those are ancient texts," she had wailed, "almost two hundred years old!"

Her father could not be dissuaded: "Here in Paris you hardly have any opportunity to speak Portuguese, and you can only learn the grammar from Vieira."

In the end Master Queiroz not only read the sermons with her; as early as the second week he gave her a book in which letters from Vieira were printed, letters that he had written in Rome, letters to Queen Christina of Sweden: "...*the last day of June 1668, last night did bring our bodies together and tear them away from loneliness, but never, never will I release my spirit from loneliness, because it is my destiny to wander alone...*"

At that time, Leonora would never have been permitted to learn that Maria Glória was reading the letters of this "devil's priest," or that she memorized some passages word for word in order to tell Clementine about them.

"Imagine, when she was warming her legs at the fire in the fireplace, he saw that her thighs were dirty! He wrote to her: '*Christina, who will place his hand on unwashed skin?*' At the time, the two of them were already so old; he was over sixty and she over forty!"

Neither her father nor her mother had reached that age. Had *Mamãe*, Dona Leopoldina, been familiar with António Vieira?

Yes. Maria Glória had once overheard a conversation.

"Here, Dadama, here is the entire indictment of the exploitation, the thieves' union," *Mamãe* whispered to Dadama and immediately stowed the Vieira book in the laundry drawer.

"Dona Leopoldina," the governess crossed herself, "don't talk about it. Otherwise there will be revolution here in Rio tomorrow! So many Portuguese live here, and that Vieira, the way he ranted about the colonial situation with his polished words. As if the Portuguese in Brazil had only stolen and exploited. That's not right. We Portuguese brought our culture to Brazil, our magnificent baroque churches. And how many Portuguese were ruined when they struggled with clearing the land and starting their farms?" Dadama could hardly control herself: "I'm Portuguese, too, Dona Leopoldina!"

Mamãe tried to give in: "But of course, and just as you remained in Brazil, even when it was no longer a Portuguese colony, so did many Portuguese, and it's a good thing. Dadama, today even you greet people the same way all the rest of us do: 'I am a Brazilian!'"

But Dadama was not yet finished with her rejection of Vieira: "Vieira wanted to destroy the Inquisition. At least they forbade him to preach."

"The fact that he denounced slavery did not mean that Vieira attacked the Inquisition." *Mamãe* shook her head. "Vieira spoke up for the Jews! He wanted them to bring the expelled Jews back to Portugal. That is why he was banished to Rome."

"Rome!" Something had also occurred to dear Dadama about that: "There he lived for weeks under the same roof with Queen Christina of Sweden, a scandal! She was androgynous. Yes, I read that somewhere," she said excitedly.

Mamãe had to laugh about that: "I interpreted that differently. Christina was an educated woman, and she was quite lonely in Rome. That's why Vieira became her preacher."

Dadama shrugged her shoulders: "Another way to look at it. But I beg you, Dona Leopoldina, hide the book."

"I won't hide it. I'll keep it in a safe place, and in a few years our children will discuss Vieira's writings in the Portuguese class."

With that the discussion was closed for *Mamãe*.

Thieves' union, a priest and Queen Christina!

Maria Glória wanted to read about that. She had looked for the book, but had not found it, and back then there was no time to think about it further.

Mamãe had died in December of 1826. She had not even reached thirty years of age.

"I would like to close my eyes, place my finger on my lips, no longer have the desire to see, no longer have the desire to speak. Can you order yourself to die?" Maria Glória had written that in her diary.

With the death of *Mamãe*, almost everything in *Boa Vista* had changed. New servants and different teachers came. Isabel, their half sister, now came only to visit. In his workroom, Father shouted and raged at diplomats and officials. Brazil had become one region smaller, for Father and his soldiers had lost a war. "The southernmost region, Cisplatina, no longer belongs to Brazil. It is now called Uruguay and is a separate state." That was the sentence that had recently been drilled into them in civics class.

With the death of *Mamãe*, Dona Leopoldina, everything foreseeable had been shoved into the room where her picture hung, the picture of Dona Leopoldina, beneath it the white Richelieu tablecloth with the constantly burning candle on it. In that room, in that room alone nothing had changed in *Boa Vista*. You could flee into that room and there you were safe from all actions, you were safe from gossip, from orders, from outcries.

With the death of *Mamãe* everything had changed, especially for her, for Maria Glória. Up to her seventh year she had been a child, a girl, someone who was growing up. Now the period of adulthood began for her.

"Control yourself. You are the oldest. If you sob, the little ones will never quit crying."

"Maria Glória, I can't spare you this reproach: You show that you're afraid! How can your siblings feel safe if you show fear? You're responsible for them!"

"Give Paula Mariana the doll. You won't be playing with dolls anymore anyway."

She was tossed back and forth between the pride of being regarded as grown up and the pain at being excluded from the children's ranks of her siblings.

"Everything around me has grown dark. I do not belong anywhere, am completely alone, and I cannot speak about it to anyone. Nor can I write it in my diary, for if anyone were to read it, they would bawl me out. '*Mais dignidade*,' - more dignity, they say that to me a hundred times a day. I am not supposed to behave like a child anymore, but to be a model for my little siblings in everything. *Mamãe*, help me to find my way in adulthood more quickly," was what she prayed, and she often added, "or let me die."

The death of *Mamãe* also became for Maria Glória the break in her chronology. She divided almost all of her memories into "before December of 1826" and "after December of 1826."

Many of her memories of the years until 1831 are wrapped in mist. Even now, more than two decades later, only the voices of her siblings cannot be pushed out of her memory: the sobbing of Januária because she had to speak only English for two weeks as punishment for secretly eating coconut sauce; Francisca's singing while sitting as model for the portrait painter; Francisca was called *"mana chica"* - she was really a "wonderfully beautiful sister." Maria Glória also hears the droning recitation of Paula Mariana. The six-year-old told herself over and over again the story of Judas Thaddeus, whom they had so often confused with Judas Iscariot. Intermingled with it was the soft weeping of the towhead Pedrinho: "I want to sleep in Maria Glória's bed."

First the death of *Mamãe,* then the endlessness of five years, and finally Paris, where she waited to travel on to Lisbon at last. In Paris she received her first lesson about António Vieira from Master Queiroz: "We will start with the sermon about the fish: '*The fish have two virtues: they listen and do not speak! You are going to practice that. Are the fish a special species?" Yes! When the flood covered the world, Noah took two of each animal. Which ones saved themselves? The fish!*' Maria Glória, we will discuss the sermons until they become for you a golden thread around which you wind your knowledge and your decisions."

At the age of twelve years, she sensed clarity, order, and certainty in the words of the sermon, all of which were conditions that existed before December of 1826. For not until Paris did the ability to see everything at a glance become part of her daily routine again, and although she had resisted the lessons about Vieira very strongly in the beginning, his words, his sentences had soon become as important as the ordering of the day's events in her diary: "*Words must be like stars, clear and sublime for everyone. The farmer finds in the stars pointers for his work, the seaman for navigation, and the mathematician for his science - that is how words must be.*"

António Vieira accompanied her all those years; the two books with his sermons were also among the first volumes that Maria Glória ordered for the royal library in Lisbon.

"Those are copies," Alexander Herculano had said, shaking his head. "In reality all of the sermons and letters are contained in one single volume, but nobody knows who possesses the original with his handwriting. It is claimed that he wrote with dark red ink, and that the power that was exuded by his handwriting would not let go of the eyes. The person who caught sight of those words had to read and read."

Maria Glória on November 14, 1853
"Lisbon, where the Tejo mixes with salty Neptune"

Just a few more turns of the road, then she will have reached the gate to the Pena dairy. She will walk for the last half hour to the tower, followed closely by Jonas, her groom. Some say that Jonas is deaf and dumb; they say it because he lives so completely removed from everything that happens outside of his daily routine. Jonas hears and sees everything, and he also speaks, to his horses and mules; only he hardly speaks to people.

He had shaken his head when she told him that she wanted to ride to Sintra, up to the castle.

"In your condition, and in this weather?"

He did not say it; he looked, gesticulated it, and got Chili, her horse.

November fog rolls up into the mountains from the Tejo to Sintra.

Today the patches of fog sweep across the city. A foggy day like this brings good business to the women who make lace on the church squares. They will tell their stories again and let themselves be paid for them, with coins, wine kegs, a ball of silk, with two or three sacks of sea salt.

"They drag themselves, they march in the fog! On the day before the great earthquake, on November 1, 1755, the fogbanks had fallen so heavily on Lisbon that even at the time of the midday bells it was not light enough for people to find their way to the church without oil lamps. Entire processions of the souls that have gone before us pressed their way through the narrow streets, and each of those souls sought for another one, one that would relieve it of its wandering, relieve it of its searching, of its poking around in every corner of the city, in every garden and backyard, relieve it from reconnoitering in the barracks at the harbor. They were exhausted from looking through every boat locker, from pushing and pulling at the stacked eucalyptus logs. They were tired of shaking wine barrels and forcing themselves between the cork slabs. They wanted to find him at last, our King Sebastian! But they did not find him. So all that was left to them after more than two hundred years was to burrow through the earth. What was deepest had to be thrown to the top, and although they had never been unified since the calamitous year of 1578 - for as the decades passed, among the souls there were many who had stopped searching, who had preferred to disappear into damnation - on this November 1, 1755 they had formed themselves into a closed procession: Sebastian had to be found; not one more sunrise should appear over Lisbon without the most noble dead man of this city being found, perhaps under a bark at the harbor, perhaps covered by layers of ashes behind the blacksmith's forge, or under the mulberry tree in front of the *Necessidade Palace*. They pressed through the city so closely packed together that the carriages could not be steered across them. The horses reared, stumbled, although no stone and no gutter hindered their trotting. 'The fog is driving the animals crazy,' screamed the people, and they ran back into their hovels and houses. They ran to the church, to the cloister, just to speak a quick prayer that this gloom would pass. They did not find the body of our king, not then, not to this day. At the age of twenty-four years, the Muslims took him prisoner. The god Chronos raged in that year of 1578 and took everything from us. King Sebastian was our hope, our future; Sebastian, Sebastianism, those were the next centuries of Portugal. Hadn't all the people, from the north to the south, given their last money, so that he received the best teachers, the best educators? They drove their cattle and sheep to the nearest monasteries and gave their pottery and their grain, and they dragged wood to the harbor at Porto. Those who had nothing gave their labor in the quarries and in shipbuilding. After the conquests in Latin America, he had been prophesied to us. Five decades after Cabral, 'He' is born, the one who liberates us from the Muslims at last, who sails across the oceans for us, who carries our language out into the world, who brings us high standing in the world, and wealth. But they took him prisoner and did not set him free again; they wanted to have one like our Sebastian. They had infiltrated their traitors into our uniform shops; they could easily be recognized by the way the iron armor was engraved, by the stamp in the leather of their sleeves. We must not despair because of it. Sebastian is not dead; Sebastian will return, in a different uniform, perhaps not with straight hair, but with dark curls. It may be that the color of his eyes has also changed with the decades. How heavily do such superficialities weigh? Only his return counts, and that event will come. On the foggy days we feel plainly how near him the souls already are. Don't the wandering souls, in their search for Sebastian, scare forgotten people, people who have gone on before us, out of the corners of the memories of each one of us? If we resist getting involved with them, inviting them to converse with us, how much heavier will the longing, the *saudade* for what is past, for Sebastian, weigh upon our senses? It is already November 1853; his 300th birthday is near. His powers are growing stronger; they leave nobody untouched, and on the 20th of January 1854 he will send a sign to each one of us. - Perhaps that venerable society lady, who prayed and wept in the chapel with her chambermaid for three quarters of an hour, wants to know which of the souls that have gone before her could help her in her need. Let her sit down with me and take these spools of silk in her hands, and I will separate the singing of the souls from the patches of fog and speak to her in our words. The man there with the leather apron and the other one in the black scholar's cloak, they stand here and smile, contemptuous, unbelieving. Noble Sir, ride down to the tower of Belem. Don't harass your horses too much to sweep over the poor, searching souls. Then climb up the tower, and up there you will sense him, you will feel that Sebastian leans against the merlons and looks toward the morning sun and toward the south. He is looking over at the other end of our language. When you climb down the stairs, feel relieved. No, not because Sebastian has taken some of your distress, your anguish from you; he has given you part of his dream, and since his disappearance, since the fourth of August 1578, his dream has been our dream: to hold this continent, Europe, in our hand, to be able to determine what happens tomorrow on our continent, to give direction at last to everything that is unstable, our direction! Just go, Milord. I'll continue to let Sebastian speak through me. Go and seek him, and teach your children Sebastianism."

Maria Glória has been living in Lisbon for twenty years, and there were periods of time, and they recurred, in which she longed so intensively to return, that in the middle of a conversation she stood up and looked out the window. Wasn't that the afternoon hour when a hummingbird was buzzing from calla lily to canna, the little black bird that Maria Glória was able to lure to the windowsill with a whispered "ziwips"? She fled into the darkened workroom when the midday sultriness of an August day swallowed all the sounds in front of *Necessidade Palace*. In front of the window of her child's room in *Boa Vista* the fruit swayed on the mango tree, and on the tree's aerial roots sat a kitchen maid. She laughed, promised, and finally walked with the boy to the hut.

Sometimes Maria Glória felt close to Rio, very close. She could swing herself up onto the horse and ride to the Santana fountain, and have the shells thrown for her: nine, a lucky number! Then she would go to Marcia, the cook, and watch her roast the coffee beans, see how she threw them into the air, smelled the beans, and let the coffee oil drip hissing into the palm of Maria Glória's hand - "That will give you a very fine skin!"

Rio de Janeiro was so obviously present for her. She closed her eyes, took a deep breath, and smelled the fresh corn pancakes; and as if strengthened by the smell, she smiled and continued to work.

Lisbon, Portugal, Europe had been drilled into her. That was what she was being trained for. She forced herself to it, but it was tough. *Saudade* choked her and again and again she needed a few breaths of Brazil.

Whenever *saudade* gnawed at her too much, she wrapped the black woolen scarf around her shoulders and rode to the lace makers.

"Maria Glória, these women also read the future. It's said that they can decipher our aura," Leonora reminded her, and each time she was disappointed when Maria Glória answered, "The future, no, I like to listen to the women, that's all."

When she sat with the lace makers for an hour, on a basket or a wooden stool, when she heard the never-changing story of the missing King Sebastian, patience, even tolerance expanded within her. Everyday things had to be taken care of, duties carried out, responsibilities discharged.

She had to discuss Almeida Faria's plans for the construction of the seaman's school; talk to the widows of the quarry workers: "It's that Eugenio, he's the foreman, and from week to week he demands more and larger blocks of stone. He has most of the stones brought to the harbor and sells them to be sent to England! Only a small portion of the stones remains for our streets. My Roberto was killed because he couldn't run away fast enough. He was too exhausted. He stumbled over the ropes."

Negotiate with Manoel and Mario Diretinho, the two officials who are brothers, one last time. For a year they stalled Maria Glória in connection with the lease contract for the monastery. "Senhor Fereira is Alentejo's largest landowner. He leaves enormous fields lying fallow and does not want to lease them to the monastery, although he knows that here in Lisbon the people are starving! There's a shortage of grain, of potatoes, of honey. All that has been in short supply for years!" The brothers were slippery around her. They talked about clauses concerning the length of the lease; they demanded from her, from Queen Maria II personally, a surety bond, and she had signed. She would have signed almost anything, if only the pantries of the monasteries were filled again and the people had something to eat. "The greatest plague in Lisbon is the beggars."

Was she surrounded only by enemies? Couldn't she trust anyone? Weren't the teachers whom they pushed off on her for her children also teachers who knew hardly any Latin, who had no command of French, or of English?

They say that you can no more get rid of *saudade* than you can get rid of foreignness. Maria Glória was born in Brazil; the places of her childhood are in the tropics, and there is excess of everything

there, even *saudade* - for Augusto, for his caresses, for his voice, which gave her, the fourteen-year-old girl, goose pimples all over her body, "Read, Augusto, please read that to me!"
"We have to learn, to accept, all the agony, all the pain, for light, love is behind the darkness; first we have to have gone through hell..."

In recent days Maria Glória has begun to put things in order, to illuminate the years of her life. Now she will meet Graça here in Sintra. Only the hours of one whole day remain to her, perhaps more; on the 15th of November she intends to be finished. On the 15th of November she intends to rest.

Maria Glória, Childhood in Rio de Janeiro
"So that the splendor of the house branches out"

"Maria of Portugal" - she had signed things that way many hundreds of times in recent years. Sometimes she wrote only an "M." But she never had the courage to write her other, her additional name, the one that she feels is her actual name: Glória.

"Maria Glória sends her grandpa many thousands of kisses on the hand," she wrote as a five-year-old to her grandfather, Emperor Franz I, in Vienna. Did Grandfather have any conception of the tropics?

"Rio de Janeiro is an enchanting spectacle, bights that line the ocean with greenery and flowers, waterfalls, cliffs, houses that flash white, streets where people of all skin colors frolic," was what *Mamãe* reported to Maria's grandfather in Vienna.

Maria Glória could never imagine living anywhere else. In Rio she knew her way around. She knew not only the streets and squares; she knew the smells, the perfume that streamed forth from the sedan chairs, the scent of orange blossoms, and the bad smell that floated from the market hall. She knew the music of this city, the singing and the shouting of the barbers and tailors, the shrieking and the praying of the lady's maids, the laughter and the giggling of the female slaves before they disappeared into the entryway of a house. In Rio de Janeiro she was at home.

But she was not destined for Rio; her destiny was Portugal.

"In Portugal they are not prepared for a jungle princess. The Portuguese expect a queen who has been educated in the European manner," was the way her first conversation with Dona Leonora began.

Leonora Fegueira, her new governess, had come from Lisbon.

"Why did *Mamãe* go away?" Maria Glória had wept, and Dona Leonora let her finish crying. She gave no reprimand for that lack of self-control. After a while Dona Leonora said, "Crown Princess, from now on I am your governess, also your chamber maid. We will spend the coming years together. I intend to do everything to make it a good time for you."

Maria Glória looked up startled.

"How do you wish to be addressed?" Dona Leonora continued and stroked her curly hair.

"Maria Glória is my name, and please, don't call me Crown Princess. *Mamãe* gave the order that we must always endeavor to behave in keeping with our station, and in personal dealings with our close friends we are to forego formalities," she rattled off, stating an educational principle.

Dona Leonora was astounded: "Good, Maria Glória. Look, I've written out the schedule. I'll give you lessons in Portuguese, Portuguese history, and regional studies. For public law an attorney will come."

Maria Glória did not understand: "I already speak Portuguese, and Master Itabuna was very pleased with me in history class."

"It is because of your destiny." She heard that sentence again and again.

She was destined for Portugal. That resulted from the fact that she was the firstborn. The firstborn daughter was destined for Portugal, the son, little Pedrinho, for Brazil. That was set down in the Bragança family rules. That it would ever become reality for Maria

Glória was something that she did not want to think about. She did not want to imagine that at all. Portugal and Lisbon were infinitely distant points in her atlas. Portugal smelled sweet and oily, that was what streamed forth from the boxes of mail. In Lisbon lived all the members of the Bragança family who had left Rio in 1820 and returned to Lisbon: her grandparents, Dona Carlota and Dom João, Uncle Miguel, and aunts as well - that was what Maria Glória had learned.

Not until Dona Leonora was in the house and explained her situation, her destiny to her, did she begin to understand the relationships. She repeated: "So it's this way: After the death of Grandfather João, I will be the heir to the Portuguese throne; Pedrinho is the heir to the throne for Brazil. That was also why Papa wanted to send me to Portugal immediately, back in the year 1826. At that time *Mamãe* was still alive, and she did not permit it. For I remember how she spoke to Papa and sobbed, 'No, not already. After all, she is only seven years old!' So Papa wrote to his brother Miguel in Lisbon that he should take care of all of the administrative business for me. In a few years, when I am fourteen, I will move to Lisbon. Besides that, it was negotiated that Uncle Miguel would be my husband."

Maria Glória wanted to know, "Dona Leonora, do you know Dom Miguel? What does he look like? Does he look like Papa? Does he sing, too? Does he compose like Papa?"

The governess answered negatively. "Your Uncle Miguel is not at all like your father, neither in stature nor in personality. Miguel is five years younger than your father, twenty-seven, and a rather dark man. He even prefers dark gray and black in his clothing." Dona Leonora broke off; then she continued speaking, almost in a whisper, "There is so much talk. Supposedly he demands absolute obedience from everyone, and piousness is the most important thing for him. It is said that the servants fear him, that they have to go to Mass twice a day, and that he sends someone to ferret out who they talk to and especially what they say. Yes, they say that even your grandfather was not safe from that son - poison!" Dona Leonora crossed herself. She stopped speaking for a few moments. Had she said too much? She just wanted to end the conversation quickly and added, "In any case, your grandfather, King João, expressly designated you as heir to the throne. And with respect to the arranged marriage with Dom Miguel we will trust in Providence. It will all turn out for the best for you."

Maria Glória was at a loss. Did she have to be afraid? No. She was still in Rio de Janeiro and she would still be in Brazil for a long, a very long time, or so she told herself.

But Dona Leonora reminded her: "So it's because of your destiny. From now on you should only have teachers and educators from Portugal." And she lovingly stroked Maria Glória's hair. "The apple of my eye" was what Dona Leonora called her.

Maria Glória sobbed. She was regarded as an adult, and the family rules were to be abided by. That is what *Mamãe* would also have wanted. To whom could she have run to tell about, to talk about what she had just heard and almost grasped? Nobody occurred to her.

All that remained to her was the dialogue with her diary: "...I also ask *Mamãe* to help me to like Dona Leonora, so that I can place my confidence in her. Her voice is melodious, and voices cannot be disguised, Papa says. But her Portuguese sounds foreign, it almost hisses. Her eyes are kind and she smells like orange blossom oil. *Mamãe*, I want Dona Leonora for a friend. I have no other friend here."

After the death of *Mamãe*, Dona Leonora had remained in Rio de Janeiro. She came every day, remained at Maria Glória's side during all those hours, and in the evening, after evening prayers, she went to the coach to ride back to her apartment on the *Campo Santana*.

Dona Leonora seldom laughed, but she smiled with her dark eyes. Her eyes talked, and when she spoke, whether in French, Portuguese, or English, she spoke correctly and without haste. She lived like clockwork. She was tirelessly active, constantly at the same pace; nothing seemed too difficult for her. During the New Year's parade she stood straight as a ramrod in the glowing midsummer heat beneath the beating tropical sun and attentively followed the speeches of the ministers and the diplomats. And she stroked the back of Maria Glória's hand, saying, "Now it's your turn, and you can do it," before Maria Glória, the eleven-year-old, stepped forward and conveyed to her father, Emperor Pedro I of Brazil, the New Year's wishes of the family and the New Year's wishes of Portugal.

Everything about Dona Leonora was permanence and seriousness. She was always dressed in the blue and white colors of Portugal; she always had her hair done up in the same knot; she smelled like orange blossoms. Every evening, before she left the house, she stood next to Dona Leopoldina's death room for the time that it took to offer a prayer.

"Dona Leonora surrounds me like a shadow. She has never reprimanded me yet. 'I wish that you would do it' - that is her strongest command. Someday, when I am fully grown, I would like to be like Dona Leonora," wrote Maria Glória a few months later in her diary.

When she had already been living in Lisbon for a long time and Leonora had become her friend, and she had turned her first children over to Leonora to teach, she often repeated these lines in her diary: "Someday, when there are no longer any intrigues and revolutions to fear, I would like to become like Leonora."

When Dona Leonora explained the arranged marriage of the grandparents during the history lesson, she began, "For generations envy, ill will, and hate were sown in the Bragança family. I pray that you will be spared that." She continued: "Your grandmother, Dona Carlota, the proud Bourbon woman, called Brazil the land of the Negroes and the monkeys! Nobody in *Boa Vista* liked her. They were afraid of her. She even had a small troop of soldiers equipped. They were supposed to deprive your grandfather of power. Thank heavens, all of her tricks were discovered in time. Of her children she loved Miguel the most. She also let him in on all her scheming plans."

Maria Glória could hardly follow her: "But Dona Carlota died a long time ago. She can't do anything bad to anyone anymore, and Papa arranged everything with Uncle Miguel. Everything is written down in contracts that are pages long, and the diplomats took those papers to Lisbon. Papa also sent a 'constitution,' a basic law to Portugal. Portugal is now a totally modern, liberal state, like France," she babbled, and Dona Leonora sighed, "Hopefully!"

On a Sunday in December of 1828, the Portuguese ambassador came to *Boa Vista*. He came unannounced and shouted when he was still on the stairs, "Senhor Emperor!"

The man was totally beside himself; soaked with tropical rain and sweat, he stood before her father.

"Your Excellency, you are very excited," Papa laughed, and he placed Paula Mariana, with whom he had just been dancing, carefully on the floor.

"Let's see what message they have sent us from Portugal." And he also shouted, "Maria Glória, stay here. These are your affairs, too, of course."

Papa read; he read many pages. And while he read she held onto the curtain, for she feared most the sudden changes in her father's moods. She could tell by looking at him: in the next moment he would scream, rage, and run back and forth through the room.

Finally her father read aloud: "...the constitution, the *Carta Constitutional*, that you, your Majesty, sent by official dispatch to Lisbon, was received with festivals of rejoicing. The climax of the celebrations took place in the liberal university city of Coimbra: Portugal finally has a constitutional monarchy as its form of government! Of course, an opposition party quickly formed: the Miguelists! Supported by the clergy, for whom a liberal form of government goes against every principle, and especially supported and promoted by the major power Austria, Dom Miguel had succeeded in taking all power for himself in only a few days. From Vienna they sent him the shrewdest negotiators, who very quickly turned adherents of the Miguelist party into fighting soldiers, and Dom Miguel had himself proclaimed king. On that very same evening began the persecution of all those persons who were close to the liberal

Cartist Party, i.e., to our future queen.

"Several hundred Portuguese succeeded in fleeing from the Miguel regime. They fled to London and to the Azores. Several thousand are still trying to flee, but the majority of the Portuguese are at the mercy of the Miguel dictate. The Miguelists are raging in the most evil ways: Honorable citizens are being dispossessed of their land and declared people without status; traders and merchants are burdened with tax demands that they can satisfy only by surrendering all of their goods; teachers and educators who were associated with the liberal spirit are prohibited from speaking in public; whoever does not attend church services regularly, whoever is on the street after dark, whoever is not dressed properly, whoever does not obey the soldiers of the Miguelist guard on the spot and without argument is put in the dungeon. They ridicule you, your Majesty, Dom Pedro I, Emperor of Brazil, in every conceivable form. They tell jokes about you and your mistress Domitila. I cannot keep from mentioning that to you. In the theater our future queen, Maria II of Portugal, is portrayed as a child without education, who has nothing in her head but her curls and her clothes.

"Since I myself am forced to flee to London in the next few hours, I will not describe further the details of this period of terror that has now dawned for Portugal. Portugal is ruled by a man who is intoxicated by the exercise of power.

"As his ministers, advisors, and officials, he has appointed men who obey him blindly, but who are mostly uneducated. Many of them are illiterate and thus depend on the advice and goodwill of scribes, secretaries, and messengers. These in turn require payment in gold coins for the slightest assistance. In my own name and that of all the emigrants, with this report I would like to record the fact that all of us, without distinction as to status or person, have sworn the oath of loyalty to our Queen Maria II, and will not stop waiting for Heaven to send our queen to us in Europe. The fact that negotiations must be started without delay, to bring the murderous Miguel regime to an end, requires no further mention. Act, Dom Pedro, act immediately! In unswerving loyalty I greet you, Dom Pedro I, and you, Queen Maria II. - Eduardo Alvelos, Ambassador."

Papa read the letter, repeated many passages. His facial color changed, but did not grow red, as it did during his fits of rage. His cheeks shimmered gray and there were tears in his eyes. As he read, he lost his breath.

"They've finally destroyed me - Miguel and Metternich! That Metternich, he prepared well and long for this! Maria Glória, your grandfather in Vienna, yes, Emperor Franz I of Austria, is now letting us feel all his power. Here in Brazil, I swore on the constitution. What's more, I sent a constitution to Lisbon - that the rights of all people are the same! In the western part of Europe a liberal spirit is beginning to sprout! That can never be allowed to happen. On the contrary, Metternich thought it out well. Those liberal, French ideas must be put down, wiped out from the westernmost point in Europe. From that westernmost region he can then lead all of Europe back into the time before 1799. And it was easy to win Miguel for that genial chess move. King Miguel, it's what he always wanted to be. That's why he even wanted to kill our father!"

Maria Glória had wrapped herself in the curtain. She just did not want to have to see how Papa became completely beside himself and collapsed.

Papa sat trembling at the table; his body threw itself into contortions. Servants came running from everywhere. They sent for the doctor; the priest rushed into the room; pitchers of juices and teas were brought. Three kitchen maids carried pottery bowls with herbs and made steam arise in every corner of the room. A groom came with a freshly picked sprig of jasmine. "A seizure," they wheezed, "he's having an epileptic seizure again."

Papa let them pour liquids into him. For a long time he did not react to any smell, to any word, and kept staring at the ceiling.

One after another, the scribes, the secretaries, the chamberlains, the coachmen, the water bearers, and the kitchen maids pressed into the room. They prayed, "Dona Leopoldina, *nossa mãe*, we plead for your help...," and slowly, after endless minutes, the fingers, the facial muscles of her father became filled with life again, and the twitching in his limbs grew less.

The seizure was over.

One after another, the servants slipped out, back to their places.

"It's his guilty conscience that sends him these seizures, these images."

"Above all, when he is perplexed, then he sees Dona Leopoldina everywhere."

"He whispered it again. I heard it: 'There she is, Dona Leopoldina. She is looking at me so sadly.'"

"At the time she said: 'I have forgiven my husband.'"

"Yes, but he did not hear that, for when Dona Leopoldina died, he was with his soldiers in Uruguay."

Maria Glória swallowed all her questions. Who would explain the labyrinthine thoughts of the adults to a nine-year-old, a ten-year-old? Why didn't Uncle Miguel stick to the agreement with Papa? Why did Grandpa, Emperor Franz I of Austria, support Uncle Miguel? Why didn't Grandpa ever write?

For two years already not a single piece of mail had come from Vienna. They received no answer to the children's letters that they regularly wrote to Grandpa.

Mamãe had always spoken of "dear Papa" with great longing, had signed her letters with "your obedient daughter Leopoldine," and decorated the picture of Grandpa with hibiscus blossoms on his birthday, on the twelfth of February. During those years the grandpa in the picture seemed to smile.

Later, when *Mamãe* was missed in *Boa Vista* more and more, later the picture of Emperor Franz I also seemed to change. The eyes no longer looked at Maria Glória when she wanted to talk to him as *Mamãe* had often done. Grandpa looked past his granddaughter.

"The picture is already quite weathered from the humidity," Dona Leonora declared, and she had the picture hung in a corner. "There it's dark. From there your grandfather can't see and hear everything that is spoken in the study. Pedrinho is being educated according to the principles of the Freemasons, which is also unimaginable for Emperor Franz I."

When the Austrian ambassador came - "the princesses and the prince are half Austrian" - they had to speak German for an entire evening.

Senhor Neuwied had the educators show him the weekly schedules.

"Shouldn't Princess Januária have started to receive riding lessons long ago? She is already seven years old. A diet plan should be set up for Princess Paula Mariana. She is becoming too full-figured. Prince Pedro should be dressed in a uniform."

"He's four years old," Dona Leonora interrupted him.

The ambassador did not react. He added, "In Vienna Princess Maria Glória would have to wear a corset at the age of ten!"

"*Mamãe* never wore a corset. We're living in the tropics. With a corset we begin to sweat," Maria Glória blazed away, and although her face became red, she could not contain herself any longer. "Besides, your Excellency, we're waiting for a letter from our grandpa. We've already been waiting for two years! You always bring greetings, but we would like to see some writing. Surely one can also smell Austria on the paper, on the letter. Why doesn't our grandpa write?"

The ambassador turned around with a start. He looked at Dona Leonora and said, "What a tone, what disobedience is getting started here!"

Dona Leonora stepped toward the dumbfounded man. "The children are not disobedient. Princess Maria Glória asked about her grandfather, and Emperor Franz should be happy about that. Everything is proceeding according to Dona Leopoldina's educational principles. She would not have forbidden any of her children to speak freely," and she signaled to the siblings and her, Maria Glória - curtsy, bow, hand kiss, farewell.

"His Excellency" surely reported everything in minute detail in Vienna.

Dona Leonora was satisfied, "That was an important lesson for your siblings. One must never knuckle under to diplomats. You reacted correctly, Maria Glória!"

"Today, on the first of January, my wish for the year 1829 is that *Mamãe* would come back. Even if it cannot be in person, she should just send her thoughts. She probably knows that this is more urgently necessary than ever. Although we all, even Pedrinho, practice carrying out our duties daily and also bravely endure both the French and the fencing lessons, we are sad. Even the flowers that Januária and I plant do not want to grow, and when they bloom, they look tired, and their colors, even the yellow and the red, do not glow."

She tied this letter into her chemise, and with this letter on her person Maria Glória went to the New Year's Mass.

The year 1829 actually had set many things right.

José Bonifácio had returned, the old man with the long white hair and the eyes in which a smile constantly flashed.

He had been prime minister of the independent Empire of Brazil. "*Indepêndencia ou morte* [independence or death]," Brazil's independence, *Mamãe*, Dona Leopoldina, and José Bonifácio had striven for that. "Maria Glória, you must never forget it. Dona Leopoldina signed the declaration of independence," she was often reminded.

Later, as Domitila, the mistress, gained more and more power over Father, Father banished the "old man," José Bonifácio, from Brazil.

"Pedro has gone crazy. He's sending away the very man to whom he owes his entire rise to power," *Mamãe* said, wringing her hands, and she also pleaded with Bonifácio in a letter to return.

A few days before she died, she wrote, "José, I beg you, come back and take over the education of our son Pedro. I can only add to my urgent plea the reminder of those hours that we spent together before you went into exile. José, where are you? I would like to be able to picture the city in which you are now rushing through the streets, striving to reach a library, a room full of books. The kind Duchess Aguiar will have many copies made of this letter and send it out into the world, to Rome, to Paris, to Salamanca, to Coimbra, and to Lisbon, to Vienna and to Dresden until my plea reaches you.

Accept an embrace from your *ama* Leopoldina."

Could "a*ma*" be regarded as an abbreviation for *amante*, for beloved? The contents of this letter were whispered through all of *Boa Vista*. Had Dona Leopoldina and José Bonifácio been a pair of lovers, *Mamãe* twenty-seven years old and Bonifácio almost sixty?

When *Mamãe* was dead, nobody held back anymore, not the officials, not the ambassadors, not the guards, and of course not the servants. "Let the whole world know that Dona Leopoldina grieved to death; otherwise she would not have died at the age of thirty."

"That vulgar man, Pedro I, Emperor of Brazil! He gave his mistress golden coaches, and Dona Leopoldina had to walk around in a linen dress."

But there was also gossip about the "blonde princess from Austria," about *Mamãe*, and "the white-haired hothead," about José Bonifácio. It was just quieter and more reserved. "She stayed over night in his apartment. Everyone here knows that."

This talk, these rumors had also not grown less over the years. They had even gone from Brazil to Lisbon.

Years later, in the *Necessidade Palace* a few days after her father's death, when Maria Glória moved the pictures of her parents closer to each other, she said, "Look, Leonora, now the two of them only speak kindly with each other." She almost did not hear Leonora sigh, "Yes, even he has probably forgiven her now."

What did her father, who lived with a mistress for years, who demanded of *Mamãe* that Isabel, the child of the mistress, grow up and be educated together with Pedrinho, Januária, Paula Mariana, Francisca, and her, Maria Glória, what did Father have to forgive *Mamãe* for?

Leonora could not be talked out of it. "It's true, Dona Leopoldina suffered much, but she also took for herself from life. Your sister Francisca came into the world exactly nine months after José Bonifácio's departure..."

No!

She did not want to remember it. Maria Glória had been four years old, and it must have been a stranger that she had observed;

that woman in the gray linen dress who permitted José Bonifácio to kiss her hand, who let him embrace her, who snuggled up to this man, whispered words to him in German, words that Maria Glória did not know, did not understand. *"Minha Leopoldina,"* murmured Bonifácio as he led that woman to the daybed, bedded her down there, and did not stop kissing her, did not stop burying his face against the woman's neck.

Nine months later, in August of 1824, Francisca had come into the world.

"Yesterday I gave birth to an especially beautiful daughter," wrote Dona Leopoldina. Everyone was disappointed, still no heir to the throne. Only Dona Leopoldina perceived nothing of that general disappointment. When she looked into the cradle, when she had Francisca at her breast, a glow passed across her face. Her eyes, the blue eyes of *Mamãe*, looked into the distance and focused on something magnificently beautiful. When *Mamãe* had Francisca in her arms, for moments she became again that strange woman whom José Bonifácio had kissed, who hid a letter from him in her sleeve.

Was it only Maria Glória who registered all that? How many persons were inside *Mamãe*?

In the year 1829 Dona Amelia had come into the house as well. Papa had finally found a second wife.

"The matchmakers had to accept a 'No' thirteen times. The sad fate of Dona Leopoldina had gotten around all over Europe. No noble house wanted to send a princess to that vulgar man."

The official report said: "Amelia of Leuchtenberg conforms to the emperor's conceptions in every particular."

Dona Amelia came from Paris. She spread her smile, her songs over everything, over the overgrown garden paths, onto the shoulders of the water bearers, into the faces of the chambermaids, servants and cooks. She not only brought with her recipes for new chocolate sweets; she had toys in her chests, toys that were the very latest fashion in Europe: painted cartons from which a dwelling, a house, an entire farmstead could be put together. With her nineteen years she was much more a playmate than a stepmother.

"Dona Amelia, Januária and I have to recite eulogies in Latin for two hours in the afternoon," Francisca complained. "Master Itabena was not pleased with our behavior in church. We looked up at the ladies in the diplomats' loge. They're wearing a new headdress now, peacock feathers that glisten green and blue and bob with every breath they take."

Dona Amelia laughed: "I've already seen that, too, and because they want to outdo each other with the length and the luxuriance of the feathers in their hats, they tickle each other with their outstretched creations."

Januária said: "We absolutely had to see if and when one of them had to sneeze."

"Good Master Itabena," Dona Amelia hugged Januária, "he takes his task very seriously and wants to make a perfect princess out of each of you. But this afternoon we're going to the botanical garden."

"Is Pedrinho coming along?" Maria Glória asked with concern.

"Of course, the little boy hardly has a free hour anyway. Sometimes I think that Pedrinho has already forgotten how to play like a four-year-old," Dona Amelia sighed, "and Dona Leonora will also get along without you for an afternoon, Maria Glória. Today we're going to indulge ourselves in a few free hours."

Dona Amelia was a good friend. They could confide in her, and with her joyfulness she drove away everything dismal.

The servants watched Dona Amelia with a critical eye. "She's beautiful, she's a very beautiful woman, but her eyes, sometimes there is a green glint in them, a clear sign of the fact that she doesn't tolerate anyone next to her. If she had her way, she would even push the kind Dona Leonora away."

"Servants' gossip," thought Maria Glória and laughed at it. She could not get enough of Dona Amelia's charms, of her smile. "If I could have the appearance that I would wish for, I would like to look like Amelia. I would like to be able to conjure that much attractiveness into my face; I would like to be able to caress that softly," was what Maria Glória dreamed of.

With Dona Amelia had come her royal household, her lady's maids and her ladies-in-waiting. Above all, her brother had come along, August of Leuchtenberg. From the beginning Maria Glória called him Augusto. She had been told of her father's plans by Dona Leonora: Once Uncle Miguel was no longer a possibility as a husband for her, they had negotiated to obtain Dona Amelia's brother as husband for Maria Glória.

Augusto, the eighteen-year-old, lived with his tutors and teachers in a house in the city on the *Rua Ouvidor*; but he came to *Boa Vista* every day, for dancing lessons, for fencing lessons, to visit his sister, the empress of Brazil, to accompany the princesses on a coach ride into the Tijuca Mountains, to learn fishing and hunting from Rafael. Above all, he came to talk with Maria Glória, to stroll with her in the garden, to weave a garland of hibiscus blossoms for her, to read lines of poetry by the fashionable Victor Hugo to her - "...give me a few rays of sunshine before I vanish into the darkness, and do not forget the rose as a comfort for me while I wait..."

"With Augusto, blue has settled in *Boa Vista* for me; everything shimmers in all shades of blue like the Bahia topazes, *tudo azul* [all of the blues]." She had entrusted that to her diary.

Since the death of *Mamãe*, Maria Glória had been forced into adult life. She had often resisted that and envied her siblings whose undisciplined acts were overlooked.

"During Papa's speech at the table Paula Mariana was already nibbling at the coconut sauce. She was not reprimanded for it. She is permitted to do that. She is still regarded as a child."

With her eleven years Augusto drew her into another realm of adult life. He hugged and embraced her. She experienced caresses that would intensify, to which she looked forward, that also sometimes frightened her.

Augusto had also brought music by Franz Schubert and the young genius Frédéric Chopin with him. He played the piano and the violin and was soon included in the house musical performances.

He also taught Pedrinho his first dance steps.

"You must all leave now. In a few days Pedrinho will surprise you," he ordered. The little boy was despondent because his dance master, Senhor Pierre, threatened him with the bamboo stick for any bodily movement that he did not carry out quite precisely. After a week of secret lessons from Augusto, Pedrinho moved freely and almost gallantly to the minuet.

Now, more than two decades later, the diplomats report from Rio de Janeiro: "The Emperor of Brazil, Pedro II, is an outstanding and passionate dancer, and it is regarded as a great honor to be invited to one of his dance parties..."

On April 4, 1830, on her eleventh birthday, Augusto stood in the line of congratulators who had come to the "public kissing of the princess's hand." He waited patiently then drew near to her. "Maria Glória," he whispered and did not pay any attention to Dona Leonora. "I would like to meet you this evening in the Glória Church. Will you come?"

"In the Glória Church," she stammered, that was impossible; besides that, the next person in the line of congratulators was already pushing forward.

"Will you come?" Augusto did not let himself be deterred.

"Yes," she nodded, and in order to appease the congratulators who were pushing from behind, Dona Leonora quickly added, "We will come."

Then in the evening a winter tropical rain came down; water from the inner courtyard streamed down the approaches and the wind shook the last winter-dried leaves from the almond trees. They started out anyway, with Maria Glória and Dona Leonora in the coach and Augusto riding ahead on his horse.

In the coach the water ran down the walls, down from the ceiling. It lay on the floor and they were soon soaked. Too bad about her curls, about the ribbons that they had braided into her hair, thought Maria Glória, too bad about the dress with the garlands of roses. The carriage was tossed back and forth and almost got stuck. Finally a wheel broke. How long would it take for the coachman to get a replacement carriage? Nobody was on the street; only a few water bearers sat on their water casks. They were probably drunk and did not feel the rain at all.

While Dona Leonora gave instructions, "Get a few more canvas covers and send an attendant with oil lamps, and above all a new carriage. No, we'll turn around and go back to *Boa Vista*," and the coachman nodded to everything, Augusto had slid down from his horse. "You promised," he said, and with that he led Maria Glória from the carriage, and she let him set her upon his horse.

"Your Highness, Augusto, what do you think you're doing?" Dona Leonora became breathless. "You simply can't, not in this storm..." But her head immediately disappeared again beneath the roof of the carriage. "I wish...," she then whimpered.

August called to her, "Kindest Dona Leonora, I'll take care of your protégée and we'll be back even before you have a new carriage."

The church was completely empty. Only by the prayer stool, at the place where *Mamãe* had formerly prayed, stood a vase with calla lilies and roses.

"These magnificently beautiful flowers, in white," stammered Maria Glória.

"I brought them here myself," Augusto began. "You know, Maria Glória, that we are supposed to marry, in three years, when you are fourteen," Augusto continued. "Do we want to get engaged today?"

Maria Glória was shivering in her wet clothes. She was willing to promise anything to Augusto, if he would only continue to come regularly to *Boa Vista*, if he would only remain close to her. She snuggled up to his heated body. Engaged to Augusto, and Uncle Miguel, could she forget him as her fiancé once and for all?

Augusto e Maria-Glória para sempre [Augusto and Maria Glória for all time] is engraved in intricate writing on the medallion that Augusto gave her that evening.

She had worn that medallion around her neck for as long as Augusto existed for her. "Augusto, your skin is much too soft for a man's skin, and nobody would believe that you, the blond young man, have the strength with which you hold, hold tightly."

In the year 1830 Papa changed. He became taciturn, locked himself in his room. He rode out and did not come back until dawn. In the newspapers they wrote scornful poems about the mistress Domitila who had finally been driven away to Minas Gerais.

Boa Vista also changed. Hostilities came at the children from everywhere. The kitchen maids, the lady's maids, the food bearers and laundresses stood together in groups and giggled. The officials shuffled sleepily to their meetings.

Maria Glória and her sisters, even Pedrinho, began to scurry through the hallways on tiptoe. They took off their shoes before they ran down the stairs into the courtyard, into the garden. In the courtyard stood the carriages, but the coachmen turned away, busied themselves with the horses whenever the children ran past them.

"Why is everybody changing? What do we do to them?" asked Januária, and Maria Glória told her what she knew from Augusto: For months there had been a governmental crisis. Many ministers and officials were oriented against the imperial family and had been incited against the Braganças. Many talked of the fact that they seriously wanted Papa, Dom Pedro I, to leave Brazil. There was no money in the state treasury, neither for roads nor for a hospital. The water from the Santana well was so polluted that they were already worried about yellow fever again, but there was also no money for a new well. Garbage was no longer taken outside the city to the garbage pits, but was being buried right in the backyards, for the garbage drivers had also received no money for months. Papa had driven all of Rio to ruin with his mistress affairs.

Of course the children could do nothing about it, but for the officials, secretaries, and diplomats it was less dangerous to take out their scorn and their ignorance toward the Braganças on the children. And the children, Maria Glória as well, became accustomed to being even more friendly toward every visitor, to speaking aloud only in the classrooms - "And grant that the crisis will soon be over," Maria Glória prayed.

Then came her twelfth birthday, the fourth of April 1831, as on every birthday, with the morning Mass in the cathedral, followed by breakfast with her siblings and later the official hand-kissing ceremony.

The line of congratulators was shorter on this birthday, much shorter. More women than men had come, and most of them were from the servant class, slaves. They pressed flowers and pictures of the saints into Maria Glória's hands. "Daughter of *nossa mãe*, may God protect you."

Everything proceeded restively, almost feverishly on this birthday. At dinner a new seating arrangement was also established: Maria Glória sat next to the ambassador of Portugal, and in his toast Papa now called her only "Maria"! She was so startled by it that she choked and Dona Leonora had to calm her by caressing her hand for a long time.

In this strange, tense atmosphere Dona Amelia handed her a remarkable gift. "Here in this wooden box I have planted a seedling of every flower, of every shrub that grows at *Boa Vista*: paradise flower, jasmine, canna, calla lily, hollyhock, hydrangea, orchids, some ferns..."

Maria Glória closed her eyes. Perhaps a person can postpone the inevitable by not asking, by not speaking; that was what she wanted. That night she hugged Pedrinho very close to her. Her beloved brother Pedrinho was soft and warm as always. When she slipped into his bed, he murmured as he did every evening, "Maria Glória, at last," threw his arms around her neck, and continued to sleep. She buried her face deeply in her brother's curls. Just never let go.

The next morning the secrecy was over.

Papa stood in the breakfast room and stared out the window. As she did every morning, Dona Amelia distributed pieces of the cake that was made with shredded coconut and corn and poured mango honey over the delicacy. Each of the children picked at it, but the yellow mass did not grow smaller.

Nobody dared ask: Why is Papa still in the house? At last Pedrinho was picked up for his classes, followed immediately afterward by Januária, Francisca, and Paula Mariana.

Now Maria Glória sat at the table without her siblings.

"Pedro, you must tell your daughter about it now," Dona Amelia admonished.

"Yes. Let's go for a walk, Maria Glória." And Father went, walked with her out of the house. He hurried with her toward the garden.

"Look, Papa, in my flowerbed the orchids are blooming most luxuriantly, in spite of the fact that it has rained so much in recent weeks. And these here will be my first cannas, the yellow ones. They bloom in the middle of the winter, at the end of July. I've dug ditches so that they do not get too much rain water."

But Father drew her away from the flowerbeds; he walked along the gravel path with her into the thicket where the parasitic plants bloomed in all shades of lilac.

"Here," Father said finally, pointing at two stones, "sit down, Maria Glória!"

He poked into the grass and under the rocks with a stick. "They are sleeping, the snakes and the spiders. Maria Glória, we will depart the day after tomorrow. On April 7, 1831 we will leave Rio de Janeiro, we will leave Brazil."

Maria Glória shook her head. No, she did not want to hear that.

"I will, I must abdicate as Emperor of Brazil, and an interim government will be formed until Pedrinho is old enough for that office."

"Pedrinho is staying here, alone with the strict José Bonifácio? And what will happen to my sisters? They're going to travel with us, aren't they? When will we come back? Isn't it dangerous to travel in the winter? Dona Leonora says it is." Questions rushed through Maria Glória's mind.

Father shook his head at all of them.

Father's hair, which usually fell in untamed curls across his forehead, clung to his temples wet with sweat. That is how he came home from a horserace. But now his face was not creased from physical exertion, but agitated and driven by the events of recent weeks. He had reached the end of the line and used up almost all his strength in doing so. He tried to explain, spoke slowly, and as if through a curtain she, the twelve-year-old, saw *Mamãe* standing behind her father, *Mamã*e in her gray linen dress.

"They have lost all faith in me, and I can't place the blame on anyone else, only myself. I was too late in sending Domitila away. I should also have replaced more quickly the officials that she fed to me. There is no money available, not even for a new well here in Rio. In recent years the taxes haven't been paid. The officials, Domitila's friends, found a way for everyone, so that each had to pay less or no taxes at all. They also say that I'm not a Brazilian and that I could never really love and defend, really organize this young Brazil that has finally been liberated from Portugal! The fact that I sent Isabel to Europe to be educated caused a scandal - a mistress's bastard, we won't pay for her. What should I have done? Amelia refused to do it - 'I'll never raise your mistress's child!' Was I supposed to turn Isabel, the five-year-old child, over to Domitila and her people?"

"It's not the child's fault," *Mamãe* nodded behind Papa.

"Isabel is an additional sister for you, and you will be good to her," *Mamãe* had said as Graça sat down with the tiny Isabel in a corner of the playroom.

Papa continued: "For Isabel everything is being paid out of my private funds, but that is now no longer important. Building the palace for Domitila ate up so much, too much money, the gifts and the slaves that I bought for her - I can no longer make amends for it. When I came here to Rio I was nine years old. I no longer have any recollection of Europe. All of the important events of my life took place here. Everything is embedded in all this green, in this blue sky. I do not remember the sky over Portugal. When I was fourteen, a Franciscan father tried to read to me from the catechism. I was a stubborn pupil. Every teacher soon gave up on me. But that pious man did not give up. He told me about pain, about the fact that the pains, the ones that we receive and the ones that we inflict, would balance out in many lives. There is so much now that I have to work off, a great deal. They have painted my face on pieces of cloth and throw knives at them, at the vulgar man. What does that matter? Not at all. Now I'll let the furious man, the wild man who is within me, perish. He'll starve - in exile."

"Are we going to travel to Portugal?" she asked, and not until that moment was she reminded again of Uncle Miguel, of the report from Lisbon, of Dona Leonora's comments - "Portugal has probably bled to death by now. The artists, the scientists - Miguel drove them all away, and those who stayed are being tormented in the work camps."

Father shook his head. "No, we can't do that. In Portugal Miguel would immediately have me arrested. He will never give up his office without a fight. And here, if I don't depart within the next few hours, there are still a few myrmidons who will shoot me."

Maria Glória became breathless as she listened, "And my siblings, do they also want to shoot them? We haven't done anything to anybody!" She almost screamed and clung to her father's arm.

"No," Father said calmingly. "Nothing will happen to your siblings. I'm the symbol for a bloodsucker of a monarch. I must leave." And after taking a few breaths he added, "And you, Maria Glória must come with me. Portugal is your destiny."

She gradually began to understand. "We must flee and don't know where we're going," she stammered. "We can't go to Portugal as long as Uncle Miguel reigns there. So where are we fleeing to?"

"To England or to France." Father shook his head. "I don't know where they will take us in. First we'll travel to Brest. Then we'll decide where to go from there."

Maria Glória pressed her lips together; she held back all her questions. She just did not want to have to hear any more terrible final things.

"Emigration, your *Mamãe* suffered so much as a result of that. How often she wept: 'Won't I ever see Europe, Vienna again? Will I die as an emigrant?' At the time I didn't understand that either. After all, I felt at home here," Father murmured.

He sat slumped next to Maria Glória, and suddenly where they would go when they fled was no longer important to her. She felt how Father was suffering, how he shrank back from the pain of departure, of letting go, how he, the man who was always cheerful, always hotheaded, was seeking comfort from her, from his daughter, and for a few minutes all the distance that separated them was gone.

Two people wept because they had to leave the place that was as familiar to them as their skin, the place where all the colors and smells, the midday heat, the winter rain, the rattling of the coco-trees, the wheezing of the aerial roots, where everything was home and security to them. They held each other's hands; they both trembled in the face of the foreign, shuddered at the unknown; and they knew that they had to walk that path, that it would not be spared them.

When they became calmer and came to themselves again, were father and daughter again, Papa murmured, "We will learn to live with it. *'It is one more color in our souls, saudade, and therefore we smile more often than the others, and with our smile we let the tears flow within us to soothe the pain.'*"

"When will we - depart?" Maria Glória asked.

"Very early the day after tomorrow. One more thing. You will not be traveling with us, but on a different ship. In you they are expecting the Queen of Portugal, and it is too dangerous for you to travel with me, with your father. The journey is long, and they can quickly buy a sailor who will use poison or a knife."

"And Augusto?" Maria Glória interrupted him.

"He will follow us in a few weeks, on the English passenger ship. Augusto will travel quite comfortably," Papa now said with a smile. You'll see each other again in Europe. You'll get your blond prince after all."

"When, how should I say good-by? How should I tell my siblings?" Maria Glória could not imagine it: getting into a boat, riding toward a ship, without her siblings, without Pedrinho?

Father sighed. He was weary, very weary. "I don't know that. Saying good-by, I can't teach you that. I can't do it myself."

Graça
"She is ready to accompany me at once"

Maria Glória hastily walks the last steps to the stone bench and finally sits at the appointed place under the parasol pine.

"Beloved Maria Glória. My time here has ended. I know now that I do not belong here. So I am going back. On November 14th I would like to say good-by to you, in Sintra, by that stone bench where you can look out into the ocean and far into the south in our direction. *Saudade* has worked hard on me. My hair is almost white. I embrace you! Graça."

Most of the letters from Graça were composed in this terse language. She had to pay for every word that she wanted to have written. Therefore she filed for days on the formulation of a short text.

In October of 1834, the first letter from Graça arrived at *Necessidade Palace*. Monteiro, the secretary and chief of protocol, pushed the tray toward her. "Your Majesty, I am reluctant to answer this letter. I will, of course, ensure that no further written communication from this person reaches here."

Maria Glória recognized the handwriting immediately. "For Princess Maria Glória, or, Queen Maria II." Graça had written the words herself, placing each letter exactly on the prescribed line. "Beloved Maria Glória, we promised each other that we would go back to Brazil, but now you are the Queen of Portugal and will remain in Lisbon. Nor will I leave Porto. My body is swelling. Yes, it is what you think. It happened because I am so alone. I cannot get used to the foreign country, to being alone. For a year Isabel has written nothing to me, although I had two letters written to her. With a tender embrace I am your Graça. And do not forget that we were born on the same day."

Monteiro watched her while she read.

Would Maria Glória give that scribbled note back to him at last, so that he in turn could pass it on, lay it aside, and get rid of it?

"Senhor Monteiro, just leave it. This letter is in order. Graça is a friend of mine."

"That can't be. I beg your pardon, isn't she almost illiterate?" Monteiro hardly found the words, "Your Majesty, the salutation alone, what intimacy!"

She had laughed. "Graça came to Europe with me from Rio de Janeiro. She wanted to find Isabel."

"The...daughter of the mistress?" Monteiro shook his head.

"Yes. That's why she wangled her way onto the ship. In Paris she cried a lot. My schedule was overfilled, and pressing and ironing my clothes was not enough to occupy Graça. She couldn't talk with anyone, her Portuguese! Later she became acquainted with the Abreu family's cook, a Brazilian. That was good. Like all of us, Graça was waiting for us to finally be able to come to Portugal. France, Paris, two years! It took a long time, but Papa carried out everything. He defeated the Miguelists, and Uncle Miguel is in Evora in the monastery, house arrest. We were able to start out at last, and Graça accompanied me, but only as far as Brest. From there she wanted to go to London. How was she supposed to do that? But she was not to be deterred from it. She wanted to visit Isabel. Isabel is in London, in the lyceum of the 'Ladies of Loretto.' Now Graça writes that she is living in Porto, a journey of only one or two days' distance. We could see each other again!"

That is what she said, hugging the letter to her as she spoke. Graça's handwriting did her good. She had a friend with whom she could talk, a friend whom she could visit, "With a tender embrace..."

In the evening, Leonora reprimanded her severely. She enumerated for her the mistakes in that conversation:

Maria Glória did not show that she was irritated at the salutation on the envelope, her Brazilian given name!

She spoke openly about Isabel, which everyone avoided; she spoke about private things with a secretary; and the most weighty matter: she talked with Monteiro about political things! Perhaps Monteiro is a former Miguelist!

"Maria Glória, as your confidante I advise you not to speak thoughtlessly," and when she wept and sobbed, Leonore held her in a firm embrace and said consolingly, "I'll help you. You are not alone."

What was she supposed to do with this smooth talk? Her sisters and her brother were at the other end of the world. She did not let the letter from Graça be taken away from her. Rather, she had fallen asleep with the letter in her hand. To hold a piece of home in her hand - that reassured her; that strengthened her.

It became known, of course, that she was corresponding with Graça. At first they criticized it with their hands in front of their mouths, and years later a pamphlet was written for the newspaper, "The queen from the jungle who carries on a correspondence with an illiterate woman!"

Journey from Rio de Janeiro to Europe, 1831
"On such a long journey, with the pain of farewell but without joy"

The voyage from Brazil to Europe seemed to be endless. Maria Glória had a fever; she fantasized.

"Your fever comes from the soul. You're afraid. You didn't want to leave Rio. You especially didn't want to leave your brother," Graça insisted to her, while Leonora discussed with the doctor which tea mixture should be put together for Maria Glória.

"Pedrinho, I was not permitted to say good-by to him. That departure, almost in the middle of the night, and now I haven't seen Papa's ship for days, although he promised me that he would signal us with the Brazilian flag."

That 7th of April 1831, it had probably rained, for when they approached the ship from the boat across the long slanted ladder, the wet dresses weighed them down. To let herself fall, to slide back. That was not possible because Leonora pushed her on ahead of her.

On the ship they were led into a salon with plush furniture, everything in dark red, with velvet covers on the little tables and the bed, and all of the velvet things were rampant with thick and furry mildew.

"What a thing to ask, to travel in the winter," Leonora wailed.

When it was daylight the ship finally moved from Guanabara Bay into the Atlantic.

The voyage began, and it would last, last a long time. To kill time during those days, Maria Glória imitated everything that Dona Leonora did. That way the hours would pass most quickly. She unpacked books and laid pieces of clothing on each other; she wound her hair tight under the hairnet; she took a second cloak, for it was cold in the cabin. Later she ate chicken with grated coconut and bananas, the rice, and the toasted manioc with peanuts. She drank watered wine and dozed for a few hours in bed. In the evening Leonora drew her into a room where a chapel was set up. Maria Glória knelt down there. She did not pray; she did not find a single word for a prayer. Her head was filled with one thought: "Pedrinho, my beloved little brother. I don't want to be without Pedrinho. After all, I'm responsible for him and for my sisters. And please, let it remain dark. Drive the hours away."

In the middle of these feverish fantasies she suddenly saw Graça.

"Here, your evening cocoa," she smiled and then said, "I wangled my way onto the ship. I hid on one of the boats that brought the water casks to the ship. For two days even the cook didn't notice me. Maria Glória, your domestic staff is large and nobody has time to count heads."

Leonora stood at the foot of the bed. She nodded at Graça, pushed a chair toward her, and said, "Talk with Maria Glória. Tell her things. Amuse her."

Graça remained with her, during the entire voyage, all three hundred and ninety days of the voyage. She set up a bed for herself in Maria Glória's cabin. She went to the chapel with Maria Glória and accompanied her to the study room; she laid out her clothes, and she talked: "The marquise wanted red velvet borders. You can only get them in Europe. The Russian ambassador, or was it the ambassador from Paris, in any case a diplomat, brought her balls of that red velvet. What he got for it? Either a brooch from her jewel box or she dictated to her secretary a letter to the emperor, to Dom Pedro I, and then the man received a title or a higher office. In that way some also earned for themselves a house on the *Rua Ouvidor*, and everyone wanted to live there. Only ministers and high officials live there. The marquise wanted to have everything that came from Europe, everything that was said about Europe. Now I'll soon see if it is true that everything extravagant can be found in Europe: the silk shoes, the velvet hats, the damask bed linens with the monograms woven into them. At the court in Vienna, where Dona Leopoldina had grown up, furnished in that red color. In addition there was also gold, crystal, and mirrors everywhere, that's what they said, and it was probably that way, for Dona Leopoldina was a Habsburg, yes, Dona Leopoldina came to Brazil from the wealthiest court in Europe! That's why the marquise definitely wanted a European lady-in-waiting, and that is why she bought my mother, Irazy, from Senhor Picard. The marquise paid a lot of money for Irazy. Of course, Irazy is no European, but she served in a European household, and that meant almost as much to the marquise. Senhor Picard, I think he's a master builder, bought Irazy as a playmate and overseer for his sons and daughters. His wife was also a European woman. She was always ill, probably *saudade*.

"In any case, Senhor Picard, that European, is my father. I know everything about the fourth of April 1819, about the day you were born, Maria Glória. Irazy told me about it. It was a day with sun and rain. The people on the *Campo Santana* had already been waiting for the shots since midnight. Dona Leopoldina was in labor, and everyone hoped that she would bring her first child into the world on that Sunday, on Palm Sunday. It actually happened. At three o'clock in the afternoon the cannon shots were fired into the air: one, two, three, four. A princess! Some were disappointed. They would have preferred to have a prince as the firstborn. On the other hand, the natives of Rio de Janeiro prefer girls. My mother had already resolved months earlier that she wanted to bring her child, me, into the world on the day the Bragança child was born. She wanted to make Senhor Picard especially happy. After she had heard the shots, she climbed up on the storage cabinet in the pantry and jumped down to the stone floor. She had to do it several times, but late in the evening, when Senhor Picard came home from celebrating the birth of Crown Princess Maria Glória, I lay in the basket! An additional daughter had also been born to him. Senhor Picard was so beside himself with joy that he gave my mother her freedom and he even had me registered in the baptismal book: Graça, Grace, and for my second name he decided on: 'Leopoldina.'"

Leonora not only tolerated Graça's being together with Maria Glória, she supported and supervised it. She would have permitted anything, if only the attack of fever would not repeat itself.

"The beloved apple of my eye, Maria Glória, has fallen into deep sadness over the pain of farewell. She broke down into fits of crying, and all that gives me cause for the most serious worries. What abysses are borne within my minx with the black curls? At the same time she constantly strives to keep a smile on her face. To bring those two faces into balance will yet require of Maria Glória a great amount of spiritual strength, and more than any book knowledge we have to work on that above all. For the position for which she is destined it is better to keep an all-too-great sensitivity hidden, and Maria Glória has to learn that, as much as it may hurt...," Leonora had written to Papa in the educational report.

To her she said, "Maria Glória, I promised your father to bring a well instructed princess to Europe, and I'll keep that promise. In accordance with the schedule, we will memorize the Portuguese constitution of 1822. Remember what we wrote in your vade mecum: However great our despair may be at certain times, it is only work that remains our reliable friend. Only work knows how to comfort. So continue to fulfill your duties and be happy that in Graça you have found a kindred spirit for your free hours..."

Like everything that was important, Maria Glória found this note next to her breakfast tea.

Naturally she wanted to learn from Graça more about Domitila, about the Marquise of Santos. In *Boa Vista* the name of the mistress could hardly be mentioned. And Graça talked. She came out with the stories the way she drew the various threads for her sewing from the bag.

"The marquise was the emperor's wife."

"What are you saying? She was my father's mistress."

"For us servants it was this way: The emperor had a wife. She was the blonde princess from Europe. And besides that he also had a Brazilian woman as his wife. That was Domitila, the marquise. What the marquise was called in *Boa Vista* was of no interest to anyone. In the marquise's palace there were strict rules: The marquise insisted that her house be called a palace. If one of her secretaries or those who read to her told her that in our huts people talked about the 'house over there' or about 'the marquise's house,' then punishments were set. Kneeling on dry cocoa beans, I had to say, 'I'm sorry, but the word *palace* is so foreign to me. It did not occur to me. Of course I know that I serve in a palace, in the palace of the noble Marquise of Santos.' While I said that, they beat me. The marquise called upon a food bearer and a water bearer to do it, and they smacked the backs of their hands across my face. If blood flowed quickly, then I was soon released, and the marquise was satisfied. She then took an amethyst from her hair or a brooch from her shoe and said, 'Poor girl, now you'll remember.'

"None of us servants really took offense at her punishments, because it was a good business. The marquise simply had her peculiarities: the word *palace*, the way she was addressed. In actuality she wasn't a marquise, not yet at the time; her chairs with the stitched monogram, and the silk slippers with the topazes sewed onto them; the water jugs in which fresh paradise flowers had to float.

"For weeks there was talk about nothing else: When Dona Leopoldina is dead, the marquise will move to *Boa Vista*, and we with her, at least some of us, the most important ones, among which all included themselves. Once the empress, Dona Leopoldina, had died, then the throne would be empty for the marquise! After all, the little Isabel, the two-year-old Duchess of Goias, was already being raised in *Boa Vista*. That was what was speculated.

"But it turned out differently.

"Dona Leopoldina was dead, and Isabel was no longer tolerated in *Boa Vista*. She was now only permitted to visit the princesses and the prince. How the marquise screamed when they shoved the boxes with Isabel's clothes into the reception hall of the palace. The marquise could hardly be calmed down. Irazy, my mother, gave her the white powder in her wine. Then she straightened the pillows in her bed for her. Irazy also selected the scribes. Whom could the marquise trust? Did they actually write what she dictated?

"And I was only tolerated in the palace because of Irazy. Most of those who were born as I was were given away, sold, or traded away. I was five years old when Isabel came into the world, in the year 1824, in the middle of the winter. It had been raining for weeks. Puddles lay on the steps, in the living rooms. The beetles and the flies bathed in it. Again and again we also found snakes that had gotten lost, for in that May there was no difference between outside and inside. Puddles of water lay in the yard under the mango tree. Puddles were in the house. Each of the servants had a place where he remained in order to catch the water in a tub during the next downpour."

"Moacir, the chief steward, ordered me to the fireplace. I fitted exactly in that corner behind the fire. Gradually I was supposed to push the sticks of cinnamon and ginger into the flames and constantly shake the pan so that dense smoke billowed along the corridor to the marquise's room. Eulalia had come with a priestess and seven assistants to set up this specific place for the fumigation fire. For two days the procession of women had moved through the palace, praying and singing. The fever was supposed to be prayed, fumigated away. Worms, snakes, and caterpillars were actually harmless because you could see them, and you could thus also kill them. The illnesses, the fever, and the paralysis could not be seen, but they were everywhere, in the water and in the air.

"I crouched behind the fire pan and heard the hissing of the wet spice sticks. My eyes had long since ceased to water from the smoke, the dense smoke. They were so swollen that I could hardly lift my eyelids anymore. In front of my closed eyes silk threads began to dance, in shades of blue, green, and yellow, some the color of oranges, the ripe ones and the half-ripe ones. I wanted to go back into the embroidery nook, back to the silk threads. We embroidered on the covers for the marquise's chairs, on the bedcovers. Only little children could do that, for the stitches had to be so fine that you could not recognize them as stitches. Adult hands were much too rough and awkward for those needles and yarns. My head was so clouded with the vapor from the fire pan, that it did not occur to me to wonder where Eunice, Lucia, and Marcia were. I wanted to run away. Then Moacir grabbed me by the hair. 'You have to do what I ordered you to do. Otherwise you'll disappear back into the low place,' he hissed. 'If you weren't Irazy's child, I would teach you obedience very differently.'

"Low place! It finally occurred to me again. The place where we embroidered was set up under the stairway. The sun shone into it all day and the sun was important. We needed the brightest light. Besides, under the stairs we didn't bother anyone. Over us there were footsteps all day. By the rhythm of those footsteps, I recognized when the emperor came to see the marquise, and when a Marcelo came. All the young men were called Marcelo, and they were all her cousins. That was what the marquise had ordered, so we called those young men cousins.

"During the last days of that May of 1824 the marquise gave birth to the child, the emperor's child. The delivery was conducted as a ceremony. Irazy had to help as a midwife, and everything, the cloths, the basin with the water, the pillows that they shoved under the marquise's body, the lace coverlets that lay ready for the child - she had to do everything exactly the way she had learned and seen it done with her white Dona from Europe. The scribe who was supposed to write down the time of birth in the document sat very close to my fire pan. He breathed in the clouds of smoke deeply. He was probably afraid that he would catch some illness. Perhaps he had been sent directly from the emperor?

"The baby had already cried. The servants were singing and

dancing, and for a time they did not continue to concern themselves with bailing the water. They whispered, 'A field slave would have taken twice as long. She squats down and throws it into the world! That was the fourth. There is no way that this child is her second or her third, the way this body is in practice - at least the fourth!'

"Not until evening did Irazy come to the scribe and report to him: 'Following a ten-hour, difficult labor and an unbelievably complicated delivery, the Marquise of Santos gave birth to a daughter. We know that afternoon births are especially painful and difficult. For that reason we thank the Heavens that the brave marquise came through everything well.'

"During the night, storm and rain swept over the palace. All the oil lamps were full of water. It was pitch dark throughout the house.

"And in that darkness the infant's whimpering could be heard. 'Graça, come!' Irazy shouted and drew me into the room where the newborn child was crying. In a corner, close to the window, so that every rain shower reached her, the marquise sat in an armchair and slept, or dozed. She was certainly disappointed, for she had counted on a son. Perhaps it really was the way the servants gossiped: 'Our emperor has only daughters in his sack.'

"Irazy pushed me into the room, and as always I was supposed to sit down in a corner of the room and be quiet. I was drawn, however, to the basket, to the newborn child. I wanted to see this newborn daughter. She had cloud-white skin, so silvery white that her face glowed in the dark. Her skin was not only white, but it was as soft as the silk threads with which we embroidered. If I bent down to the child, the little girl stopped crying; and when I went away she screamed again. No matter how much the two nurses endeavored - they sang and whispered - the child that was only a few hours old screamed all the louder. They were all perplexed. That is why they didn't shoo me away when I took the child, the girl, out of the basket and sat down on the floor with her. She smacked her lips a few times and then she went to sleep.

"Did I like her or didn't I like her? More than likely I didn't like her back then. With that tiny thing I sat on the floor, which was wet with rain. If I didn't hold still, that little person would immediately begin to scream again. So I held still and let the rainwater run over my legs, over my feet. 'How will I get rid of you again?' I thought.

"That first occupation with the little girl brought me a Bahia topaz from the marquise. I gave that stone to the sailor who helped me to wangle my way aboard the ship.

"They called the girl Isabel. And because the two nurses with their overfilled breasts accomplished nothing with Isabel and Irazy took over nursing her, Isabel had become my milk sister. Was it an order from Heaven? Was Isabel now my concern? If Isabel cried, I was to blame. If she developed bedsores, it was my carelessness. If she spit the porridge onto her clean shirt, it was my inattention. Later, much later, when she ran down the path from the mango tree to the pond, fell in, screamed in deathly fear, and spit out water after I had pulled her out, she blurted breathlessly, 'Now they will punish you. You didn't watch me!'"

That was the way Graça talked; Graça, who had become Maria Glória's comforter on her voyage to Europe. But Graça herself also needed comfort when she came to Maria Glória and cried in despair: "When will we finally be in Europe? I have to find Isabel. After all, she's only seven years old and completely alone. Where? In Paris? Is it cold there? She's as unhappy as a rock. I can feel it. Do they also call her 'mistress's child' in Europe?"

Maria Glória is still sitting alone on the stone bench. She wanted it that way. She wanted to be in this place ahead of Graça, and lines from letters that she wrote to Graça in past years run through her mind. Sometimes Maria Glória worked on a letter for several weeks, added, and began over again, for she had to wait for an opportunity to be able to pass on a private letter, to be able to pass it on dependably and confidentially.

"Beloved Graça, you married Abrão. Let me embrace you! The Braga family is a respectable family. Here in Lisbon they say only good things about all of its members. Naturally I feel that a quiet, reserved love, or more likely friendship binds you to Abrão. You find that passion is missing? Believe me, it is better that way. I loved Augusto passionately. When I became a widow at sixteen, the cheerful part of me perished. Graça, I am surrounded by intrigues, by people who do not stop at anything. Unfortunately I did not heed your warning about Dona Amelia soon enough. You write that Abrão owns a book by António Vieira. I often read the passage about salt: *'You people are the salt of the earth, and salt prevents spoilage. But when we see how the world is spoiled today, although there are so many people upon it, wherein lies the cause for all of the evil? Either the salt no longer seasons, or the earth can no longer be salted...'* Porto is so close by, but I do not know whether I can leave Lisbon in the near future. For that reason I am sending you a box with clothing and dishes by ship. I personally selected and packed everything that you will find in it. There is nothing among those things that you must have for your kitchen. I am certain that you obtained everything necessary for your household long ago. So I have sent you pieces of clothing and porcelain that should make you happy. These things should have no other purpose but to make you happy. Accept a hearty and firm embrace from your friend Maria Glória. In July of the year 1836."

Few letters came from Graça; usually they were kept brief, "Isabel sent a photograph. She is magnificently beautiful and the good education shows...," but a few letters came that were pages long.

"Beloved Maria Glória, today the honorable Mother Ines will write for me, which is why I can write to you in detail. This year of 1843 is a good year for us. In the mulberry trees the fruits shine more luxuriantly than in any year before. The cocoons of the silk worms are filled with silk fibers of the very highest quality. Abrão has been so skilful in trading our silk that we can set up a weaving mill. Now we no longer have to give away the less valuable marabou and casing fibers as a bonus, but can weave them into sailcloth, into cloth for tables and beds, and some even into cloth for the theater. Maria Glória, it is already September again and this month is the last working month of the year. The European calendar, the European seasons, I am still not used to them. The months of October, November, and December. The trees have no leaves, the silk worms are asleep, and it constantly grows colder. I often sit for hours at the harbor, but no ship comes to Porto from Rio de Janeiro. During the winter months, Abrão will again read to me the sermons of António Vieira. I like to hear them. After all, I know that at the end of his life Vieira returned to Brazil. The book has been lying in the wooden casket for two hundred years. The paper is brittle and full of spots, but the ink is not faded. Letter follows letter in a blood-red line. '*Saudade*' is written on the first page. Vieira did not take this book with him, why? Maybe he was just able to save himself on a ship for Salvador, and he could no longer bother with the book.

"I want to remember the sermon on the fish, word for word: '*The fish that pursues the weaker ones should be careful not to wind up in the mouth of a larger one; he himself will be swallowed.*'

"Sometimes I want to write myself, write a letter to you with my own hand, but it is so much trouble. The words run through my head so rapidly that I cannot follow them. As if two languages had nested within me, the inner one that I brought with me from Brazil, and the other one that I speak here. So when I write, things get tossed back and forth and the letters, the words become illegible. Sometimes I become afraid. Will I not find my way back anymore in the end? I have already been here in Europe for twelve years, and I cannot imagine that I will remain here. Isabel will marry Count Max Treuburg and live in Munich. She wrote me a letter: 'My beloved soulmate, Graça!' How thankful I am to Isabel for every word. Beloved Maria Glória, may Heaven protect you and your family, and be to yourself, as Vieira teaches us, a good gardener for your soul. I send you a hearty embrace, your Graça."

António Vieira, the devil's priest, accompanied both of them, Maria Glória and Graça through all their letters. What strength is emitted by this writing; what power draws us to the words, the letters, which shimmer blood-red in the shadowy writing: "*The thieves' union...they steal, they bend the word steal in all directions and according to all the grammatical rules: they steal in the indicative, in the reality form. As a first indication, they demand knowledge about the treasures that they can carry off. They steal in the imperative, in the command form, for they have at their disposal an empire in which theft is permitted, yes, is ordered. They steal in the subjunctive, in the possibility form. They establish their union, the connection, with their copper coins and take for them cold and precious stones. They steal ad infinitum, so of course they steal in the infinitive. If they go away, then they leave behind the roots, the patterns for future stealing. They themselves steal, so in the first person; and their servants steal, thus in the second person; and they steal in the third person. Those are the ones that have a special gift for stealing. They steal in the present, for that is their time, of course. They also steal from the past, for from there they dig up crimes, damages, and debts, and from these they derive the right to steal. They make contracts concerning fruits that still hang on the tree, so they also steal in the future. They steal, they stole, they have stolen, they will steal, they would have stolen much more, if there had been more to steal..."*

    Maria Glória has been able to recite this sermon since Master Queiroz read it to her for the first time in Paris, more than two decades ago. "Maria Glória, don't tell anyone that you are familiar with this passage, that I'm giving you the book with this sermon. Promise me that you will be quiet. Otherwise I will have to flee from Europe. Otherwise the colonial rulers will banish me as they did Vieira, whom they ousted because they did not want to hear what he preached!"
    Run away, flee; perhaps she should have confessed her great fondness for Vieira; then she would finally have been expelled, southward across the Atlantic. She would no longer have to consider the question: Which place is more important, the place of destiny or the place of birth? Or the question: When should one stop adapting?
    How much *saudade* has distorted her face. Will Graça recog-

nize her now? Surely even Graça has become more corpulent, and Maria Glória wants to let herself fall into Graça's corpulence and softness. To take in the fragrance of her clothes; everything about Graça is familiar, and she, Maria Glória, wants to hand over at last what she has kept back for more than two decades.

CHAPTER II

*Sometimes in poverty that we abhor
and then dependent on strangers' aid
and sometimes seized by hope one more
with heavier consequences on us laid.*

Drizzle is coming down, fine drizzle, so fine that it immediately disappears into the pores of the stone bench, so that it hardly dampens the stone. The stables behind the castle are lighted. The lights move back and forth. Perhaps a foal is being born or a steer has broken free. In the autumn, when there is less work in the fields, the farmhands often drive a steer to the wooden partition behind which cows in heat are bellowing. When the animal that is tortured by the rush of its drives breaks away and runs wildly snorting through the stable yard, then the young fellows demonstrate samples of their courage to each other, trying to lure the steer back into the stall to the cow that is in heat. Sometimes a cow is trampled to death in the process. "Rape, she didn't want it any other way," the farmhands laugh. "Too bad about the meat, it stinks. The strongest vinegar will not draw out the taste of the cow in heat."

The morning sun glows red-orange through the fog from Lisbon on up here to Sintra. "In Lisbon you will miss the tropics. You will not find in any street, in any park the many shades of green that were so natural to you in Rio. Nor is there in Lisbon that market life where the blood of freshly slaughtered pigs and cattle steams and the steam mixes itself with the clouds of smoke from the spice pans. But there is something substantial that you will find in Lisbon - the tropical light. It shows itself every day, for only a few minutes, in the morning, when the night is replaced by the day and the sun rises out of the Tejo. Then the city is bathed in the tropical red-orange of the tropical light," was what Dona Leonora had told her in Paris about her new home.

Maria Glória in Brest and London, 1831
"And destiny abducted her into a different world"

She had spent two and a half years waiting in Paris. Only then did she travel to Lisbon.

First was the voyage from Rio de Janeiro to Europe. That voyage lasted for three hundred and ninety days. They plowed through the waves, encountered thunderstorms and tempests. They had to sail in a wide arc around the Azores.

"The emigrants wish for nothing more ardently than to see their queen at last, but it is too dangerous. Then Miguel will immediately send a ship with soldiers and will have them shoot at us. Only when Miguel has been ousted, when your father has defeated him, will you be safe, in Portugal and on the Azores," Dona Leonora explained.

Maria Glória did not ask anymore: "When will that be?"

She knew the answer.

"First an army has to be put together. Not until then can Portugal be liberated from the Miguel regime."

To shorten the time, the days that stayed the same and did not want to end, she wrote letters to Januária, to the sister who was now the oldest of her siblings in Rio. She wrote, added, formulated anew, taught Graça letters while doing so, and led Graça's hand in curves and loops to words: "Beloved Sister, I have finally stopped counting the days. We have been sailing toward the continent of Europe for sixty days. I cannot complain about anything. Everyone here on the ship takes pains to make my daily life as comfortable as possible. But nobody can tell me whether the ship on which Papa and Dona Amelia are traveling is headed for France or for England. We have lost sight of each other. Yesterday a stay on land came to an end. We landed for three days in Senegal. In the city of Dakar the barrels were filled with fresh drinking water. They also drove calves onto the ship; they are the meat supply. As you know me, I shall not eat a bit of meat. When I think of the eyes of those animals, which are full of trust, tears come to my eyes. They only permitted me to go ashore for a little while. Everywhere I am in danger of being abducted, they say. The faithful followers of Miguel would lie in wait for me to prevent me from traveling any further. So nothing is left to me but the strict, daily fulfillment of my duties: the Mass, the classes in French, geography, and history, the piano and dancing lessons, the lectures on rhetoric, and in all of these things Graça is at my side. That consoles me in many instances of melancholy.

"To give you a picture of life here on the ship: Many of the passengers are business people who lived in Rio for a few years and are relieved to escape from the tumultuous political climate in Brazil. They have acquired fortunes for themselves in Rio, and now they show off with their jewelry, the rings and the bracelets. Even the gentlemen wear bracelets set with all the precious stones of our homeland, with emeralds, aquamarines, and topazes. Some of them constantly have little cases with them, and it is rumored that rolls of money and precious stones wrapped in cloth are hidden in them. When I walk with Graça and Dona Leonora on deck, they are friendly toward us. But they imitate everything. Right now on the ship it is fashionable to curl their hair as I do! They scrounge sugar water and coconut oil from the stewards, and many a lady gets too much of everything; then we hear her squabbling with her maid, and the latter has to run for water so that she can free her mistress from her filthy hair. Most of the businessmen have one or two servants with them. They are freed slaves. Those colored people are used for all kinds of service, some for dice games, some to carry water, and some, according to what Graça told me, are partners for the bedroom. There are married couples where each partner brought along a slave for his or her cabin. Graça is a good observer of some involvements that we follow with amusement. Among the sailors, the servants quickly find friends and people of equal station with whom they can converse. Loving couples are formed, involving the servants of the businessmen and the sailors, and some no longer want to be separated. So the rich feel that they have been seriously hoodwinked, because they freed their slaves before our departure, and now the latter refuse to perform the services that were agreed upon, but prefer to languish in the sailors' cabins with their lovers. Some even call themselves engaged. Dearest Sister, you see that aboard ship things go as they do in Rio de Janeiro, only here we are right next door to the showing-off and the mendacity, as well as the intrigues; and that is the thing that I fear most, that on the new continent, in Europe, I will not be able to place my trust in anyone but Dona Leonora. I pray to Heaven for a few people who will be sincere with me.

"The ship is setting a course for France; a wide swing is being made around Portugal, until we arrive in Brest. There, as the future Queen of Portugal I have a text to recite, while I have never seen my new homeland. I send you a most intimate embrace, your sister Maria Glória."

At the end of the first week in July of 1831 they had arrived in the harbor of Brest in Brittany. Everywhere there were flags, bands, and festively clothed people who waved with their hats at the sailing ship from Latin America.

Maria Glória recited the text of her greeting in French and Portuguese: "I thank France, the French people, the King of France, Louis Philippe of Orléans, his family, and his ministers, that this grand reception has been prepared for me. Since I am prevented from entering my homeland of Portugal, I am especially thankful for protection and refuge. I greet especially my Portuguese people, the emigrants. Dear countrymen, you had to flee from the Miguel regime. You fled to England and now you have come here to Brest to greet me. No queen of Portugal before me ever received such an honor..."

She was interrupted by shouts of "Viva!" A rain of flowers fell on her. Everyone wanted to see the twelve-year-old Queen Maria II of Portugal close up. In a white muslin dress with blue ribbons, dressed completely in the colors of Portugal, she shook hands, waved, and listened attentively as the speaker of the Portuguese emigrants read the oath aloud: "...that we here promise and swear to support in every way our Queen Maria II in her efforts to transform Portugal into a prospering realm ...have faith that our queen will liberate our homeland, for with her youth she brings both peace and freedom, equality and fraternity; long live the *Carta Constitutional...*"

For hours Maria Glória was passed along from one delegation to another - on every corner a different manifesto, arms full of flowers, blossoms that they stuck in her hair, and all the while Dona Leonora was constantly at her side, caressing her arm and smiling - at last, at last the whole world could see how she had raised this growing girl to become such a perfect queen.

In the evening the first official reception.

Dona Amelia and Papa had been in Brest for weeks. Dona Amelia was expecting a child; that was already visible. She smiled as always. Papa looked strange. Everything about him had become gray, his hair, his skin, and his eyes.

He waited patiently until it was his turn to be introduced.

"Duke Pedro of Bragança!"

Father had actually renounced all claims, and he bent his knee before his daughter to kiss her hand like the others, the diplomats, bishops, and officials.

One of the ambassadors eyed Maria Glória especially closely and for a long time. "That was the Austrian! He will now report to Emperor Franz I in minute detail how well instructed and well formed his granddaughter is. You're half Austrian. Don't forget that," whispered Dona Leonora to her.

July, midsummer in Brittany, with the days when the sun does not go down until ten o'clock in the evening and when the bays and fields and hills are bathed in a veil of mist during the hour before sunset; the fields small and lined with trees and shrubs.

Father had climbed the lighthouse of Brest with Maria Glória. She wanted to see Europe; she wanted to see France, this first part of it. Above all, she wanted to hear her father laugh again. At one of the bends in the lighthouse stairs he would disappear into a niche, imitate the whistle of a small armadillo, and finally dart out of his hiding place and be standing at the top window even before Maria Glória got there, with his curly hair falling untamed across his forehead. "Well, where have you been, Maria Glória? I've already been her for a few minutes," he would laugh.

But Father walked behind Maria Glória step by step, stair after stair up the lighthouse stairway. "Paris lies in that direction," he declared halfway up, and, "there, toward the northwest, lies London. It is very near."

Father did not transform himself again into that father, into Papa, whom she knew from *Boa Vista*.

"Europe is a wonderful continent," this new, serious father said comfortingly to her. "In the beginning everything seems closer together. Cities and landscapes change rapidly and have new faces every few hours. But soon this closeness will become nearness to you, and nearness is the good sister of closeness. Here different languages and cultures live next to each other very closely."

She had nodded to that. The man who now stood and walked next to her was a stranger. It was Father, but first she had to get used to him.

They remained in Brest for only a few days. Once Maria Glória had ridden up a hill alone. Grass and trees were so easy to bend; most of them had no thorns and could be broken, torn off with one tug. The smells that surrounded them were milder. Nothing here had the sweetness, the spiciness that intensified itself to the point of burning at home. Nowhere did she find the brightness that hurt her eyes; none of the blossoms spread a fragrance that made a person dizzy.

She wanted to become accustomed to Europe; she had assigned herself to do that in her diary. When she wrote that, she did not know how difficult it would be. Again and again she made mistakes: "You embrace too much." "Do not present yourself as being so open, so cordial." "You have confused the seasons again. August is summer here and not winter!"

Sometimes she was quite despondent about it. She missed Brazil so much. "Brazil will remain in your heart. Nobody can take that from you," Dona Leonora had often said to her during the voyage, trying to console her. Nor could Brazil be pushed away. Maria

Glória grasped that fact in France. For whatever she saw, heard, or smelled, she drew a comparison. All of her senses weighed things, and Brazil came off better in those comparisons. "Drive the *saudade* from me," she prayed.

Even in Brest, Graça remained at her side, slept in her room. "When are we going on to Paris? It's because of Isabel," Graça often whispered, but even she soon no longer expected an answer. Everything was delayed.

Back then Graça had become smaller, or so it seemed to Maria Glória. Graça had retreated from Maria Glória in her new ruffled dresses, retreated when Maria Glória spoke French. But even in her withdrawal she remained the Graça that she had been in *Boa Vista*, the one that she had been on the ship. "Maria Glória, try the sweet baked goods. Here, I swiped them from the kitchen," and she pulled round and square sweets and delicacies from her bag. "We have to eat them all, so that the strict Dona Leonora doesn't find a crumb."

Already on the fourth day after their arrival in Brest, Father stated at the evening meal, "Tomorrow we'll travel on to London."

Everyone took note of that; only Maria Glória dared to ask a question: "Why? We intended to go to Paris. After all, Dom Louis Philippe and his family are expecting us. And Clementine, I'm already looking forward to meeting her!"

Dona Leonora looked up startled. How forward Maria Glória was in speaking.

"It will be better for our cause if we go to England," Father stated as he pushed back his plate and left the table.

With that Maria Glória had received her reprimand. Silence spread across the room; they all looked at their plates. It was an unpleasant situation. Was dinner now over? Pedro I, the Emperor of Brazil, had left the table. Or was that rule no longer valid for Duke Pedro of Bragança?

When the emperor ends the meal, everyone present has to leave the table. That was an iron rule. The servants were already moving. Shouldn't they carry the dishes away?

But Maria Glória was hungry; the chicken soup smelled delicious, and there were platters with vegetables and bowls with sauces on the table. The breads smelled of anise and caraway. She bent toward the soup bowl.

"The queen wishes to have some of the soup," said Dona Leonora, and everyone, the officials, the two ladies-in-waiting, and the clergyman, breathed a sigh of relief and continued the dinner.

Once and for all the hierarchy was established.

Maria Glória did not grasp that fact until she saw that tears were running down Dona Amelia's face. Nobody paid attention to it; they did not want to see it. Even Maria Glória continued to eat her soup, took some of the chicken and the creamy dessert. With every spoonful that she ate, she became more conscious of the situation into which she had brought herself, into which she had brought her father. Her face burned under the blush that had risen in it. She wanted to smile at Dona Amelia and hand her the bowl with the creamy dessert; she wanted to comfort Dona Amelia with some kind gesture. But she felt Dona Leonora's eyes on her arm, on her hand. Maria Glória felt the sentence that Dona Leonora was thinking, that she had hammered into her so firmly: "We must never flinch from decisions that we have made, but have to prove that we have courage and a sense of responsibility..."

If she had tried to comfort Dona Amelia with a smile, or to placate her, it would have brought her a rebuke from Dona Leonora. She did not want that; she feared the staccato of Dona Leonora's doctrines more that anything else. For that reason she continued to eat without looking up.

Dona Amelia did not let herself be served anything. She ate nothing. She watched, she caught a word here and a sentence there, until Maria Glória got up and left the dining room with Dona Leonora. With that the meal was over.

Dona Leonora praised her, "That was important. You acted boldly and correctly. I'm proud of you."

"Your stepmother is dangerous," said Graça after the evening prayer. Only in the darkness of night did Graça speak so frankly.

She pushed aside the screen behind which her bed stood. "Maria Glória, she doesn't like you. She wants to be in your place!"

"Oh, no," she said to Graça reassuringly, "she watches Argus-eyed to see if I behave properly at the table. She wants to know what I say to the bishop. Woe be unto me if I were to make mistakes. Then she'd blame Dona Leonora, and she wants to hatch some plot to get her out of the way."

"Nevertheless, I don't like your stepmother," Graça repeated. "She's dangerous. She wants to be in your place, Maria Glória."

"Why does Father think that England is more supportive of Portugal's affairs than France is?" Maria Glória asked because she did not understand.

"Dom Pedro is offended at King Louis Philippe for sending only officials and not being present in person at your reception," Dona Leonora sighed.

She continued whispering, "In reality it's this way: Neither Wellington, the prime minister, nor the English King William will seriously support the cause of 'the Queen of Portugal,' in other words, your business, and give money for an army with which battle can be waged against the Miguelists. Neither England nor France wants to get involved with Portugal's affairs."

"But the Portuguese emigrants are living in both England and France," Maria Glória said. She had learned so much about the ties and also about the dependencies between Portugal and England, between Portugal and France, and now she did not know what to do. She felt sorry for the emigrants.

Dona Leonora continued to explain, "They want to get rid of the emigrants again, of course. On the other hand, we know that those who fled from Miguel have meanwhile established business connections in London and in Brest, and that will be advantageous to Portugal, to the new Portugal, when Dom Miguel is finally gone...," Dona Leonora corrected herself, "has finally been deprived of political power."

Maria Glória tried to follow. "And they don't want that either. Neither France nor England wants that."

Dona Leonoara nodded, "A delicate matter."

The crossing from Brest to London was stormy. In the thunderstorm the sailing vessel lost its direction for hours. The masts for the sails burst; a sailor was thrown overboard and drowned. And when the harbor of London was already in sight, another severe storm moved in, and the ship reeled again for hours without direction.

The boats with Father and his secretaries, with Dona Amelia, Maria Glória, Graça, and Dona Leonora, and the ladies-in-waiting entered the harbor in pitch-black darkness. A few coachmen were on the quay; they were half drunk and looked at the group of travelers. "Those are the Brazilians," one of them bawled.

Maria Glória, Graça, Dona Amelia, and Dona Leonora were crammed into a coach and rumbled toward the city. Masses of water fell from the sky as they did during the heaviest winter rains in Rio de Janeiro; thunder and lightning chased each other across the skies.

Finally the four women were dropped off at the *Hotel Clarendon* and directed into the foyer of the hotel. There they stood, dripping wet. Dona Leonora asked the doorman for a pot of hot tea.

The doorman shook his head: "No, it's after midnight. They're all asleep. Besides that, I was notified of the arrival of the Emperor of Brazil, and now two ladies-in-waiting and two young ladies are standing here," he murmured.

They stayed in London for a few days, and every day they were treated as poorly, as ignorantly as they had been treated during the very first hours after their arrival.

They all froze; their dresses did not dry out, but nobody offered them any help or gave them a piece of wood for the stove.

"Give me your slip and your petticoat. If I lie on them in the night, everything will be dry by morning," was the way Graça tried to help.

In the morning, Father left the hotel to meet with officials and with ministers. But they put him off. They spoke of a fever epidemic and talked about economic problems. There was a crisis in the production of iron; they had put a lot of money into the development of the steam locomotive. Why was Brazil denying itself this new technology? Would it not be appropriate for the Portuguese emigrants who had found a safe place of exile here in London to travel to Brazil with their knowledge of the language and the culture and promote the English steam locomotives? In all earnestness, they wanted to use Pedro Bragança to engineer business ties with Brazil, but nobody had an ear for Pedro Bragança's concerns or for his daughter's concerns.

"They don't want to grasp the fact that Brazil has been independent for ten years. They don't want to hear that I speak for Portugal, that Portugal and Brazil are two separate states, that I need support for an army against Miguel." Father was despondent and immediately ordered their departure.

At Windsor there was still a dinner to attend. Even there everything remained ceremonial. King William praised Portugal. Maria Glória recited her memorized words about the liberal spirit of the major power Great Britain. The good wishes were received with smiles. Then Queen Adelaide stood up and approached Maria Glória. "This will be the welcoming gift for the Queen of Portugal. Here, Maria."

Queen Adelaide smelled of lavender; she even tried an embrace. Maria Gloria did not want to be embraced by this woman. What did the English woman know about the Brazilian custom of embracing? Nothing. It was only imitation. Maria Glória busied herself with the wooden casket. Jewels lay within it. All of the colors of Brazil shimmered up at her, red, blue, green, and yellow. Even Bahia topazes were included among them. The stories about precious stones from Brazil were repeated: From Ouro-Preto these stones had traveled to Rio de Janeiro and then on to Lisbon. In Lisbon they had been purchased for a song by an English gemstone dealer and had been brought to the goldsmith in London. "Queen Adelaide especially loves the precious stones of the Portuguese."

For a few seconds Maria Glória said nothing. The food bearers and servers were already becoming agitated. She reflected, stared at the glitter of the precious stones from Brazil. Would she find a sentence, a memorized sentence for this situation? "I thank you, your Royal Majesty. You know what these jewels mean to me, precious stones from my first homeland! I will give them to the emigrants when they return from London to Portugal, return home to a liberated Portugal, which will hopefully happen soon."

She did not worry about the glances, the clearing of the throats. Father reached for the wineglass. She could not hold back the tears for another moment and let them run down her cheeks. None of those who were present said anything. They all stared at her. Would she completely lose her composure in the end? When would she finally sit down, so that they could begin serving? At that time, for the first time she felt alone on an official occasion, left alone by everyone. If she had sunk down next to her seat, nobody, at least for a long time, would have helped her.

"First homeland!" After that dinner Dona Leonora was beside herself. "Never say that again!"

"I shall always say that. Portugal is my second homeland!"

"Second!" Dona Leonora wrung her hands. She tried to convince her: "Portugal is '*a minha Pátria adoptada* [my adopted homeland].' I beg of you, Maria Glória, express it that way."

And as much as she had resisted it in the beginning, as much as everything within her had balked at it, these words soon became extremely natural for her: "I shall always do everything for Portugal's best interests, for the best interests of my '*Pátria adoptada.*'"

Maria Glória and Graça in Paris until 1833
"The world still lay wrapped in the light of dawn"

Maria Glória has not noticed Graça's approach. There are still a few steps between her and the stone bench, and Graça stops at that distance. Her wide, black skirts billow in the morning wind, and with her gaze she holds Maria Glória tightly, holds Maria Glória down. Power and inflexibility come from Graça, and the person Graça whom she wants to embrace, but whom she cannot reach, is infinitely far away. She is not strong enough to overcome that distance, to walk the two or three steps to Graça.

Graça finally sits down on the stone bench. She remains at quite a distance from Maria Glória.

"And what came after that," Graça asks, and Maria Glória picks up the thread of her narrative again.

From London they went to Brest again and then on to Paris. August of 1831, midsummer in Europe. They rode past fields in which the grain stood ripe, ready to harvest. When Father had them stop for a rest and Dona Amelia, Maria Glória, and Graça sat under a shrub to recover from the jolting, a few men and women soon came. They brought a jug of wine and placed a basket with bread and cheese in front of the strangers. Maria Glória could hardly understand their French.

She reported to her sister Januária in Rio de Janeiro: "The people who work in the fields here are full of pride. They approached us quite freely, spoke with us, and joined Dona Amelia in looking forward to the baby that she would soon bring into the world - at least that is what we gathered from their gestures. You know, Januária, we know only the strict separation of the worlds: the slaves who work in the field, the kitchen maids, and the stable boys - they all stop at a distance from us, and they immediately stop speaking when we are in their vicinity. Their world has nothing to do with ours. We are the commanders, the coercers, and we have no part in their huts or their conversations. That is different here, and I think that I am now beginning to understand the statement 'that the rights of all people are the same.' Here in August it is as hot as it is there at home in January, but the air is oppressive, because the wind is missing, our good friend the wind, into which we so much like to hold our faces and our bodies - oh, yes, for me it is really: into which I so much liked to hold my face..."

They traveled to Rennes and remained overnight in the capital city of Brittany. "Dona Amelia is already completely exhausted. We should stay longer," sighed Dona Leonora.

Father met with city officials, with military men. There was good news at last: In Paris financial backers had already been found who would equip an army for the Duke of Bragança.

The next stop was Laval, a sleepy town, then along the rivers to Le Mans, and finally they arrived in Chartres. The entire Orléans family had come to meet them there: Louis Philippe, Dona Maria Amalia, and Clementine. Bands played and toasts were exchanged: "We thank you for the hospitality that France, that you, your Majesty, Dom Louis Philippe grant to us. After a long journey from Latin America we are now received by the liberal nation..."

That was what Maria Glória had to say, and it fell easily from her lips, for in Chartres she felt herself surrounded exclusively by people from whom benevolence radiated. She spoke without fear and without hesitation. As a welcoming greeting, Dona Maria Amalia, the Queen of France, had placed flowers on each of their pillows, even on Graça's pillow. At dinner there was bubbling fresh water and strawberries with sweet cream; the steam from the bathtubs smelled like rosemary. How many charitable acts could be done to a person on one single day?

For a few days, the *saudade* was a little less painful. In the Pilgrimage Church Maria Glória lit four thick candles: "For Januária, for Francisca, for Paula Mariana, for Pedrinho. I hope that they are doing well and that it just does not rain too much during this wintry August, for then the roads and paths from *Boa Vista* into the city will be muddy for days, and that makes everyone fearful. The servants are fumigating the rooms again with ginger roots. They cannot be deterred from it, although it has never helped. They could not accomplish anything with it to ward off the death of *Mamãe*, and it didn't help against Domitila." That was how Maria Glória often spoke and prayed during the months when she lived in Paris. Somehow she had to pacify her guilty conscience, and she did have a guilty conscience, for the charitable deeds that had begun in Chartres did not stop. The bath in water steaming with rosemary became routine, the visits of the seamstresses and the milliners the same; a new ribbon in a more intensive blue, a hatpin set with a tiger's eye, a second ribbon of lace sewn onto her stockings, and the gloves that she wore every day had mother-of-pearl buttons.

Only Graça reminded her that outside of this perfume-clouded world there was another part, one that Maria Glória pushed into the background for weeks.

Graça had become a member of the family. During their initial days in Paris she slept in Maria Glória's room. She sat in a corner while Maria Glória attended her classes.

"When will we visit Isabel?" she asked, and Maria Glória put her off, saying, "Dona Amelia will do that, tomorrow, or next week."

She pretended to sleep when Graça murmured or even wept in the night, "*Saudade, saudade* for Rio."

Maria Glória could hardly keep back the tears herself. She was relieved that she could commit herself to her schedule, to the tea parties and dance parties. Everything was a diversion, an anesthesia. Her thoughts had no time to wander.

After two weeks Graça had moved out of Maria Glória's room. "I'll sleep in the servants' quarters, next to the kitchen. It's warm there, and I'll help the dessert cook. Here I have nothing to do all day. The employees don't want me to help them. They don't even let me take out the ashes. Everyone has his place and I'm superfluous."

Maria Glória was relieved. She just did not want to have to hear that voice in the night.

Saudade, often the only Portuguese word that Maria Glória heard, for she only spoke French anymore for hours and days at a time. *Saudade* - in that she heard Pedrinho crying, she heard the clatter of the palm trees when the night wind blows through the fronds. She heard the laughter of a chambermaid who amused herself in the courtyard with a stable boy. *Saudade* - when the small armadillos fight in their mating battle during the early morning hours; *saudade* - running in the garden with her little sister Francisca, "I'll stick the first open hibiscus in my hair"; *saudade* - fighting with Paula Mariana over a larger portion of coconut-corn cake, "I'm going to tell Dona Amelia. You'll get fat because you pour so much coconut milk over it."

At the end of October, when they had all acclimated themselves to Paris, Graça rode with Dona Amelia to Montparnasse, to the boarding school where Isabel lived.

Maria Glória knew only this about it: Isabel lived in a building in which she went to school, and in which she slept and ate. Did they like Isabel there or treat her badly? Did they call her "mistress's bastard" there, too? Maria Glória felt that things were not going well with Isabel. She dreamed about Isabel, and in her dreams she saw Isabel emaciated, with dark eye sockets from which tears ran, pleading. Maria Glória awoke from those dreams sobbing, with her eyes red from crying. She did not talk to anyone about it.

After the visit to Isabel, Graça talked. She did not let anyone interrupt her: "Isabel is sick. They have put her in a sick room. There is nothing in it but a bed, a washstand, and a prayer stool. And the nun was not friendly to us at all. They didn't even offer Dona Amelia a chair. They just wanted to have us outside again quickly. 'It is probably consumption. She surely brought it from Brazil, and, as you know, there is no medicine to combat it.' Dona Amelia had grown pale. I had to hold her up, and only when Dona Amelia pulled a bundle of banknotes from her bag and held it out to the nun did the sister become kinder. We were at last permitted to sit. Dona Amelia received a bowl of warm milk. I only caught this much: The two governesses who brought Isabel here to Paris two years ago paid the institution for only a few months, although Dom Pedro had given them enough money for at least two years! Those two snakes also departed from Paris after a few weeks. The one is in Rome, and the other, I think, is in Vienna. Maria Glória, nobody has taken care of Isabel for two years! She's freezing. 'I'm letting myself die,' she said. You wouldn't recognize her. At the age of seven she is as small as a four-year-old, with transparent skin. Her voice has become strange. It sounds hoarse. Maria Glória, you must help her. You must!"

How was she supposed to do that? She had no money. Besides, Dona Amelia would take care of it, and Papa, of course, so that things would go better with Isabel. Maria Glória did not want to interrupt a schedule that held so many benefits, and diversions as well.

"She will die of *saudade*. I must visit her, and you must come with me and talk to the nuns. I can't speak French. You must impress upon them that I have to be let in to see Isabel and that the doors have to be opened for me. You're the Queen of Portugal. You have stationery with golden coats-of-arms on it. We'll take it along, and I still have a few precious stones from the marquise. I'll pay for Isabel with them. Then they will be good to her and heat her room. I'll also take a brick along, one like you get in your bed so that you don't freeze."

The image from her dreams of Isabel could not be pushed away. Perhaps if Maria Glória knew how Isabel lived, perhaps then Isabel would also laugh and sing again in her dreams, the way that Maria Glória remembered her little half-sister from Rio.

So she rode with Graça out to Montparnasse. "Nobody must know that you are visiting Isabel. That would be a scandal. You are visiting the daughter of your father's mistress. Be back for afternoon tea. Please!" The kind Leonora had become engrossed in the Bible. She knew that nobody would dare to interrupt her in that, to ask her about Maria Glória.

The coachman cursed because he had to turn around twice. The streets of Montparnasse were covered with ice. The horses slipped, shied. They almost crashed into a coach that was coming toward them.

"Here, I want to get out here already," Graça stated, and she slipped through a gap in the fence. Maria Glória could hardly follow her. They ran across the icy grass toward the building, and when they got there Graça threw small pebbles at a windowpane. Behind the window glass was a grating and between the bars of the grating Isabel's small face suddenly appeared.

"No!" Maria Glória cried out. This little child could not be Isabel. A white chemise trembled on her body; the ties at the neck were open, and below them was only naked skin. The little girl trembled with the cold. She did not react; she only looked. She gave no sign with her hand or with her head.

"We're coming," Graça waved to her and drew Maria Glória along to the main entrance.

"We request permission to visit Isabel of Goias," Maria Glória stuttered at the mother superior, and she laid an amethyst on the table. "May I give you this stone, Mother Superior. It gives strength to anyone who possesses it," she added. She had carefully removed the amethyst from the slip into which she and Dona Amelia had sewn several dozen precious stones on their last day in *Boa Vista*. "Who knows how we will fare in Europe? And with those you can pay."

They were in Isabel's room for almost an hour. The little girl did not say anything. She let Graça embrace her and rock her like a little child. When Graça held her in her arms, she trembled so much that Graça lay down with her in the bed. Graça caressed Isabel, told her the story of the mango tree and the fairy that lived in it, and Isabel became calmer. For a few minutes she even went to sleep. Maria Glória sat on the floor and watched Graça, watched how she caressed Isabel, how Graça tried to give warmth and life to Isabel from herself, how Graça pulled the chemise over little Isabel's head.

"What are you doing?"

"My underwear, my undershirt, my underpants, my slip, I'll put it all on her. She will get well from that because with that I give her more of my strength. Maria Glória, give your underwear, too. You have so much cheerfulness in you from recent weeks. Isabel must get some of that. It will ease the *saudade* for her. Quickly, get undressed before that nun comes." And Graça and Maria Glória helped each other open the ties and the hooks and eyes. Off with the coat, jacket, shawl, and dress. The chemise with the long sleeves undone, the knee-length overpants and the stockings, the slip. Isabel watched them. She let them roll the stockings up her legs and put the chemise and pants on her. Everything was too big for her, but she held every piece of clothing pressed tightly to her body.

"And these things here?" Isabel finally asked, pointing to the pieces of underwear that lay on the floor.

"Of course they will stay here with you. Look, I'm also putting my muff with them. It's cuddly. You can lay your head on it and hide your hands in it." Maria Glória would have given the little girl everything but her coat and the shoes with the leggings, if she had only spoken, if she had only shown that she wanted to live, wanted to continue living and get well.

When the nun came and said, "I must ask the noble young ladies to leave our Isabel alone again now," Maria Glória stood freezing, without any underwear and without any stockings, holding her coat firmly together in front of the giant nun. "Reverend Mother, Graça has the assignment, the assignment from Isabel's father, the Duke of Bragança, to visit Isabel regularly. I'm sure that I can convey your permission to my father!"

Dona Leonora had drilled this sentence into her: "Maria Glória, if you really want to help, you must threaten the nuns with your father, and take money along, or a precious stone."

The nun nodded, "Of course the lady's maid Graça will always be welcome here. What is the meaning of this underwear?"

"The Duke of Bragança sends it. With your permission, Reverend Mother, Isabel will be allowed to put this underwear on," Graça said, and the nun also agreed to that.

Isabel had followed this conversation attentively. She sat on her bed, and her small head protruded from the ruffles and ribbons of the overly large pieces of underwear that she was wearing. And she held the muff and the bundle with the second set of underwear from Maria Glória tightly to her.

The nun was already holding the door open. They should go; these two adolescent nobles should finally go away. That was what she was thinking. They could clearly see that in her face.

Go away. Maria Glória could not do that. She rushed to Isabel and embraced her. She wept with her face buried in the emaciated body, and all the tears that she had held back burst forth. Her siblings were so far away, Januária, Francisca, Paula Mariana, Pedrinho. She caressed and hugged all of them as she held Isabel in her arms.

"Isabel, get better," she stammered into the little girl's ear, and when the nun wanted to pull her away from Isabel, Maria Glória resisted: "Leave me alone!" For Isabel already felt livelier. She wrapped her thin arms around Maria Glória's neck: "Stay here."

Paula Mariana had shouted that after the evening prayer, and in just the same way that Isabel held her with her clasped in her arms, Pedrinho had held her: "Come into my bed, Maria Glória. I'm afraid."

Maria Glória was so completely absorbed in the memory of her siblings, of *Boa Vista*, that she almost fell down when the nun grabbed her firmly and separated her from Isabel.

"For Heaven's sake, your Majesty, are you having a seizure? We need a doctor," cried the nun and ran for help.

Slowly Maria Glória became conscious of reality again. Once again she snuggled up to her sister, half-sister, and said, "Get better again, please." Then she also reacted to Graça's timid coaxing, "Maria Glória, we must go."

She wrapped her coat tightly around her body again, so that nobody could see that she had nothing on under it, and walked out of the room with Graça. Isabel breathed deeply and quietly. She seemed to be asleep. A terrible nightmare was finally over for her, had gone away.

The nuns were relieved that the two disturbers of the peace, Graça and Maria Glória, had disappeared. They did not report the incident to anyone.

As they were driven home, Maria Gloria also grew firm again. "More dignity! You must maintain your composure. Such an outburst, almost a scandal," she would be reprimanded. And when they arrived at the house that was her home in Paris, she had calmed down outwardly, and she was smiling again.

On the way home, Graça held her hands. "You poor girl. Nobody really knows how much you suffer. Don't you have a place where you can cry? You must find a place where you can cry. Tears water the soul. Otherwise it turns into stone, poor sister."

Of course, Maria Glória told Dona Amelia about that visit: "Horrible, the poor little girl! We'll report it to Dom Pedro."
"When?"
"In the next few days. At the moment Dom Pedro is very busy."
Meanwhile, from hour to hour it became colder; at least it seemed that way to Maria Glória. When she closed her eyes she saw Isabel in front of her, with her little head behind the bars of the grating. An hour away by coach, Isabel lay in her chilly bed, and in the house of the Braganças on the *Rue Aboukir* they were talking about the decorations for the Advent soiree.
Three days after the visit to Isabel, Graça came into Maria Glória's room in the evening.
"I want to write Dom Pedro a letter. Please write for me," she said, no, she ordered it.
Shouldn't Maria Glória have written to her father herself, one of those official letters that were laid on the breakfast tray, and which he had to read and answer, because only the urgent, the most urgent matters of all lay there?
How should she tell her father about it? Above all, how would Dona Amelia react? After all, two years earlier in *Boa Vista* her stepmother had hissed: "I will not raise your mistress's child. Isabel will leave the house!"
Did Dona Amelia really think and feel differently now?
Maria Glória did not have the courage to talk with Dona Amelia about it. Her stepmother would purr: "We'll do everything for Isabel, don't worry. Maria Glória, I find it touching how you worry about your half-sister."
She was afraid of those flattering tones: "When Dona Amelia speaks so kindly to me, I can't resist, and in the end I betray to her the fact that Augusto has written to me, or that Clementine is meeting Pierre. I miss *Mamãe*. I miss my siblings. Above all, I miss *Boa Vista* and Rio, and Amelia breaks open all this longing that I

otherwise keep well locked away. And as if she could ease my pain, I then want more and more of her spoken caresses, and afterward I don't feel relieved, but weighed down. Does that happen because her words are not genuine, not meant to be true?" she entrusted to her diary.

Therefore, when Graça asked her to write the letter, she immediately let her dictate it to her: "I humbly ask the Duke of Bragança, Dom Pedro, to help. You know that I traveled here to Europe because of Isabel, the Duchess of Goias, and now that I have finally found her, I know that Isabel's situation is very bad. She is seriously ill with *saudade*. Dom Pedro, Isabel will die if she is not moved to a different institution. Isabel needs affection like your other children. Pardon my openness. Please act, Dom Pedro. Isabel cannot speak for herself. At the age of seven, she is too despondent. I was always responsible for Isabel. For that reason I now plead for the little girl. Your obedient servant, Graça."

Maria Glória added, "With an embrace, your daughter Maria Glória. I know, dearest Papa, that you will help immediately."

Father had acted, as quickly as he could. As early as a few months later, at Easter, Dona Amelia drove to London with Isabel, to the Institute of the Ladies of Loretto.

Until that time, Graça visited Isabel almost every week. "She's growing. Yes, I think she has gotten bigger, and sometimes she laughs. In the mornings she is now together with the other girls, in class," she said joyfully.

Then letters came from London, letters with flowers drawn on them. "My most dearly beloved Graça. Since the 26th of May, my eighth birthday, I have been participating in ballet and dance classes, and my teachers praise my talent greatly. Now I also have two good friends, Aglaia and Abigail. We have our beds standing next to each other, and sometimes we hold hands when we cannot fall asleep. London is fabulously beautiful, and the governesses and teachers are friendly and patient. I am even receiving Portuguese lessons, so that I do not forget my native language. Graça, I embrace you. Will you visit me sometime?"

Graça memorized those letters. She had each line read to her very often, and she sewed them into her bag. She prayed aloud, "...and protect Isabel, so that she doesn't freeze and that she doesn't suffer too much from *saudade*."

Maria Glória envied Graça because of those letters, because of the letters and because of her task to be responsible for someone. For Graça nothing else existed. Everything she did was tied to Isabel. For that reason no work seemed difficult to her. For that reason she shrugged her shoulders at the malicious acts of the kitchen maids. Graça lived, worked, and thought: "Until the next letter from Isabel," "Isabel would be amazed at that," "I'll tell Isabel that. You'll write the letter for me, won't you?"

For Maria Glória the months in Paris continued on, theater, attendance at concerts, crystal lights, mirrors, gold, and plush. The villa on the *Rue Aboukir* was only a few blocks away from the residence of the Orléans family. So Clementine and Maria Glória could see each other every day. Clementine, the youngest member of the Orléans family, was almost sixteen. Every day she bore the fragrance of a different perfume, and she had love letters in her bag. "His name is Albert, and he's the jeweler's son. Next week he will deliver the tableware for the reception of the minister from Turkey. Listen to what he writes: 'Then I shall again walk up the stairs and through halls where you, beloved Clementine, walk every day...will arrange it so that I come next Wednesday at the time when you have Latin class. It will be easiest for you to escape from the old Latin teacher. Perhaps a handkerchief will point the way for me to your chamber...'"

Maria Glória sighed, "Is he blond or dark, this Albert? What will come of it? After all, you can't marry him."

"Marry! My parents will arrange that. That isn't important yet." Clementine looked at her impatiently: "You're thinking about marriage, about Augusto! Where are they keeping him hidden from you?"

"He's in Rennes, in a Jesuit monastery. There he's studying constitutional law," said Maria Glória. "We weren't allowed to see each other for even five minutes, when we were in Rennes."

Clementine considered: "Isn't he your stepmother's brother, Dona Amelia's brother?"

"Yes, and after nothing happened with the arranged marriage to Uncle Miguel, I was supposed to marry Augusto. Dona Amelia wanted that. She wanted to engineer a marriage by contract, as it was done for her. But when she saw that Augusto and I like each other," Maria Glória bit her lips, "she became jealous and sent Augusto away."

"I understand," Clementine nodded. "Dona Amelia acts sugar-sweet. Those women are the most dangerous ones! Besides, she can't stand it when another woman is happy. Then she destroys."

Clementine thought about it: "You need an ally. I think Graça could be the one. She would jump into the ice-cold Seine for you. So she will also carry letters between the two of you. I'll talk to our courier Victor. He's as silent as a grave. He has to be. Anyway, he has a family on the *Rue Drozda*, and here he dances around Mademoiselle Valerie in the kitchen and disappears with her into the pantry." Clementine giggled, "If his poor wife knew about that."

Soon letters and notes actually did go from Rennes to Paris and back. "Dearest Maria Glória, I had better not write about my longing for you, for then I will never reach the end of this letter. The faster I complete my education, the sooner I will see you again, in Paris or somewhere else. I have successfully passed the examination about my knowledge of contemporary, modern constitutional law. Since they want special supervision for my education, a father came from Brussels specifically for me, to examine the colloquium. Now nothing will stop me from getting an education in agriculture as I promised you. In the very near future we will run a dairy farm in Lisbon, with horses, sheep, cows, and even guinea fowl, which you like so much. I am also progressing in the disciplinary exercises. My bed is only forty centimeters wide now..."

"Augusto, dearest, how thankful I am to Graça for arranging for our letters to be passed along. Clementine is also an angel of discretion. Of course I send you kisses and embraces, but when I consider that Father or Dona Amelia might intercept our letters, I begin to sweat. Father is very strict in everything. I do not want to say anything about Dona Amelia, because she is your sister and beyond that is expecting a child. But I think that it would be better for me not to trust that woman, Dona Amelia. I actually did not want to say that so openly.

"My teacher Marcel, who teaches me economics, speaks a French that I hardly understand. He explains to me the principles of performance and quid pro quo, the free social economy and the economics of production and consumption, the examination of objects regarding their usefulness for satisfying demand. Oh, I try to retain all of that in my head, even though nothing has yet assumed a practical form in my mind. To be honest, I am reciting these sentences like Gino, our parrot. October will soon be over, and I will experience my first autumn in Europe, with the hoarfrost on the leafless branches, the way that *Mamãe* drew it for us..."

Dona Leonora warned her about Dona Amelia just as Graça did.

"Don't tell her which color you like, or then she will go to the theater wearing that very color." And she also said, "Don't say a word to her about the fact that your father received the pledge from the Rothschild family, money for soldiers and for his trip to the Azores!"

"Dona Leonora, I don't understand that. Dona Amelia wants to travel to Lisbon just as quickly as I do," said Maria Glória.

"Of course she wants to do that," Dona Leonora looked at her for a long time, "but perhaps she wants to enter Lisbon as the queen!"

Maria Glória did not understand. "Father renounced all his rights in Portugal. That is why he is now the Duke of Bragança. How does Dona Amelia intend to engineer that?"

Dona Leonora answered, "We'll be on our guard, Maria Glória. May Heaven protect us from intrigues!"

Maria Glória remembered that a few weeks before their departure from Rio de Janeiro, Father and Dona Amelia argued with each other. The siblings paid no attention to the screaming of the adults; they were busy with homework and playing music. Only Maria Glória happened to be walking along the hallway and down the stairs. "Queen of Portugal! She's a brat who is not even twelve years old!" Dona Amelia had sobbed.

"She's the firstborn daughter!" Father screamed back at her.

"Yes, and she is thoroughly spoiled," countered Dona Amelia. "Everyone knows that Dona Leopoldina was too indulgent with the children." Dona Amelia scolded vehemently, "A governess had to come from England to teach her to sit still in church. And have you forgotten that at the age of six she used a whip to force slave children to dance and to play? They are still talking about that. Queen of Portugal? Impossible!"

For several seconds it was quiet. Then in a strange voice Father spoke, as if he were reading aloud a text from a book: "To promote the children, to study their abilities and to seek out the best teachers for them - that is what Dona Leopoldina and I promised each other before Maria Glória was born. Then that calamitous decade descended upon me. I will not be able to make up for it. But I have entrusted little Pedrinho to José Bonifácio. The old man despises me, but he is the best educator for our son; and I have asked Dona Dadama, who detests me, who also calls me a *vulgario*, to take over the education of our daughters. Dona Leopoldina would have wanted it that way. I will do everything to secure for Maria Glória her rights as Queen of Portugal. Amelia, I forbid you to speak the name of Dona Leopoldina, the name of the mother of these children, ever again."

For a few hours Dona Amelia walked around with a tear-stained face. Father had locked himself in. The doctor was summoned. The servants whispered, feared: "An epileptic seizure?"

At dinner everything had been swept away again. Father played his jokes, "Francisca, what color is our kind Dona Dadama's green dress?" And Dona Amelia distributed extra portions of the freshly whipped chocolate. Maria Glória almost did not believe what she had heard. Had it been a bad dream? But she noticed that from that afternoon on Dona Amelia spoke only of "the empress" when they were talking about *Mamãe*, about Dona Leopoldina.

Her first November in Europe, with snow flurries, frost patterns on the window panes, and glowing stoves that always gave off too little heat.
"First Maria Glória has to become accustomed to Europe," Clementine laughed, displaying her woolen coat with the fur collar, felt-lined ankle boots, and fur-lined shawls. There were sled rides to Versailles. There they drank tea that made them dizzy, tea with cognac. Her strict schedule, the weekly examinations in civil law and economics, having them listen to her diplomatic conversation, the rehearsing of audiences. Soon French gave her no difficulties any longer. Spanish was especially easy for her. English and German remained cumbersome for her and often brought her punishments: "From eleven o'clock until four o'clock in the afternoon you will speak only German and English!"

Meetings with Father were rare. He often remained away from the house for days to prepare for his departure to the Azores, to Terceira.
Nor did anything remain of that father with whom she had grown up, of Papa, who taught her to drive a coach when she was seven years old, who composed songs for her, who talked about Great-grandmother Maria I: "All the furniture, curtains, and cloths in her room had to be black. She sat motionless on her bench for hours, her face covered by her unkempt hair. And when we children crept into her room, she suddenly jumped up and screamed, 'The devil has gotten into me!'"
Papa, to whom she confided her fears: "Please cut off the branches of the bougainvillea there. In the night wind the thorns scratch so eerily on the wall and on the window, as if a fairy with long fingernails wanted to climb up to my room." And Papa cut the shoots off. He also promised, "Tonight I'll sleep in your room, and

if that fairy comes back, then we'll sing and clap so loud that she will flee."

In Paris all that remained of Father was the weekly letters that they wrote to each other. "Your handwriting is not pretty. I must criticize you," wrote Father. And another time, "The lack of a good education, as I came to experience it, can hardly be made right again." And when she did not meet expectations in her examination on canon law, Father also wrote: "...it is necessary for you to work harder and not waste so much time trying on clothes. You should study the book by António Vieira more intensively: *'Kings can only obtain respect through good qualities and virtues. If they are vain, they will soon be surrounded by sycophants. They are small and lithe and do anything to live among the supposedly great ones. For that, any intrigue, any deception is right, and the vain ones are defenseless against them...'*"

On December 1, 1831 Dona Amelia gave birth to a girl. The little girl was christened Maria Amalie. She had Dona Amelia's delicate face and Father's dark hair and dark eyes. From the first day on, this sister was a beauty. Besides that, Maria Amalia was a child who never got sick, who scintillated with cheerfulness, a girl who was immediately at home everywhere. This girl's life seemed to run in a perfectly straight line. Tenderly cared for by two governesses, even the constant moves to new quarters by her mother, Dona Amelia, did not seem to throw her out of balance. Maria Amalia remained cheerful.

Two years ago, on her twentieth birthday, she became engaged to the Prince of Austria, Maximilian von Habsburg. It was supposed to be an arranged, perfectly organized marriage.

Nevertheless, once she wrote to Maria Glória: "Dear Aunt Maria, the invitation to the dance party is a great honor for me, but I lack the inner joy for dancing. For that reason I had best decline, since otherwise I would disturb the entire party with my too serious behavior..."

Maria Glória turned the letter back and forth. What did these lines mean? And after they attended Mass together Maria Glória answered in a letter: "I still have the clear ring of your voice in my ear. What gifts Heaven has bestowed upon you! But the dark colors of your dress, you are engaged! You know the meaning of the colors black and gray. Is some resignation troubling you in a way that I could be of help?"

Maria Amalia answered quickly: "Dearest Aunt, I do not share your belief that the colors gray and black point toward an inner resignation. For several weeks I have taken great pleasure in those colors. Do not worry. I only love the color black. I do not want to hear anything about resignation."

But Maria Amalia became weaker, more transparent. The doctors said that Madeira would help, heal, and in February of this year, 1853, nine months ago, she died of tuberculosis on Madeira. "...I seldom confided in my mother. Perhaps it is the natural course of things that a person makes friends more easily with her aunt than with her mother. It was probably right, what you said to me about resignation. My fiancé loved me so dutifully, and that was too little for me. Besides that, my mother did not leave my side. She wanted compliments from Maximilian, and as I soon learned, she wanted and received from my fiancé much more besides. We lived as a threesome in a terrible entanglement. I did not know what power my mother could exercise. I had no idea what power of attraction came from her. I knew only that I did not want to share Maximilian. He fled to Vienna for a few months, and now that he is gone, I am even less able to get over what I experienced. What woman is inside my mother? Dearest Aunt, you told me about the powers that we have at our disposal. Can one also use those powers to leave this world? Nothing can be straightened out with my mother. Everything would happen all over again, and I am not strong enough for that..."

Finally, in January of 1832, Maria Glória was led into the reception hall in the residence of Dom Louis Philippe Orléans. Father's house was not large enough for an official ceremony.

Was the waiting for action now over? Would Father turn his plans into deeds? Would there be a timetable for how many months they still had to live and wait in Paris?

For months Father had been working out the strategy with financial backers and advisors for the toppling of the Miguel dictatorship. No country in Europe actually wanted to have anything to do with a military venture; above all, they did not want to make enemies of each other. If France supported Dom Pedro too openly, it would have difficulties with England. The Spaniards, on the other hand, sided again with the English, for a weakened Portugal could be rapidly integrated into the Iberian great power. There was no reaction at all from Austria, which did not promise anything good and made the strategy more difficult, for in the year 1832 nobody wanted Austria, Metternich, as an opponent.

The hall was decorated with flowers, and with the exception of the Portuguese ambassador all of the diplomats had come, even the Austrian. The bishop with whom Maria Glória discussed the Bible during her classes spoke the words of introduction: "As the military leader of those Portuguese who feel committed to the *Carta Constitutional*, Pedro, the Duke of Bragança, is going to war for the rights of his daughter, our Queen Maria II. May God's blessings..."

Maria Glória stood alone on the podium. She had only two sentences to say: "May everything go as Providence has ordained for us, Duke. Greet my emigrants; my thoughts and wishes are with you."

Father was in his highly formal uniform, but the pants and jacket were too large for him. The clothing hung loosely on his emaciated body. Father had been thirty-three years old then. She would have most liked to walk a few steps toward him. She could not do that under any circumstances. He came slowly toward his thirteen-year-old daughter and then he knelt before her and kissed her hand.

The year 1832, with its many months of waiting: "...I thank you very much for the pressed violets. Did you find rose oil in the monastery? Even over the long path taken by the mail, the fragrance of roses was not driven from the paper. Oh, Augusto, perhaps your surroundings are less strict with you than mine are with me. Father has reports sent to him in Terceira about my learning accomplishments. In his last letter he criticized my handwriting again. Beloved Augusto, when will we see each other again at last? I love you immensely..."

Meanwhile dispatches arrived, official news from Terceira: "It will still be several months until Pedro Bragança readies an army that can confront the Miguelists."

Delays, delays, and the year 1832 trickled onward.

In November Dom Louis Philippe received a delegation of merchants from Brazil. They had interrupted their voyage for a few days in Terceira, and they reported: "The Portuguese emigrants were waiting for the soldier emperor, and then a man who was exhausted from that short trip by sailboat landed on Terceira, a man who steals away from a round of drinks with the soldiers because the liquor wearies him so much. They said he was a hero. With his speeches, his orders, he could convince the soldiers that they would be victorious. But Pedro, the Duke of Bragança, does not hold any meetings. He sits in small groups with the officers. He says little, has lists written up, and has weapons and munitions inspected. He inspects ships, and he does everything slowly and with much deliberation. The soldiers are downhearted. Some no longer believe in a victory. How can they be successful in driving the dictator Miguel out of Lisbon, with this weary man? Dom Pedro dwells, he lives in the house of Ana Peregrino, the widow, and in general people are relieved about that, for he could not have endured being alone. That would have weakened him even more."

At the end of July Clementine wanted to organize a summer soiree.

"The students from the ballet school are coming, a few of my girlfriends from the lyceum, young army officers from the cadet school, and Albert, of course."

"Clementine, I don't want to. Papa is in Terceira, and I'm dancing - no."

"Do you intend to wait until you have white hair?" Clementine could not be talked out of her idea. "You'll see. During the next year at the latest he will storm Lisbon with his soldiers."

"Clementine, Father will land with his soldiers in Porto, and there the liberals will receive him with an army. In spite of that, in the Azores there are too few soldiers to topple Miguel. Miguel's soldiers outnumber them," explained Maria Glória impatiently.

"Fine. You're better informed about the strategic plans. Nevertheless, we don't want to forget the soiree. I think you should wear a green dress. That will cause your dark eyes to glow," Clementine raved.

"That's not a good idea. Green is the color of Brazil." Maria Glória shook her head.

"But you are a Brazilian, after all," Clementine laughed. "I mean, here in Paris that simply sounds more interesting. Besides, What are you actually? On your mother's side Austrian, on your father's side Portuguese, by place of birth a Brazilian! Henri Laliche will be very interested in you. He comes from Genoa. He'll teach you to flirt!"

Maria Glória did not react. She let Clementine lead her in a few dance steps. How many years older was she? By how many events was she more serious than Clementine? The cheerfulness and candor of her friend did not rub off, did not touch her.

More endless months in Paris. August, September, October, and Maria Glória had no news from Father.

"Today is the 12th of October. It's Father's birthday! Should I light a candle in the church, as if he had died?" she wept. The waiting was already unbearable for her.

"I understand," Dona Leonora nodded. "Even your hair can no longer be curled. We'll go to the *Sacre Coeur Hospital* twice a week and visit the women in the maternity ward there. We'll take baby clothing. Clementine's mother has filled three baskets and made them available for that. You can pick out the little shirts, pants, and cloths. Perhaps you can help our Simone with the embroidery. All that will shorten the waiting time for you."

Dona Leonora had also taught her that, just never to permit a standstill. "When your mind can't take in anything more, then you must occupy your hands," and: "When we're despondent, then we should do good deeds for others."

At the end of October the trees were leafless again; now it would soon snow again. For Maria Glória the second winter in Europe began with the November and December mornings when fogbanks rose from the Seine and the sun held itself back for one or two hours longer; the Masses in ice-cold churches, where the cold slipped in through the soles of her feet and spread into her fingers. The awkward winter clothing, stockings and underpants made of sheep's wool, over them the linen underpants that were tied below the knee, a little vest of sheep's wool and a linen slip, a woolen shawl wrapped around her torso, and only then the street dress, with wristlets that matched the color of the dress. Why was it not permitted to wear gloves in the church?

Two weeks before Christmas, Francisco de Almeide, Father's official emissary, arrived. "...that the Duke of Bragança has landed in Porto with the soldiers from Terceira. They feared resistance from the Miguelists. They were prepared for battle. Nothing of the sort can be reported. The liberals were received indifferently in Porto. They were permitted to take quarters and no cannons confronted them. But on the second day it was already apparent how treacherously they had prepared for the liberals of Pedro of Bragança. Only beds were allocated to the duke and his soldiers. They refused to give them food, or even water for drinking and washing. Those who give the poor soldiers something to eat anyway are in the greatest mortal danger. Such almsgivers, who were suspected of having liberal inclinations, were publicly executed. They also cut off the duke's retreat back to the harbor to his ships. So, by depriving the liberal army of food and any news, they intend to force them to surrender..."

Maria Glória could hardly follow the words. Father was in danger. Father had not fought until they had finally celebrated him as a liberator. They had lured Father into a trap.

She interrupted Francisco de Almeida, "Your Excellency, did Dom Pedro give you a message, a letter for me, or for Dona Amelia?"

"Yes," the white-haired man bowed. "Here, a dispatch, the seal of which is supposed to be broken by both of you, by Dona Amelia and you, Crown Princess. There was not enough time," he added, "for two letters."

Maria Glória shoved Dona Amelia's hand aside; she immediately tapped the seal open. A miniature oil painting fell out. "If you, my beloved wife Amelia, and you, dearest daughter Maria Glória, find that my portrait shows me to be thin, that should not make an impression upon you. Obtaining food is awkward, to be sure, but we have arranged things well for ourselves in all aspects of life."

Father's handwriting was the same as that with which she was familiar from all of his letters.

"Your Excellency, when will you travel back to Porto?" she wanted to know.

"Before Christmas," answered the emissary.

"I shall prepare a letter and request, your Excellency, that you take it to my father as quickly as possible," and without coming to any further understanding with Dona Leonora through eye contact, she added, "and tomorrow you will come to dinner in the evening. You must tell us exactly how Dom Pedro is doing."

Dona Leonora could hardly follow Maria Glória, when she left the reception room so quickly and ran so quickly to her desk.

"Maria Glória," the governess tugged at the sleeve of the almost fourteen-year-old girl. "You should apologize to Dona Amelia. It would have been better if you had talked with her about it before issuing the invitation."

She looked up: "I won't apologize to Dona Amelia. She will be just as interested in hearing how Father is doing in Porto as I am."

"But formally it would have been appropriate," Dona Leonora continued trying.

"Dona Leonora, I think nothing of formalities when things are going badly for my father." She dug around looking for stationery. For a few moments Dona Leonora said nothing. Then she said, she spoke: "And, your royal Majesty, whom do you intend to invite to tomorrow evening's dinner besides Clementine and Dona Amelia?"

Maria Glória jerked around: "Dona Leonora, what's the matter with you?"

The governess embraced her: "Maria Glória, you made an independent decision. You decided quickly and correctly. You didn't retreat faint-heartedly from your decision! Although," she caressed her protégée, "with your direct and spontaneous manner you will breed enmities."

Leonora was right about that.

Dona Amelia was furious about Maria Glória's highhandedness. She did not come to the dinner: "Little Amalie does not want to be without her mother for even a minute in the evening," she wrote as an excuse.

Did this evening meal with Francisco de Almeida mark the beginning of petty jealousies and taunts by Dona Amelia? In December of 1832 that was not important for Maria Glória.

José Bonifácio, the old white-haired man, would have laughed uproariously about "two estranged females," and with that Maria Glória pushed everything aside that Leonora suggested with regard to reconciliation.

"The only thing I want to do is travel to Porto." She could not think about anything else. This standstill that had gone on for months, the waiting, the anxiety; how long would this condition continue? When would she finally see Portugal?

The New Year's parties and the Carnival balls of the first few weeks of the year 1833 bored her. Did she suddenly see the same faces and the lavish robes in magnificent colors everywhere in Paris? Did she suddenly hear whispered talk from every corner?

"She sits up there. Her poor father is fighting in Porto. There is no good news. It is simply harder to fight and to negotiate in Europe than in the jungle."

At that time she began to read António Vieira on her own, no longer as a duty, no longer as homework. She enjoyed reading him; she liked his language. With a few sentences from the Vieira correspondence she could divert herself, she could mentally escape: "*Vanity is the cleverest angler among the vices; it deceives the human being most easily. As bait, it fastens flattery on the tip of the lance. How greedily the person swallows the flattery and then hangs on the hook and does not escape. Christine, you should fast for a period of time that lasts for a few tens of days. You should move from your bedchamber to a cell and seek your truth. Did you convert to the Catholic faith because it conformed to the fashion and satisfied your intense need to appear interesting? Examine yourself! It has also been reported to me that of late you prefer young priests as conversation partners. Those poor farm boys will throw you every kind of bait, of flattery! Pray for common sense. The sweet words are not addressed to the woman but to the Queen of Sweden, from whom those novices expect advantages. Chasten yourself before you hang totally on the hook of vanity.*"

Maria Glória felt sorry for Queen Christina. Almost two hundred years ago she had lived in cold Rome, without friends, without family.

"*My very dear one, in your latest letter you complain, and although I despise the tones of complaint, I understand. As a flame sometimes bends for a few moments and then rises straight toward the sky again, so our souls sometimes bend. When we have overburdened ourselves, do we demand from the spirit powers that torment the soul too much? These moments of being drawn down are necessary. We need them to remember that we have brought ourselves onto our path. Christina, as a seven-year-old, you had to live as an orphan after the death of your father. You laid the child Christina into the coffin with your beloved father. But your mother needed the comedy of a seven-year-old child, so you played the role and whis-*

pered to your mother the words of that child. What was your mother Maria Eleonora to you other than a person who had long ago withdrawn from the world, one for whom you performed small acts of charity by playing the child, and then immediately fled back into your reality, to your Aunt Katharina, to your tutors Axel and Gustav? But the child in you, beloved Christina, was mortally injured, died prematurely, and the pain of that death is what torments you. I cannot offer you any medicine, only the comfort that I am familiar with your suffering. At the age of fifteen I prayed for inspiration in the church in Salvador, that Heaven might open my spirit, open it so wide that I would understand, that nothing would divert me from my studies anymore. To leave my parents' house for that, never to embrace a weeping mother, a distraught father again, that seemed to me a small price for the blessing, the inspiration that Heaven gave to me. But, Christina, even my soul squirms sometimes; then I kneel in my cell, incapable of finding a single word, a single expression for my defense paper, and only prayer and silence give me the strength to overcome the pain that I feel regarding the youth that I never experienced and to return to my own path again after a few days. So lock up your mouth, your pen, and your room and pray, beloved Christina...Rome, the fourth day of February, 1670."

At the end of April, two weeks after her fourteenth birthday, Clementine came to the *Rue Aboukir* early in the morning.

"Maria Glória," she waved a paper, "Papa has news from Porto, good news from your father, from Dom Pedro! Here, read it yourself: 'All of the streets in Porto leading to the harbor and to the interior of the country are open to travel. A new, liberal mayor was installed, who immediately swore the oath to support the *Carta Constituional*. The Miguelist army has retreated to Lisbon...'"

Clementine danced with Maria Glória. "Your father has liberated Porto, and from Porto they will go to Lisbon!"

"Father kept his word. In his last letter he wrote: 'You will not spend the year 1833 in Paris. I promise you that.'"

Clementine looked at her: "Surely you're happy. Or has the eternal waiting made you forget how to be really happy?"

"No, but what is there to do now?" Maria Glória became completely confused inside.

"We'll eat breakfast together, and you'll listen to me. Henry is coming to Paris for a whole year, as the finance minister's secretary. You understand, Maria Glória, that it will give us a thousand opportunities to see each other. I'll miss you so much, Maria Glória. I'm sure that there isn't such a true friend anywhere in the world anymore. You could easily have snatched Henry away from me, easily!"

Clementine talked about letters and secret meetings in the church, about exchanged fans and handkerchiefs, about a garrulous lady's maid and a reprimand that she received from her religion professor. And for the time that it took to drink their morning coffee, Maria Glória forgot about Porto, about the fact that she now would soon depart.

"How often do I have to say good-by in order to learn how to do it, so that it is less painful?" she wrote in her diary.

The months of May, June, and July were filled with anticipation of the journey to Lisbon and simultaneous pain at letting go of Paris.

"We all hope that you, dear Maria Glória, have, to a small degree, become a Frenchwoman," Louis Philippe Orléans wrote in his farewell dispatch.

Then came the last lessons in Latin, French, and Portuguese, the hearing in canon law, and the recitation of the *Carta Constitutional*: "...which, to be sure, concedes to the Queen a veto right, but even then only a right of postponement, and that must, moreover, be justified in writing..."

Then, in August of 1833, came the departure to Brest. Marquis de Loule had come from Lisbon to accompany Maria Glória, Graça, and Dona Amelia with the one-and-a-half-year-old Amalia from Paris to Brest and on to Lisbon.

Clementine rode with Maria Glória as far as Brest. During the journey they were inseparable. Packed tightly together, they sat in the coach, held each other's hands, and Dona Leonora oversaw this lack of discipline. "We always have to sit up straight, without leaning against anyone, and place our hands gracefully in our laps." That rule was not valid for this trip.

"You promise to write at least one letter a month, and you'll write me everything, really everything." That was how Clementine comforted Maria Glória, how they comforted each other.

In Brest the Bragança family was received boisterously.

"Paris did her good. How self-confidently she moves now."

"Just look! The chubby child has become an elegant young lady."

Some also murmured: "Loneliness is eating at his wife, at Dona Amelia. How serious she looks. The poor woman."

Maria Glória let herself be pushed toward the important people. She recited her memorized lines: "I am grateful for the hospitality that was bestowed on my family and me."

She looked for Clementine once more. How was she supposed to be able to travel on without her best friend? "Let's exchange our perfumes," Clementine whispered in her ear and pressed her tear-streaked cheek against that of Maria Glória.

"Swallow, swallow," she ordered herself, just no tears in public.

While Maria Glória watched through her curtain of tears, as Clementine went away, a figure separated itself from the crowd, a young man, Augusto! With a few quick strides he stood in front of Maria Glória, and without paying attention to the people, he drew her into a doorway and embraced her. At last they felt each other; each felt the skin, the lips, the hair of the other. Greedily they sucked in their breath. It had to happen quickly and their bodies wanted to become acquainted with each other. Everything pressed toward being touched, caressed.

Only a few moments of ducking away remained to them, but for a few minutes they had disappeared, one into the body of the other, and in those moments they became close to each other, so close that they emerged from that embrace reassured and strengthened.

"I'll follow soon," Augusto whispered. "Do you have the lock of hair for me?"

They exchanged letters. "Don't let me wait too long."

"Don't forget our star, every evening before falling asleep, our gazes, our eyes will meet up there."

Suddenly they were jostled, almost driven apart. Dona Amelia stood next to them. "Augusto, do you also have a letter for me?"

Her stepmother's face was ash-gray: "Where is Dona Leonora? A scandal!" she gasped and tried to push Augusto, her brother, away from Maria Glória.

But Augusto bent down to Maria Glória once more, kissed her again, and said, "*Até* logo. See you soon," so that Dona Amelia groaned aloud. She would probably have fainted, if Augusto had not taken her, his sister, by the hand and pulled her away.

Augusto had been twenty-two years old at the time, and Maria Glória had felt herself protected by him as she had been by her father. By how many years had Augusto gotten ahead of his life? She had not known that, not yet back then.

When Augusto had gone away, she looked for Graça.

"Why do you want to stay in Brest, Graça? Here in Brest you will be all alone."

Perhaps she could still get Graça to change her mind.

"Alone, that's how I've almost always been in recent months, and now I want to visit Isabel. London isn't far away."

Maria Glória was not able to say a word. She could not imagine being without Graça. Graça had to come along! Since they had departed from Rio de Janeiro, she had always felt Graça's presence. Maria Glória needed only to reach out her hand, and Graça was there.

Maria Glória wanted to say that. She should have told Graça that long ago, but in Brest, with a repressed sob, all that she uttered was, "Please write to me."

Maria Glória wept, and everyone saw it; and Dona Leonora permitted those tears. "It's the farewell to France," smiled her strict confidante.

When she went aboard the ship, Maria Glória turned around again and again, waving. She saw Augusto. His blond hair gleamed in the sun. He waved the letter in which she had enclosed a lock of her hair. She looked for Graça, but Graça was no longer in sight. Graça had ducked away, ducked away as completely as if she had never been there.

CHAPTER III

*She stays then many days within the land,
as moved upon by chance or even purpose;
mulberry, the fruit that's raised by Persian hand,
thrives better here than in its native land.*

How naturally Graça decided upon this place for their meeting, for saying good-by: "...in Sintra, by the stone bench where you can look out into the ocean..."

Maria Glória loves this place. She also told Graça about it in a letter: "Fernando bought the Pena Monastery in the mountains of Sintra. It is dilapidated, and after decades of sleep it is overgrown with trees and climbing vines. A wonderful, mystical spot of earth. We will carefully free the monastery walls from the trees and plants and revive the building again. It should become a peaceful place, and I shall appoint those master builders who will realize my innermost desire in the construction: the good and peaceful coexistence of the cultures. We must succeed in expressing the Egyptian, the Arabian, and the Gothic, but also the Manuelian culture in this building, in arches, courtyards, towers, gates, stairways, and everything else. No architectural style should press against another, but each should live for itself, and on the whole only the conciliatory should be found here. There is one place that we will leave untouched, a stone bench beneath the parasol pine, from where you look out into the ocean. Graça, in Sintra there is a point from where we can look in our direction..."

Graça searches her face: Did she, Maria Glória really experience everything that she talks about? Did she really experience it that way? Or were some things told to her, told to her for so long that she took parts of them, the easily narrated ones, extracted them, and put them together?

Maria Glória can hardly withstand the look that Graça gives her. Have the two decades during which she has lived far away from Brazil, has *saudade* distorted her memories, even transfigured them? She remembers a letter that António Vieira wrote in October of 1669: "*My beloved Christina, how do you describe your childhood in the college? I cannot follow you. You present Gustav Adolf II as an affectionate father who even forgave you for being a daughter. Ask your cousin Karl Gustav. He will tell you that your father persecuted the Catholics, had them publicly hanged, and called us Jesuits devil's spawn! Enough reprimanding - Stockholm is too far from Rome, and it appears that you suffer from homesickness...*"

Graça listens attentively to her, then she says: "Maria Glória, you can write down the words so rapidly that they fly onto the paper. You can decipher diplomatic expressions, and you have learned so many important things in lessons, and later from letters and reports. Refugees from Miguel, Azores, your Uncle Miguel - words, all just words! What do you really know about it?"

Graça in Brest and Porto, 1833-1835
"Tell us where the angry sea took you"

Graça smoothes out her black skirts; she twists the mist-damp, white strands of hair up under her hairnet; "*the fish listen and do not speak,*" and Graça spreads out her story, her years. Without effort she finds her way into the language from which she already believed herself to be excluded through years of silence, of suppression.

"There I sat at the Brest harbor and wept; back then, in August of 1833, I still wept. The drying out, the acceptance of the unexplainable, and the swallowing of the days and years didn't begin for me until much later. Where should I go? For hours I sat on my chest with the sewing materials, probably all night. It must have rained, for my smocks and chemises were wet. I had put on four or five of them over each other. My clothing lay heavily upon my body, but those smocks and chemises were all I had. Nor was there anything in my sewing box that I could have offered for sale, a few pieces of thread that were left over from the embroidery work on the evening gowns, needles that were all rusty, and the ball of bits of cloth.

"Where should I go? Dona Leonora had led you, Maria Glória, up the steps onto the ship, and this time you didn't leave during the night wrapped in dark clothing so that nobody would recognize you, as you had done three years earlier in Rio de Janeiro.

"'I'll wait for you,' I had said to you, 'until you return again, back to Rio, to Francisca, Januária, and Pedrinho, to Dadama and Rafael.' That was what I had insisted to you, and you nodded at that until Dona Leonora finally drove us apart.

"If I had learned to read and write, in really long sentences and in words like the ones I used when I talked, I could have written down those words and would not have had to repeat them to myself out of fear that the words would transform themselves or that I would forget them.

"'I'll wait for you and we'll return.' I had fallen asleep while constantly reciting that sentence, and when I awoke, in wet clothes, the square in front of the harbor was almost devoid of people. A few fishermen toiled with their nets, and two sailors were hitting each other. They had probably stolen from each other or cheated one another during a game. Everywhere lay heaps of garbage, remnants of meat and fish, oranges, figs, turnips, everything overripe and half rotten, and pigs and goats rooted around in it.

"Which of the ships that lay far out on the ocean would sail to London? I wanted to see Isabel again. She should know that I had decided to return to Rio de Janeiro, that Maria Glória and I had promised each other to wait for each other and travel back together.

"A few men came tottering out of the tavern.

"'You get her for breakfast,' they bawled. 'Isn't she very old?' 'No, that's the rain. That's why she looks so wrinkled,' they laughed, and I didn't grasp the fact that they meant me.

"When they were standing in front of me, I asked, 'Can one of the gentlemen write? Could one of the gentlemen write a letter for me, a letter to London?'

"I said that in Portuguese and also tried it in French. They stared at me. Then each one wanted to be the first to reach for me. 'She is a philosopher. You have to pay her in letters.'

"'Take note, you Indian, we can write if we want to, but we don't want to now.'

"They tugged at my clothes and kicked at my sewing box, which burst open, and the needles and threads, the spools and the rolled-up cloth remnants lay in the mud. They dragged me toward a shed, and they did not react to my screams and my blows, they were laughing so hard. 'I'll write you a letter now!'

"Suddenly Abrão came out of the shed. He dumped a tub of water out at the men and said, 'Beat it!' And to me he said in Portuguese, "To whom do you want to write, Miss? I'll be glad to help you.'

"'I must write to Isabel. She's in London. Perhaps she is as unhappy as a stone again. Where I come from we say: unhappy as a stone, but stones are certainly not unhappy. They have hardened and pressed their souls so long that they can only be seen as glitter anymore, and you can scratch at those points and veins of glitter until you bleed,' was how I talked in order to prevent this man from calling me 'Miss.'

"I was not a Miss but a seamstress, and ever since I had stolen my way onto the ship in Rio de Janeiro I had constantly felt caught.

"'You're a Brazilian,' Abrão pulled me out of my reverie. 'I mean, I can tell by looking at you.'

"I knew that I take a lot after my mother, after Irazy. 'Indian face' they had called me in the sewing room. I have often compared the color of my skin. Weren't the palms of my hands just as rosy as the backs of my hands? Did the brownish red come not only from the sun, and wouldn't my hair curl like that of Isabel? Was it really straighter? Did it lay in my name, Graça? Could I simply rename myself? After all, the name came from Mother Earth; she selects and forms the human being accordingly. Can you simply - like Maria Glória, as you had to do - erase the 'Glória' and in so doing erase the Brasilian woman?

"How much of all that I thought did I say aloud? I probably told Abrão everything about myself during the first hour. They, the thoughts, don't take form except in speech. Later I would learn to write; later I would surely have time for it, but at the Brest harbor I only wanted to write a letter to Isabel, have a letter written. I no longer wanted to travel to London. I wanted to go to Lisbon, to the place where you, Maria Glória, were taken.

"Abrão continued to treat me like a young lady. He wiped off the bench with his leather apron before I sat down, and he smiled at me when he came to the table with a stack of paper and the inkpot. He also gave me a mug of wine and put a wooden plate on the table, with cold, half-burnt potatoes and salt on it.

"'To Princess Isabel of Goias-Santos, my dear, much loved, little Isabel. For days I have not been able to sew a stitch or to speak a word without thinking about you, you pound so firmly on my soul. Maria Glória has departed for Lisbon, and with that she will fulfill her destiny once and for all, and she will be the Queen of Portugal. Dom Pedro, your father, is in bad health. The months in the Azores severely ate away at his strength. He can urgently use prayers and good thoughts from you. I am convinced that he will not regain his full health until he goes back to Brazil, to Rio de Janeiro. For three years we have experienced so much that is unfamiliar, unaccustomed, and that weakens all of us. But we will all remain steadfast and wait patiently for the voyage back. Maria Glória and I promised each other that. My beloved little Isabel, I send a thousand embraces from your milk-sister, Graça.'

"Abrão wrote four pages full. The black ink ran; the paper was damp, gray, and rippled.

"'Finished,' he said, looking at me, and I wrote my name under what had been written. Then I had to take off my clothes, for I had sewn Isabel's address into an undershirt. Abrão helped me out of my clothes, copied the address, and tied up my ribbons again. While he folded the paper and sealed it with sealing wax, I asked him, 'Can I work that off? I can cook or even mend the fishing nets. Should I sew a vest for you, or a new leather apron? I have no money.'

"Abrão shook his head. He went to the market hall with me and gave some coins to the sailor from the postal service. My debt

grew larger and larger.
"What was I supposed to do? I let him lead me to the sheds of the sailors. In the next to the last row stood his hut, one room without windows. In the semi-darkness the few objects were visible: boards that were laid across each other to form a table and a bench; two baskets, in one of them: wooden plates, nets, and pieces of clothing made of leather, in the other: potatoes and grain. Two rats rooted around in it. For that room there was nothing to sew. Where in that room was I supposed to begin working off my debt? The earthen floor was dry. What could I use to fetch water?
"'Will you cook something?' Abrão asked, and he took my sewing box from me.
"'Yes,' I nodded, 'but the rats,' I said, pointing at the basket.
"'Are you afraid of rats?' Abrão asked with amazement. 'These here are tame. I leave everything in this basket to them, and for that they leave me everything in the second basket. Look, they're listening to me!'
"The two animals really did look in the direction of Abrão's voice. While I still stood there in the room, hesitant and dumbfounded, Abrão had slipped out, and moments later he came back with an iron pan full of fire. He pulled an iron rack out of the basket, out of the basket that the rats had left to him, and set up a kettle over the fire pan. He hurried away with a wooden tub for water. Then I, too, began to dig around in the basket and found cornmeal, salt, onions, and cheese. While I crouched next to the kettle and stirred a porridge that gleamed yellow as the sun in the hut, Abrão began to talk.
"'Your name is Graça. Is that actually a name? Is there a saint with that name?'
"'I know nothing of a saint,' I explained. 'My mother called me Graça, Grace, out of gratitude because I came into the world on the same day as Princess Maria Glória. On our plaques was written "*de Neto*," that was the agency.'
"Abrão interrupted me. 'You're a slave, and you're writing to a Princess Isabel. Do you belong to the Bragança family?'
"'I'm no longer a slave,' I cut him off, 'nor is my mother. Sen-

hor Picard gave us our freedom long ago. There is a document about that. Irazy has it, sewn into her green and yellow smock. When will Isabel receive the letter?' Nothing else was important to me.

"'In fifteen or sixteen days the letter will be in London, quite certainly. Graça, your friend will be happy.'

"Abrão was suddenly out of breath: 'When will the little girl, the child queen Maria be in Lisbon? When will we, will I be able to return? I have already been waiting in Brest for so long. A few hundred Portuguese are waiting here like me. Some departed too soon from London, others too soon from Terceira. Nobody endures it there any longer than is absolutely necessary. We believed that when Pedro Bragança was in Porto the years in exile would be over for us. Graça, we refugees from Miguel have been waiting for five years for our return to Portugal!'

"'Refugees from Miguel' - I had already heard that term so often. I wanted to ask Abrão, but he did not wait at all for my question. He talked: 'Look, Graça! The rats no longer react. They already know every word. For days they have been hearing the same thing. I can't endure the waiting any other way. My family, the Bragas, have been living in Portugal for almost two hundred years! Since António Vieira preached in Lisbon in 1640: *"Never again will Portugal allow itself to be swallowed by Spain. The Lusitanians have sworn allegiance to themselves for all time!"*'

"'In 1650 the Bragas moved out of Spain, out of Grenada. They wanted to live where Vieira preached, António Vieira, who took the liberty to speak from the pulpit about the tricks of the mighty, to castigate the greed of the colonial rulers: "*...one of the great events that we experience in the modern world, and about which we are not astonished out of sheer routine habit, even more, to which we pay no attention, is the enormous migration from Africa to America. They are bringing Africa to Brazil. What inhumane trade, in which the goods are human beings, what a devilish business. The rulers wear gold and silver. The slaves carry iron and die a wretched death in the sweet hell of Bahia...*"'

"'That's the sugar mills, I know,' I interrupted impatiently.

Back then in Brest I didn't want to hear anything about that devil's priest. I wanted to go to Lisbon, wanted to go to Maria Glória, and I didn't know how I could escape from Abrão again. After all, I was in his debt. Perhaps I could work off my letter debt by listening?

"'The Bragas began in Lisbon with a shipping agency. They organized the first postal agency. The Braga family shipped the pieces of mail to London, to Brest, and to Brazil. The second branch of our family settled in Porto. There they planted mulberry trees, on which they later intended to lay out the silkworms, in order to get started in the silk spinning business. But that took two decades. The mulberry trees were very sensitive. Years came when it rained too much and the leaves became moldy; and there were years in which the dryness caused the new shoots to wither already in the spring. After twenty years they were able to place the eggs for the first time. Thousands upon thousands were laid out in the leaves of the mulberry trees, and a progression of months and seasons began, which was not interrupted for over a hundred years, until the year 1828, until the Miguel dictatorship. The eggs were laid out. Two weeks later the caterpillars were gathered in again and spread out in the drying house. Then the butterfly was peeled out of the cocoon and the silk thread was wound onto the spools. The spools were wrapped in silk cloth and stowed in boxes on the ship, loaded onto our own ship, and then sent to Paris and to London. My grandfather, Senhor Adalberto, ran the freight agency at Belem Harbor in Lisbon. In the year 1807 he had to vacate it when Sir Taylor came from London. In that year, 1807, many people left Portugal. They sailed with the king to Brazil, and with them went officials and ministers, craftsmen and merchants, teachers and priests. They were not driven away. Nobody threatened their lives, but they didn't want to have anything to do with the English. It was the case that the Portuguese had to tolerate the English in the offices. Some feared that before long they would also have to speak English. My grandfather had remained in Lisbon. He had reached an agreement with Sir Taylor: He shared the profits from the shipping agency with the Englishman. In the Rossio quarter, Taylor owned a tavern, under the name of a respectable landlady, of course. In that dive rum was served, blended, obviously. After all, rum from Brazil was unloaded by the barrel. A person could also easily distil it himself, and who bothered to count the sugarloaves? Besides that, with every cargo some women from Brazil arrived in Lisbon, women with brown, reddish, or black skin. They had fled as slaves, and after a three-month crossing they were driven from the ship. Some were simply laid in a corner to die. Those Brazilian women who had survived the crossing were placed in the households of the English officials, as cooks, as maids, as lady's maids, as diversions for the householder. Taylor earned a lot with his tavern, with his placement service.

"'Grandfather was not interested in that. He thought only of the Braga family business. He had specific plans for his two children: José, my father, was sent to Porto to continue breeding silkworms there, and Beatrice, my aunt, was raised to be the proudest of Portuguese women! She received teachers who taught her both French and English. A professor came from Coimbra, who taught her astronomy. She studied song and dance at the theater and was supposed to marry the son of the famous Mendez olive family.

"'The marriage was already arranged, Braga and Mendez, silk and olives. One could live well with that, and the next generation, Beatrice's children, would study in Coimbra and the Bragas would establish a library for themselves.

"'Graça, that was my grandfather's dream, a room full of books, a room where it smelled like books, a room in which you could open a book and leave it lying there, perhaps continue reading tomorrow, or in a month. In that room with the books, in the library, an open book would be in nobody's way.

"'But things turned out quite differently: Beatrice had a child by Sir Taylor and went to London with the Englishman.

"'In spite of everything, Providence arranged everything well, for in 1829 my father fled from the Miguelists with my mother to London, to Aunt Beatrice. Who else would have taken the two of them in?

"'My father sent me to my grandfather in Lisbon. What was to be done? "Fight," said the old man, and as a twenty-year-old I joined the group that traveled to the Azores to put together an army against the Miguelists. That was in 1830.'

"While Abrão talked, I stirred the yellow porridge, which became more and more dry and crumbly. The onion rings were now only visible as threads anymore. That story that Abrão told me, I wanted to remember it word for word. Later I would perhaps understand the relationships. For me the year 1830 had not differed from any of the preceding years. We were embroidering on a wall hanging for the marquise. I remembered April of 1830 precisely. It was the rainy month, and in the palace boxes and baskets were all standing ready for the move, once again. Irazy had run to the *Campo Santana* to get hold of a few handfuls of coca leaves, for the marquise had been almost out of control. Every few hours she had a fit of weeping or burst out screaming. She did not know where she should move to this time. In Rio she had already changed her address, her palace three times. They did not want to tolerate the mistress anywhere, and they embittered her life everywhere. They put coral snakes on the landing, delivered moldy flour to her, and infiltrated wastewater bearers who did their work half drunken and stumbled, pouring the stinking brew over stairways and corridors. Again and again men in elegant uniforms showed up and conversed with Domitila for hours. Each of them brought promises such as a house in Vazouras, where they would greet the marquise with respect! Some visitors said they were friends of the emperor. They lead her to believe that they were writing letters for her to the emperor. They passed on gossip: Since his marriage to Amelia Dom Pedro had supposedly been writhing in epileptic seizures every week, and during those seizures he called out her name, 'Domitila'! And each of them left with a package or a box. Gradually the silver and porcelain cupboard emptied itself. Back then most of those men were brazen enough simply to demand. They no longer waited to see what gift would be offered them for their story, for the help that they offered in seeking an apartment. 'The velour that you have on the windows - I would ask the venerable marquise for that velvet.'

"But I did not want to think about the marquise. I wanted to listen to Abrão. Finally the corn porridge was also done. I dumped it onto a wooden board and then we began to eat; and even while Abrão filled the clay mugs with wine and water, he continued to talk.

"'We Bragas lived well in Porto. The breeding of silkworms and the spinning of silk thread were a good business. They smell sweet, the silkworm pupae, and there is a crunching sound, as if one were grinding sand, when the cocoons are broken open. I grew up with those smells and sounds. In the drying house, my father built me my own stand, where I could easily lay out the pupated silkworms next to each other at arm's height. So at the age of five, I learned to open the cocoons at the right time. If you miss those few hours and wait too long, the fiber dries out and breaks. If you are impatient and open the cocoons too soon, it is sticky and for that reason it cannot be spun. Our silk fibers were only of the yellowish white organzine quality. Five dozen men worked in the spinning mill, on the mulberry plantation, and in the drying houses.

"'Mother, Dona Carla, was responsible for the house, for the kitchen, to see that the codfish in well spiced sauce was put on the workers' table, that only black and ripe olives lay around the cheese, and that the wine was not too severely watered down. Until my sixteenth birthday there is nothing more to tell. In some years the fruits of the mulberry trees were juicier, more deeply violet. Then the syrup that the kitchen maids cooked from it attracted entire swarms of insects and wasps. In the year 1826, King João had died. We read that in the newspaper. But that event had taken place in Lisbon, and Lisbon was a day's voyage by ship from Porto. Lisbon was the capital city. There the laws were issued, and my father had to send the taxes there. But his place, our home, was in Porto. I worked in the crew that laid out the silkworm eggs, and on Saturdays I brought the boxes with the spools of silk to the harbor in the horse-drawn cart. There I saw Fatima. She was the same age as I was, and she was the daughter of a weaver who lived in our neighborhood. For a few weeks I was thoroughly confused by her caresses, and only gradually did I begin to listen to her. She talked about how the people in Lisbon were starving, that most of them lived on the streets. She told of men who lived in her father's house and held meetings there: "When Miguel finally becomes king, all that will change. Miguel will put things in order," she often said, and I stood in front of her dumbfounded, and as a reward for listening to her I was permitted to grope her breasts and to feel the warm moisture between her legs again. A few weeks later Fatima began to change. She no longer wore her hair open, but hidden under a gray net. One Saturday she came dressed in a way that I almost didn't recognize her. Pants and a jacket of gray cloth, Fatima's body was clothed in them. That body was no longer recognizable; everything feminine was so coarsely packaged. She told me about a very important assignment that her father had received from the men in Lisbon. Her father now had to weave gray, heavy cloth like she was wearing, as quickly as possible and of the very best density, from a mixture of sheep's wool and flax. What did that mean? In the first week of February in 1829 Bento had come. Bento was as old as my father. He had grown up in my grandfather's house, and after the death of my grandmother he took care of all the chores in Senhor Adalberto's household. He brought a letter from Grandfather in which it said: "My dear son, here in Lisbon much has changed. We have a new king, Miguel, and with him we received a new government to which we must, as subjects, be absolutely obedient. My shipping agency is now being run by officials of that government, and I am helping them with it..."

"'Father shook his head. Grandfather had turned his shipping agency over to outside officials? He picked up his eyeglass to make sure it was the handwriting of the old Senhor Adalberto. Finally Bento began to recite his text. Bento had a long text in his head, which he repeated to my father again and again: "Dear Son, by the quickest possible means I am informing you that Miguel, Dona Carlota's favorite son, seized all power and had himself proclaimed king. Unfortunately, all of us ignored this political development for too long. The people are doing very badly. They have no place to live, and they have nothing to eat. The only ones who have earned money are those who obtained commissions for themselves, and for every piece of wood that came from a ship they took commission after commission. We discussed this situation in the lodge. We talked, but we did nothing! On the first day of this new year of 1829 they came to my office. Two men in the new official dress - soon those gray suits will also be worn in Porto! I had to place on the table all documents and records pertaining to the ships that are sailing under contract to me. They took the box with the banknotes, the files of correspondence, and finally the ring of keys, yes, the entire ring with all the keys, both to the warehouses and to my home. They allocated a shed to me behind the lumberyard, and because of my age they left me Bento. Dear Son, I do not tell you this because I am moaning about my lost fortune. I am sixty-five years old, and my shed is large enough to die in. I want to warn you: In a few weeks they will be in Porto. They have their followers, their loyalists in every city, and they are well prepared, the Miguelists. When they come, give them everything and go to London, to Beatrice. I expressly order you to do this. Go to London! They slaughter anyone who resists them. They lock up anyone who speaks a word against Miguel or who opposes his ideas of a new, disciplined Portugal. They lie in wait for denunciations. For that reason, say nothing to anyone and go!"

"Abrão stopped talking for a while. He shook his head and finally continued: 'Bento had recited the text from Senhor Adalberto many times, but Father couldn't believe all that. Grandfather, the old Senhor Adalberto, who grabbed the collar of any merchant who wanted to cheat him regarding the fee for a cargo space and threw him out of his office; the old Senhor Adalberto, who screamed at any official of the Office of Weights and Measures, who skimmed too much of a "handling fee" from the customs duties, and forbade them to come to his office - that old Senhor Adalberto had let a few rebels take away his key ring? Grandfather had to be confused, severely ill. But Bento continued to talk for days about those men in gray jackets. "With cudgels they pushed the old man along in front of them, to every cabinet, to every table. He himself had to display the papers and count out the money, and when he wanted to take the picture of Sebastian with him - 'May I ask the gentlemen for this picture? It has been in the possession of our family for three generations.' - that is how the mighty Senhor Adalberto spoke to those myrmidons, who were hardly capable of properly inspecting the business records because only one of their group could read and write - and when he took hold of that picture, they struck him on the fingers."

"'My mother finally urged Father to divide up our silkworm enterprise and the silk spinning mill among the laborers and underlings. In each case a dozen men received the drying houses, the mulberry plantations, and the huts in which the spinning stools stood. Mother sent me to the harbor. I was supposed to find out when the next mail ship went to London. Mother did not spend hours lamenting about the health of Grandfather, of Senhor Adalberto. She would go to London with Father. There they would surely find work with Redborn. Redborn had been buying our silk for more than twenty years. And Father made me promise to go to Lisbon and look for Grandfather there.

"'Everything had been discussed, and that was good. Nothing had to be repeated, for a few days after Bento had arrived at our place, a fellow from our mulberry plantation told us that Senhor Antunos, the wine merchant, had disappeared. An official of the new government was now sitting in the office, and the wine would now be delivered only to the monastery anymore. The next day, Marilia, a kitchen maid, told us that they had shipped Senhor Assandro, the lumber merchant to Lisbon, driven like a piece of cattle to the harbor at dawn. Nothing could be learned about his servants, fear! It was dangerous to talk too much; then a person would disappear. Immediately after that noon meal Mother had everything removed from our home. She took only one bundle with her. Not a single piece of personal clothing was packed in it, but a glass filled with silkworm eggs, then five mulberry tree seedlings, and a sack of mulberry leaves as food for the silkworms. The furnishings of our home, all the furniture, pictures, vases, candelabras, the table and bed linens, the porcelain, the clay jugs, the water tubs, and the silverware - we carried all of it from my parents' home into the kitchen house, into the huts in which the laborers and maids lived.

There everything was pushed and stacked together. "Take for yourselves, take for yourselves," Mother urged the chambermaids and the workers from the spinning stools. "They won't take anything away from you!"

"'The next day, very early in the morning, I took Father and Mother to the harbor. "Faster, faster," the guards of the new government could come any moment, and the captain was risking his life when he allowed passengers to board the ship, for the order was in force: The Portuguese have to work in Portugal for Portugal! Mother stopped for a moment and drew a cross on my forehead. And in the very next moment, she and my father grabbed a sack of mail and dragged themselves as mail sack bearers up the gangplank onto the ship.

"'While I followed my parents with my eyes, someone tugged at my sleeve. Fatima! "Put that on," she whispered, and in the next moment she ducked away. It was a gray pair of pants and a gray jacket. Had that really been Fatima or only a hallucination? For at that moment the sun had come up, blood red and orange, as it did on every clear day in Porto. Look into the morning sun, into the morning sun of Porto, for as long as it takes to pray the rosary, and your head will be clear again - an ancient sailor's song.

"'When I climbed down from the coachbox in front of our house, they were already waiting for me: Arantes, the weaver, and a few soldiers. Everything went very quickly - here are the keys, yes, the uppermost layers of cocoons must be broken open in a few hours, then the next layer and the next. Of course I'm a Miguelist. Obviously I agree to have the honorable Arantes run the business now. My parents are ill. They are lying in the hospital ward of the monastery. Leave? Flee? Never! From what? Back then they still could be outwitted. While Arantes and his bullyboys greedily tried the keys to determine which ones opened which drawers and which cabinets, I put on the gray clothing and walked out of the house.

"'They would not find the box with the Vieira book. Our greatest treasure was well hidden in the secret compartment of Mother's china cupboard, and that china cupboard was screwed down tight to the floor and the wall. I walked slowly down to the cupola. There I took Mira, my horse, and whisked away to the harbor. Graça, in the beginning it was that easy to escape from them.'

"So many questions shot through my mind: Were the Bragas the only ones in Porto who bred silkworms? Did he have to wait a long time for the voyage to Lisbon? Where had he found his grandfather, and how did Abrão get to Brest? Why was he in Brest?

"I did not ask any of those questions aloud. I was quite dazed by the wine and by the darkness in the shed. The corn porridge had almost been eaten up. I had not noticed it at all. It had to be night soon, and Abrão would now take my body for himself. In this shed he would lay himself on me on one of the boards. Just not too close to the rats, and it should be done quickly, the way the shoemaker had done it for the brocade shoes and the doorkeeper of the convent in which Isabel starved and suffered. Now the letter had to be worked off. Listening alone could not have been sufficient as payment.

"But Abrão did not touch me, not in that first night, not on the following days and nights. He tied his leather apron together into a ball, so that it became a pillow for me, and he dug two other pieces of leather out of his basket, large and soft, and they were my pad and my blanket.

"During the first night I thought: This strange person is still treating me like a young lady. During the next three or four days I often asked myself: Was I repulsive? Did I smell strange and unpleasant? Was it because of my Indian face? It hurt me not to be noticed as a woman by Abrão at all.

"He brought fish and fat, a few panicles of sweet-smelling herbs. From those ingredients I made us a sauce. He brought a sack of barley kernels and roasted them in front of me, so that they smelled like coffee, almost. From some neighbor or other he had obtained syrup, and we sat before the fire pan, brushed syrup onto the greasy, freshly baked corn cakes and drank with them the transparent brown liquid from the roasted barley kernels.

"Every evening Abrão prepared my bed for me and rolled his leather apron into a pillow. In the mornings he left the shed and went out with a few fishermen. After several hours he came back, stopped in the open doorway, looked for me in the dark, and came to my corner with a stride or two. I crouched next to the fire pan. From there he pulled me up for a few moments and embraced me. He embraced me out of gratitude that I was still there, that I had tended the fire, and that a meal steamed in the kettle over the fire. From one day to the next, I looked forward to that embrace more and more. I liked what he said. I liked to listen to him.

"On the fifth and on the sixth day I was no longer angry at Abrão because he did not reach for my body with any movement of his hand. I wanted to know more about the Braga family, about his grandfather, and I was really thankful when Abrão continued to tell his story.

"'I didn't find my grandfather for days. Where was I supposed to look for him? I didn't know my way around Lisbon. Bento was also at a loss. He walked along beside me. He was completely confused at not finding his employer in his hut any longer. My coins had long since been spent. Where were we supposed to spend the night? *Guesthouses* were what they called the stalls in which benches were set up beneath which pilgrims could sleep. At five o'clock in the morning the benches were tipped over; at five o'clock in the morning everyone was driven into the church. My stomach was empty. My knees gave out because of weakness, and while I made an effort not to stumble over the cobblestones, Bento was already beginning to pray the rosary next to me.

"'In front of the entrance to the church there were guards, soldiers. They held out the bowl with the holy water to everyone. One of the guards reprimanded me, "Again." I did not understand. Then an underling sprang toward me. "You're supposed to cross yourself again," he barked at me and then pushed me into the interior of the church. All the pews had been removed from the church. The men stood on the right, the women on the left. Two cords marked a corridor where soldiers, men in black uniforms, stood. I was certainly the only one in my row who looked at the men in black so carefully. During that first Mass in Lisbon I didn't yet know that we subjects had to look at the ground. How was I supposed to find my grandfather, Senhor Adalberto, in that crowd of people who were clad in gray, all with their hair cut short, with clean-shaven faces? The Mass lasted two hours or even longer, because the liturgy was constantly interrupted by sermons and speeches. A priest ranted and raved against the English who had transformed all of Lisbon into a single tavern with their liberal lifestyle. With the women from the jungle, illnesses had been brought into the country, by which the best men had been carried off. The next one talked about help and grace, about change. He held the picture of King Miguel in his hands. Above all, he spoke about food for everyone, about one's own house, which everyone would soon have. The incense pressed down upon our heads. I could hardly breathe. The man in front of me sank to the floor. Bento jerked me back when I wanted to help that weak man. The next preacher talked about obedience and work, about the fact that a road to Porto was being built and that all strong arms in the country were needed. He thundered the order down on our heads to speak only the Portuguese language, and threatened everyone with the dungeon who mixed Portuguese with Spanish, with French, or perhaps with English. The liturgy went on and on. For a few moments I leaned against Bento, then he leaned on me. The man behind me did the same thing, and when it came time to kneel down, many sank to the floor and were no longer capable of getting up again. When we were finally permitted to move out of the church, a man dressed in black pushed me into a group of men, and with them I shuffled out of the church, with Bento next to me. At the gate, during the transition from incense smoke to sunshine, many men and women fell to the ground. They were too weak to cope with that transition into the morning air. None of those who were pressing along from behind was permitted to help them. Outside it smelled like bread, like soup, but our group was driven on past those kettles and baskets toward a barrack. There we had to line up. On a wooden plate we received greasy codfish and potatoes. I watched the man in front of me. He crossed himself before he began to eat, so I did it, too, and then finally shoved the first piece of fish into my mouth. Suddenly Bento cried out next to me, "Senhor Adalberto!" Bento had recognized Grandfather.

"'From that day on I worked in the group of men who were building the road from Lisbon to Porto. I worked with my grandfather and Bento. For six days, from sunrise to sunset, we grubbed, we hewed, we dug, and we hauled stones and drew water. For decades nobody had penetrated into that area. The brush was thick, and the ground was firm and hard. On the seventh day we were taken to the church in horse-drawn carts. After the Mass we had the greasy fish with the potatoes, and until sundown we loitered around behind the barrack and waited until the cart brought us back to the camp. Grandfather, Senhor Adalberto, didn't fill his work quota on any day, but the overseers overlooked that. The overseers were former harbor cleaners or had driven the wastewater barrels out of town as coachmen's assistants. They had been stable boys, had cleaned fish, or salted cattle hides. And now they stood before Senhor Adalberto in black uniforms and boots and listened attentively to him. They felt flattered when he said: "Mister overseer, would you give me permission to continue my work assignment tomorrow? For today my strength is exhausted!" The old Adalberto was not exhausted, not with respect to his physical strength, and especially not as far as his mental powers were concerned. He always arranged it so that he could dig or saw next to Bento and me, and next to Carlos Mendez, his former business friend. The two old men, Carlos and Adalberto, talked every day about resistance. They explained to us that a group had to be organized, a group consisting of those men who had been driven from their homes and from their offices; and soldiers had to join them. The old man often forgot to whisper, but talked his way into such enthusiasm and in so doing became loud and clear: "That has to be taken care of in a few days, Miguel sent into the mountains or across the water. There an accident can easily occur. And his faithful followers and lickspittles can be sent back to the places where they always were before." It was very dangerous to talk like that! Every week some disappeared from our camp. They had raved too loudly about bygone times, perhaps used an English expression, or discussed the constitution. We are no longer subjects!

"'For me the months in the Miguelist work crew were a good time, in spite of everything, for when I woke up I was already looking forward to Grandfather, to his stories of women who sit at the window deeply sad until they have lured a man into the house. I looked forward to his curses, "Just wait, you whore's son of a boulder." I looked forward to his craftiness with respect to the overseers.

"'It became October and November. We made only sluggish progress with the road construction because nobody knew exactly how to lay out a path, how to lay out a road. A master builder often declared to us in the evenings, when we lay exhausted on our pallets, that it would be best to drive a flock of sheep northward from Lisbon. "Then you wouldn't need either a plan or a mathematician. The sheep would wind their way along and find the most favorable path." We shrugged our shoulders at that, and the next day we continued to dig where the supervisors placed us. Two days before Christmas a mudflow occurred, and everything that we had leveled and laid free for several weeks was covered with a thick layer of earth. So we began all over again. In the second week of January in the year 1830 the messenger finally came! Carlos Mendez had dependable people, above all ones who brought news from our camp down into the city of Lisbon, from there to the Belem harbor, and on across the Atlantic Ocean to Rio de Janeiro, and then the entire way back into our camp. "Maria Gloria will be sent this year yet, in 1830. She will be proclaimed Queen of Portugal. The loyal supporters of the queen are to expect her arrival in the Azores, on Terceira." The debate was so vigorous that there was almost an uprising in our camp. So weapons and money as well would be sent to the Azores, so that we would be equipped for a battle against Miguel, against the Miguelists. But who would notify the refugees from Miguel in London, who surely wanted to participate in the struggle for a liberated Portugal? On the other hand, wasn't the queen just eleven years old? In the end, would a relative from Austria...? No, never. They, of course, had already helped Miguel come to power. Carlos Mendez sent the messenger off again. Now he brought wine and liquor, "A gift for you for the new year, Mr. overseer," and we had to accomplish less work for the day. Now all that we debated anymore was our escape plan: from the camp to

Belem, and from there by ship to the Azores to prepare ourselves for the fight for freedom. And I would be there. I would accompany Senhor Adalberto.'

"So the years 1829 and 1830 had cut notches in the souls of each of us. Abrão and his parents had been driven out of Porto, away from raising silkworms; and a new era had begun for me as well. Dona Amelia had arrived in Rio de Janeiro, and Isabel had to be taken away from *Boa Vista*. Soon after that, Isabel had been taken to Europe by the two governesses.

"'Isabel will write to you, Graça. Don't worry. Things will go well for Isabel. She won't forget you.'

"Those words were my only comfort. For days I recited them to myself: 'Things will go well for Isabel. She won't forget you.' But then it occurred to me how urgently Isabel needed her cocoa in the evening, how easily she made an ink spot, and that she fell asleep most quickly when I sang to her. In those moments I felt so strongly that Isabel needed me, because she would surely be weeping and sobbing. I ran out of the palace, ran as far as the *Campo Santana*, and from there I rode to the harbor in a horse-drawn cart. From Rio to Europe, how long did that take? And which ship was sailing to Europe? How often did ships sail there? The sailors laughed at me, but old Valinho, the dog breeder, explained to me that the mail ships from England came once a week, and that ships from France and from Portugal came every two or three weeks. In the dirt he drew the country of Brazil and far outside of our country another land, a continent, Europe.

"For me, the year 1830 was the year when I did not know where Isabel was. I felt that Isabel was suffering. In my dreams I heard her crying. But I could not tell anybody that. Isabel was no longer my affair. I had to embroider and polish the Dutch tiles. Besides that, anybody who talked about Isabel, about the mistress's child, was beaten.

"With an embrace Abrão drew me out of my thoughts and back into his hut, into the shed at the Brest harbor. He pulled me back into his year of 1830.

"'Actually, we didn't have to flee at all. It was easy to get the guards drunk with liquor and wine. There were two dozen of us, and we marched to the city, walking through streets that were almost devoid of people. There were no longer any beggars to be seen in Lisbon. The beggars now lived in the monasteries or in the houses that had been taken from Miguel's opponents, the supporters of the constitution. At the entrance to the harbor stood soldiers. It would have been better to make our way here at night and individually. In the end they would now throw us all into prison, or they would shoot us on the spot. Grandfather, Senhor Adalberto, shook his head: "They will be happy if we leave, if they no longer have us in the country. With each one of us, it was only important for them to take everything away from us, and the quicker we disappear, the more unconcernedly they can settle down in your house, Luiz, in your wine cellar, Carlos, and in my office." And that is how it actually was. We were ordered into the harbor administration office and asked our names and what we wanted at the harbor. "We have been ordered by the prefect to work in the lumber storage area," was what we had agreed to say. The official sneered, opened a book, and stared at the series of names. He couldn't read. Finally he whistled for the scribe, who wrote our names one below the other: "Braga, Mendez, Mendonça, Abreu, Costa, Pereira," and after each name our vocations as well: "shipping agent, olive merchant, master builder, Dutch tile maker, master carpenter, carpenter," and finally blurted out: "Get out of here." Nobody else paid any attention to us. Two days later we rode in the boat to the English mail ship, which took us to Terceira in the Azores.

"'Graça, for those who possessed or had possessed anything, it was easy to escape from the Miguelists, at least in the beginning. For they could take something away from us. They could park themselves in our houses; they sent their people to our workshops, our offices, and our wine cellars; and they let us leave quietly. The others, and that was the majority, who raged aloud against Miguel during those initial weeks and months, or against the uniforms, against the curfew in the evening, against the strict requirement to attend Mass, those who perhaps talked about freedom of thought, but didn't possess anything, they were driven into the camps to build roads and dig wells. Grandfather often talked about one of those forgotten men, Mario, a painter and poet. He had begun to translate our *Os Lusíadas* into French. Mario often sat for a week over two lines. He filed on the words and the expressions. None seemed to him to be close enough to our text by Luís de Camões. Then he knocked on Senhor Adalberto's door in the middle of the night and read to him: "*Should we sing of Lusitania's realm that blossoms there on the western shore, that already sees the sun when it is barely rising?*"

"'Of course, Mario raged against Miguel. And he was one of the first whom they took. In the early weeks many were hanged.

"'On Terceira, in Vilaforte and in Horta, we quickly found our way around. The refugees from Miguel who had arrived ahead of us had already built a small settlement of wooden huts, a garrison building, and sheds for the weapons and our meetings. We wrote down our strategy. We drew maps, already marking out the best travel route back to Porto and to Lisbon. Each of those who had newly arrived had to report precisely about the situation at home, about the situation in Lisbon. Was the coach service functioning? Did the ban on speaking in public still exist? Who was living in this or that house now? Where did they deliver the sea salt? And what was ordered in the last sermon? All of that was discussed, and in ceremonies the oath of allegiance to our queen was renewed: "... to fight with all my power for the rights of my homeland Portugal, and to give my life for Portugal and for our Queen Maria Glória." We did all of that to shorten the waiting for ourselves. Some began to cultivate fields, but in the Azores everything grows poorly. The weather changes too often. Some worked at setting up salterns. On some days the sun blazed, but they were hardly finished with the enclosure and had poured the first tubs of sea water into the wooden boxes, when the storm began to howl and rain and snow swirled down from the sky for a few hours, and the saltwater moldered for a few days.

"'We went out with the natives to catch fish. Most of us soon lived with an Azorean family. When the first refugees from Miguel arrived, men were still scarce on Terceira, but in 1830 men were in the majority and the women could be selective. I lived in Louisa's house. She reminded me of Fatima, and she only let me into her room and later into her house because I was related to Senhor Adalberto, whom everyone called "Consul Adalberto." A few weeks after his arrival on Terceira, Grandfather had become active in his business again; he ran a trade agency. He inquired of the sailors, when which ship was expected. Then he rowed a group of sailors out and gave flag signals: Put in at Terceira. There one could do business! In a short time, most of the people of the villages of Vilaforte, Horta, and Lajes, who had lived in idleness and bitterness until our arrival, were involved in the business dealings of Consul Adalberto. Ships that were on their way to Lisbon with lumber, sugarloaves, and cotton interrupted their voyages for a week at Terceira. Part of the cargo was liquidated, transferred to an English ship, or put in storage. Banknotes and certificates of indebtedness were exchanged, parties were held, and the captain sailed with the rest of his freight to Lisbon. Our share of the goods went to Plymouth or to Brest. What Consul Adalberto was doing was dangerous. We knew that, but it didn't matter to us. A year after our arrival on Terceira, we were all so busy inventorying cargo, correspondence, storing goods, building unloading ramps, and constructing platform and beam scales, that we hardly had any time left for our military meetings, for our shooting practice and strategy discussions.

"'In the pieces of mail that reached us from the English, the same thing always appeared: We should wait for our queen. In June of 1831 we learned that she was on her way to Europe! Maria Glória with her royal household, also her father with his new wife Amelia. We went into joyful rapture! Now it would only be weeks or a few months until we could sail back again, return to our old life. The streets of Lajes, of Vilaforte were cleaned, the cobblestones replaced, the manure heaps moved outside the city, the wells cleaned, the houses freshly painted blue and white. I thought about our silkworms, about the mulberry plantation, about the crackle when the cocoons were opened by the hundreds. Where should I go first, to Porto to put our breeding site in order, to check the placement of the eggs, and to examine the silk spools? In the end, had they mixed less valuable marabout silk with the organzine on the spools and angered our customers? Or should I first go to England to my parents and bring them back? Each of us was thinking about the first tasks and actions that he wanted to perform immediately after his return to Lisbon, when we gradually grasped the fact that our Queen Maria Glória had sailed in a wide arc around the Azores to Brest. She had not interrupted her voyage on Terceira to speak with those people who had sworn to give their lives for her, for that twelve-year-old girl.

"'"Just what does she know about us?" many said, shaking their heads and hardly able to hold back the tears. "She's not a Portuguese woman, after all. How should she know what we feel, what we have to endure?" Some did not want to believe it and didn't stop practicing the welcoming song; they continued to press and clean their uniforms and their Sunday clothes. But in September, in October of that year of 1831 everyone had accepted it: Our queen had traveled directly to Brest, then to England or France, in any case, straight to safety. How the refugees from Miguel lived with the Azoreans had not interested her. She didn't want to become acquainted with the weather changes, the icy winds, or the scorching sunshine. She didn't want to know that we received almost only fish to eat, that we had to wait for weeks for the ship with oil and potatoes, that a liquor distilled from moldy grain sent people into a delirium from which some didn't awaken again.'

"'The travel route,' I interrupted Abrão, 'the travel route was altered several times. Dona Leonora often had arguments with the captain because of it. Portuguese territory cannot even be touched. If it is, they will immediately take Maria Glória from the ship and arrest her - that was what he said. Abrão, Maria Glória didn't know that they were expecting her in Terceira. She would have accomplished it, but nobody told her that faithful followers of the queen were waiting for her in the Azores.'

"Abrão shrugged his shoulders: 'Who will blame a twelve-year-old girl for anything? But what kind of advisors surrounded our queen? We fell into despair. In reality nobody would take us back to Portugal. We began to grasp that fact. And then it was a long time, of course, for Pedro, our first soldier, our liberator, did not come until months later!

"'We had been so weakened by *saudade*, that after the first meetings where Pedro explained his strategy we left without saying a word. Nobody believed in a return anymore, and if there were one, what would await us? Besides that, Dom Pedro was ill. He lay for days in a darkened room. He was feverish, could not get up out of his sick bed. Word soon spread that it was not only his body that had come from Brazil in a thoroughly weakened condition. Above all, it was his soul that had been gnawed down to the point of powerlessness by the events.

"'His thoughts now revolved only around the idea of "making amends." Everything that he did on Terceira, every conversation in the arsenal, the appraisal of the maps and the weapons, he carried out without the enthusiasm, without the impatience that they had raved to us about. His embraces were not passionate and heartfelt. That is how he had been described. His embraces were polite, and again and again he said, often completely out of context, "I'll make amends for it." A few weeks after his arrival some people were already beginning to grumble: "What should we do with him? The man is confused. How are we supposed to drive out the Miguelists with this man?"

"'Senhor Adalberto, my grandfather, flew into a rage about it. He was convinced that if anyone could lead us back to Portugal it was only Dom Pedro. He also visited him in Ana Peregrino's house. Dom Pedro lived there. Grandfather pushed aside all the spectators, stormed into his room, and slammed the door. Now it would come to a terrible argument. Dom Pedro's fits of rage were feared. But it remained quiet in the room, and soon the two men came out and walked in the direction of the beach. Dom Pedro spoke and Grandfather listened. Some of my comrades had joined me in following the two of them. They soon turned back. Once more the soldier-emperor had disappointed them. What kind of a hero was that, who told a perfect stranger about himself, who almost cried his heart out in the presence of Senhor Adalberto?

"'A week later my grandfather had died. He had put the freight records and his desk drawer in order, and then he had me summoned. He instructed me to offer myself to become Dom Pedro's personal adjutant. I still wanted to ask my grandfather so many things, but no time remained to us for that. How often I had reached for his hand during the tempestuous crossing to the Azores. What a good thing it was when Grandfather patted me on the shoulder, when he pinched my cheek like a child. Grandfather's hands radiated so much security and safety. Above all, from those hands streamed the certainty that I would always be caught, held, and led safely through all of the chaos. I never wanted to let go of those hands. Grandfather probably gave off power and strength through his hands for decades. For decades the thought had probably not come to him at all that it would ever be he who reached for another hand, that he needed the benefit of a hand that held him, that gave him security. In the last minutes of his life Grandfather reached for my hand. He was moving toward the unknown, and he wanted to hold onto something while walking across that bridge. One single time I was able to give him strength and security from me, and with all the love, all the tenderness that I felt for that old man, I held his hand until he was on the other side and let go of my hand, because over there he no longer needed my support.

"'Dom Pedro was tormented by *saudade*, *saudade* in every hue, we knew that, especially by *saudade* for Brazil, from where they had driven him away.

"'When everything was finally ready for us to leave for Porto, we had to postpone our departure again for two weeks. Storms and fogbanks held us back, and Pedro, our first soldier, writhed once again in fever.

"'We would now march against his brother Miguel. Everything had been discussed and written down. We were equipped. But he was only concerned with a postponement. He was waiting for news that Miguel would voluntarily abdicate. Yes, that is what he was waiting for. That is why he looked for the clouds in the sky that brought snow and storms. They would again prevent his departure for a few days.

"'It was not until the end of November of 1832 that our three ships landed in Porto. No watch ship, no boat opposed us. Were we mistaken for freight ships? When we drove the horses ashore and distributed the weapons, the fishermen hardly looked up. They continued to busy themselves with their nets and pushed each other's boats into the ocean. Nor were there any Miguelist uniforms visible. Where were the dark gray jackets and pants? There was actually no battle in Porto. Graça, we, the soldiers of the queen, marched into Porto and roamed through the streets. My comrades took up residence in inns.'

"What was Abrão saying? It could not have been that way. 'In Paris it was reported that they almost let the soldiers starve to death. There was talk of executions! We prayed every evening for the liberators of Portugal.'

"'There were deaths. A few comrades had also injured themselves. Some of our comrades shot at each other, but that happened because of a woman, because of rum. The men were too starved in everything. Graça, we Azoreans, we Miguel emigrants, we felt that we had been deceived. We had held out, while the people of Porto had long since been living in harmony with the Miguelists! There was almost a revolt in Porto, Azoreans against the inhabitants of Porto whom we wanted to liberate! A month after our arrival, in a pompous celebration, the mayor gave Dom Pedro the key to the city gate. The officials and all the important people of Porto swore allegiance to their queen and rushed back to their businesses, and nothing was to change there. The distilleries, the wine cellars, and the oil factories, even the little workshops where shoemakers, tailors, and sail-weavers worked at their crafts - they all belonged to Miguelists. But they didn't stagger in the direction of the church in the evenings. They didn't go to the city office with their heads bowed to pay their tithes. The Miguelists lived well in Porto. The previous owners had been driven out and that was how it was supposed to remain.

"'I went to our estate, of course. At the entrance to our silkworm farm a wooden sign hung in splendor: "Arantes." They didn't even take a new board, for on the back it still read: "Braga." Arantes set his dogs on me, and a manager shot in my direction. The whitewash on the house was peeling off. Cabinets from the dining room stood outside in the open, even my mother's favorite cabinet. The back of it, the secret compartment where the book by António Vieira lies hidden, was undamaged. Everywhere lay spools with sticky silk thread. Unopened cocoons were stacked in a basket, covered with mold. In the office were piles of half-crumpled papers.

"'When I told Dom Pedro about it, he nodded. He had been hearing the same stories for days. So did we have to fight to liberate our own houses? Should I shoot at the members of the Arantes family, at his laborers? Dom Pedro did not know the answer to that. In memory of my grandfather, of Senhor Adalberto, he gave me a letter: "By order of her royal Majesty, Maria II, it is decreed that the silk spinning mill with all of its buildings, as well as the mulberry tree plantation, be restored to the possession and responsibility of the honorable Braga family. All powers of the police and the military are to be employed in carrying out this order." I went to the mayor with a copy of that letter. He shook his head and laid the sheet of paper in his desk drawer. I knocked on the door of the vestry. The priest crossed himself when he had read the letter. He would never tell Arantes that he should give the silkworm breeding business and the entire farm back to me. Today I was there; tomorrow it would be the wine merchant, the day after tomorrow the owner of the oil mill, then the boat builders, and the master builders. So that was the truth about our struggles for a new constitution, for liberation from Miguel. We were concerned only about our property. That was the only reason why we, the emigrants had returned, today those from the Azores, in a month those from London. That was how he railed at me as he sent me away.

"'It was not the time to negotiate. I boarded the next ship that sailed for London. I wanted to see my parents, to tell them that our Vieira book was still safe, that our silk spinning mill still existed, but that we would have to fight to get it back, sometime.

"'But then I decided to do something different and left the ship already in Brest. I could write to my parents in London and tell them what there was to report. Could I convince my despondent father to travel to Porto with me and retake our estate? Hardly. My father could not shoot. So I stayed in Brest. I intended to wait here until the child queen traveled to Lisbon. Then perhaps a new era would dawn. Then I would get back our estate in Porto. That is why I am here.'

"I had listened breathlessly to Abrão. I was so agitated by what he had told me, that I had not noticed that a rat had jumped into our kettle. Abrão dumped all of our corn porridge into the basket and gave it to the rats, while I was hungry and cold. For that reason Abrão pushed a mug of liquor toward me. He himself drank of it, a lot, much too much. He belched.

"'And did you find Isabel, that mistress's child? Where? Talk, Graça, talk.' With that, he thrust himself upon me, awkwardly taking off his leather apron. In the next moment he would fall upon me. Today, on the sixth evening in his shed, his hands would feel their way along my body. He would smell of fish and liquor, thrust, and immediately afterward roll sleepily into the water puddle that lay between our two sleeping pallets.

"I didn't want that. I didn't want to feel that stinking, drunk Abrão. I pretended to submit, but then I slipped to the fire and poked around in the fire pan until he was snoring. I immediately got my bundle, which was hanging beneath the roof, and stepped out of the hut barefoot. I just didn't want to look at him; I didn't want to remember this Abrão. Every person has an animal inside. You simply must not ever lure it out. Irazy had also taught me that.

"When Abrão has slept enough, then his animal is locked away again in the furthest corner of his soul and everything in his voice, in his eyes, in his touch is tenderness and patience again.

"I just slipped quickly into my stockings and shoes.

"'Where are you going in such a hurry, young lady?' a fisherman asked me.

"'To the nearest ship,' and I was already letting myself be pushed toward the pier. Some women and men with baskets and packs were already sitting in the boat. They were half asleep and smiled kindly. We went toward a sailing vessel. I tied my bundle around my neck and pulled myself up the rope ladder onto the deck. Nobody asked me my name. So had I wangled my way onto a ship again? No, I went down and up the steps with the other passengers, stumbled over hawsers and ropes, and finally found a place next to the galley. It smelled like fish soup. It smelled so deliciously like fish soup that my knees became weak and I sank down next to a pile of wood. On that ship I ate codfish for the first time. What a meal for my stomach, for my body, which was already dried out down to the last fiber. I ate two plates of that delicacy and fell asleep.

"Sleep lay upon me like a veil, very lightly, and beneath it I was awake. I saw the children's room in *Boa Vista*, and in it Isabel, who was fighting with the two Bragança princesses, with Francisca and Paula Mariana, over the little well that Rafael had carved for them. It was raining and I ran outside, into the corridor, as far as the gargoyle that poured the rainwater in a wide arc into the courtyard onto the hibiscus bush with the yellow blossoms. I held my head under that rainwater that was shooting down. I let it run through the strands of my hair, and in a few moments the layer of salt had been washed out of my hair. Suddenly I heard a man's voice: 'Not the mistress's child. She doesn't want to see the mistress's child.' Those words rang out through the howling of the wind and rain. I ran back into the children's room where several officials were already standing. The mistress's child must leave, quickly, right this minute. And I could not immediately distinguish Isabel. She was dressed exactly the same as Paula Mariana, in a white dress crisscrossed with blue ribbons and the same ribbons braided into her hair. Isabel, no, not you, that is Francisca. Why does she also have that white dress with the blue ribbons on today? Isabel, finally I pulled her away from the basket with the building blocks and ran outside with the five-year-old girl, down through the rain toward the stables; no coach anywhere. The mistress's child must leave. Where could I take Isabel? Where could we go? No stable boy anywhere. The mistress's child must leave! Then the cook shook me awake. He held out a wooden board to me, with pieces of codfish lying on it. They dripped with grease. 'Eat now, before you leave the ship,' he said, and I ate, swallowed, still quite dazed from my dream. With the salty taste of codfish still in my mouth, I dragged myself with the others to the rope ladder, swung down to the boat, and went toward the sheds on the dock. In front of them, tables were set up with mountains of fish lying on them. Baskets that were filled to the brim with olives were being pushed toward the sheds in pushcarts.

"I was finally in Lisbon.

"Whom should I ask in this throng of people? 'I want to go to the palace to Queen Maria. I have here a letter from her. We're sisters, almost. Take me along. In which direction is the city, toward the sunrise or toward the sunset?'

"They did not understand my Portuguese, and although they sounded like Portuguese, I couldn't make head or tail of their answers. When Luiz Arantes stood before me, it was already pitch dark. He talked to me, and his words sounded amicable. He pulled me along with him to a building with walls of stone, a tavern. There he pushed a bowl of codfish soup and a mug of wine toward me. Gradually I began to figure out what he was saying.

"'You probably don't know where you should go. Here at the harbor there is enough to do. My friend Clotoaldo is looking for a woman to clean fish. For that you can set up a place to sleep in the shed. Just what do you want here in Porto?'

"Porto? I was in Porto!

"I was still separated from Lisbon, from my princess sister by so many hours of sailing. I had to get away from there, Isabel in London, Abrão in Brest, and Maria Glória in Lisbon!

"Luiz comforted me in my sobbing. He led me to the shed of Clotoaldo, the fish merchant, and he helped me set up a bed in the farthest corner of the shed. Beneath the roof he sawed a skylight through which I could look up into the sky. He brought a clay jug full of water, fresh water. For all of these services he took my body. That was obvious. I had nothing, of course, to pay him with, and during the first night in Porto I preferred him to Abrão, who had talked to me for days and had hardly reached for my hand.

"Luiz never asked me my name, not in the first night and not in the following nights. He obtained work for me. I could clean the fish for Clotoaldo. I turned them in the salt tray. I stirred the codfish sauce. And every day I ran to the harbor several times. 'Which ship out there is sailing to Lisbon?' And always the same sneers on the sailors' faces. 'To Lisbon? What do you want to do there? No ship sails from here to Lisbon. We want nothing to do with them.'

"In the process, three or four weeks passed. During the day the drudgery and the stink of the fish, in the evening Luiz. He usually came drunk. 'Do you still want to go to Lisbon? There they are working out laws so that they can take everything away from us. Down there, in Lisbon, there they have time for that.' That was how he babbled before he threw himself on top of me. There was no longer any trace of the tenderness with which he had embraced me during the first night. Perhaps I had only imagined those embraces. I wanted to be embraced that way by Abrão. Somebody had to take Abrão's place for me, provide a substitute for his hands and his body. What an insult. Abrão had spurned my body, so from Luiz's every breath, every thrust I formed for myself that Abrão whom I had never felt. A few weeks later, when I vomited in front of Luiz, spewed the fish soup and the wine in a wide arc, he cried out and left.

"Now that I was pregnant, Luiz didn't come into my shed again at all. Sometimes, when I dragged two baskets full of fish to my table, I saw him sitting on the box of a barouche. He pointed to my belly, lifted his thumb - 'Victory' - and sneered. Where should I go? Why had I stayed in Porto? Why hadn't I gone to Lisbon? Surely I could even have gone to Lisbon on foot. It would not have been more arduous than dragging the baskets with the fish across the harbor landing. What child would I now bring into the world? Could I take it out to the garbage pits with the fish entrails? Every evening I pulled the cart to the garbage pit myself, and I stood in front of that hole in the ground where rats and vermin moved across the remnants of fish and meat. I could throw my body in with that, and just at that moment of wavering about going in and down I felt the child within me and turned around, pulled the pushcart back, and fell into my bed that way, stinking of fish offal. 'Nobody knows exactly when he begins to die, and they are especially punished whom Heaven lets toil for a long time, for a very long time among the living, among those who are truly living.' Irazy, my mother, had murmured that, and for many months I had fallen asleep with that sentence. The autumn turned to winter, 1834. I probably gradually forgot how to talk, for Clotoaldo sometimes looked at me in horror when I indicated to him with hand gestures that there were enough fish in the basket, or when I shook my head - no, I did not tip over the salt tray. And instead of 'Yes' sometimes a 'Lisbon' blurted out of my mouth.

"The child in me grew. Where should I take the child? I didn't know.

"In the last week of August in the year 1834, on a Sunday, I saw Abrão again. He got out of a boat that was lying next to the one from which the fish were being shoveled into my basket. Although Abrão looked at me, he didn't recognize me and went straight to the man who had coaches for hire. Abrão was in Porto. Abrão was in my vicinity. Abrão, who could talk, talk for hours and for days, as I had forgotten how to do during the previous weeks and months. I left my pushcart standing there and ran after him: 'Abrão, talk to me again. Continue to talk to me. Perhaps then I can find them again, the words, and can speak entire sentences again.' I had fallen down. Meanwhile my fish baskets had been shoveled full, and I pulled my cart to my cleaning table as I did on any other day. Abrão hadn't noticed me at all. The scales brushed off - Abrão, I must see Abrão again, I want Abrão, I want to hear him talk - the fish's belly slit open, the entrails pulled out - Abrão, that very evening I would ask my way to him, Abrão and the silkworm farm - the fins hacked off and the fish thrown into the salt tray - Abrão, I'll wash myself, let water run over my body as long as it takes for the fish smell to be washed off. Abrão will recognize me again and continue to talk to me. Cramps suddenly drew me to the ground. The child, this child had finished growing. It wanted out. Between the cramps I hoisted the basket with the entrails, the offal onto my cart and pushed and pulled it toward the church. At the back was the hatch with the wheel and in front of it the oleander bush. It did not take long. I crouched under that bush for perhaps one or two hours. Then I had my son in my hands. I wanted to remember his face, Luiz, the hair that grew low on his temples, the hands that didn't seem small and tiny to me at all, but rather large and powerful, his screaming, which had already become a crying after he took a few breaths, a crying in which the tears of my newborn son mixed with the slime, the blood that still stuck to his face.

"'Look at him closely. They don't change,' said a woman, a nun.

"'What name should we give him when he is baptized,' she asked, as she peeled the child out of my hands.

"'Luis,' I said. And Ines - yes, it was the nun Ines from the foundling house - Ines led me to the well. There she washed Luiz, helped me wash myself, and even brought a pot of soup and a piece of bread.

"Luiz's face, his hands, the hair - I could push all that away. But the crying, that bitter crying, I couldn't get that out of my ears, the tears that had welled up from the tiny eyes. All these years, all nineteen years I have carried that bitter crying with me.

"I could only deaden that crying. At first I did it with the search for Abrão, and that lasted a long time, weeks, months, into the following year."

Graça interrupts her narrative. She is silent, tracing the irregularities of the stone bench with her fingers. "Nice," she murmurs. She is still sitting at a distance from Maria Glória. Now Maria Glória is supposed to continue telling her story, and Maria Glória almost becomes panicky about it, for the events, the ones that are really painful for her - they did not come until after 1833.

Graça smiles. She understands, and she is also the more courageous woman, for she finally embraces Maria Glória. It is good that we meet here in Sintra. This stone bench is a special place, so solitary, and the solitariness is important. Graça recites a few lines from a Vieira letter, and she listens attentively when Maria Glória continues: "*My beloved Christina, when a philosopher was asked where the best place in the world was to find the truth, he answered. He answered that it was the remote, the solitary place. So you, honored Christina, should seek out a cell and distance yourself from amusements, from the daily routine. And you should not wait for answers that you can separate into heaven and hell; the matter is not that simple. You should change your dress, change your name, and so that you no longer stand there as a show-off, you should hide your immense knowledge behind silence. Christina, only in that way will you learn the many truths that live in one and the same day, in one and the same deed...*"

CHAPTER IV

*When the pomegranate opens deeply red,
this competition, ruby, you'll not win;
the vine winds lovely, with the elm branch wed,
now bearing grapes that are red and green.*

Graça remains sitting at a distance from Maria Glória. Nothing has remained of the intimacy with which they had embraced each other in August of 1833, in Brest. At that time, as fourteen-year olds, they had promised each other to return to Rio de Janeiro, soon, when Maria Glória had fulfilled her duties in Lisbon. They knew that this promise could not be fulfilled, but they could not have let go of each other without including Rio de Janeiro in their embrace. That piece of earth was part of them, was part of their language, both their spoken and their unspoken words, part of their outbursts and their prayers.

Start out, separate from one another, and arrive. How often that sequence would repeat itself. Being strangers upon their arrival and learning about each other's lives and daily routines by watching for weeks and months, and in so doing creeping more and more into dreams, living out their lives in dreams. Finally, each learning to divide up her own personal nature into the one who laughs and weeps, walks and dances in dreams, and into the one who she is perceived to be, into the one who she presents herself as, the taciturn, demure, and cumbersome woman.

Now they sit next to each other on the stone bench under the parasol pine in Sintra. The November cold creeps into every crease in their skins. During the whole twenty years the two of them have never become accustomed to the European seasons; during the whole twenty years the two of them have rarely talked about it with anyone.

In November they think of spring blossoms. In November the almond trees clean themselves; they leave the salt-hardened, hand-sized leaves to the wind and let it blow them from the branches.

When the winter months of June, July, and August have been weathered, then during those weeks the tree has gathered all its strength for something new, for an additional level of leafy canopy. Its branches will grow more outstretched, its foliage more dense than in the previous summer. If they were now sitting under an almond tree that was unrolling its November spring shoots into leaves, they would hold each other's hands, lean against each other, and talk, letting their thoughts roam freely. But here, on the stone bench in Sintra, they draw their woolen shawls tighter around their shoulders. Here they need to stop for breath.

Graça and Abrão in Porto, 1835 and 1836
"The search for the stream guided me"

Graça finally lets her story continue. For Maria Glória it is no longer important that Graça speaks about the events aloud, audibly. She can feel Graça's thoughts, in every breath, in the swaying of Graça's body back and forth, in her hand gestures, when Graça sits with her face propped on her hand, when she wipes her forehead and eyes, when she covers her face with both hands, when she reaches for Maria Glória's arm. With these things she expresses herself, and it is easy for Maria Glória to read Graça's movements, to follow Graça's story.

"To find Abrão, I didn't let anything else enter my mind. It took a few weeks, but I didn't notice the time. Even thoughts of Isabel came to me only in the moments when I was falling asleep. 'Help her, so that she doesn't freeze,' I prayed. It was September. I had not heard anything from Isabel for over a year. For more than a year I had not written to her. Who in Porto would have written the letter for me? And for an answer I would have had to give my address. But I didn't have an address. Hardly anyone knew my name. 'Go way, leave.' They didn't say any more than that to me.

"The tavern owner's wife, Dona Paola, gave me a few linen

cloths. 'Graça, wherever you left your baby, you can surely use these linens.'

"I cut those cloths into strips and bandaged my body with them, more and more tightly. Only after I had seen Abrão again did I notice the changes in my body, belly and upper thighs swollen, and two varicose veins moved downward from the hollows of my knees. I pulled the cloth firm and tight; to bind away that year of 1834, the months from my departure from Brest until the day when I had seen Abrão again. I wanted to erase those months. Luis Arantes, he didn't exist, and the child, what child? Within two or three days all of my powers, those of my body and the powers of my soul, assumed one single direction: I had to get work in the kitchen of the tavern; only there would I have the opportunity to see Abrão again. He would come into that tavern after he had taken the boxes with the spools of silk to the ship, or when he was waiting for the arrival of mail from London. I didn't want to carry the fish baskets and clean the fish for even one more hour, both in the tavern's back yard. Four women stood at the soup pots and in front of the oil pans in the kitchen, and each of them had thrown taunts at my back: 'Have you shown Arantes the jungle boy yet?' 'Look how she laces herself up. That won't help her. Luis Arantes doesn't even know her anymore.'

"That's how they laughed, and they pushed a fish basket toward me. Quick as a flash I reached for the piece of wood that was lying halfway in the fire. I threw that piece of wood at the kitchen maids and they flew apart and shrieked.

"I hit the oldest one of them, Marisa. She fell and remained lying there. She tugged at her smock, which immediately began to smolder. I felt sorry for the poor old woman. I didn't want to do anything to her. I just wanted her place at the hearth, in the kitchen, near the bar. So therefore I immediately dragged her outside and wrapped her leg in one of the linen strips that I took from around my belly. It looked serious, a charred spot from which blood seeped. Perhaps something had also happened to the bone. Was it broken? So I didn't worry about it any further, but immediately went to Marisa's water jug, took her cooking spoon, and continued to stir the codfish soup, trickled olive oil into it, and crushed the salt in the mortar. The other three kitchen maids crept back to their water jugs and pots. They never taunted me again. They looked at me and they shrugged their shoulders when Dona Paola scolded: 'Just what happened here?' They stirred, chopped, and continued to grate. Nobody looked in Marisa's direction when the laborers came and carried the whimpering woman across the yard to the shed.

"From that day on, Marisa probably cleaned the fish instead of me. I was sorry for her, and late at night I often remembered her and prayed 'that Marisa doesn't get a deformed leg.'

"What should I have done? I needed that place in the kitchen.

"From my side of the hearth I could watch them all: the wine merchants who constantly complained about prices that were too low, the olive farmers who lamented about the weather, the fishermen who stared into their liquor and shook their heads for hours because the ocean had been too stormy or too calm. It had driven into their nets fish that were too large one day and too small the next. The ship owners came. They slammed their leather bags of coins on the table and stomped over to us in the corner of the kitchen. 'Put out the large bowls full of codfish, and bread, freshly toasted, and with it the Menezes olive oil,' they ordered, and soon they sat at the table with a few officials from the city office.

"From morning coffee until the last pitcher of foam-covered wine, I didn't let the barroom out of my sight for a minute. I had even set up my bed behind the fire pit and nobody, none of the kitchen maids, none of the laborers dared to assign me a different place. They were afraid that I would throw a piece of wood at them again.

"On a Sunday in January of 1835 these two men in dark jackets came. They organized papers at the table. They hastily spooned up the fish soup, hardly looking up from their papers. They spoke with each other in a foreign language. They were neither from Porto, nor were they Portuguese at all. French? English? Both in dark overcoats, with manicured fingernails, with well cared-for hands. So they were officials. I took the two pieces of codfish out of the simmering fat, garnished them with olives, and put the plate at the edge of the table. The gentleman and his scribe looked up with astonishment. Had they ordered baked fish?

"The two of them were master and subordinate. Nobody deceives me. I watched carefully how the one hastily pushed the papers back and forth, how he listened with his eyes open wide and nodded, endeavoring with every movement of his hand to do things correctly for the other one, his master.

"Were the two of them passing through?

"The barroom filled up. The harbor workers shuffled in. A ladle of soup, two or three mugs of wine. Sailors had a saltcellar placed in front of them and poured blended liquor into themselves. The sailors, the harbor workers, even the fishermen didn't sit next to each other as they did on other days, randomly, the way they came through the door. Two groups sat across from each other. In the one group they licked salt and slurped liquor. The others ate soup and sauces and drank wine. The ones with the liquor mugs at their lips were silent. The others handed each other the wine pitcher, laughed, and talked indiscriminately.

"'Today we retook Braga's silkworms for him. Tomorrow we'll march with Menezes to his oil mill.'

"'And in the evening old Menezes will be able to trickle his own oil onto his bread. Who knows how those Miguelists watered down his oil? They don't know anything about pressing oil.'

"'Just as Arantes knew nothing about spinning silk. How he ran to stuff one more basket full of silk spools, all of it inferior threads.'

"'What does he want with them. Nobody here will buy those sticky threads from him, and on the next ship to Brest there will no longer be any cargo space for an Arantes.'

"'Even here in Porto the time of the Miguelists is finally over.'

"So the silent ones were those who now had to depart from their positions at the harbor, in the silk spinning mill, in the wine cellars and the oil mills. And the others, who sang and celebrated, were those who were taking over their old places, their property. They were the coachmen, vintners, olive pickers, and scribes; they were the laborers and managers of Menezes, of Lendonca, of Braga, yes, even of Abrão Braga.

"The mood became more excited. The one group roared louder and louder and the other remained silent and grew more and more sullen. The three kitchen maids pressed close to me. They grasped my apron tightly. Now it would have been all right with them if I had reached into the fire and thrown a half-burning piece of wood into one group or the other.

"I was interested in only one thing: When was Abrão going to come? After all, they talked constantly about him, so they were his assistants, his cronies, those who were celebrating here. A kettle of soup, quick, yes, and there, a wooden tray with olives, and a plate of scallions. Of course, I'm already bringing the wine. Two more dishes of the spicy sauce. Water? No, I'm not handing out any water today, only the wine. Yes, it's the best that we have, the same wine that we send to the church. I ran back and forth that way, with the three frightened women holding tightly to me and moving with me.

"Finally he came.

"Again he had a leather apron tied around him, his hair sticky with sweat. Abrão did not look up. He didn't pay any attention to either group. He stood at the door, looked for a vacant seat, and sat down with the two strangers, with that master and his scribe.

"I had already forgotten those two figures. They were still organizing papers, stacking them differently, and putting them in a different order.

"'Sit down somewhere else. We need quiet here,' they said, turning Abrão away.

"For me there was no longer any holding back. For days I had put aside the silver pitcher. Now I filled it with wine. The only glass that I had found in the tavern was well hidden under the pack of straw in my bed.

"'To your health,' I uttered when I put the pitcher and glass down in front of Abrão. I had memorized a long sentence: 'The goddess Iemanje probably showed you the way so that you can tell me the rest of the story of your family.' That is what I intended to say, but I couldn't talk, not in those moments.

"Abrão looked up, 'Graça,' and as if we had only been separated for hours, he put his arm around my waist and pressed me to him. I just had to escape from his embrace! Wouldn't he feel my bandage? Had my breasts soaked my chemise again after all? Didn't I still smell of Arantes? Couldn't they tell by looking at me that the traces of Arantes's hand marked my entire body? That is how I wavered back and forth.

"'Find another seat. We want quiet!' Now the stranger was shouting.

"It sounded like Portuguese, but he also shouted words of a foreign language, and Abrão answered him. It was English.

"'Abrão Braga, and what is your name?'

"'Richard Leão,' the stranger blurted out and rushed toward Abrão. 'Braga, you are the son of Adalberto, the ship owner from Lisbon! The Braga family, the silkworm breeders!'

"He became completely beside himself. The papers slid to the floor. 'My grandfather learned Portuguese in your family, from the original copy of the sermons of António Vieira. How often he told about that. The book has been preserved in a box made of Brazil wood, for almost two hundred years. Words must be like stars, so clear and illuminating.' Now Richard Leão was speaking Portuguese.

"Abrão let himself be embraced, but hesitantly. He kept Leão at a distance.

"'What business brings you to Porto? A pitcher of wine for the friend of my family, for Richard Leão from London.' With that he pressed Leão down onto the bench, onto the seat where he had previously sat next to his scribe.

"Abrão and I sat across from him. Abrão did not let go of me again. He pushed his mug of wine over to me. We sat that way for a few minutes. Behind us we could feel a wall of people, a wall of men, for in that moment when Richard Leão had spoken Portuguese they had gotten up and moved closer.

"Now they quit talking and stared at Abrão and the Englishman.

"Abrão, you said earlier... Permit me, we have both studied António Vieira, and for him it is only a matter of brothers and the informal mode of addressing one another. I heard earlier that freedom prevails in Porto. Here anyone can sit where he wants to. Moreover, they are in the process of restoring the old order. That may be valid for Porto, but is Porto really so far away from Lisbon that here you don't know how the people there live, that they are starving and suffering?'

"'Oh, Lisbon,' some of the men shuffled back to their wine. 'In Lisbon they're lazy and don't work. In the evening they go to the theater and during the day they sleep. They're all officials there. They sit in their offices at the harbor and watch the captains and the sailors run around from one office to the next until they have finally delivered the tariff money everywhere.'

"'Exactly, and then they're permitted to sail out again on their ships or finally unload the cargo. And they had better do that with a bundle of banknotes in their hand again, because they must figure that somebody from the customs office will come by again and want money, or else he'll file a complaint about something or other. It doesn't matter what. Payment is made. Everyone is powerless against those customs officers. Oh, Lisbon.' That's what they murmured and actually didn't want to listen anymore at all.

"Richard Leão did not let himself be interrupted. 'The child queen is in difficulties, with beggars everywhere on the streets. There is too little seed stock in the storage bins. It is urgent that it be obtained. Otherwise there will be a famine next winter. The streets are so rundown that they are hardly passable any longer. How will the farmers go back out to their villages, to their fields? For five years the order was: everything for the Church! In any case, she needs money, the child queen. That's why her advisors wrote to us. Yes, Abrão, I've been sent out as a money messenger.' Leão smiled and drank wine.

"'But she doesn't get it, because here, all these papers are certificates of indebtedness. So many certificates of indebtedness are lying here, that with them we could buy for ourselves the entire backcountry, all of Lezirias. She has no choice, the little Queen Maria II. Either she has to start paying the money back, or she'll have to agree to the sale of Lezirias. In any case, she will not receive any new certificate of indebtedness, and for the country that probably means civil war, at least in Lisbon.'

"'Are you passing through?' Abrão didn't listen to Leão's words. 'Lisbon is far away.'

"'The people from Porto must help. Food has to be delivered to Lisbon, fish, potatoes, and grain.'

"'That would really suit them,' now the wall formed densely behind us again. 'We'll never do that. They won't pay us anything.'

"Leão began to push the papers away. 'How old is the child queen? Sixteen? Is she already married to that Leuchtenberg? Oh, well, half German, half French. Is that a good move? She is said to be well educated, the little Maria II. Will that help somewhat? Who knows what advisors, what prompters they have lined her up with.'

"'What is she supposed to do? She doesn't have it easy,' said Abrão, leaning forward. 'A few months ago her father died! And here in Porto we know nothing about the political plans. We don't even know the finance minister's name. Nor is it important for us.'

"'Portugal has claims against Brazil. Maria II can get the money from there, and with that she can pay off a few of our old certificates of indebtedness. Then we will gladly help her.' Leão did not let himself be deterred from his purpose.

"Brazil? 'Brazil has no debts,' I said. A few half-drunken men behind me laughed out loud.

"'Yes, they hatched that out well, back then in 1822. In order for the Brazilians to obtain their independence, they would have signed anything,' the men said in their discussion.

"'Right! So they signed certificates of indebtedness, but they have no intention whatever of paying.'

"'The jungle is far away. Besides, the brother of our queen is there. He's the Emperor of Brazil, isn't he?'

"'Pedrinho is still a child, not even ten years old.'

"'Our Queen Maria II is a Brazilian, and now she has to demand money from her brother,' the men sneered and toasted each other. 'That's how the Braganças live, in every generation intrigue and deception. First Miguel was supposed to marry the little Brazilian. Then Miguel discussed it with the Austrians and they advised him to have himself proclaimed king. After the Miguelists enslaved us for five years, the fine Dom Miguel received another bundle of money so that he would finally go away, finally leave our country. Now the little Brazilian girl is in debt. No, we won't deliver a single jug of olive oil to Lisbon.'

"Leão listened attentively to the men. At the same time he fixed his eyes on me. 'Brazilian woman, Indian blood,' he thought. I could read it in his face.

"'So,' Leão began, 'either I get Lezirias for these certificates of indebtedness, or I sail to Brazil and get our share there. We could become partners, Abrão! Let's settle in Brazil for a few years, and we'll come back as wealthy men. Everyone says that. The father of our child queen, Pedro, willed an entire region to his mistress's daughter, Goias! The little girl even received the title of "Duchess of Goias." She's also still a child, of course. Imagine, in the Goias region there are two topaz mines! Abrão, topazes that glisten in all shades of red and golden yellow. We have a business friend who showed us a handful of those precious stones. We can deliver those treasures to all the noble houses of Europe.' Leão closed his eyes. 'Gold topazes,' he whispered, and immediately he continued stridently. 'With these certificates of indebtedness I could also have the Goias region signed over to me, and even if not the entire region, at least the two topaz mines. We'll be able to find the little duchess. I don't think anyone knows where they are keeping her hidden.'

"'Isabel isn't hidden. What do you intend to take away from her? We Brazilians don't owe you anything. What are you saying?' Everything had become confused within me. What did this stranger want from Isabel, for whom I was responsible?

"'Isabel is in London,' I screamed, and I shook Abrão. 'You wrote to her. You must remember the letter. Tell him finally that Isabel is not being kept hidden anywhere. He can't take anything away from her'

"The men pressed toward our table.

"'He's a money collector!'

"'Let him go back down to the capital city. We don't have anything to do with all those machinations here!'

"Abrão slowly stood up and drew me up with him. 'And you, Richard Leão, say that you've studied the sermons of António Vieira: "...*they steal in all relationships...*"'

"'Abrão, I'm not stealing, here, we have a right to it,' the Englishman gesticulated with the papers. How fluently he was speaking Portuguese now. 'Abrão, come along. You already have a little Brazilian dove,' he said, and none of the men moved from the spot. They all simply gawked.

"Even Abrão wanted to leave instead of throwing that man out. My princess sister was threatened! 'Maria Glória is not a child queen! She's the Queen of Portugal. And Isabel is crying her eyes out because she misses Brazil, the flowers and the warmth, and here, this man from England, what ideas he has!'

"Perhaps I didn't just think all that, but screamed and sobbed it. I pounced on those papers, on those damned documents that made this man so powerful that his face did not cease to smirk.

"'Into the fire with them!' I clamped my fists tightly around the fragments of paper. I stepped toward the cowards who were still standing in my way. I stepped toward Abrão. Did he also intend to prevent me from throwing that packet of papers into the fire pit? I was already throwing a handful of them into the flames. The tongues of flame shot up red-orange. They twisted the second pack out of my hand. Several men were necessary to wrestle me, the madwoman, to the ground. When I was lying on the floor and still screaming 'Into the fire with those devil's papers!' from far away I heard a man's voice. 'Fire!' someone shouted. That voice shouted again and again, 'Fire! There's a fire at Braga's place!'

"'Braga, your farm is in flames, fire!'

"They were all concentrating so much on attacking me, staring at me, this woman who, as if in a cramp, did not release her fingers from the papers, that they didn't react. The feet around me remained motionless. Even Abrão, his boots, the ones where he had cut holes in the sides - he had worn those same boots in Brest - even Abrão's feet didn't move.

"I was the first one to react: 'Abrão, your house is burning!'

"On that Sunday Luis Arantes had set fire to the house, the barns, and the cocoon drying sheds of the Bragas.

"The flames shot into the sky. Showers of sparks came down. Abrão and I ran. The heat of the fire came toward us in waves. So many people surged toward the house, the Braga farm. They ran toward it from every street. Nobody screamed. Nobody shouted. In hell there are no human sounds, no weeping, no begging, no pleading, no caterwauling, no barking of dogs, only fire and running. At the entrance gate the people crowded together. We were driven to the well. What a relief in that heat, amid that crackling and the flying sparks, to hear the splashing of the water, the squeak of the crank with which they pulled up the buckets. A chain of people moving water to the house. Farther over stood a second line of people. Take the bucket, pass it on, take it, and pass it on. The men at the crank had to be relieved. An old man and I cranked the bucket upward, fast, faster, the bucket gets heavier the higher it climbs. The palms of your hands burn. Keep cranking. Keep cranking. It's only skin that breaks open. Skin grows back and blood scabs over. It is a superficial pain, crank, crank. This bucket is too full. Don't stop cranking, and the next bucket into the well, the next one, and another one. Now the pain in the palms is already less.

"Suddenly a woman's voice: 'The mulberry trees! He set them on fire, too!'

"Back then I didn't yet understand anything about breeding silkworms. I only saw that far away on the slope trees were turning into torches. The fire sprang from tree to tree.

"When the well had been scooped empty and we were only bringing up mud anymore, the people left, one after the other. There was nothing left to save. The Braga farm was burning down, and they didn't want to watch that burning, that extinguishing any longer.

"Where was Abrão? Where should I go now? Just like in Brest, I was completely alone, and I cried. And in my crying I found Abrão. I heard his sobbing, a sobbing in which laughter gurgled. He lay beneath the mulberry tree that stood in the yard next to the coach barn. His hair was singed, his face was black, and in some places his flesh lay open.

"'It's safe, I saved it,' he laughed and sobbed and pointed to a wooden box that lay next to him. I didn't understand. Back then I didn't understand even that.

"In that night Abrão had lost everything, but he had saved the book with the sermons of António Vieira, the book that had already accompanied his family for generations, the book with the priest's handwriting. And that book is unique in the entire country. Only that one copy with the red handwriting was the first, the original, and as long as that book was in the Braga family, it would not perish; the family would not cease to live, to continue living.

"Two dozen of the mulberry trees remained. The January of 1835 had been very dry. That is why most of them had burned like dry logs.

"Yes, in January of 1835 we began, Abrão and I began anew, with everything. We planted mulberry seedlings. We built a shed, then soon a hut, and later a house. We built barns and drying sheds. We did everything together, just the two of us. We didn't have a single coin to pay even one assistant. We carried the silkworm eggs to the mulberry trees, thousands of them. We collected the cocoons and removed the precious threads. We slept under trees, next to the barn. We slept where we sank to the ground with exhaustion. We ate mulberries and corn pancakes. We drank water and watered mulberry liquor. Maria Glória, for a year and a half, until far into the year of 1836, we didn't reckon according to daytime and nighttime. Braga, the Braga silkworm farm had to be built again. We didn't talk, breathe, or think anything else. In August of 1836 the first two boxes were full of spools of the finest organzine silk threads, and Abrão and I pulled the handcart together to the harbor. For our first cargo we had to sign a certificate of indebtedness for the cargo space. Our name was never on such a document again.

"In all those months I never asked myself who I was for Abrão - worker, friend, wife? Only when Abrão signed the certificate of indebtedness did I understand: I had become part of the Braga family, for he wrote, 'Abrão and Graça Braga.'"

Maria Glória in Lisbon, 1833 and 1834
"Who could cleverly escape from the danger that lay in the machinations?"

Maria Glória remains caught up in Graça's narrative for quite a while. She considers: Of what group had she become a part? They had separated her from her family, from her homeland, and she was supposed to fit into the new homeland as a part of it –

"Christina, you plead for my advice. You complain about how much you suffer because you have not long since become a part of the society of Rome. You say that they still call you the Nordic woman, although the overfilled four decades of your life have drawn a map on your face and on your habit that no longer allocate you to a certain region. My dearly beloved woman, I want to speak gently to you. Your pain is a deep-seated one and incurable. Rome and the society of Rome are not the problem from which you suffer. Christina, you feel rootless, and that causes you pain. Is there relief from that? Dearest friend, no! If only you had never left Sweden! You want to go back, back to where you grew up, where you went on sled excursions with your father on lightless winter days. That is why you write about Hamburg, about Bremen. Those areas near Sweden seem attractive to you, since you know that Stockholm remains closed to you. The Queen of Sweden left her country in the lurch, and therefore nobody there wants to see her anymore. Do not give yourself over to an illusion anymore. You have to live with the pain of rootlessness as with your natural eye color. Rootlessness is part of our task! And what medicine do I prescribe to you for relief? Work, Christina, work!

"Now I must reprimand you after all! For years you have been cultivating associations almost exclusively with scientists and theologians. For everything you want an explanation that is as sophisticated and unrealistic as possible. Christina, leave the auditoriums and go to those who are down below, who are poor, helpless, and miserable. Give support and consoling words there. With that your pain at being rootless will not decrease, but you will experience a new sense of belonging. They will admit you into the society of the

helpless and miserable, and once you are finally a part of them with your soul, you will bear the saudade *more easily. And do not forget, you can acquire the* doctor gentium *anywhere in the world. Start with that, dearest friend. Do not disappoint me..."*
António Vieira wrote that in January of 1670.

For years those letter texts that she had memorized in Paris as a thirteen-year-old girl had lain fallow within her, unused. A book laid out ready and not read. Only in recent years had those words taken on form and meaning for her, had she begun to understand them.

Maria Glória wandered back in her thoughts. From Brest they finally went to Lisbon, at the end of August of 1833. The first stop was Plymouth. There they celebrated "Maria II of Portugal" for two days. Gifts were on tables, gifts of silverware, porcelain, carpets, and paintings. "All this is supposed to make going home easier for our future queen and remind her that in England she has a loyal ally."

From Plymouth they traveled to Lisbon in seven sailing ships, one with the royal family and six with the emigrants who now, after four years of exile, were traveling home again at last.

The captain of the *Seho*, the Portuguese ship, sailed far out onto the Atlantic. Maria Glória could lose herself with her gaze in the many shades of blue of the ocean and the water. The wind blew the sailing vessel briskly toward its destination. From the British ships flag signals were sent: "Viva Maria II."

"The strip of land that you see now, your royal Majesty, that is already Portugal," the captain, Senhor Bertrand, smiled.

"Captain, you chose the best route. The ship is as clean as a whistle, and all the sailors are well instructed. They brought roses to me in my cabin and a small cup of coffee. How difficult it must have been to obtain coffee. I thank you." Maria Glória spoke, looking into the face of Senhor Bertrand, a face that was almost still young; at least the eyes glowed like those of Augusto.

Senhor Bertrand had tears in his eyes. "How beautiful your Portuguese sounds with your Brazilian accent," he said. "Princess

Maria, I am now bringing the new Portugal to Lisbon! You are the symbol for the new beginning! Maria, what a good name. We know that your name is Maria Glória, but only your family is permitted to call you that. This voyage is my first in three years! Miguel introduced new and higher taxes and assessments for everything. He constantly needed more officials and soldiers who spied on the people, and hundreds, thousands of policemen were necessary for that, and a lot of money, a very large amount of money. Because I couldn't pay the high taxes for my ship's license, they confiscated my schooner. Princess Maria, I didn't want to go away. I grew up in Lisbon. Lisbon had formerly been a free city. In the taverns there was singing in the evenings, and they played dominoes. If there was something to celebrate, and there was always something to celebrate, we waited into the early morning hours and helped the farmers erect their fruit and vegetable stands. That brought us a few mimosas or lilies that we gave our wives. Nobody could imagine that in less than two weeks the *Rua da Ouro* could degenerate into a lifeless street. Very early in the morning and in the evening the people moved through the streets toward the churches, dressed in gray and black clothing, with even their necks covered with a scarf. The prohibitions came so quickly that we could hardly follow them. I walked down to the harbor in broad daylight, wearing dark clothing. There I met my wife's sister. She was coming out of the church, and we stopped and talked. We laughed with each other. To converse shamelessly laughing with a strange female person was prohibited. Clemency was applied because the encounter had taken place in the middle of the day, but I was put in prison. And not until three months ago, when your father, Pedro, our liberator, had the prisons opened for those of us who had been persecuted by Miguel, did I learn that my entire family died. My parents and my wife wanted to flee to Terceira and the ship went down. My wife's sister hanged herself, and her family died, like many others, in the labor camp of the Evora monastery."

Senhor Bertrand stopped talking and looked into the ocean. "We'll begin anew, all of us."

She was ashamed of her idle talk from earlier. "Captain, I have a great deal of remedial learning to do. Everything that I know about Portugal comes from books."

It was easy for her to speak quite openly to Senhor Bertrand. "Your uniform fits you well," she smiled. The sailcloth was bleached; blue and white wooden buttons had been sewn onto the white captain's jacket.

"Cloth is still scarce in our country, but the dyers can't resist the orders. You will soon notice that, Princess. Twenty dyers have set up shop on the *Rua Madelena* and each of them wants to prove to his neighbor that he knows better how to transform gray cloth into a green or red piece."

He bowed. "They will cheer you, Princess Maria, but you won't have it easy. You are... I beg your pardon. It's not appropriate for me to talk this way, but people do not believe that a beautiful woman works and thinks. Heaven will help you."

The tower of Belem at the entrance to the harbor at Lisbon, the entire bay was lined with people. They surged back and forth with their shouts of "Viva!" Cloths and flags in the blue and white colors of Portugal were waved.

The September midday was hot, and Maria Glória was stuck in a dress that was almost too tight for her. She was supposed to enter Portugal with firm strides and walk to her father, the Duke of Bragança and Portugal's military chief. Everything swayed. She forced a smile to her face and felt Dona Leonora's hand hard against her back.

Maria Glória hesitated when she saw her father. She had not seen him for a year and a half. Father looked sick and emaciated. The dress uniform seemed to press him down. Beads of sweat gleamed on his face. In spite of that, they endured the reception ceremony well; a bent knee and a kiss on the hand from Father, her memorized sentences of greeting: "...thank Heaven that I am in Lisbon, in Portugal at last. I promise to give all of my strength, my entire life to the people of Portugal..." Then the welcoming greetings of the ministers, the bishop, the diplomats, and finally Eulalia.

The young woman with the smoothly combed black hair was the

only one still wearing the gray gown of the Miguel era. She did not bend her knee before Maria Glória.

"Princess, I speak for the Azores emigrants. We thank your father for his victorious struggle. You came late, your royal Majesty. Many of us died in the Azores. I can't spare you. I must talk about it, because we now place all our trust in you that we will never have to leave our homeland again. Welcome to Portugal!" She handed Maria Glória a little basket of olives. Over it lay a slender book, a hand-written notebook.

"A book?" Maria Glória marveled.

"Yes, it is by Herculano de Carvalho. He will become one of our country's greatest poets, quite certainly. For Herculano everything is language, everything is poesy. He was also in exile." Eulalia spoke that candidly in the presence of all the diplomats and dignitaries, and immediately there was intimacy between Eulalia and Maria Glória.

After that first day, which was loud and full of superficialities, when she wrote in her diary, she remembered the slender booklet by Herculano. In it she read:

"Is it not a city that would prefer to sleep in order to safely dream its way past the era of the tyrant? The light in it does not tolerate an evil eye; the people are skilled in disguising themselves. You have to see through their camouflage..."

Eulalia, that woman wanted to win Maria Glória for a friend.

"Eulalia comes from a very good family. Now she lives impoverished and has no relatives. The entire da Costa family perished. For generations they were respected judges and attorneys," explained Dona Leonora as she thought about it. "You need a second lady-in-waiting, Princess. You will have many duties, and I alone will not be able to cope with everything. Besides that, my area of responsibility is the catechism, discipline, and the observance of the diplomatic rules. Dona Eulalia will bring literature, art, and free thought into your house."

That, too, was a part of Dona Leonora. "Yes, dearest sister Januária, you remember her only as strict, and she is that, but I understand more and more that this strictness and discipline is a great help to us. Otherwise I would never have endured standing up straight for hours and listening earnestly today. After all, everything took place in my honor. That she wants to tolerate a second lady-in-waiting, and at that, one that I am free to choose, is evidence for Dona Leonora's magnanimity. She herself would reject the word magnanimity. 'It is my duty' would be her words. So I believe very firmly that *Mamãe* reveals to us her way of conducting life through the most diverse individuals: Dadama, Leonora, José Bonifácio... "

With her first day in Lisbon an additional new era had begun: "Your royal Majesty, Dona Maria, you have now arrived safely in Lisbon. You're at your destination. I was permitted to accompany the girl Maria Glória as a governess. Now I shall look after your royal Majesty, Dona Maria, as a lady-in-waiting," was what Leonora said when they rode home to *Necessidade* after the reception festivities. Leonora became more and more her confidante, almost a friend.

The walls of the castle were illuminated with torches. Footmen, servants, stewards, water bearers, laundresses, and scrubwomen stood ready to receive them. The stairways and the corridors leading to the reception hall on the second floor, to her personal chambers had carpets laid out on them.

"Why the many carpets?" Maria Glória wondered.

Leonora explained to her, "They wanted to decorate the castle sumptuously. Perhaps Maria II became too much accustomed to gold, crystal, and tapestries in Paris. They even brought everything displayable from the other residences. It is supposed to gleam, look luxurious and above all valuable. They ordered twenty mirrors and borrowed a chandelier from the Florentine ambassador!"

During the lighting of one of those candles the fire started. Maria Glória had not understood it, had not wanted to understand it yet at the time. But two weeks after her arrival they already struck for the first time.

"Outside the room of Queen Maria II a fire was set. Thank heavens it did not develop into a catastrophe." That is what Minister Palmela wrote in the official diplomatic report.

Maria Glória shook her head: "That is not formulated correctly. I am still the daughter of the Duke of Bragança." Was everything coming too soon for her? Was everything happening to her ahead of time?

Her initial months in Lisbon, with audiences where she was showered with praise and good wishes; visits that she undertook with Father, to the astronomy department of the university, to the arsenal, to the hospital, and nowhere was there any sense of discord or servility. "Viva our immortal rescuer," Father was greeted, and they called him "Father of the homeland" in their speeches. And all that admiration and gratitude was really meant that way; but so many things existed simultaneously, and Maria Glória still had to learn that painfully.

Immediately after the expulsion of Dom Miguel three parties had formed: the Miguelists - they saw themselves as having been deprived of all their rights, for most of them had to give the houses back to the emigrants who had returned home; and the Miguelists withdrew again into the wooden huts, into the stone houses in which they had previously lived and worked.

The second party was that of the *Carta Constitutional*, the party of Dom Pedro, and almost everyone professed a feeling of belonging to this moderate party, to this moderate constitution.

But there were also the ultraliberals for whom this constitution, the *Carta Constitutional*, was much too soft. "The kings must not be given the right to veto," it was said in the taverns.

"Why do we keep kings at all?" they asked in their discussions. "Only so that we have somebody to show off in case another king visits us."

"Exactly, but our kings have to do what we order!"

First came the fire outside her bedroom, and a few weeks later, during an evening meal, Dona Amelia said: "Have some, Dona Leonora," and pushed the plate with the sheep's milk cheese toward the lady-in-waiting. "It's delicious. It has the proper ripeness."

"If you'll permit me, no thanks. I tasted it and it made me quite ill. I believe it is too rich for me," Leonora answered.

At that moment Eulalia had jumped up: "The color! It's greenish! The cheese has been poisoned!" she screamed.

Everybody jumped up. Water glasses fell over. Father jerked the plate with the cheese out of the dining room supervisor's hand.

"Who else ate some of it?" they shouted in confusion, and Eulalia dragged Leonora to the door. "Quickly! Quickly!" she screamed, and: "Come, help, Maria Glória!"

Eulalia ran down the stairs and barked at two water bearers: "Come with us! We need freshly milked milk. Only freshly milked milk can help."

The water bearers with the torches ran ahead: "Here, this one here, she gives the most milk," they gesticulated and retreated when Eulalia ran to get ropes and ordered the stable boys to tie up the hind legs of the cow. The cow bellowed; it was not milking time. Without paying attention to that, Eulalia pushed Dona Leonora under the cow's udder. "Open your mouth!" she screamed, and the maid milked with firm strokes into Dona Leonora's mouth. The cow tried to kick. The barn was brightly illuminated and full of people who finally helped to hold the poor animal still.

Dona Leonora lay as if lifeless beneath the enormous cow's body. "She's choking," Maria Glória screamed. "She's not swallowing!" But the maid did not stop milking. In thick streams the milk flowed into Dona Leonora's open mouth.

Outside, in front of the barn, they were praying: "To prove that you will return through helping this poor woman, Sebastian, use your influence with the Almighty for this poor soul..."

In the rhythm of her heartbeat, Eulalie pushed her fists into Dona Leonora's belly, four, five, six times, until the woman convulsed and vomited.

Later they carried Leonora back into the house.

"Into my room, and water, a lot of water in my bath tub," Maria Glória ordered, and: "Go back to work!" she shouted into the crowd that was standing around.

Dona Leonora held her eyes tightly closed.

"Get out!" Maria Glória screamed, when they wanted to help

her undress the governess. She took piece after piece of clothing from the body of this woman whom she had never seen other than in a bodice, in the most proper clothing. She freed Dona Leonora's hair from the net. Pieces of straw and manure fell on the floor. Leonora did not fend off any manipulation of her body. Her skin was white and soft; her body looked younger than her face and lacked the strictness that Dona Leonora always had around her mouth and in her eyes.

"Cut off my hair," she whispered when she lay in the bath water and the apple of her eye, Maria Glória scrubbed her body with cloths soaked in lavender oil.

"No, Dona Leonora, we'll wash your hair until it smells like lavender again and glistens like silk."

Father fed the rest of the cheese to a pig. He did not have to wait long; only a few minutes later the animal began to twist and turn. When they heard the shot, they crossed themselves: "Saved."

From the next day on, at dinner three cooks stood at the table as tasters, and for a time there was a new eating ceremony. The tasters had to eat a few crumbs of every portion that a member of the dinner party placed on his or her plate. Then they waited a quarter of an hour. Meanwhile the soup and the lamb were cold and greasy.

"Papa, who was it that wanted to do such a thing?" After they had remained silent for two days, Maria Glória could not hold out any longer.

"There is no use talking about it," Dona Leonora had said, shaking her head. "We will never be able to determine for whom the poison was really intended and from whom it came."

Father was also at a loss.

"Sit down, Maria Glória. Look, Pedrinho wrote us a letter: '...that you are greatly missed everywhere, beloved Papa. Dom José Bonifácio does all he can to cheer up my sisters and me, but nobody knows how to ride and play hide-and-seek as well as you do...' Here he drew his flowerbeds, and if he didn't exaggerate, our Pedrinho is a good gardener. I count twenty canna blossoms here."

The two flowerbeds that Rafael had set up with Pedrinho, behind them the blue and white walls of the horse stables, between the wild orchids only a little of the red earth visible anymore, *terra roxa*. Maria Glória sniffed at the drawing paper. Yes, it smelled like *Boa Vista*, like orange blossom oil and dried jasmine blossoms that lay between sheets of paper and pieces of clothing everywhere.

"On the day after Christmas we'll ride out to Queluz. The air is better out there," Father murmured.

"Yes, in Queluz the winter jasmine is in flower. Although it has no fragrance, the yellow is almost as intensive as that of the mimosas in the *Rua Ouvidor*," she said to herself, looking toward her father, who walked slowly to the window and opened it.

So, standing at the window, he finally began to speak with the voice that had lacked any radiance since he had returned from the Azores. He thought about every word, every expression. Occasionally he fought for breath. "This morning in the state council they presented the request to have your marriage organized as soon as possible." He gestured with his hand for her to remain silent. "They are not willing to accept Augusto von Leuchtenberg, at least not immediately. On the one hand he is too German for them, and on the other he is too closely related to Napoleon. He is also my wife's brother, and he is a Freemason as I am. Some ministers want an Englishman, while others would prefer a son of the house of Naples-Sicily. The Austrian ambassador even brought a suggestion from Metternich! No matter, I immediately forgot the name of that Austrian prince. Metternich and his tricks? Never!"

For several sentences, Maria Glória was unable to continue listening. She and Augusto had promised one another to wait for each other. "That was all already arranged a long time ago. I'll marry Augusto and nobody else!" she shouted. "Father, your brother and his people are the ones who are behind all these intrigues, the fire, the poison. Why don't you finally send Dom Miguel away, out of the country? His followers will not stop threatening us, seeking to take our lives, as long as they see a chance of installing Dom Miguel as king again. I believe it's this disorder that is heading us for disaster. Father, I don't know my way around, and nobody knows how things will go here in Lisbon, in Portugal. You're the military chief, and the head of the state administration is Senhor Palmela. And what is my task? The hospitals and the schools? Then I intend to start the visits and the checks with Dona Leonora. Why does the bishop avoid our castle? On the sixth of December a priest read the birthday Mass for Pedrinho - an affront!"

Father nodded; even that he did slowly. "The emigrants want compensation for damages, Maria Glória, but the state treasury is empty. The bishop doesn't want to do without the tithe that the people payed during the Miguelist regime. But Palmela immediately did away with the tithe. That's why we have the bishops against us. Everything is lacking. Maria Glória. Our harbors are avoided because there are too few boats available to bring a load of goods to land quickly. The roads to the harbor are washed out and have not been repaired for years. The mills in which our olive oil was pressed are dilapidated. In the north, in Minho, too little grain will be available for the winter. The farmers there have stopped cultivating the fields."

"When will we begin? When will you begin organizing things?" Maria Glória interrupted her father. "Everything depends on when Miguel is expelled from the country! He lives well in Evora. Every evening he has sacred choral music performed, and he gives paintings to his faithful followers. Eulalia told me about that," she remembered. "She also told me that you, Father, shouted, ordered, when you marched into Lisbon with your troops: 'Don't shoot in that direction. My brother is there!' Why did you do that? He was able to pack calmly and withdraw into the Evora monastery."

She was quite startled at her own outburst. Now one of her father's screaming fits would order her back to obedience. If only her father's rage did not cause him to have an epileptic seizure.

Nothing of the kind occurred.

"He's my brother. Was I supposed to take him prisoner or have him shot?" Father sat down, and without another word he began to write a letter to Alvaro Freire, the man who conducted the negotiations with his brother.

Maria Glória, September 1834
"The years flee away, the summertime will soon be gone"

Father had remained walled off during all of the months of the year 1834, until September. Maria Glória found no common ground for communication with this new father; he remained a stranger to her. She could not get used to his pensiveness, his deliberateness. For as long as they had lived in *Boa Vista*, they had had the same temperament, in anger as in joy, always shooting out beyond moderation, and impatient in everything. Now, in Lisbon, Maria Glória uneasily stayed away from any audience together, any visit, any walk, and dinner with questions, and she got into the habit of talking with her father in letter texts, in letters that she never placed on the silver tray for dispatches for him to read. The letters, the unwritten ones, joined together, and on the 24th of September in 1834 those letters yielded a whole, and with them all the questions were answered.

"Beloved Father, Dona Leonora has already repeated today's date to me several times. Today is the 24th of September 1834. Governesses have to ensure strictly that we do not forget any important day. The day is only a few hours old, and perhaps today you will brush off your lassitude and get up late in the afternoon, when the sun floods your room and turns it green, and want to come back to Lisbon, to *Necessidade*, for a visit to the theater. A week ago you wanted to be taken to Queluz, and that very room where you came into the world thirty-six years ago in October had to be transformed into your sickroom, into your death room. Was it also a late summer day? The light that the sun brings up from the ocean was still red, and in less than an hour it would lighten up into white, and the houses on *Rossio Square* would stand in tropical light. You should not talk about the tropics. They often remonstrated with you about it during the last year: How are you supposed to understand the soul of Portugal, when you grew up in Brazil. 'Father of our homeland,' they cheered at you a year ago, when you had driven Dom Miguel from Lisbon; and a few weeks later they called you '*Vulgário*.' As if that expression, that word had followed you here from Rio de

Janeiro, it clung to you, and during the past twelve months it has constantly pressed its way to the surface. Father, they trusted your military moves. They cheered you for those, but when you talked about national law they did not believe you. How can someone who is a *vulgário* be a statesman, someone who, over there, in the jungle country, ruined his family and his court through his dealings with his mistress? A *vulgário* who lived his life in fits of rage, one who sent Maria Graham, the English governess Maria Graham, away from Rio because she refused to make the deep and formal curtsy; one who drove his best advisor, José Bonifácio, into banishment in Europe, because Bonifácio had rejected the advisors who had been infiltrated by the mistress; a *vulgário* who did not have a single line of farewell for Dona Leopoldina when she already lay dying; a *vulgário* who had to leave Brazil during the night in the fog because none of his ministers and advisors trusted him anymore? Isn't Portugal an exile country for the Duke of Bragança? Isn't he a refugee who fled back to the land of his birth? Yes, Father, nobody could prevent me from hearing all these murmurings. I began to put the pieces together for myself. Concerning your years in Rio de Janeiro - and they form the greatest portion of your chronology - there are deeds to be reported that are unexplainable, for which you will find no defender. Why did *Mamãe* have no money for the household, no money for better dresses, although the Santos woman showed up in *Boa Vista* in silk robes? All of these old and faded things from the past are brought up against you here by the ones who are disappointed, and there are many of them; there are almost only disappointed people. The Azores emigrants are disappointed that although they used the last of their money to equip an army to topple Dom Miguel, they were not immediately restored to their old positions in the bureaus, customs offices, and freight offices. The ones who languished for years under Miguel are disappointed that you do not punish the Miguel loyalists severely, that you do not have them thrown into prison. 'There are no victors and no defeated people; there is only one Portugal and its people who want to live in peace with each other. What I can do to achieve that, I shall do,' you said at the reception on Epiphany. The people broke out laughing. From the gallery they let a rain of play money fall, newspaper cut into small pieces. 'Gather them, Dom Pedro. Gather up the bills. Perhaps it will be enough for your brother's coach.' You accepted all those gibes. The negotiations with your brother dragged on; it was not until May, four months ago, that Miguel signed. I sat next to you in the first row. Mundane things were discussed. A new form for olive sales was decided upon. In Porto the harbor road would be widened. The monastery of Covilha in the Estrela Mountains was granted a license for an orphanage. Then Saldanha, Gregorius Saldanha stood up and read the agreement that had been reached with Dom Miguel: "...that within eight weeks he will leave his current residence in Evora and the country of Portugal with the intention and the promise never to set foot or even to travel in it again, and in all foreign countries to refrain from all political activities concerning the country of Portugal. For his subsistence is granted to him in accordance with his rank...' The sum had hardly been stated when a tumult broke out. The men dove forward over the seats; papers flew over our heads. Some of the representatives vaulted onto the tables and stomped on them to make themselves heard. 'That's how the Braganças are. First we have to let ourselves be enslaved for years by that Miguel. Then a fat bundle of money is packed up for him so that he can live it up! We don't have enough money to buy seed. It's May and the fields haven't been plowed yet. Next winter we'll suffer from hunger, but Miguel will stroll in Venice!' For several minutes those shouts hailed down on us. Slowly, very slowly you stood up from your chair. In May you were already trembling with weakness, also with loathing. 'He is my brother!' you shouted, you screamed. 'He is losing his homeland. With that everything is paid for at a price that is high enough.' For the time that it took to speak a few words you were once again for me that father whom I knew so well, that man who ranted and raved when people did not want to follow his will. For the ministers and representatives it was the first time that they experienced you so agitated. Whether or not the tumult then quickly ended I do not remember. We had to support you and accompany you out of the hall. How many times you were hurt in that way during the few months that you lived in Portugal. On the way to the theater they catapulted dirt at you; you entered your box in a uniform splattered with mud. You accepted everything without saying anything. 'The people must be conscious of stability and continuity. Then they will trust,' you often murmured, and when they suggested Saldanha to you as prime minister in June, you agreed. Saldanha! That ambitious man was supposed to control you, keep an eye on you, Father. 'Saldanha is the guarantee that it will not come to the point of a revolution,' you explained, and you accepted that as well. Two months ago, in July, my fiancé was approved: Augusto von Leuchtenburg! You were so relieved about that decision that you had a fever for two days. 'It is only joy. Now Maria Glória will get her tall, blond prince. Now there was only one thing left for you to accomplish, the acknowledgment of my premature majority. '...taking into consideration the fact that the development of Maria Glória from the physical and moral point of view appears to be sufficient that she can be named Queen Maria II of Portugal, with all rights and responsibilities that the *Carta*, the constitution gives.' Two weeks ago, in the first week of September of this year 1834, with that letter you asked the ministers and advisors to acknowledge that recommendation, '...since my weakness is such that I can no longer completely fulfill my responsibilities.'

"All the months that you lived in Portugal, from your arrival with the emigrant troops from the Azores in March of 1833 until now, in September of 1834, you let Providence work on you. You avoided no humiliation, no pain, and only now is your image, the man Pedro, a whole. Now everything is in order; everything has been finished. You are lying in the next room, and in the next few hours you will let your spirit, your soul glide across to the other side. In the last few months your hair has become thin, but your face, your hands will soon look as if they have been revived. You are finally the one that Providence intended for you to be. How many lives raged simultaneously within you during three and a half decades? How many versions of human being you were: the soldier, the lover, the beloved, the husband, the friend, the opponent and enemy, the comrade, the musician, and the composer. Who could have followed you? They changed too quickly, the people inside you. Only a few know that during all the years, even in those years when you lived away from Brazil, the father in you always remained the same. We drove through the *Rua da Prata*, and suddenly you ordered: 'Stop!' And you jumped out of the coach and ran to a mother with two children. You crouched down to the boy, to the girl, and pushed the two of them in dance steps around in a circle. 'How old are you?' you asked. 'Eight years old, just the same age as my Pedrinho, and you're ten years old, so a year younger than my Chicinha Francisca.' When you had to tell me that my sister Paula Mariana had died in Rio, you sought for a place, a spot where you wanted to tell me that. You rode with me to Sintra. For an hour and a half you drove the coach southward. We went up gentle hills and were soon surrounded by a forest, a tropical forest, quite near Lisbon. We walked past giant ferns toward the walls of the Sintra monastery. Aerial roots and parasitic flowers shimmered in the evening sun; small waterfalls murmured. 'Here there are as many greens as in Tijuca,' I shouted, and there you told me: '"Our little Paula Mariana died in Rio de Janeiro in January of 1833. She expired as quietly as she lived," Januária writes'

"When today, the 24th of September 1834, has run its course and you have breathed your last, I shall ride out to Sintra and remain at the place where we sat last October until I feel that you have gone in the same direction that my little sister Paula Mariana and before her *Mamãe*, Dona Leopoldina, went."

Maria Glória stood at her father's bedside for a long time. He appeared to sleep; above all he seemed to sense that she was there. With the greatest effort, after a few minutes he motioned with his hand for the last time: "There, on the little table, something is lying there for you."

A diary. "What I want is to do everything as well as I am able," Father had written for Maria Glória in trembling script on the first page. When she kissed her father's hand, kissed his hand one last time, he whispered: "Sintra, Maria Glória." Then he died.

While standing at her father's deathbed, she immediately closed her eyes. She did not want to picture the body of Pedro Bragança as a cooling corpse. She had not let *Mamãe* be taken from her as a conversation partner; she would also continue to converse with Father. It was not easy to talk with *Mamãe*. *Mamãe* spoke so often of duty. One could emulate her attributes, but Maria Glória could never attain that goodness, that will to achieve reconciliation and peace. With Father it was easier. He was constantly in conflict, in a struggle with himself against a part of himself, and that made the conversation easier. It was trouble and work to bridle his temperament, not to give his trust to everyone, and he was destined to begin anew tomorrow, and again and again. From her father she adopted his terse, unadorned mode of speech and the lower case '*eu*,' 'I,' that he used in all letters and documents - entirely against the customs and the inculcated rules.

Graça has trouble following Maria Glória. She tries to put the narrated images in sequence. "In Porto we didn't learn of Dom Pedro's death until February of 1835, five months later. Actually, it didn't really interest anyone. Most people were slaving away like Abrão and I, day and night, in order to restore their ships, their oil mills, and their weaving mills. Everything was ruined. Even the road to the harbor had to be repaired first. The rain of four years had washed it out, and they had to take their first baskets of olives, the first barrels of olive oil, and the baskets of cloth in the new, glowing colors to the harbor on donkeys. The Azores emigrants had to complete all of those tasks themselves, without help, because the Miguelists refused to work for the Azoreans. Abrão tried to explain it to me when we leaned exhausted against the cistern. Usually he was too tired to talk, and for me all that was hardly understandable.

"A month after Abrão and I had begun to lay out the silkworm eggs and to set the mulberry tree seedlings, the priest visited us. He said he was going from house to house and wanted to reconcile the Azoreans and the former Miguelists again. Everyone was supposed to come to the church. Abrão went after the man with the mattock: The church had sided with the Miguelists for years. Every priest had collected the tithe and pounded the fear of hell into the people. The idea of working, really working had been virtually driven out of them. The Azores emigrants had left enough behind. With that they could live comfortably and even cheat each other in trade besides. To the church only the tithe was important, and obedience; and obedience meant standing in the church for a few hours every day and not walking on the street anymore after it began to get dark. And now, after the Azoreans had returned to their businesses, the priest would only come because he could no longer feed the Miguelists through the winter. The church did not have enough monastery soup! Abrão also spoke a sentence that had been written by Vieira: '*For a church can never be as important as a school, and a church can never be as necessary as a hospital.*' The fact that Abrão could quote so fluently from that Father António Vieira frightened and angered the priest more than did the axe that was raised against him. For suddenly the man of God was no longer sordidly friendly. He pointed to me:

"'And she, did you have a slave sent to you from the jungle?'

"Abrão almost jumped at his throat. The two men shouted at each other.

"'As a priest, you have a task here. Come back tomorrow with the marriage certificate. Graça is my wife.'

"'Oh, are the respectable citizens of Porto now mixing with Indians, with illiterates?'

"'One more word and I'll throw you out. Graça is related to Maria Glória, to Princess Maria Bragança.'

"'That is easily possible. Pedro, that *vulgário*, died of syphilis a few months ago. It is certainly probable that he also fathered children with Indian women.'

"'Graça is not a blood relative. She is the milk sister of Maria Glória.'

"'How well you have worked that out. The old Adalberto would not have arranged it better. Now you are as good as related to our Queen Maria II.'

"'Go, and bring the marriage certificate tomorrow. We have no time to come to the church!'

"'Abrão, you are confused because of weariness and despair.'
"'Bring the marriage certificate!'
"'How do you intend to prove that this Indian woman...?'
"'Here, her name is Graça. She was born on the 4th of April 1819, on the same day as Maria Glória.'
"With those words Abrão undid his belt. He had a packet of papers and documents tied around his waist, and he peeled off a sheet of paper. It was the stationary with the queen's coat-of-arms, the coat-of-arms in gold and blue with the intertwined letters M and B (Maria Bragança).
"'Maria Glória gave me that stationary,' I shouted at the priest, 'in Paris, when we were packing the clothes and the books!'
"The priest didn't say another word when he saw the coat-of-arms. The next day he actually did bring a document, and with that I was the wife of Abrão Braga."

Graça pauses, but she does not want Maria Glória to take up her narrative again yet. Graça struggles to find the words: "Maria Glória, I wanted to write it to you in a letter. I wanted to have it written to you when I heard about your father's death. Now that your father is dead, you will hear many things about him, things that they kept secret from you. Or have you known for a long time about the disease of his untamed lust? Good or bad, the fewest people can be divided up that way. Abrão explained to me that we should rather ask if he was necessary or not. And he was necessary, and specifically in the manner in which he lived. Otherwise Isabel would not exist, and without Isabel I would not have sailed to Europe with you. And in the same way Dom Pedro was probably necessary in political things, and we want to leave it at that for all time, Maria Glória. Dom Pedro, your father, was necessary."

Now Graça smiles. She has finally rid herself of those thoughts that she had preserved within her for so many years.

One more question presses forth before Maria Glória continues her story:

"Why, Maria Glória, have you never traveled to Porto? Why have you never gone further than Lisbon, than Sintra?"

Maria Glória nods. She has also often read about that in Vieira's writings: *"My very dear Christina, I have already hinted to you several times that you should not think that Rome is the world. Whoever is entrusted with a public duty must not hide; he must go forth! He must not just look toward heaven and hide in religion and philosophy and family. He must go to the people, travel through the country. There is something else that I do not want to hold back, my beloved Christina. I must correct your hard words about the kings. The situation actually is bad with some kings, but it is not the kings who seek robbers for themselves. It was that way hundreds of years ago. Nowadays the robbers seek their kings; at least the robbers seek to pull their kings down by making the kings submissive to them. If the kings do not do as they are told, they are pushed off the throne. If the kings obey, that is not better, for then, by nodding their heads, they confirm the evil works of the robbers. But that is still not the worst thing. Some kings do not fulfill all their duties. And I repeat: Whoever is entrusted with a public duty must not hide; he most go forth!"*

"Next year, after the next child, when the housing tract is finished in Sintra, then I will travel through Portugal, first to Coimbra, then Porto." Maria Glória had often said that. But she was always warned: "Don't leave Lisbon. You're the symbol for the independence of this country. Don't forget that they are already talking openly about a unification of the Iberian Peninsula. And here the people are so worn down from the civil wars that they won't even fight against it anymore. Dona Maria, you must not leave Lisbon during these months, in two or three years perhaps, or in five..."

Father was dead. Maria Glória heard voices praying. There were clouds of incense in the room and a priest's hand held a cross above her father's face. White linen was carried into the room in baskets and Leonora pulled the curtains closed. In the next room, where she had sat the entire previous night in conversation with Father, with that part of Father that nobody, not even death, could take from her, in the next room they had cleaned things up and rearranged the furniture to create an office. On the desk stood the two candles and the crucifix, and under them lay the stationery with the mourning border. In broad sweeping letters her name was printed on it: Maria II, Queen of Portugal.

Minister Palmela pushed her to the table and said: "I have the duty to read the will of your highly esteemed father, the Duke of Bragança, immediately: 'That all rights and privileges that I held go to my daughter Maria da Glória, for Portugal "Maria." I expect my son-in-law Augusto von Leuchtenberg to assume command of the Portuguese army, and with it the qualities of a military leader...'"

Maria Glória listened, recited phrases, and raised her hand for the oath. She had memorized everything thoroughly; she made no mistakes and committed no acts of carelessness, but her thoughts were in Sintra. She wanted to escape from the daily routine, from the ceremonies for a day or even a few hours, but in October of 1834 that was not possible.

"Then the walls of the monastery, the little chapels, and the prayer booths will be overgrown with plants for one more year, and soon we won't see them anymore," Maria Glória complained. "Why didn't anyone concern themselves with Sintra after the earthquake?"

Maria Glória had known the answer for a long time. There had not been any money available. Even the Order of St. Hyronimus, to which the monastery belonged, had not had any means. After the earthquake the monks had fled north, to Covilha and Guarda. It was said that even in Sintra, since 1578 the young King Sebastian had wandered through the gardens and the rooms and the courtyards, constantly seeking a new place to hide in order not to be captured by the myrmidons of the Sultan Abd El-Malik. "Sebastian isn't dead, he's just keeping himself hidden. He will enlarge our empire far into Africa and expel the Muslims from our culture forever."

In October and November hardly any time remained for mourning. "Six weeks of mourning clothes is sufficient," Leonora decided, and at the end of November she laid out the blue and white dresses and jackets for Maria Glória again. She was engaged. She had to be prepared for the wedding, and she had to keep to her daily schedule. The positions of the officials had to be filled again. Her question: "Wasn't he a Miguelist?" always received a negative answer, and nobody could explain to her where the Miguelist followers had gone.

Minister President Palmela explained impatiently, "Dona Maria, we are living in a transitional period. No better, no more loyal officials can be found."

So were the principles that had been drilled into her not valid after all? "When a system of government is changed, and not all positions are filled by men of the new direction, the old dictatorial spirit will destroy any renovation through revolts and revolutions..."

She trusted Palmela. Surely he also wanted peace and quiet at last. Besides, the next reception for the mayors from Minho was pressing. The roads in the north were partially impassable. New cisterns had to be dug and constructed. There was a shortage of everything, even tools. Almost daily the treasurer came to inform her that there was no money. The pay for the bodyguard had not been paid. The mayors of the rural communities went away disappointed. They had expected more for themselves than delaying tactics.

"Never make a promise that you cannot keep." She had brought that instruction from José Bonifácio with her from Rio de Janeiro. Perhaps it would have been better if she had not adhered to it so strictly. If the mayors had returned to their people with promises, it would have calmed the people for a while.

Within a few weeks food was already in short supply in Lisbon. "The farmers from the North are not selling anything into the capital city anymore. They receive no money for roads and water, so they give no flour, no potatoes, and no slaughter animals."

Whenever Maria Glória drove down to Baixa early in the morning with Leonora and Eulalie - "I want to go as far as the Tejo. I'm still far too unfamiliar with the city" - the people followed her with suspicious eyes. The shoemakers, the dyers, and the weavers who set up their equipment, their kettles and stoves, halfway on the street, the farmers who straightened up their boxes with the chickens and lambs - they all acted busy and looked away. "We've never had it so bad. Under Dom Miguel we had to knuckle down, but what kind of freedom is it that those Braganças have brought us from Brazil. The streets are full of beggars." That was what people were saying.

In those last weeks of the year 1834, the Menino Deus Church became an important place for Maria Glória. As in the Glória Church in Rio, in that little nave she felt safe and secure, screened away from all hostilities for the time that it took to say a few prayers. And she corresponded with Clementine; she wrote to Paris - that world was also still there: "Dearest friend, receive my embrace for the two dolls that you sent me. I could like the new fashion with the wide, embroidered sashes. I also find the hat with the wax cherries fabulously beautiful, but here in Lisbon I would have no opportunity to show off these works of art. Clementine, I live in a completely different world. It is not possible to dispel the strict, dull, and gray life that Miguel declared to be a routine duty. The former luster is still visible in the buildings. Walls do not wear down as quickly as people. I do not want to complain about anything. After all, I am watched over by my two good fairies Leonora and Eulalia. Soon we will also be writing the year 1835, and in the very first weeks Augusto will arrive here. You can surely imagine how much I long for him to be here. Clementine, write back to me soon. Paris glitters in my memory..."

A mild January of 1835, a first winter in Lisbon, without snow and fur caps. "The arrival of Prince Leuchtenberg has been delayed. Perhaps he has had second thoughts about it," it was whispered.

Count Lavradio reassured Maria Glória: "Prince Augusto still had to travel to Munich, family matters."

"Why doesn't he write? Augusto has always written to me," she asked in despair.

Lavradio had no answer for that. He would never have said what he thought: "Perhaps someone is keeping the letters back somewhere."

And that was the way it had been.

Much later they surreptitiously passed on a packet of letters from Augusto to Maria Glória. "...that you do not forget what you promised me, at least six children, and if we work at it, next year, in 1836, we will already be carrying the first one to its baptism. Your blond Augusto sends you affectionate kisses..."

In another letter he wrote: "Be patient with my sister. Amelia was always the most ambitious one of us siblings. That is why she took everything upon herself to become Empress of Brazil. And now, at the age of twenty-two, she has nothing left but widowhood and a sweet little child..." A book was enclosed: "I am sending you a few poems by Baudelaire. Let's read them every evening before going to sleep. The French will help us into our dreams. My Portuguese still sounds awkward, although I study most diligently. How good it is that in the language of our bodies we will easily find the right vowels and consonants..."

When Augusto had finally arrived in Lisbon, they hardly had any time left to follow up on the lover's oaths that they had exchanged in Brest. The official program had to be completed, and at that time, in March of 1835, Maria Glória was still planning on a long life for herself. She wanted to become sixty, perhaps even seventy years old, and she would never let go of Augusto, her beloved Augusto. She would reach out her hand and touch his body and submit herself completely to him.

First there was the Mass celebrating their official engagement, and the announcement: "The marriage ceremony will take place in the Menino Deus Church. Since they are still in the months of mourning for Duke Pedro of Bragança, they will dispense with a banquet and an official reception. The bride and groom will go to *Rossio Square* and celebrate with all who are present, without regard for rank or origin, the happy union of the house of Bragança with the house of Leuchtenberg..."

A first excursion to Sintra, with a wreath made from the early-blooming paradise flowers plaited around her curls, embraces, kisses, and dance steps, "Their spying eyes do not reach this far into this wilderness."

A night when they stayed awake and made love to each other all night in the prayer pavilion, "What a bridal bed you have selected for yourself, the March sky and the ruined walls. You must listen closely. The stones speak with the wind. Our first child will be a daughter!"

For several days Maria Glória also sensed the blessing of feeling a husband next to her. She was not mistaken; since Augusto had been sitting next to her, the delegates spoke to her in a different tone, and memorized answers were no longer expected of her, but they waited for her answers, her decisions.

"Dona Maria, the people can no longer feel safe. For that reason, when it gets dark they flee into their homes as they did in Miguel's time. The assaults are increasing." Peixoto looked at her questioningly.

"I've been told that the assaults are only a bad spectacle that our opponents carry out to make the police look ridiculous," Maria Glória stated. Then she continued: "It is also said that weaklings are sitting in our highest offices, and that the people can't feel safe for that reason."

Peixoto was startled. How was he supposed to answer that?!

Maria Glória let a few seconds pass before saying: "As the supreme commander of our army, my husband, Dom Augusto, will place several divisions of soldiers alongside the police as support troops. In the next few days Lisbon will again be a quiet, safe city."

Two and a half weeks later she visited the barracks on the *Campo Grande* with Augusto. A meal was shared with the soldiers, lamb and olive oil on freshly toasted bread.

"Viva, Dona Maria! Viva, Dom Augusto!"

During the toast: "...I would like to express my thanks, as well as the thanks of Dona Maria, my beloved wife, to all our comrades..." the sudden pause in his speech, the hand at his throat; Augusto struggled for breath. People pressed toward the collapsing body. They called for water, for a doctor.

"Away," screamed Maria Glória and thrust away from her everyone who wanted to hold her back. The collar, the tie, the shirt, and the jacket were ripped open, cut open. She tugged at the body and dragged it in the direction of her coach. It was not until many moments later that the men roused themselves from their immobility and helped to bed down the twitching body of Dom Augusto in the carriage. None of them had the courage to stop her. They still managed to shove an adjutant onto the seat to ensure that Augusto would hold on.

She knotted up her skirts and heaved herself up onto the coach box and began to whip the horses, so that the animals rushed with the carriage toward *Necessidade* as if they were rabid. There it was a long time, a very long time, until they brought a stretcher to carry Augusto into the house. Meanwhile she had him bedded down in the short spring grass. He was breathing; the pains and cramps seemed to have passed. When she cautiously placed her face against his neck, he opened his eyes. "Too bad," he whispered.

He had another day and a half to suffer, to struggle, and on the 28th of March 1835 Karl August Eugen Napoleon, Duke of Leuchtenberg, Prince Augusto of Portugal, died at the age of twenty-five years.

Until after the last minutes of his life, Maria Glória held the body of her beloved Augusto in her embrace. "Augusto, if you are leaving, then take me with you. Don't leave me behind. Without you I live in hell here. Augusto, don't turn away from me. Why are you letting go of my hand?" That is how she stammered and pleaded, and they had to use force to separate her from that body. She watched as they drew the white linen over Augusto. She watched and spread a part of herself, the part that was familiar only to Augusto, across the lifeless body. "Take me with you!"

They said it was diphtheria. Some asked if poison had played a role.

When Maria Glória had cut off her hair and shorn her head, they quit talking about a cause of death; they quit speculating. The dead man would have been quickly forgotten, embalmed, squeezed into his uniform, given the last rites, and wept over, a horrible fate, but everyone could have lived with that. The queen's deed, however, was it not an act of insanity to cut off her curls, to have her head shaven? They had to look at that deed every day. They shuddered at this strange Dona Maria.

Had she turned to stone, and could she therefore not tolerate anything soft, anything smooth on herself? Had she turned to stone, and was it for that reason that no tears flowed from her eyes? "I am sixteen years old and a widow. They will sew a few pleats in my widow's bonnet for me, so that nobody will see that I have cut off my hair. From now on I intend to live only truthfully in all areas. The new hair will be without waves, without curls. My fingernails will remain unpolished. Nothing on me will be beautified anymore; my eyebrows will not be drawn in a better direction with dark paste; my waist, which is too fat, will not be hidden by seams," she had written in her diary.

New dresses had to be procured, without ruffles, without ribbons, smooth and with stiff collars, the color, black for six weeks and then blue with a white belt. The portrait painters were shocked. They were supposed to paint that darkened, serious face, and in ten or twenty copies the countenance of this woman would hang in Lisbon, in Porto, and in Coimbra? All of them who had oiled their way in around Maria Glória for a year and a half, since her arrival in September of 1833, the servants and chamberlains, the secretaries and coachmen, the officials, the senators, the members of the diplomatic service and the clergy, the food bearers and the stable boys, the gardeners, the tailors, and the letter carriers - all of them now had to take the daily instructions and orders of this strange woman. That did not please them, and they began to mistrust and lie in wait for each other. If a vase fell on the floor, if a document was misplaced, if a window wing was left ajar and not closed, if the food was too sweet or spiced with too much coriander, they blamed each other and they scolded and shouted curses at each other.

"Dear Sister Januária, you would not recognize me anymore, for I sent a part of me with my beloved Augusto over into his world. That giving away of the 'beautiful things' was easy for me. During the long hours when he was dying and in the initial hours afterward I sought for people to whom I could flee in my pain, people, friends, and confidants who would weep with me. I prayed for five, just as many as the fingers on one hand. I did not find four. Except for my good fairies Leonora and Eulalia and my true friend Bertrand, I did not find a single one, Januária. They hold everything against me, that I am a Brazilian, that I lived in Paris, that *Mamãe* was an Austrian, that I married a German Frenchman, a French German; that I treat my stepmother badly because she moved out of *Necessidade*; that I show partiality to my stepmother because I pay the bills for her tapestries; that I use fiery eyes to make Minister Palmela tractable for our house of Bragança; that I incite General Saldanha against the monarchy with a provocative hairdo. Yesterday, two weeks after the death of my husband, in the state council they gave me the evidence of all the disrespect that they have left for the person Maria Glória, for the human being in Dona Maria II. The chairman read a manifesto in which I was requested to marry again in the immediate future and to bear children as quickly as possible, so that the monarchy will remain the symbol for continuity. They have no word of comfort for me. If I could entrust myself to the powers of our Brazilian earth, I could let myself die. Beloved sister, I am sending you a portrait that was painted two days ago, so that you can see what I have let myself become..."

Maria Glória also sought comfort in the writings of Vieira:

"*My highly esteemed Christina, a very close friend of yours has died, and you are suffering. I feel for you. I do know that among all the pains that we must bear, the parting from a body is the most tortuous. You do not expect polite consolation or a quickly uttered word from me, for you know as I do: in order to attain love we have to go through hell. It is not for us to ask how many chambers are appointed for us to go through. Christina, let the spirit of your noble friend be resurrected within you. Love, smile, and remain silent. With a comforting embrace I am in loyalty your friend, António Vieira. Let yourself be assured of that once more in November of the year 1669.*"

After the death of Augusto she had been thrown into another, a new era. Everything pressed to be dealt with. Every evening she

examined things in her diary: Had hours been spent unused?
"Senhor Minister," she said as she received Palmela, "let's spare ourselves the formalities. I have prepared here two pieces of legislation."
"Pieces of legislation?" Palmela flinched. The trained diplomat began to tremble when a conversation was not wreathed in the usual greeting ceremony.
"Yes, my father instructed me that these two laws must be established first of all: freedom of the press - Lisbon needs an independent newspaper - and the obligation to attend school, the literacy of all the children of Portugal." Maria Glória placed the four sheets of paper filled with writing in front of him.
"Of course I will pass this along," Palmela answered.
"I wish to have these bills read yet today in the state council."
"Yet today," Palmela repeated breathlessly.
"Yes, and tomorrow I want to speak to Duke Terceira. He has to select the teachers, and Minister Linhares de Rego will negotiate with the bishop and ask him to make rooms available for the school classes in one of the monasteries." Maria Glória had already stood up.
Palmela remained seated and slid back and forth on the chair.
"Your Majesty, permit me, allow me, Minister Linhares was a Miguel supporter, and the bishop will not voluntarily..." The poor man found no words. These assignments were impossible to carry out.
"Minister, Senhor Palmela," she placed her hand on his shoulder, "I shall never again ask who was a Miguelist, who is on my side, or who could obstruct my wishes. I shall do what my conscience prescribes!"
Palmela had stood up and had nodded at every word. She had prepared the sentences well, had often recited to herself: "Senhor Palmela, nothing is left for me but to fulfill my duty. I will comply with that assignment, and if people do not do what I wish, then I shall seek others who will do it."
On October of 1835 the first edition of the newspaper *O País* appeared. Maria Glória wrote an appeal, an article, on the front

page: "Citizens, countrymen, and friends, this newspaper will appear three times a week and every journalist who writes for *O País* will be able to express his opinion uncut in this newspaper. Many questions will be addressed to the powerful and the influential, and they will have to practice maintaining calm and discretion if they are criticized. Free access to knowledge and education and the freedom to express opinions are written down in the *Carta Constitutional*, in the constitution that was introduced by my beloved father in the year 1826. Beginning today Portugal possesses liberality of the press. Libraries and schools will follow. When there is talk of obligatory school attendance, I am immediately presented with the lack of teachers as an obstacle. I cannot see this lack of educated people, for how many of them were in exile and had to let their minds starve there. Now a task is waiting for them..."

The first editions of the newspaper were cheered. At last the questions that stirred the people could be read in a well-formulated form: the country bankrupt; for months the soldiers had received no pay. How long would Spain still be able to resist the poorly defended border? How much land had been transferred to the church during the Miguelist period?

The enthusiasm about the newspaper, however, soon turned into anger and fury. It did not help anyone to read about the deplorable state of affairs. They were conscious of the injustices, the powerlessness every day anyway, when they had to fear for their lives because they were not protected from beggars and riffraff on the streets, when every day they received less fish and less sweet potatoes for their few coins.

When the first school was opened in November of 1835 on the *Rua Sebastião* in accordance with the "new law of obligation to attend school for everyone without respect to station," many shook their heads about the enthusiastic article in the newspaper *O País*.

"Will the children fill their stomachs if they know the ABCs?" "Should orphan children and children of citizens perhaps be taught in the same room?"

Maria Glória did not worry about the talk. "I shall continue to pursue the points of all my plans with perseverance and work daily on them," she commanded herself in her diary.

To Clementine she wrote: "You know that you remain my only friend from my childhood. The correspondence with my sisters is difficult, for the mail ships are not dependable, and besides that the letters are en route for four or five months. Those are eternities in which people sometimes die. I like to look at the journals that you have sent me. I find the latest fashion with the mantillas extravagant; I like the attached bonnets and hoods, although I do not feel the slightest wish to dress that way..."

The everyday duties increased. In May of 1835 she had begun to attend the sessions of the state council regularly. Almost every day she walked through the streets of another part of Lisbon with Leonora. She visited both of the prisons. Every two weeks she turned up in the public hospital with Eulalia; there, too, there was a shortage of everything.

"At the harbor there is a cotton storage place," Eulalia knew. "My father and my uncle had it walled up before they fled to the Azores. Perhaps the cotton can still be used."

The Miguelists actually had forgotten it. The cotton from Brazil was hardly mildewed. It could be used and woven. In the hospital every additional piece of clothing was desperately needed.

"How slowly everything develops. This year of 1835 is dragging along," she often murmured.

Dona Amelia, her stepmother, continued to change her places of residence and constantly sought for new governesses for the four-year-old Maria Amalie. "This woman's French was bad," and "That liberal woman wanted to teach the child the English handshake," she complained.

At the weekly official dinners, at which Dona Amelia was present, the delegates and diplomats admired the wife of the deceased "Emperor of Brazil." They very seldom called her the Duchess of Bragança. Clothed in Brazil green, with her medium-brown hair in curls and falling to her shoulders, the twenty-three-year-old Dona Amelia formed a sharp contrast to Queen Dona Maria II. The sixteen-year-old widow sat with an austere hairdo at the head of the table. Everything about this young, so very young woman was unadorned. Her voice was hard, her sentences short and terse, and hardly had the coffee been served when she got up and left the room. Delicacies remained untouched on the table.

Soon after the appearance of the first edition of *O País*, Maria Glória had driven out to the Menino Deus Church with Eulalia, as she did every Friday. When she arose from the prayer stool, she saw Dona Amelia standing there.

"Congratulations," her stepmother began on the church square. "The writer who wrote the newspaper text for you is good."

Maria Glória was not expecting that. She had been waiting for weeks for a single comforting embrace from Dona Amelia. At the death of Augusto, at the death of Dona Amelia's brother only a note had come, and at the funeral services only the stepmother's curtsy before the queen.

"Dona Amelia, I wrote that text myself," she responded. "Leonora checked my formulations. With my text I wanted to give evidence for free speech, for freedom of opinion."

"That's very praiseworthy, and nobody will learn from me that dispatches of the Queen of Portugal actually come from the pen of her governess," Dona Amelia said with a smile. She gave a brief curtsy and disappeared in her coach.

Everything began to spin and grow dark around Maria Glória, although the morning sun was shining. From far away she heard Eulalia speaking: "Dona Maria, I beg you. She didn't know what she was saying. She didn't intend to hurt you so."

No, she did not need a doctor. She had just sunk down for a few moments. On the way back into the church she was already walking as straight as a ramrod.

On the sixth of April 1831, on her last evening in *Boa Vista*, José Bonifácio had slipped a letter to her: "Maria Glória, I cannot give you anything to take along, only my good wishes, my good thoughts. But you will live very far away from your family. You no longer have a mother, and how long your father will remain to you we do not know. There will be moments in your life when you will have the urge to scream for a mother, for a father, for your siblings. I cannot give you any comfort to take along, even for that, but you should know that I, that all of us empathize with you. Dona Leopoldina entrusted herself to prayer and to work. In the darkest hours, I, too, have found comfort only in that..."

She had remained in the church for a long time. As if she did not want to leave that cave anymore, she did not react to any sign or any appeal from Eulalia.

The kind lady-in-waiting was completely beside herself. She had never before seen Maria Glória so shocked. She had the coachman rush back to *Necessidade* to get Leonora. Perhaps Leonora could help. Her two confidantes stared distraughtly at her as Maria Glória came out of the church toward noon.

"We'll eat our noon meal now together, and this afternoon I want to speak to Count Lavradio," Maria Glória decided.

The women nodded. Leonora had brought an herb pillow to calm her. Eulalia poured wine from a wicker bottle into a cup: "Drink this. It will give you strength." Maria Glória seemed to have calmed herself.

Maria Glória, Second Marriage
The Revolts Begin, 1836
"My flesh is transformed into hardened ground"

Count Vicente Lavradio suspected why he had been summoned. A man of elegance, his full, dark hair glistened. On his dark red diplomatic robe there was not one gold braid too many; no button glittered in an inappropriate place.

"It is much to your credit, honored Count, that you permitted yourself to be summoned to me on such short notice," Maria Glória said in greeting him. "We'll speak privately. That will shorten our conversation."

Lavradio needed only a few moments, for he had grasped the situation. "Your Majesty, Dona Maria, you wish to get to the point immediately. May I nevertheless permit myself to mention that your new clothes and your new hairdo are very suited to your nature?"

"With that we have already touched on an important point," she began. "When you, when your diplomatic negotiators look for a new husband for me in the European noble houses, do they still show the curly-headed portrait of me?"

Lavradio shrugged his shoulders. Was he supposed to tell some sort of lie?

He found the curly-headed portrait more suitable. After all, it was a matter of finding a groom for Dona Maria. Lavradio said nothing about his thoughts.

"Is that wise? Whatever prince is found will feel that he has been deceived," said Maria Glória.

"But, your Majesty, perhaps you will feel different in a year," Lavradio interjected.

"A year? Senhor Vicente, in the next few months a second husband must be found for me!"

She raised her hands: "For two weeks I have not received any report. It is already June. What is happening with my case?"

Lavradio cleared his throat: "To summarize it: We will not find an Orléans. The brothers of Princess Clementine are all promised already. Besides, to speak quite candidly, we don't have an easy task. In most of the noble houses, your Majesty, fear of a union with you prevails. The poisoning affair cannot be gotten rid of, and for that reason many princes lack the courage. We had contact with the Russian ambassador. He declined. From the house of Naples-Sicily we received another rejection. Metternich has placed a prince under consideration..."

"Out of the question," Maria Glória interrupted him immediately. "Whoever becomes my husband, he must swear on the constitution. Metternich would never sanction that! In Portugal no kings rule by the grace of God any longer. We're selected by the people." She shook her head: "Austria - no, unfortunately."

"The house of Habsburg also has good principles," Lavradio said, trying to placate her, "Dona Leopoldina..."

"*Mamãe* was one of the exceptions. She brought the Freemasons into the government. She dispensed with the possibility of going home, just so that Brazil could come to political order, at least temporarily." There were tears in her eyes: "Once *Mamãe* waited for two years for mail from her father, twice three hundred sixty-five days!"

Lavradio remained silent, nodded, and then finally said: "It's very difficult. The gossip ran out across our borders so quickly."

"What are they saying? What are they reporting? Speak, Senhor Vicente!" she ordered.

"Dona Amelia is not interested in having you, your Majesty, marry and have children. That would definitively place succession to the throne in your line, and for Dona Amelia would remain once and for all nothing but the position of the near relative to the Queen of Portugal."

"That is well known. That is why she could hardly endure the fact that the marriage to her brother Augusto did in fact come true."

Lavradio looked at her in amazement. The indifference with which she talked about Dona Amelia frightened him, as did the tone in which she continued: "Is it not so that Augusto was also in Minister Saldanha's way? I know precisely that this Saldanha cannot be trusted. Today he is a fiery monarchist, tomorrow he will be a reactionary, the day after tomorrow an ultraliberal. That man wants power and followers. Augusto was very popular among the soldiers, and that was the case even though Saldanha, during all the weeks before the wedding, said only the worst things about the 'stubborn German.' For a long time already Saldanha has been planning a revolution in every detail, a revolt against the royal house, but he would never have aroused the soldiers against my husband, against Dom Augusto."

"It's true, the political situation will not endure a postponement of your marriage any longer, your Majesty. You are surely also informed about the fact that Maria Christine of Spain is having her speculations sent out: If Dona Maria of Portugal remains childless, there will finally be nothing standing in the way of a union of Spain and Portugal."

Lavradio stepped back a pace. What he had just said was too daring.

But Maria Glória remained unimpressed by that as well: "Those are two cultures that will never unite. The Spanish and the Portuguese cultures are basically different. Where the Portuguese spirit has taken root, there it will remain, in Brazil and Portugal. The Spanish element could never flourish in such ground!" With that she drew a line under these deliberations. "So, Senhor Vicente, whom can you offer me?"

He placed the portfolio that he had held tightly in his hand for the entire time on the table and struck a pose: "Prince Ferdinand von Coburg, he is nineteen years old, raised and educated in the best fashion, perhaps somewhat too much in the direction of the arts and sciences, but from his family we can expect a 'Yes.'"

Lavradio leafed through his portfolio and presented letters. Even a miniature of the prince had been prepared.

"Another German," she said. "Aren't they negotiating with a Coburg for Victoria of England?" she asked without paying any attention to the laid-out papers and the miniature.

"Yes, a brother of Ferdinand, Albert, is supposed to become the husband of the English queen. For that union as well, the Belgian king led the negotiations," said Lavradio quickly.

"That is outstanding," Maria Glória considered. " A good, almost familial relationship with England is very important for Portugal. Ferdinand - Fernando," she said a few times. "Which portrait did you send the Coburgs?"

Lavradio did not answer.

"The little curly head?"

Lavradio nodded.

Now Maria Glória had to laugh: "So we're all being deceived, and if Ferdinand, Fernando, doesn't see my face under the head of curls, that is actually not our fault. Do you have something written by him? I would like to see his handwriting."

Fernando's writing was very similar to Augusto's writing, with the letters exactly the same height and the sweeps broad: "...have decided to concern myself more deeply with the matter. It should not remain unmentioned that I actually did not want to follow the path of the prince consort, but was educated in the direction of the fine arts. The sequence of my birth would also have made a marriage of lower rank possible..."

All that sounded true. There was no indication of a lie or flattery anywhere. "Fine, Senhor Vicente. Now I request you to carry out the marriage negotiations with the house of Coburg, with Senhor Fernando." She clasped both of his hands and said, "I ask you to do that, and do it with all necessary haste." Then she embraced Lavradio. He stood helpless before her. "I didn't expect you to decide so quickly," he said with a bow and pushed the portrait toward her. "Later, later you will perhaps want to look at it."

The portrait showed a very young man with blond hair draped luxuriantly around a face in which only symmetry could be seen.

"You should not burden yourself with worry because of his handsomeness. Consider that portraits always even things out and also conceal. Yes, beloved sister-friend, even you in your portrait cannot be recognized by a tiny twitch of your mouth as that Maria Glória who frightened the servants here in Paris in February of 1833 in the clothes of the good Leonora..." wrote Clementine.

Letters went hastily back and forth between Paris and Lisbon: "Clementine, now I know at last what relatives this marriage brings to me! So I will soon be related to the Grand Turks and perhaps even to the Emperor of China! I will not have a wedding ceremony arranged the way it appears in Gotha. What a baroque program! Celebrating with controlled faces does not suit us southerners, and to tell you the truth, I will let all the celebrations happen to me. Hopefully that will bring a few days of quiet and the absence of intrigues..."

She had soon gotten into the habit of talking with Fernando, with his portrait, and of telling him things: "What should I do? I don't have a single friend here, so you must be everything to me, both husband and friend. Count Lavradio reported to me about the engagement celebration in Coburg and how strictly everything proceeded. You know, here we had only a *Te Deum* and afterward I took a walk with Leonora, Eulalia, and Count Lavradio through the streets of Lisbon. The people made every effort. An October day full of sun and ocean wind, with cloths waving from the windows and flowers that people gave me from every side and strewed before me. The important thing to say, however, is that all of them, in those moments in which they wish me happiness, pray with me, rejoice with me, and truthfully mean it. That is why I often stop in such situations and plead with God: Let it stay this way. Let them begin to have confidence in me, and drive away the malevolent ones. There is no money available for large celebrations. There is actually no money available for anything at all. You will notice it immediately, the bad roads, the heaps of garbage that nobody transports out of the city, the people who lean against their houses day and night in their despair. There is no lack of work, but they know that they will receive no pay, neither coins nor goods. Fernando, I wanted to offer the east section of *Necessidade* as a hospital. There are so many rooms that are not used, and we have enough room for guests in spite of that. Imagine! They rejected my offer, and they did not mention my intent in the newspaper. The people need a symbol to which they can assign guilt, and I have to be that. Fernando, when you are here at last, as commander of the soldiers you must prohibit this swaggering. Early in the morning they thrust their way through the streets where a few emaciated women exchange a few self-dipped candles for bread and suet, where midwives carry the stillborn out to Alfandega, and men, farmers and workmen, sleep in the street. These people have toiled for days at the harbor or in the arsenal, and they were sent away without pay; they were not even given a few coins for a drink of liquor with which they could have drowned their sorrows. For the soldiers, however, liquor and wine are poured immediately, and they are given olive oil and bread, and nobody would expect a coin for it from the soldiers. Fernando, it will soon be Christmas. The year 1835 is finally used up. Fernando, why do you never answer? Why don't you lay aside your formality? Your face is so fresh. It gives me a guilty conscience, as if I had not told you about the things that I have already experienced. You know that I was married and that since Augusto's death I have devoted myself completely to the fulfillment of my duties. But sometimes there are stretches of time when I want to be embraced and caressed, and then I am alone, and the December nights in Europe are cold and endlessly dark. I cannot warn you enough about the intrigues. Mouliniere, Dona Amelia's lady-in-waiting! In her mind she breeds rumors of the very worst kind. Since I am not compliant and no longer sign bills for Dona Amelia's tapestries and silverware, Mouliniere concocted a story: Dona Maria married Lucio da Silva, a plebian, on the day before Christmas in 1835. That report was printed in the newspaper. Yes, in Portugal anyone can write what he wants in the newspaper..."

During all the months of waiting only one single letter came from Fernando. One day before the wedding by proxy this dispatch was brought to her by his ambassador:

"Revered Maria, highly revered Maria Glória, for the day of my arrival, which will be at the end of March 1836, I ask you to proclaim a general amnesty as evidence for everyone of my good will as well as your own concerning the confidence of the Portuguese people..."

She did not really notice the fact that this letter came so late, that it had been the only one, because she was so intensively immersed in her conversation with Fernando. He assumed all forms, that of Father, that of Augusto, and that of José Bonifácio. And they all helped her to push away the malicious comments: "That Coburg wants to become King of Portugal. Dona Maria, the woman, doesn't interest him." This gossip came from Belem, from the home of Dona Amelia.

Maria Glória did not depart from her strict daily schedule: "Work is the only true friend."

When she drove out to the Menino Deus Church early one morning in the week before Christmas, still in the year 1835, a coach stood there that was unfamiliar to her. The women, prayer leaders and fortunetellers, glanced kindly at her, attempted curtsies and bows, and then drew back when a man dressed in black got out of the foreign coach and reached Maria Glória in two or three strides.

"Your Majesty," he said with a bow. "Dona Maria, I wanted to speak with you alone," he said softly. She nodded at that and walked to the olive tree with the black-robed man. "This tree has already been standing here for three or four hundred years. Not even the earthquake could hurt it. I think it supported the church with its roots." The man smiled and while doing so did not let her out of his sight.

It suddenly occurred to her who was standing before her: "You are Senhor Costa Cabral, the judge," she cried, "and you come from Coimbra!" She had recognized him by the black university clothing.

Costa Cabral was a delegate in the ministry of justice. She had signed that decree only a few days earlier.

"Dona Maria, in the next few days, even before your wedding, they will suggest to you that Lezirias be sold."

She knew about that already.

"Don't do it," Costa Cabral whispered.

She drew back. She could never let herself become involved in such a conversation. "They are actually swamps. There is no good usable land between the Tejo and the Sado. A sale will bring hardly any money, and if money comes in it will be used again for the soldiers' pay and for cannons," she said. "But, Senhor Cabral, I cannot refuse. You know that."

"You have a veto right," Cabral insisted.

"That exists on paper," she said, shaking her head. "If I were to make use of it, it would be a scandal!"

She thought about it and recited: "According to the *Carta Constitutional*, the king's veto right has the exclusive function of postponement and cannot be employed in any case to thwart a plan of the state council."

"In spite of that, your Majesty," Cabral said with a bow, "do it! I shall help you select the adjutants for your husband. Do you like to ride? It's beautiful around Queluz now, in late December." And within the next few moments he had disappeared in his coach.

So much strength had gone out from António Costa Cabral that Maria Glória walked into the church as though strengthened, as though uplifted. Did the winter sun actually shine more brightly on the whiteness of the marble? Did the light from the oil lamp glow more intensely? Were the pews polished? How luxurious the lace altar cloth with the gold border was. "That I always do everything as well as I am able," and she did not find more than this plea, this line of prayer. Nor did she kneel on that morning; she remained standing during her worship. The look from António Cabral could not be laid aside, could not be pushed away. Did that light and airy world that she had briefly experienced with Augusto still exist outside her world of duty, a world that she had left and into which António Costa Cabral placed her again? How often she remained below stairways and let herself be carried along by the whispers, the promises of a pair of lovers, a lady's maid and a scribe. Often, while in the middle of writing daily reports or greetings, she had the face of Clementine in front of her: "His name is Raymond, and nobody has kissed me that way before." During the dinner commemorating the first anniversary of her father's death, she watched Eulalia and the way her confidante's face grew red when Rodolfo seemed to accidentally brush Eulalia's hand while serving the coffee. Maria Glória had always felt herself excluded. The realms in which there was kissing and caressing were not appointed to her. She had to fulfill duties and live a disciplined life, and her heart, where it glowed and sometimes burst into flame, she had to keep that heart tightly locked up.

The conversation with Costa Cabral had stirred Maria Glória up. She intended to write him a letter and was unable to give the accustomed sweeps to her handwriting. She trembled as if she would want to write to him. "No!" she called herself to order aloud and finally wrote: "I urgently request, Senhor António, that you be present at the session of the state council in the coming week."

The meeting room was full of people. Many had come to bid on the "swamps." The delegates ranted once again in their speeches against the extravagance of Dom Miguel.

"To put everything into the church and the army, so that today there are not enough cisterns and too little seed."

"We emigrants received no thanks. We endured in the Azores

and joined Dom Pedro in forcing the tyrant Miguel to flee, and to date we haven't gotten our houses back."

"Dom Miguel is living in Germany, in Baden-Baden. He married his way into another dowry!"

Maria Glória waited for the sale of the Lezirias swamps to come up on the agenda.

Leonora had wrung her hands: "Maria Glória, don't make use of your right! Don't forget that you are surrounded by so many envious people! In the end..." Leonora held her hand in front of her eyes, "Your great aunt, Marie Antoinette, she was also so gullible! Remember Dona Amelia. Now she has accepted Belem as her place of residence, but she is having it renovated and she tried to foist the bill for the gilded Dutch tiles and the windows made of Murano glass off on you! 'The queen supports the extravagance of Dona Amelia with tax money!'" Leonora had hardly been able to calm down: "Forget your veto right!"

Now Leonora sat erect next to Maria Glória and watched and listened.

Then a gentleman slipped up to her, an Englishman. Maria Glória recognized that immediately by his frock coat, by the gold pin in his collar.

"Your Majesty, may I introduce myself? Richard Leão."

What did he want? Why was he pressing up against her?

"My family, we are a banking house. We loaned money to your esteemed Bragança family." He was almost whispering. "Now, since the political situation here is clearing up, we would like to submit recommendations to you for settling the matter."

Maria Glória pressed her lips together. A money collector! What should she say to this man?

"If it comes to the sale of the Lezirias swamps today, with that we could eliminate part of the certificates of indebtedness as paid off."

"Lezirias will not be sold, not under any circumstances." She could hardly keep herself under control. Where was Costa Cabral? Where was Palmela?

Leão looked up: "We are also prepared for that situation. Portugal has claims against Brazil and those are also easily dealt with and would not burden your esteemed brother, your ten-year-old brother. We could negotiate about the mines that your honorable father left to Isabel of Goias, his mistress's child.

Maria Glória finally began to understand. "What are you saying? My half-sister Isabel received the title of a Duchess of Goias, but no land. Isabel is eleven years old and is being educated in London. Father also arranged for her marriage. What do you want?" Her voice broke. "Should I steal from Brazil to satisfy you with your certificates of indebtedness?"

Eulalia dropped a glass to divert attention from the outburst, and Leonora walked up to Leão: "Senhor, go to Minister Palmela or to the Brazilian ambassador about this matter." Then she drew Maria Glória to her seat in the first row.

But Leão could not be shaken off so easily.

"Here, Dona Maria, the certificates of indebtedness. They are copies, just to convince you that we are not demanding anything improper," and he pressed a few sheets of paper into her hand.

She should not have taken the certificates of indebtedness. She should have let them fall to the ground. But she already had the papers in her hand, and Leão had immediately ducked away.

Maria Glória sat alone and well visible to all on her seat in the state council meeting room. An artist hopped back and forth next to her: "This day must be captured. Our country is selling the river bottoms between the Tejo and the Sada. That has never happened before in history."

The documents, the contracts were read aloud. The ministers were already pressing through the rows to sit down at the table and sign.

Then Maria Glória stood up and said: "In the name of the *Carta Constitutional* I am exercising my veto right!"

Some officials and delegates paused in their pushing and their simultaneous talking. Where was that female voice coming from?

Maria Glória added to what she had said. It was difficult for her to restrain the trembling in her voice: "I object to the sale and to an auction, to any form of disposal of the river bottoms from the Tejo northward, and to any form of disposal of a part of our country..."

For several seconds it was quiet. Then a tumult broke out. Businessmen and speculators shouted at the same time. Maria Glória stood surrounded by the blue-robed delegates, diplomats, and ministers.

Costa Cabral, the chairman of the state council, rang his bell and admonished them to be quiet. He asked Maria Glória, shouting every word into the hall in order to drown out the angry people:

"Your Majesty, Dona Maria, will you insist upon your veto right?"

"Yes!"

She did not get another word out, for she was suddenly surrounded by furious men. She felt hands grasping at her dress. A book was flung at her feet. Balled fists were raised toward her, and finally Leonora stood next to her and pushed her out of the room.

In the coach Leonora pressed the rosary into her hand. "Pray, pray!" Leonora whispered. "I beg Heaven for help, for we know well that monarchs are sometimes shot for such a reckless act!"

Leão and the certificates of indebtedness did not let go of her for years. She actually had to correspond with Pedrinho about them: "...came with renewed demands for interest and compound interest, and he constantly presses me to demand money from Brazil, from you, beloved brother...," she wrote in despair.

When Pedrinho, the 'young Emperor of Brazil,' informed the English, all English banking houses in 1846, "...that the payments to England that have been made since 1807 are terminated as of this date...," Maria Glória embraced the Brazilian ambassador who brought her a copy of that letter by her brother. "My beloved brother, I cannot admire your courage enough. Pedrinho, we will join you in your decision. First the people here must have work, homes, enough to eat, and then we will negotiate with Leão and the others..."

On January 1, 1836, the wedding rites took place in the São Vicente Cathedral by proxy. With her hand in the hand of Costa

Cabral, she swore the oath of faithfulness, faithfulness to her still absent husband Fernando Augusto Francisco Kohary de Sachsen-Coburg-Gotha.

With António Costa Cabral a man had been woven into her life, a friend who was present during those times when she saw herself at the mercy of the mob. Both as a politician and as a friend, for seventeen years he did not deviate from his principles. "The republic cannot be stopped, but the monarchy still has an important task. Portugal must first learn the art of self-determination. We have lost colonies and we have lost influence. Now prices and profit margins for colonial goods will no longer be discussed: at what price the sugar from Brazil can be resold to Holland. Now the goods themselves have to be procured, in our own country, or bought through good trade relations. We must learn all that."

The months from the marriage by proxy to the arrival of Fernando in April of 1836 had whisked by, and she wanted to force his arrival on her 17th birthday, April 4, 1836, but the ship entered a calm that lasted for days, and Fernando did not land until the 8th of April.

The political situation began to boil. Her veto of the sale of Lezirias had aroused ministers and officials against her.

"In the lower city cartoons are circulating in the taverns, Dona Maria," Eulalia reported nervously. "A little child - yes, that's how you are portrayed - is holding Portugal in her hand like a toy ball, and the jungle is drawn in the background."

She immediately pushed those comments aside: "We can't sell the country in pieces, ever!" But Eulalia did not let herself be deterred. She warned, "The liberals are using Lezirias as a reason to combine against you, Dona Maria. Some are talking of revolution."

During those weeks Maria Glória did not want to hear anything about that. Fernando would arrive soon. She wrote to Clementine in Paris: "I have also laid aside my hatred of my outward appearance. Clementine, I no longer brush my hair - it is not very long yet - straight, when it wants to twist into curls. Don't I also have the responsibility to present a good appearance for Fernando? After all, destiny has appropriately endowed me. I owe all that to António Costa Cabral. With a few glances he slipped the woman onto me again. Clementine, you wicked girl, I can hear you laughing. But he is at least forty years old..."

The occasion of Fernando's debarkation on April 8, 1836 had been prepared as an important national holiday. The tower of Belem was decorated with pennants. The diplomats were in their official robes. Everything came together in an image of feathered hats, scarves, and flags. At last they would get to see what had been negotiated for so long and so comprehensively.

Fernando was almost hidden behind his companions. Carl Dietz, his educator and priest, and Friedrich Kessler, his personal physician, were posted like two cabinets next to the prince. The boat rocked toward the harbor and the men had visible difficulty in maintaining their balance while standing.

"That slender, blond man, yes, that's how I know him." Maria let the words slip out, and even the first, furtive touch of his hand was intimate. She, both of them had waited for that and they were brought together at last, one half joined to the other. The welcoming ceremony, words of greeting back and forth; the medals that they presented to Fernando as evidence of their confidence in advance; the Mass, the ride in the open coach from Belem to Lisbon, past the waving people to *Necessidade*, everything only a postponement of the first embrace. "How was your voyage? Tell me about Paris. How does Clementine look now?"

Fernando spoke: "In London I also visited Isabel Goias. She is an especially pretty, well-educated girl. She gave me two letters to bring along, one for you and one for Graça. And here is my present, an amber necklace. There is no amber in Brazil." And Maria Glória let herself fall into Fernando's kisses and embraces. Hadn't he always been here, just briefly absent, out of town on important matters and now returned at last? Everything about him seemed familiar to her. She wanted to find that familiarity, and she devoured Fernando with overwhelming joy and passion, at least during the initial weeks. She had then soon learned to adapt to his reserved endearments and to accept his quiet embraces almost obediently.

Graça rouses her from her thoughts: "Which letter? Maria Glória, I never received it. So back then Abrão was already beginning to keep letters back from me, to use those letters with the royal coat-of-arms."

She leans her head against Maria Glória. In the past Graça would have reacted to it with fury and screaming. Now, as a thirty-five-year-old, after almost twenty years in Porto, she accepts and she takes note, but it really does not concern her anymore.

She would just like to know what Isabel had written at the age of twelve in the year 1836.

Maria Glória tried to remember: "My beloved friend and sister Graça. I am doing well here in London in every respect. I have wonderful teachers and three girl friends that are dear to my heart. Since you liberated me from the prison in Paris, Heaven has been giving me all kinds of blessings... From our Brazilian ambassador I learned that my father died. Many speak badly of Dom Pedro. I shall never do that because he provided for me... Graça, he selected a prospective husband for me, Count Max von Treuberg from Bavaria. As you can see, beloved Graça, everything is turning out for the best for me...and nobody here in the Institute of the Ladies of Loretto calls me the mistress's child. A hearty and firm embrace, always your Isabel of Goias."

Graça lets the tears flow: "She actually did marry him."

"Duchess Augusta wrote to me two years ago," Maria Glória tells her. "Isabel is the dearest daughter that I could wish for. She is very refined and so warmhearted. She also takes the greatest care in raising the two children Leopoldina and Peter. Isabel and Max compensate for many disappointments that I had to experience with my other children..."

For a few moments Graça closes her eyes. She fulfilled her assignment to watch over Isabel, to keep evil fairies away from Isabel. And now, after two decades, on the stone bench in Sintra she can let go of all her worries about Isabel.

The first weeks of the marriage full of duties, the visits to the hospital, to the scientific academy, the shipyards, the cartography institute; the celebrations of the Mass in the cathedral and the secretly attended morning Masses in her church, in the Menino Deus Church.

"One daughter will be named Antonia, after your mother."

"And one Leopoldina and a son Pedro, and one daughter will have to put up with the name Maria Glória."

"But only if we also have a Fernando."

"I want seven children. Seven is a lucky number."

In the state council Fernando's swearing in as commander-in-chief of the army, "*Chefe do exercito.*"

"The uniform looks good on you," she teased Fernando. "Today they will envy me even more because of you."

"But you know, I'm not a military officer," he protested one more time. "I was trained only theoretically in strategy, and that only in the very last months."

"You take after your mother completely," Maria Glória knew. "Dona Antonia is a real aristocrat! The princes of Kohary concerned themselves exclusively with culture."

"Yes, Mama also offered me an appanage," Fernando began to rave. "I can buy myself something here, an estate or a dilapidated little castle, and I shall rebuild that for us, renovate it! That is my passion, Maria Glória, to ferret out and restore the original characteristics in a building that gave up on itself long ago."

"Do you know how to work with bricks?"

"Of course! I can calculate complicated roof constructions. I worked with a master carpenter for half a year. I like to work with wood most of all. Brazil wood, I've never had that in my hands."

"In Queluz there are a prayer stool and a desk made of Brazil wood. My father brought both of them from Rio; salty, yes, the salt wind can still be smelled on both pieces.

"You miss Rio a lot, don't you? Even in your Portuguese you cling to it. It sounds much softer than the way I was taught to speak it," Fernando said.

"Brazil – when I was sad, then I could go out into our garden at *Boa Vista* and talk to a cook and let her shake freshly roasted, greasy coffee beans into my hand. What pattern do they form? It doesn't matter. It means luck. I also miss Brazil when I'm happy; riding to Botafogo with my sisters and Pedrinho and asking a water bearer or a gardener to get coconuts down from the tree for us, the ones that are not hard as rocks yet, so that the water in them tastes sugar sweet; stopping and sitting in the sand until the sun has fallen into the sea, and at that same moment Rafael stands behind us, our guardian angel from *Boa Vista*. He has come to ride back with us in the darkness."

Fernando listened attentively to her: "Were you thinking of those images when they painted your portrait? Very few people know you the way you are when you have your Brazil in your face."

After the initial duties a few summer weeks in Sintra, Sintra at last.

"A dilapidated monastery," said Fernando breathlessly. "Can it be purchased?"

He wanted to lay out a tropical forest for Maria Glória, as she had had it in *Boa Vista*, with rerouted watercourses and waterfalls and ponds where water lilies bloomed, those stars that had fallen to earth. He would draw the glazed tiles out of their disintegration piece by piece until all the stories were again visible in the blue and white tiles; then he would clean the overgrowth from the stone floors, the pergolas, and the atria. They had worked their way around the Pena Monastery in Sintra in those initial weeks together, climbed every hill, and explored every cave opening and every path.

"...I can report to you, dearest Clementine, that in Fernando I have found that husband who is the only one suitable for me. That is why I have promised Providence not to complain about anything else in my life. With Fernando I have been compensated for everything that has happened until now and that will yet happen, will certainly yet happen. We differ in only one point: his inclinations toward art and nature have taken hold of his entire being. He also wears those inclinations outwardly, and for that reason I must protect him from military matters. From my early childhood on, of course, I learned that I often had to be outwardly gruff and to hide my inner portrait that way..."

At the beginning of September they drove back to Lisbon, still quite intoxicated from the parties and excursions, the rooms without guards, and the walks without adjutants.

They had only reached Amadora when a company of soldiers came toward their carriage train. "Your Majesty, Dona Maria, for your own safety I have to inform you that your army has deserted to the revolutionaries. General Bandeira is leading the rebels!"

"General, I thank you for informing me," said Maria Glória. She had immediately gotten out of the carriage. "Is Senhor Costa Cabral in *Necessidade*?"

"He is waiting for your Majesty with great impatience." The General added: "I, we, have orders to ride back immediately."

"That is in order, General," answered Maria Glória without batting an eye. "We will continue our trip home. I'm sure that we will arrive safely in *Necessidade* even without the protection of the soldiers."

The streets empty in places and on some corners crowds of people; they dumped out water tubs at the royal coach, threw burning foliage in the direction of the royal carriage. Shots whipped through the air. The road to *Necessidade* was still long, very long.

The coachman stopped. "Onward, drive onward, Manoel," Maria Glória urged him. He shook his head; he could never pass through the *Passeio Rossio*. "They will hang on the coach like grapes. Get out, your Majesty. They will give you refuge in some house."

Until then Fernando had remained silent, but now he blurted out: "They want to kill us, Maria Glória! Down to the harbor. We must leave. We must leave Lisbon!"

"No," she said shaking her head and climbing up on the coach box. She was wearing a dress whose neckline was too deep; the golden yellow of the amber necklace glittered in the sun. "Go on!

Let's travel," she urged Manoel, and they drove along the usual route to *Necessidade*. They dumped one more wastewater barrel out at the coach. "Go on, stop them at last!" shouted some in the crowd, giving the command to storm the coach. "Don't, it's actually her," others shouted.

In the palace chaos. Just not to have to flee once more as she had fled from the revolutionaries with *Mamãe* in the year 1822; not race to the harbor at night and in the fog, as she had done in April of 1831, when she left Brazil with Father.

"I have committed no crime. We won't flee," she said to the servants, the few who were still in the house. Most of them had already fled.

"Why should we flee to England, Fernando? Nothing will happen to us. This revolt was to be expected. It's the response to the fact that I rejected the sale of Lezirias."

Fernando waited in his room. He walked back and forth, clinging to a book. "I've never experienced a popular revolt before. Only a few weeks ago they were cheering us, and now they've shot at us."

Maria Glória remained firm. "We must remain steadfast now. Come, dinner is waiting."

"There are only pancakes. The cook with his assistants was one of the first to join the ultraliberals," they were told.

Half the night spent awake and in the morning the arrival of the delegation from Bandeira. The revolutionary representatives of the people were able to press their way unhindered into Maria Glória's office.

General Bandeira bumped his secretary; he had to read the manifesto: Queen Maria II of Portugal was to come to the city hall immediately to confirm by oath and sign a new, radical constitution, and after that to greet the passing troops of the new, liberal government from the balcony of the city hall.

"I request a few minutes," she said and pushed aside the soldiers who came running up. "I want to pray by the picture of my father. We will not flee."

The soldiers of the palace guard held their eyes half shut as

Maria Glória and Fernando were shoved past them down the stairs to the coach. Nobody was there to accompany her, to defend her, to protect her. Maria Glória looked for Palmela, for Costa Cabral.

"Minister Palmela is waiting for you in the city hall, Dona Maria," said General Bandeira with a smile; and as if he had heard her thinking, he added: "Costa Cabral is under house arrest for a few days."

The September morning of the year 1836 was very cool. The coach of the state assembly, of the people's delegates was wet with dew, even inside. The coachman turned to Fernando; he swayed drunkenly: "Here's a rag for you. You can dry the seat with it," he said thickly.

Fernando did not understand the dialect. He stood undecided next to Maria Glória and waited.

"Open the carriage door," she hissed at him, and when he did not react, she pulled back the door herself. The steps got stuck and did not fold down. None of the assembly soldiers moved. Bandeira conversed with his adjutant and acted busy. Nobody wanted to miss the scene of the queen and her prince standing in front of the open coach unable to get in. With a jerk Fernando finally lifted her up and shoved her inside the carriage. Then he hoisted himself into it.

"Your Majesty, Dona Maria, here, your cloak." Eulalia had run after them and wanted to hand the hooded mantle into the carriage.

"He will probably need it more than she does. Our commander-in-chief is trembling," someone shouted from the crowd that was pressing toward the forecourt of the palace. In carts and on donkeys they had ridden out to *Necessidade*. "She doesn't know our country at all, but she wants to decide whether or not something can be sold!"

"They're only sour meadows, the Lezirias lowlands. Nobody needs them!"

"Right, and we would have received good money for them."

"But that doesn't interest her. After all, she pays no taxes. She has no debts with the loan shark on *Rossio Square*."

General Bandeira left the coach standing there for endless minutes. "Thank you, Eulalia," Maria Glória said to her lady in waiting. "Meanwhile, get things calmed down in the house. We'll return soon."

Eulalia crossed herself. She let tears run down her cheeks, and when she did not move away from the coach immediately, a soldier prodded her with the barrel of his rifle. "Get away from me, you bastard!" Eulalia screamed, and she struck out at the totally dumbfounded soldier with her fists. "You were a Miguelist, like most of those here. You want to live without work, without responsibilities. I'm an Azores emigrant. You don't have any idea what it means to go into exile for a liberated country. Which of you is even interested in that? You run after anyone who promises you liquor and idleness!"

Eulalia's voice broke; she did not cease striking out around herself. Without exchanging a word with each other, Maria Glória and Fernando jumped out of the coach. Maria Glória's knees gave way briefly and she almost fell, but it did not matter. Fernando walked toward the soldiers who were tugging at Eulalia, peeled the lady in waiting out of the scuffle, placed his arm protectively around her, and led the sobbing woman back into the house.

The mob pressed in. Bandeira planted himself in front of Maria Glória: "She will be put on trial," he shouted. "In the palace she agitates against our new state!"

"General, I ask you to spare Dona Eulalia. I'll vouch for her. Like me, Dona Eulalia no longer has any parents. Her parents died in the Azores," her voice took on a totally foreign pitch. She said nothing more. She felt Fernando's arm.

"Dona Eulalia has calmed down," said Fernando. "Now, General, we wish to be brought to the city hall."

Bandeira nodded. He jerked his head back and forth. He did not want to obey that order, but on the other hand he had to do, still had to do what Dom Fernando ordered.

For a few minutes yet, until the two royal scions were in the city hall, until then Dom Fernando was the commander-in-chief.

The crowd remained silent until Maria Glória and Fernando sat in the coach again and drove off. The trip carried them past yelling people to the *Praça do Carmo*. They did not speak a word to each other. Hand in hand they entered the meeting hall. Minister Palmela received them with the portfolio containing the new constitution under his arm.

"Your Maje..." He broke off for a few moments. The new government had no longer provided this form of address for Maria Glória.

Finally Palmela said: "Dona Maria, I shall now read to you the new constitution of September 1836, adopted by the new ministry chaired by General Bandeira. Your sanction, your oath is expected," he hesitated. "It is requested," he added softly.

She stroked the upper arm of the humiliated man. The elegant cavalier's cheeks were bloodless. "Our country can be proud of its queen. She is not only well instructed, she is also extremely beautiful," he had often said to her.

The members of the assembly did not spare any of them a single humiliation. He, Palmela, a loyal follower of Maria Glória, had to read the new constitution aloud, and Lavradio, her most intimate confidant, the matchmaker, had to sign as a witness. "...that beginning immediately it is no longer the function of the monarch to impede or delay resolutions of the people through the exercise of a veto right...but from now on to attend only to the honorable obligations of representation..."

She signed; she raised her hand for the oath.

There remained nothing for Fernando to do but stand there. Lavradio pointed to the balcony, and for half an hour, perhaps it was hours, they stood in the sun and had to receive the salute of the army of the new state of Portugal.

"Father, you would have acted differently, I know. You are not pleased with me. I should have sent an army, several divisions of soldiers against those rebels. How you would shake your head at having all of your rights knocked out of your hand by such uneducated fellows who were stuffed into a soldier's uniform. In your will you wrote that your son-in-law, my husband, has to be the supreme commander of the army. That was valid for Augusto von Leuchtenberg. Who could dream that he would die so soon? You know the truth about his death and from what direction the poison came. It is no longer important. You would have approved of Fernando. Like you, he loves music and the theater, but he is no soldier. Now that I am married for the second time, I have been to the theater again. During the months of my widowhood, I missed it very much. I should have had the courage to sit in our box in defiance of all the rules of propriety. I did not have that courage. Dona Amelia cannot be figured out. If I had asked her, she would have encouraged me to attend the theater, and the next day that scandal would have reached the bishop and the diplomats and would have perhaps frightened away my prospective husband. How lost in thought Fernando now stands next to me. He is in Sintra with his thoughts, and tomorrow he wants to visit a young painter with me and buy at least three pictures from him. The landscape in Algarve in the month of January, at almond blossom time, Fernando wants to hang that picture in our bedroom. Father, Fernando and I are alike even in that trait. We want to close our eyes to violence and falsity. Fernando has never experienced revolution before. I remember being driven out twice, pushed out of Pedrinho's bed and taken to the harbor at Botafogo with Leonora at dawn. Never to see Rio de Janeiro again - those were only words. I had to maintain my composure. We were not even traveling on the same ship. I can have no memory of the Revolution of 1822. I was three years old when *Mamãe* fled with me from the assembly forces to Santa Cruz. But in my dreams some images have buried themselves. How bitterly my little brother wept. Yes, he obediently wept softly. Had not *Mamãe* said to me: 'Please hold his mouth shut.' I never heard those words from *Mamãe* again later. How she swung the whip at a stranger. The room was small, a salamander was climbing the wall. *Mamãe* had placed me on the table; I had pressed João Carlos to me. That stranger came toward us. He wanted to take my brother and me with him, and *Mamãe* struck again and again, so that the man fell down. He was bleeding. *Mamãe* did not stop; she continued to strike him; she ran after him - *Gesindel* [rabble] - I know that German word only from my dreams. João Carlos died after that flight. 'The representatives of the assembly have taken everything from me. They killed my firstborn son.' That was what you sobbed in despair when they placed the abdication decree in front of you. Father, you know that I also would now have signed such a thing in order at least to postpone revolution and revolt. That situation of standing on the balcony, greeting the troops of my opponents, confirming by oath a new constitution and another new one, that situation will repeat itself. There is no illusion about that anymore. Miguel's years of terror confused the people. They do not trust me. They do not think that my advisors and I are capable of serious effort and work. Father, I am talking about it with you because I do not reach *Mamãe* with my thoughts. There must be many heavens, and *Mamãe* is probably in the most remote one. Would she excuse my weaknesses and the times when I close my eyes? It is difficult for us children to speak with parents who are no longer among the living. Now I have told you that I shall fulfill my duties and do everything as well as I am able, but I shall accept many things with my eyes closed. Like Fernando I want to be unreachable for ruthless things, for cruelties. In a month the Academy of Fine Arts will be opened, and Fernando will contribute the first ten pictures. Father, there is one fear that I cannot conceal from you. Keep Dona Amelia away from me. I have such a severe lack of devotion from a loving family, and when Dona Amelia speaks to me in her honeyed tones, walks with me in the garden, and praises my handwriting and my appearance, she opens within me a chamber of my heart that I otherwise keep well locked. She talks to me like a sister, like a mother, like a grandmother, like a brother, like a father, and I cannot get enough of those acts of kindness, and it is possible that I let her steer me in the wrong direction. However, I know no prescription against it. Like a person who cannot resist rum, I absorb every endearment from her. I am defenseless when she dumps poison into my spirit and soul in a situation like that..."

They were brought back to *Necessidade*, and now, after Maria Glória had bowed to all the demands, the human grapes no longer bobbed up and down yelling and singing. The people held the cleaning rags that they had swung against the queen only hours earlier absent-mindedly in their hands: "What kind of a woman is that who fearlessly steps up in front of an army of soldiers, a woman who swallows her pride and rides back to her residence sitting erect?" Curiously they followed the coach with their eyes and shook their heads. They had anticipated more, haggling by the queen for a paragraph in her favor, a resistance, or a refusal. But the way everything turned out, by accepting without a fight the queen had deprived the people of a spectacle.

"They are all back at their posts," Leonora reported. "The news arrived like wildfire. Not a single shot, not a drop of blood. The queen ratified the new constitution."

Leonora crossed herself. "The baker will bring you fragrant, warm olive bread this evening. With a delegation of people who are loyal to the queen he will express his admiration and his gratitude for that woman, our queen, who cleverly and generously retreated in the face of the blind exercise of power and in so doing avoided the shedding of blood!"

"How is Eulalia doing?" Maria Glória wanted to know.

"She has a high fever. It came within a few minutes, and she is fantasizing.

"Has Senhor Melo already been notified? Eulalia needs a doctor immediately." And Maria Glória ran with Fernando into the room of her lady in waiting.

"People who lie ill, die," she had sobbed as an eight-year-old when Dona Dadama had gone to *Mamãe's* sickroom with her every day for a week.

"She looks so strange. I don't believe that *Mamãe* will get up again," she had sobbed.

Her feeling had been right. *Mamãe* had died.

Father had also died when he let himself be bedded down in Queluz.

Not to have to watch a person die again; she stopped stiffly in front of Eulalia's bed. The woman lay on the bed with her hair down. Two maids stood pressed against the wall shaking their heads. The bed was rumpled, but she would not let anyone near her.

She struck out around herself, and they had not even succeeded in cooling her forehead or her cheeks.

Maria Glória stood motionless. That strange body frightened her. Fernando waited a few minutes and then he sat down on Eulalia's bed and spoke to her. "Eulalia, we'll drive to Sintra. There we'll show you a pavilion with paradise flowers in every shade of orange winding around it, and a gargoyle bubbles inside it. Eulalia, you don't have to be afraid. There will never be a return to the Azores. Nobody will have to flee. Look, Dona Maria has a light blue dress on. There is no longer any ordinance that prescribes gray and black clothes."

Fernando, whom most people called a weakling, an unworldly man, Fernando brought Eulalia out of her unrealistic fantasies. He was courageous enough to ease the cramps in her hands and her legs by rubbing them. He wiped the drops of sweat from her forehead, massaged her wrist, straightened the pillows, and poured sugar water into her mouth. With every touch, with every word more calm entered Eulalia's body. Now and then she smiled. For a few moments she fell asleep. Then suddenly she opened her eyes and looked at Fernando: "Dona Maria, Maria Glória, I feel it. They want to harm her. She is being led astray. They will try to persuade her that she should resist, that she should send soldiers against the regime, that she should sanction a counter-revolution. She must not do that. They want to harm her!"

Eulalia did not die. Later she had no recollection of those hours of her confusion. She tried to explain it to Maria Glória: "Sometimes our souls pick up thoughts from other people that can only be vented violently. The more malicious the wishes are that are thrown at us, the more severe are the convulsions to become free of them again. In those moments Heaven lets us see more deeply and broadly, but for those on the outside everything is dismissed as fantasies, and the soul has hardly purified itself of all the malicious things that have been thrown at it, when nobody wants to remember anymore and nobody wants to think about those signs."

"They want to harm her." Maria Glória had not forgotten the

sentence." She prayed every evening: "God protect me from intrigues," and she was convinced, back then in September of 1836, that they all had been satisfied, that they could not require anything more from her. She had ratified the constitution of the Septemberists, the ultraliberals. She was only window dressing now; now the tempers would calm down.

Now there had to be time enough at last to undertake excursions with Fernando in the vicinity of Lisbon, to read with Fernando in the books of António Vieira. He was not familiar with those texts. "Two hundred years lie upon this language, unbelievable":
"*Words must be like stars, clear and sublime,*" Maria Glória began and recited a letter: "*My dearly beloved, I almost cannot believe what they report to me. Christina, your passion for pictures and miniatures clouds your spirit. The nuns of the St. Francis Convent in Perugia are complaining to the Pope that you, the Queen of Sweden, sent out fences to steal pictures for you. Can it be that you freeze in your bed to the extent that you have to tempt yourself with other kinds of forbidden fruit? I shall not criticize you for that, but prescribe my gaze for you. It is nice to look at you, Christina. Your body is well formed. Is it still that way, or is it true that you have partaken of too much wine and fat? My beloved friend, my gaze is punishment enough, as I well know. Cover your body. Go into a cell and take only a jug of water with you...*"

CHAPTER V.

*On ever changing, arduous long trails
upon high seas against the winds to sail,
I fear, if you bring no help to me,
my little boat will sink into the sea.*

Graça rummages in her bag. "Look, Maria Glória, a mulberry tree seedling. I'll plant it here." She holds the little tree, which is two spans tall, in the sunlight. "When you enter the house of a friend for the first time you bring a tree or a shrub along."
She expects Maria Glória to continue talking, but Maria Glória remains silent. She fiddles with the folds of her dress, and when Graça reaches for her hand, she gratefully leaves her hand lying in her friend's hand. Maria Glória did not know how arduous it is to illuminate, to dig out the years and the events once more.
"It smells like bay plums here," Graça says. "Did you plant bay plums in your Brazilian garden? I'll send you a basket of bay plums, the firm, yellow fruits with the ruby-red meat, and if I lay *mamão* leaves between them, they will stay fresh for weeks and will endure the journey from continent to continent well."
Graça takes a few deep breaths. Some things can no longer be held back. The years, the events can be read from her hands, her skin, and her white hair. And as unadulterated as hands, skin, and hair are, so she continues to tell her story in an unadulterated way.

Graça and Abrão in Porto, 1839
"For those mulberries that have decided in favor of love grow better"

"They say that Porto is a beautiful city, and that is probably true, too. I didn't notice any of it. During those first years my sadness hung so heavily on me that I hardly went to church from our farm. I very seldom accompanied Abrão to the harbor, and when there was a lack of flour and wine in the kitchen, I sent the maids out. I mourned, for whom? I mourned for Rio de Janeiro, for Irazy, for Isabel, for all the people that I had left behind there, and not until Mother Ines from the convent said to me, 'Graça, you are suffering from *saudade*," did I cease to resist the heaviness, the fog that had laid itself upon me.

"In the first years I also watched my face, the way it changed. My eyelids halfway covered my eyes and a downward crease formed around my mouth. My hair became thinner; it lost its powerful unruliness and let itself be twisted and pinned up in any roll, in any knot.

"In the year 1838, three years after Abrão and I had begun to rebuild the Braga farm and the first deliveries of silk spools were on their way to London, we also began making the Sunday and holiday visits. The Assis, Mendonca, Menezes, and Fontoura families had already been business acquaintances before the Miguel era, and beginning in 1838 there was a dinner at least once a month in one of those houses, and at our place as well, of course. On those occasions the prices were calculated and helpers, laborers, and maids were offered and exchanged. On such evenings I was also less aware of my *saudade*, for I was soon familiar with the rules and therefore saw myself less as a foreigner. At the table, we women spoke only when we were spoken to, and later, when we sat at coffee in the next room, we complimented each other's dresses, exchanged names of cooks, and talked about the sermon from the previous Sunday. There was never any talk of family matters or even anything personal - content or not content, sad or joyful, fearful or confident, not a word about those things, everything always "*tudo bem* [all right]."

"In October of 1839, so in the spring, no, autumn, at one of those dinners Richard Leão was standing in the Menezes' drawing room. He told about an office that he had set up at the harbor. He praised the organization of the harbor, inquired about the olive harvest, had the smoking of fish explained to him, and distributed to each of us women, as we rose from the table with liqueur glasses in our hands, a small gold topaz. He even gave me a gold topaz that flashed and glittered reddish golden. He told about the two years that he had spent in Brazil, about the lithe female slaves and the depraved Donas who open their chamber doors to every European. Finally he drew drawings from his jacket pocket. He was having the jewels that he had brought with him from Goias made into necklaces and bracelets according to the latest Paris fashion. Then he enumerated a list of names and said that he would furnish all those noble families with jewelry. It could be felt in the salon. Abrão wanted to go and the others were also probably looking at the clock. Then Leão finally got around to talking about the business that he wanted to suggest to the men of Porto: In Rio de Janeiro he had established contact with a ship owner, and now it was possible to make a profit on the lumber and sugar cargoes.

"The men did not understand.

"But Leão had worked everything out. 'In the first European harbor the goods must be registered, and duty must also be paid on them, of course, and for decades that harbor has been Belem at Lisbon. But, as we know, in Lisbon there are only civil wars. The child queen is pushed politically first in the radical liberal direction by her advisors, then in the moderate one. The officials are constantly replaced. Hardly has a captain reached an arrangement with a few harbor officials - for a small fee, a few sugarloaves, or a few logs you can then get any kind of freight documents - when there is already a new face sitting in that musty booth. I told my friend Magalhães that in Porto a person can register and pay duty on his load of lumber or sugar very quietly. Who remembers the child queen in Porto? You perhaps, dear Abrão, out of sentimentality, but that has not rubbed off on your business sense!'

"That's the way Leão talked, in the same tone, with the same polish that he had had back then in the tavern. The men asked questions. Soon only a murmur could be heard anymore, then laughter and handshakes, and finally the '*Saúde* [health]' with which they congratulated each other on the new business contract."

"'I don't want to have anything to do with Leão,' I declared to

Abrão as we rode home. He didn't answer.

"Three weeks later Abrão laid out for me a dark woolen dress and a black scarf for my head.

"'Put those on, Graça,' he said tersely. 'The first delivery is coming today, and you will talk with Captain Magalhães. He will understand your Portuguese better, and he will also know that you are sent by us.'

"I didn't understand immediately.

"'Two hundred and fifty sugarloaves, fifty cords of Brazil wood, and a hundred baskets of cotton.' That was written on the sheet of paper that Abrão pressed into my hand. 'Besides that you will give him the bag. The money is in it. Everything else will be taken care of by the sailors, and by us, of course.'

"So Abrão and his business friends wanted to resell part of the goods, the sugarloaves, the wood, and the cotton that was delivered from Brazil to England, themselves, to deliver it to Brest in small ships, and from there to dealers.

"'No, I don't want to do that, Abrão. Leão is behind that, and he wants to harm Maria Glória and Isabel!'

"I always felt that menace radiated from Leão. But I couldn't talk about that with Abrão. He expected obedience from me.

"In all the years Abrão never raised his voice to me. He told me what there was to do. He praised my work. He patted me for my codfish sauce. He admired my walk and my singing voice. He took my body and went back to his bedroom. I couldn't complain about anything, not anything at all. It was actually the case that I was in his debt. Abrão had taken me away from the tavern, from the toil at the fire pit in the tavern's kitchen, and had given me a better, a good life. Abrão was always quiet and thoughtful. Nor did he react - he seemed not to hear it - when they told him about little Luiz in the convent whose mother was an Indian. He did not lose his patience when my body did not obey and no baby made its nest there. He dressed me up for the Sunday dinners, brought brocade, muslin, and velvet ribbons for my formal dresses. I, Senhora Graça Braga, stood at his side when he talked to the mayor. And now I wanted to refuse to perform such a minor service for him. *Saudade* had completely clouded my spirit. How often Abrão reminded me: 'Forget your princess or queen sister. She hasn't written you a single line for an entire year. She doesn't send you money for passage so that you can visit her. Believe me, Graça, she's doing well. She hardly thinks about you anymore.'

"The black market trade with Magalhães soon flourished. I was the one who delivered the orders and the money, and after a year the business friends founded their own shipping agency. Now we, the Bragas, also owned a share in a ship.

"Only a few weeks after the founding of that shipping agency the business friends came into conflict with Leão. He wanted a larger commission, and on a Sunday evening he waved papers around in the air, and again his voice became shrill: 'With these I can...'

"I didn't want to hear any more of that. I only thought about how I could take his sheets of paper and documents away from that man, how I could finally get at that case that he constantly carried with him like a treasure."

"Leão usually stood next to Magalhães when I went aboard the ship with the order and the money. Waldemir, our coachman, drove me to the pier, stopped, let me get out, waited, helped me back into the coach, and took me home.

"A week before Christmas in 1839 I decided, 'I won't wait another week. He won't possess those papers for even one more week.'

"After the next errand I didn't scurry off the ship immediately, but pressed myself against the wall of the cabin. It would only be minutes until Leão would come and stroll whistling from the ship.

"When he bumped against me in the darkness, he was startled. I reached for the pouch - either the pouch in my hands or the pouch into the water. However, he didn't let go of the pouch, but began to hit me, and I resisted. I resisted so violently and struck out around me until I felt the handle of the pouch in my hand and had freed myself from his strangling fists. For a few moments I stood relieved. I had warded Leão off, forced him away. I had kicked, hit, and pushed, and suddenly I became aware that I was standing alone.

He didn't even scream when he fell into the water. I thought: just get away! The pouch was heavy and shapeless. I could hardly hide it under my woolen scarf. I rushed to our coach and barked at Waldemir, 'Fast, faster.' And at home I ran into the kitchen shed. There was still a glow in the fire pit. I quickly stuffed the papers into it, page after page, pack after pack, until everything was finally transformed into flames that glowed orange and blue. In the pouch I also found a rolled-up piece of leather. Gold topazes and emeralds were sewn into it. Where was I supposed to put it? Even the pouch was in my way. It wouldn't burn quickly enough. Initially I hid everything under my bed, and a few days later I buried the pouch together with the piece of leather under the winter jasmine in front of my bedroom window.

"Now, after the fire, I dug both of them up. Leão's pouch is my travel bag. With that bag I'll travel back to Rio de Janeiro, and with some of the emeralds I bought passage, and there are still enough topazes. With those I'll set up a sewing shop for myself in Rio."

"They found the body of Leão already the next day. The mayor came to Abrão personally. 'No, Graça didn't notice anything. Everything was the same as ever. Here, Mr. Mayor, your commission."

"My guilt with respect to Abrão had now become even greater, but I was so relieved. 'My beloved Maria Glória, I have finally freed you and my protégée Isabel from that cutthroat, from that profiteer. Leão will never wave certificates of indebtedness at you again. Nobody will call you a child queen ever again.' Maria Glória knows about the power of thoughts. Maria Glória will sense that Leão can no longer harass her, and that I freed her from that - that is what I convinced myself.

"Besides that, I was certain that they reported it to Queen Maria II. After all, in Porto it was the topic of conversation in the bars for months. 'We can hope that this Leão doesn't have a few accomplices. Let's wait and see which profiteer turns up now! In any case, nobody will involve himself in our business anymore, and if someone wants something from our queen again, then we'll send him to Lisbon. Let him go directly to *Necessidade* and knock.'

Graça looks at Maria Glória and nudges her: "For a year, two years, until into the year 1841 I waited for a letter from you, a message in which you would inform me in your well-formulated words that you knew what had happened in Porto. Maria Glória, do you know, did you know what they say about you in Porto?" Graça is waiting for an answer: "You don't say anything about that even now. Some say: Dona Maria II has never gone out beyond Lisbon. Abrão explained to me: The fact that she did not seek the people weighs much more heavily!"

Maria Glória 1836-1845
"Bend down a bit, your Majesty, and show me the tender face where old age is already written"

Maria Glória remembers the years after the Revolution of 1836. She only wanted to flee from a daily routine in which new decrees were laid before her every hour. New ministers, almost all the delegates were replaced; every day she had to receive new members of the government.

With closed eyes and no longer looking at people, at papers that were no longer the ones that had cheered her and the *Carta Constitutional*, the moderate constitution. "Nothing will deter me from waiting for the *Carta* to be reinstated," she wrote again and again in her diary.

In order to escape into a different world, she and Fernando visited the two painters Tomas Anunciação and Francisco Vila-Franco. They lived in an isolated outpost. "...that there is a piece of primeval forest so close to Lisbon."

They spent an entire afternoon with the artists. Maria Glória did not want to leave that world anymore, a world where there was

nothing unharmonious, where intrigues and falsity were absent.
"We want to buy some pictures from you, Senhor Tomas," Fernando revealed to the artists. "There will soon be an academy of fine arts in Lisbon!"
"An academy of arts! Wasn't there a revolution? Didn't you have to abdicate, Dona Maria?" asked Francisco.
"No, I didn't abdicate, but I'm only a decoration anymore," she answered.
"They don't trust you, Dona Maria, and that pains you," and Francisco explored her face, lifted her chin toward the sun, turned her head against the light. The sculptor explored every muscle: "Your eyelids, your eyebrows, everything drawn extremely tight. At what age in your childhood was time brought to a stop in your face? Did you also quit growing when you had to leave Brazil?"

Do not touch that mystery: "She misses the fruits, the bananas and mangos. The change of food can be the only reason why Princess Maria Glória has not grown any more for two years." Dona Leonora was despondent. "They take such good care of us here in Paris. They extend every kind of kindness to us, but Maria Glória can't get used to Europe. Will she attain the size of her mother Dona Leopoldina?"
The doctor shook his head. "It can also be the sun. They attribute special powers to the sun in Latin America." He was also at a loss. "So she will simply remain small in stature. She is physically quite healthy," he reassured Dona Leonora.

She also took other diversions, an evening in the theater. She was so starved for gaiety, for merriment.
Dona Amelia came into the box with Moulinier, her lady in waiting. She embraced Maria Glória and Fernando and whispered: "Terrible, that revolt. It almost came to a civil war! How farsightedly you acted, Maria Glória, accepting everything and saying nothing."
She continued talking intimately to Maria Glória, caressing her cheeks. The patrons in the boxes and in the orchestra observed the

scene. There were shouts of "Viva, Dona Maria." Hand kisses were thrown at the two women. "They're getting along with each other again, the two women, how exemplary!" So it was all only evil gossip that after the wedding Dona Amelia avoided the house of our queen.

Maria Glória could hardly follow Dona Amelia's words, her bubbling tone. Her stepmother's perfume smelled like vanilla. "I have already spoken to Manoel Passos. He's the most capable soldier and he'll fight for your rights. He will free you from the dictates of that General Bandeira. He needs a few weeks and that counterstrike will be devastating. How happy you must be. You have blossomed like a hibiscus blossom since Fernando has been in Lisbon. That blue that you're wearing is the color of Bahia topazes. Did Clementine send you the material from Paris? Oh, I live rather isolated in Belem. We should see each other more often," Dona Amelia cooed. She sat down in the furthest corner of the box, rubbed Maria Glória's neck, and fanned cool air toward Fernando with a lace handkerchief.

As if she had fallen into pleasantly warm water, Maria Glória now saw everything only blurred and very distant. However many sprites and water monsters tugged at her in the following weeks, she was incapable of resisting.

She had become caught up in the maelstrom of Dona Amelia's kindnesses, and that meant: sanctioning a counter-revolt, following a conversation of Manoel Passos: "...I shall have two hundred soldiers march against the army of General Bandeira. The storming of the city hall will take place on a Tuesday when the Bandeira people, those ultraliberals, your opponents, your Majesty, conduct their weekly meeting..." - and not to react to any shaking of Leonora's head.

Dona Amelia's kindnesses intensified into caresses: "Maria Glória, you're so tender. With your seventeen years are you really already right for rough masculine hands?" Dona Amelia caused a string to vibrate in Maria Glória that made her defenseless. She did not want to do without those caressing hands anymore, and soon she was no longer capable of weighing suggestions from Amelia: "Isn't it about time for Dom Fernando to become acquainted with his new homeland and to travel into the North for a few weeks?"

Right, Fernando has wanted to visit the Monastery of Batalha for a long time now. "I'll be back before Christmas. I'm not traveling alone, anyway. My friends Eschwege and Dietz will accompany me..."

Yes, yes, Fernando should travel, so that Maria Glória could have all the hours for herself at last, and for Amelia: "Come, dearest, many landscapes on your body are still untouched. Let's explore them."

Amelia had kindled in Maria Glória all the passion that she had hidden so well from Fernando. She quivered at Amelia's touches and let herself fall into embraces in which Amelia transformed herself for Maria Glória into Augusto and Fernando.

The walked in the garden and picked the fully developed rose blossoms: "Hidden under rose petals I shall seek your body."

For three weeks Maria Glória floated in a cloud of desire and longing, joy and pain. Would she ever again be able to live without Amelia's touches, without her caresses?

On a Tuesday in that November of 1836 she was awakened by pounding and knocking.

"It's five o'clock in the morning," Eulalia spat at the sentry. The door was opened further, a few firm steps: "Dona Maria! I beg you to get up. I must speak with you immediately!"

António Costa Cabral stood in the doorway.

"Senhor Cabral, why are you here? Where have you been for so long?"

"Dona Maria, they are going to start a civil war today, and it's said that you, Dona Maria, gave the order for it! What a mistake! Where is your husband? Who sent away the man who is commander-in-chief of the army?"

António Cabral looked at her in horror: "Dona Maria, did you actually sign a manifesto for the organization of a counterrevolt?" With his eyes he followed Amelia, who slipped behind the screen: "Your stepmother is with you, in your bedroom?"

With every breath that Maria Glória took in becoming more awake, finding her way from sleep back into the day, the events of the past days and weeks came more and more together.

"How long has your stepmother been living here?" António Cabral was horrified. "Nobody in the city knows about that."

"That's how she wanted it. Nobody was supposed to find out that we are living like good sisters under one roof." Maria Glória looked around in the room: "Everything here smells like Amelia, the sheets, the pillows..."

Eulalia finally tore her away from her dreams: "Come, a bath has been prepared." And to Cabral she said, "Senhor Cabral, if you would please wait for an hour, then Dona Maria will talk to you."

Eulalia poured jug after jug in the tub. She scrubbed Maria Glória's body. "You should have been pregnant long ago," she hissed. Maria Glória let everything happen to her. She just needed to wash Amelia's caresses away quickly and tightly close and lock once more that door to her heart, behind which a fire burned and sometimes blazed up.

Then stockings, underwear, shoes, gorget, undershirt, and slip were donned, everything smelling of almonds, and then finally the dress, the ribbons tied in bows, her hair combed smooth and tied up as always in two rolls under the net.

"Senhor Cabral, I thank you for coming."

Maria Glória reflected and tried to explain: "Senhor Cabral, I wanted, I don't know, I wanted to go back home. I haven't received a single line from my sisters for a year. Perhaps they are keeping the letters from me. I can't write anything but superficialities to Clementine. They read everything. Besides, would Clementine understand what I am suffering from? I am at home here, of course, and I have my handbook, and Leonora and Eulalia are around me. I should probably visit my father's grave more often."

Costa Cabral listened attentively to her: "*Saudade* can eat our souls. Maria Glória, this failed political action, this counterstrike would not fill a line in the history books. They will forget it. You have been left so alone, surrounded only by flatterers and intriguers.

Whom could you trust? However, Dona Maria, we are waiting for offspring," and Cabral added: "You know the saying - we need a wound, a wound that draws us. What else would drive us toward our duties but the constant flight from the pain of that wound and the incessant labor at suppressing our unfulfilled wishes?"

He embraced her and she let herself be held by the arms of António Costa Cabral. She let herself be carried south by the waves into the other part of the world. To creep among the lilies and the hibiscus blossoms, to wait in the midday heat for the iguana that creeps on the wall, to run barefoot up the stone stairways - nobody should awaken from his siesta. They lean and doze, Rafael, Dona Dadama, the Aguiar woman, and José Bonifácio. Watching her siblings: Januária is writing math exercises. Francisca stares at an empty page; she has to fill it with sentences in Italian. And Pedrinho is sitting at the window watching the shadow of the mango tree - reading the time in the November sunshine from the slowly creeping shadow. If only she could float past those people who are so familiar to her, stop briefly, dream with them, bite off a few morsels of the air of *Boa Vista*, and give nourishment to her soul with it.

António followed her images. He felt with her. He understood, and in the time that it took to draw those few breaths all the distance, all the unfamiliarity was wiped away. "Maria Glória," and she carefully freed herself from his arms.

Some weeks later Manoel Passos stood before her. Maria Glória did not recognize him immediately.

"Your Majesty, Dona Maria," he bowed in front of the doorway to the Menino Deus Church. He was in gray and black prison clothing, with his hair cut short.

"General Passos," she cried in horror.

Passos had led the failed counterrevolution.

"Dona Maria, I need only a few weeks of rest. But after Christmas I shall put together an army, and the next storming of the city hall will not last two hours."

"General Passos," she said, pushing the poor, confused man away from the church doorway to the olive tree, "you made a courageous effort. You meant well, but there will be no repetition. The government is recognized, and there will be no further revolt."

"Your Majesty," he stood at attention, "my blood for the honor of the Braganças. I swore that to your father."

"General," she tried again to calm the man down, "there were no wounded and no casualties, and I owe that to you. You will be honored for that."

But Passos did not listen to her at all.

"That Saldanha, who is now our prime minister, he was a Miguelist, Dona Maria! He settled in the Azores to win the emigrants for Dom Miguel, to spy on them." It was such an effort for him to string words together that Passos almost lost his balance. "Dona Maria, Saldanha is like a chameleon from the Pantanal. I shall fight against him. I shall free you, Dona Maria, from this personification of falsity." He did not let himself be interrupted; he wanted to kneel before Maria Glória.

"The coachman, quickly," she cried, and with ease José, the coachman, pulled the former general to the carriage. She followed and reached inside the carriage: "Senhor Passos, we'll find an important task for you in *Necessidade*."

His hand was cold and cramped itself around hers. For several seconds he did not let go of his queen's hand. The November sun shone on her shoulders, and behind the coach was the magnolia tree with its pink blossoms halfway open. "The tree has lost its inner clock since Dom João went to Brazil. Since that time it only blossoms in the late autumn," murmured Manoel Passos, and the coach with the general moved slowly away from the church square, down into the city.

"The rebels lie in wait for her even in front of the church."

"Who knows, maybe she slipped a letter to him and is already planning the next revolt. The Braganças can never be trusted."

"Pretty faces are dangerous, and she always tries it with her pretty mask. He knelt before her!"

They were saying that, and none of the church visitors made an effort to do it so softly that she was spared hearing or listening to it.

"Fernando, dear Fernando, you have been away on exploration

trips for weeks. You have already visited who knows how many monasteries, and you don't have a single line for me. I can imagine that they do not bring me your letters. The very first thing that we have to do is to find dependable adjutants and couriers. You will not be able to believe the political chaos, about which they surely report to you. Unfortunately, the truth corresponds to the worst embellishments that they use when they tell you about it. Only Providence and all those who have gone before me have prevented the worst. Fernando, being alone is crushing my soul. I can't say any more about it. In all the time that lies ahead of us it should be my, our task to promote science, art, and education. We promised each other that when we returned from Sintra and revolution was raging in the streets of Lisbon. Tomas's pictures of the landscape covered with almond blossoms give comfort, but too little..."

And it was only a few days later that she received an answer to it: "Beloved Maria Glória, I am informing you as quickly as possible that I shall be with you in *Necessidade* by St. Nicholas' Day at the latest. You write of political chaos! Well, we both lack the qualifications for the intrigues of politics. I have become acquainted with a young poet, Alexander Herculano. We will read his book, *A voz de Profeta* - the voice of the prophet."

The trembling in her knees when the coach with Fernando drove up, his footsteps, his kind words to Eulalia, to Leonora. "Roses for us, now in December, Dom Fernando." The two ladies in waiting were flattered.

And finally for her: "Maria Glória, I stopped in Sintra for a few hours. Look, the Glorioso lily is blooming. We planted it only a few months ago."

Never to let go of that body again, to devour it and wander over her own bodily landscape with him. How many pleasures and pains were now more familiar to her, how many tones of the language of her skin she had kept back from Fernando. Nothing would be hidden from him anymore; she had to succeed in drawing him into the vibrations of her body. She intended to be patient; for that she wanted to summon up all her patience.

The initial months of the year 1837 with spring festivals in Queluz. "A good omen. The spirit of her father flows through Queluz. It will fall upon the child that Dona Maria is expecting in September." Walks and coach rides, supper by torch light in the open, discussions with Senhor Carlos Dietz: "The melting together of the cultures could be successful in the reconstruction of the Pena Monastery in Sintra. The Moorish element is still too little in evidence. Eschwege will have to plan for a long time."

Speculations with Fernando's personal physician: "Dona Maria, you will bear a son. Sons make their mothers more beautiful. Daughters already begin to take from their mothers during the time of expectancy."

A letter came from Amelia: "I did not yet have the strength to accept that first invitation to a spring festival. Too much remains unsaid. With this letter I would like to close our diary of life together. Good, bad, it weighs differently today than it did during the time that we spent together in *Necessidade*. Nothing bad was intended. Nothing was supposed to hurt us, but it hurt you, and to write that down and in so doing satisfy the need for truth is painful enough. You can believe me when I say that I am looking forward with all my heart to an infante or an infanta..."

She left that letter unanswered.

On the 16th of September 1837 Pedro came into the world.

"The pregnancy was easy," Eulalia said as she patted her during the contractions, "almost too easy. You could have pretended to suffer a little more, Dona Maria. Here it is actually a part of good form to be a suffering pregnant woman."

"Eulalia," she had to laugh, "you say that to me now because you know that I will whimper again in the next few minutes." And she breathed deeply and slowly, let the sweat run, and let herself be pressed into the crouching position by Eulalia.

"Of *Mamãe*, Dona Leopoldina, they said that she gave birth to Januária all alone."

"A scandal," and Eulalia pressed down again. "Like the slaves in the fields."

Eulalia drove the midwife, the doctors, the priest, the scribes and secretaries, and the maid with the water jugs out of the room. "Bring the screen here," she ordered, and: "Dom Fernando, sit down!"

She caressed and reprimanded Maria Glória: "Dona Maria, how you carry on! Haven't you ever watched the horses?" She willingly let herself be bent, pressed, caressed, and tickled by Eulalia: "Dom Fernando, stay here. You are the only witness. We don't need another one. Push the scribes and the curious people out of the room."

Two hours later she shouted, "A healthy son, a magnificent child! I have never before had a mother giving birth who endured the pains as bravely as Dona Maria did. Everything went easily and without any difficulties because Dona Maria followed my instructions strictly." Eulalia also dictated that to the doctors and the officials as a first official report.

Little Pedro slept a lot. As early as the second day the doctors claimed, "The child is physically strong, but his nerves and his disposition are weak. We will have to see how his mind develops."

Maria Glória and Fernando vied with one another at alternately caressing and carrying the child.

"I want to bathe him," Fernando decided, and when Maria Glória took the baby out of the cradle Eulalia rushed up. "Dona Maria, you can't get up already on the second day!"

"I'm fine. I don't want to lie any longer."

"Nobody must hear about that. Every lady of station remains in her childbed for at least ten days," insisted Eulalia.

"That's just the way it was with Domitila," Maria Glória laughed. "That's over with. I'll drive to the church tomorrow."

Eulalia laid the baby boy, fragrant and wrapped in cloths, in Maria Glória's arms. "In the initial weeks a baby must be able to move freely. It must gradually become accustomed to all restrictions," said Eulalia, and she sang and prayed with Maria Glória and Fernando. Eulalia also spoke to the little boy and told him: "Pedrinho, I can tell by looking at you that you are dreaming of an excursion to Queluz. The roses and the lilies, they stretch their heads toward you, and the butterflies light on your little fingers. They all know that you won't do anything to hurt them because you can hear them much better than we can." Then a piece of *Boa Vista* could be felt in the room of *Necessidade*. "A pot of hot, thick cocoa, please" - that smell was still missing, a few swallows of the sweet liquid, a tiny drop of it on Pedrinho's lips, "so that he also feels *Boa Vista*."

The bulletins of the doctors continued to report things that caused them to be concerned: "...it must also be noted that the prince never screams the way infants normally do, which is why we cannot conceal our great concern about the development of his lungs."

Tickling the baby so that he finally screams, not laying him at his mother's breast at the usual time on one occasion - Pedro did not scream in spite of that. He sucked noisily on his thumb and at three weeks smiled at everyone who looked into his little bed. He actually did sleep a great deal.

Maria Glória and Fernando made it a habit to walk around cautiously in the room. At every smack of his lips, every gurgle from the crib they ran to Pedrinho and caressed the little boy.

"There are felt slippers by the door. Why don't you put them on over your boots?" "You opened the window wing too loudly, and you still have the tobacco smell on your clothes from the officials that you were just talking to," they reprimanded each other.

Two weeks before Christmas the physicians composed an additional bulletin: "...the physical condition of the prince is good, but his need for sleep remains too great and the infant's lack of crying presents a disquieting outlook regarding his character, for which reason..."

Fernando and Maria Glória listened to the doctors and tried to follow what was being read. "Not so loud, please. Don't speak so loud," said Fernando.

At that moment Eulalia had rushed forth from her corner: "What kind of sly intrigue have you cooked up again now against Dona Maria? Senhor Batisto, who's paying you to write such non-

sense in the official books? I've never seen a healthier baby, or one who smiled so happily, who is so patient. The little boy feels protected. He feels his parents, his aunts, yes, me, Aunt Eulalia and Aunt Leonora around him. He has no reason to scream," and she beckoned the gentlemen to come to her. "Come, just look!"
Eulalia let her amethyst necklace swing back and forth in front of the alert Pedrinho. The baby smiled and followed the glittering ball with his dark eyes.
"Here, you try," Eulalia said, nudging the physician. But hardly had the face of the stranger thrust itself over the crib, when Pedrinho closed his eyes and began to scream with all his might.

The next year, in the year 1838, the joy regarding the second pregnancy, excursions to Mafra and Queluz; experiencing the European spring without homesickness. The first roses bloom in April. "That is the rainiest month in Brazil, but that is far away," Maria Glória remembered.
Fernando sat over the plans of the monasteries of Tomar, Jeronimas, and Batalha.
She walked in the garden with the poet Alexander Herculano and admired the first edition of the newspaper *Panorama*.
"Perhaps there will be only ten or twenty editions of it. Who knows how long those who are loyal to the monarchy will be able to afford their own cultural newspaper? But now we have something that exists elsewhere in Europe only in London," the young poet said with a smile.

A very hot summer that did not interrupt the pleasant life of the year 1838 with a single day. In the state council the events of the years 1836 and 1837 repeated themselves: shouting matches because of taxes that were too high, balled fists against the unjust awarding of ship licenses and warehouse tariffs that were too high, a law against the dreadful problem of the beggars. From the cities of Coimbra and Porto came threats of overthrowing the government. Repeated tax increases, a law on the duty to collect taxes - political chaos had become routine.

Sometimes high officials were found stabbed in a side street. The sale of poison was prohibited. "Only doctors can administer it anymore, and that exclusively in person," it said in the newspaper. Thieves and bilks were no longer locked up: "The prisons are overflowing, and actually those people are neither bad nor evil. They have no work and nothing to eat. So it is better to sentence them to ride the garbage coach for a few weeks, to carry the waste water barrels to the gutter, or to clean up the garbage on the bank of the Tejo near Vadoura."

In September of 1838 Maria Glória once again had the seams of her dresses opened. "Will it be twins this time?" she wondered.

During the year 1838 she brought all of her projects to realization: "Lisbon has no surgical institute. In Lisbon there was no school of pharmacy. From today on those two educational institutions will exist, and I thank the government, all the ministers for approving my recommendation and the recommendation of my husband, Dom Fernando, and for joining together in the invitation of professors from London and Brussels..."

Senhor Costa Cabral warned her: "Dona Maria, you have here a list of scientists from London, from Paris, from Brussels, even from Florence!"

"Victoria sent me those names - 'Dearest friend, I am happy to give you the names of men with appropriate knowledge and the necessary experience, who will gladly pursue your project of promoting science in all areas in Portugal...'"

Costa Cabral became impatient: "Who will pay these men? No minister will dare to bring up such a suggestion."

"The scholars will live in Queluz. We will provide food for them. There is no money available for a salary. They are private scholars. They will learn our culture, our language. Victoria knows that that is sufficient for these men," answered Maria Glória almost defiantly.

"Dona Maria, your thoughts run in such a straight line! You completely overlook the political situation and point at a light that is far removed from our continuous everyday quarrels. But you're absolutely right," Cabral nodded. "Lisbon needs a polytechnic institute and a chemistry laboratory. We are a sea power and have no observatory. A botanical garden should have been established long ago. Since 1807, since Dom João moved to Rio, everything here has been at a standstill."

"The English lived especially well in Lisbon," she said, shaking her head. "By the way, she is afraid of having children," she said to António Cabral with a wink and smoothed out another page of the letter.

"Queen Victoria of England? She isn't even married," he said, failing to comprehend.

"But the whole world knows that she will marry Prince Albert von Coburg," she replied.

"Oh yes, the two husbands are brothers, your Dom Fernando and Albert, who is going to London," Cabral reminded himself. "In London they will employ attorneys from the entire world so that Albert von Coburg doesn't have the slightest right to anything."

"Listen: '...I also wanted to ask you if you have already heard of a birth under the influence of ether. There are supposed to be doctors there in Lisbon who ease the raging pain of birth for a woman with it...'" Maria Glória read aloud. "I shall write to Victoria that she should send a midwife. My Eulalia will train her, and then she can forget all her fear."

Costa Cabral reflected, then quoted - Senhor Cabral was also familiar with the letters of António Vieira: "*Christina, do not complain about physical pains, otherwise I must assume that the lauded common sense of the Queen of Sweden is only a rumor. The pain of the body does not exist; only the idea of it exists and the fear of pain. The flesh twitches and strains, but nothing more! Compare this indisposition with the torment that your soul experiences when Cardinal Decio declines your invitation to a dinner. Do not waste any further reports on pains of muscles and limbs. Dearly beloved, the twentieth day of November 1670.*"

She did not want to let Cabral go yet.

"Senhor Cabral, are you familiar with those times in life when a person wants to stop time? I often wake up in the night and try to drive a bargain with my father, with *Mamãe* - because you have to earn everything after all, and this year my blessings do not end. What could I do, what could I give so that this time of blessings continues? How could I earn it for myself for a longer period of time?"

Cabral smiled: "Lifted up, thrown down, how often a person asks for something in the middle. Dona Maria, I don't believe you're destined for that."

He added the question: "Will you entrust the library to Alexander Herculano?"

"Of course. Senhor Garrett is a delegate, and his second soul, his friend Herculano, needs an assignment. He will become the first librarian of the royal library."

She had already conversed with Cabral for too long. "Have you seen it yet? Our Pedrinho is already attempting his first steps, even before his first birthday."

"They say he has his temperament from Dom Fernando, and that everything about that child is gentle," Cabral said.

"The next one will take after me, and it will be a son. I sense that."

Between António and Maria Glória there was a harmony from which neither of them could escape any longer. Even when they sat across from each other in silence, each of them felt the thoughts of the other, the affection that they had for each other, and they both made an effort to hold back their innermost feelings and to be quiet about them.

Maria Glória should never have been allowed to be alone in the room with António Costa Cabral. But Leonora brought wine and freshly roasted chestnuts and then left the room. Even Leonora did not want to interrupt the harmony in the year 1838, with anything.

Fernando's birthday, on the 29th of October, was still celebrated outside in the open. In the stormy sky, with Dietz and Kessler, they looked for the wish cloud for Fernando. Maria Glória was also sitting by Senhor Eschwege and listening to him: "I am a German, but have already been at home in Portuguese for decades. The return from Brazil was painful. A person does not believe in addiction to the tropics and has long since been stricken by it. Here, in Portugal, Europe is easier to endure."

Baron Wolfram Eschwege had taken over the assignment for the renovation of the Pena Monastery. Every stone, every arch, the windows, the towers, and the little courtyards - everything in the former Pena Monastery bears his mark.

Maria Glória had written to him: "Pena, that centuries-old monastery must become a place whose architecture presents the history of Portugal. Senhor Eschwege, unite the architectural styles of the Mudejars of Spain and the Arabian buildings of Algeria. Bring stones, woods, tiles, and glass together in such a way that no epoch, no culture, neither the Islamic nor the Christian hinders or constricts the other. The most important thing, leave the stone bench untouched in that place from which King Manoel looked at the discoverer Pedro Cabral three hundred and fifty years ago, the man who reported to him about Brazil..."

It was two days after Fernando's birthday, on October 31, 1838, when Luís came into the world.

Eulalia ran back and forth in the room, straightened out tables and screens, called for water, for soap, and pressed Fernando onto a chair: "The doctors later. Remain in the room as a witness."

Eulalia expected a long and strenuous birth phase, but then the cut-glass bottle of lavender water fell out of her hand: "It's coming," she cried, and half an hour later, "An extremely beautiful child, Maria Glória. He has your dark hair!"

In Fernando's embraces Maria Glória whispered: "Now you will buy it. You promised that when this child came into the world you would buy the Pena Monastery in Sintra,"

"I've already done that. It already belongs to us. We'll plant the arbor vitae for Luís in Sintra."

She had the newborn child lying on her belly. It whimpered softly, and Fernando placed the one-year-old Pedro on her bed. "Look, you have a brother."

In Sintra the park is so dense and large that you can get lost in it and you can find refuge in it. You can float up and down the hills. Was the year 1838 a woman or a man or a tree that waited for her in front of the Pena Monastery and invited? "Come, there is a place of refuge for everyone, and yours is here."

To rotate once through the twelve units, the twelve years of the clock of life. "How often can you begin anew?" she had asked Leonora as a thirteen-year-old when she wanted to travel from Paris to Lisbon at last. "You don't know how often you will be drawn through the ebb and flow, some people seven or eight times, some only twice, not even three times."

The year 1838, "It is my best year. What could I use to beg for myself an expansion of this year into my next one?" she wrote in her diary. She needed glistening things around her. She had the frames of the pictures gilded. She wanted to have a mirror on every wall, and on the ceiling she had them paint the hibiscus bush behind which she had hidden from her sisters with Loirinho, with her brother Pedrinho in the garden of *Boa Vista*. "Paint here four hummingbirds, Januária, Francisca, Paula Mariana, and Pedrinho, each a hummingbird, a flower-kiss."

She gradually learned to accustom herself to Fernando's deliberateness, his circumspection: "Sometimes my impatience misses a similarly quick-tempered disposition in my husband. It costs me some practice to adjust to his tempo," she wrote to Clementine.

The organization and distribution of duties began: "I shall focus my entire effort on the erection of schools, of all places of education, as well as the hospitals..."

Fernando collected works of art: "The pictures and the three sculptures will be purchased by my husband Dom Fernando personally and placed at the disposal of the academy for instructional purposes."

Then the year 1839, a year of recuperation. Her little sons grew. Pedro was already forming his first words and Luís attempted his first steps already at the age of ten months.

In the year 1840 she began to display flowers, to drape flowers everywhere, on consoles, in bowls and vases. She longed for the presence of a girl, and it had actually been a girl. On October 4, 1840 Maria had come into the world - "an extremely beautiful daughter born." Nobody could answer the question of why the lovely child had died hours after her birth.

The year 1840 exhibited hostility. It showed her that she could not bar the door to hostile things: "I inform the state council that the money for building the road to Sintra and on up to the monastery building of Pena comes without exception from my husband's private fortune. In addition, the claim that begging people were being gathered from the streets like slaves to carry out the work is shameful! My husband brings men of youth and strength to Pena, who beg for their daily sustenance in the streets of Lisbon and who earn their living for many months doing road construction. I can hardly give enough expression to my indignation. I shall not sign the next 'ordinance' for dealing with the severe problem of the beggars in Lisbon until the poor people are told through criers and intermediaries that work and pay are available for them in the new paper factory, in the dye works and tanneries, as well as in the construction project in Sintra..."

In the city the harvest festival was celebrated, the first one in years without demonstrations by revolutionary groups. The god Chronos danced as the main figure among the pushcarts and barrels that had grapes and olives hanging all over them. Maria Glória had driven to São Vicente with Fernando and the three-year-old Pedro. A white child's coffin, prayers, and not letting go of Pedrinho in the process. "Maria, Marininha, she's weeping. Nene is weeping," cried little Pedro and sobbed for his little sister.

During the few hours in which Maria had lived, they had all become so accustomed to her crying, to her whimpering, that they noticed it everywhere where they knew that the little body was.

How often she had already practiced, almost drilled letting go: her mother, her father, Augusto - they had died, been torn away from her. The only thing missing had been her own child.

"I ask myself if there are pains for which you can train until you are insensitive to the constant repetitions. I pray that my soul will grow a shield that makes me insensitive. Clementine, we find no comfort..."

After the death of Maria she let the flowers in the room wither, and only when their rotting scent turned sweet did she pack everything that was wilted and dried-up into the basket.

In November a letter came from Rio de Janeiro: "Beloved sister Maria Glória, I am sending you a mango sapling that I raised from a pit myself. Even if it will never bear fruit in the cooler Lisbon, it will surely bring you blossoms, our smells, and our green. No day passes when I do not think of you, my favorite sister..." Pedrinho had written that. In that year 1840, at the age of fifteen, he had been proclaimed Emperor of Brazil. He was called the emperor with the sad eyes.

In the year 1840 a friendship also began for Maria Glória. Victoria of England married Albert, a brother of Fernando. "So we are not only almost the same age to the month, but we also have the same parents-in-law," wrote Victoria.

This relationship with England was judged to be an especially good chess move in the state council. So it had paid off to accept Fernando, the artistically minded German, as the husband of Maria Glória. Now Fernando Sachsen-Coburg-Gotha brought the good connection to Great Britain, and that was important. The house of Rothschild would continue to give generous credit. How else was Portugal supposed to pay off its debts?

But there were also problems with England: Mediators from London settled down in the harbor of Belem and shamelessly conducted illicit trade in fish, olives, and cork.

"Again one of the new aristocrats from England has settled in Belem. They wave currency around and cheat our farmers..." was how that development was castigated in the newspaper.

"Senhor Bertrand, without dwelling on formalities, I urgently request that you visit me," Maria Glória wrote to the captain.

"Dona Maria," he bowed and did not let her out of his sight. The creases in his face had grown deeper. He also had difficulty standing at attention.

Maria Glória stood before him in a light green linen dress, without a belt and jewelry, with her hair pinned up in two rolls without any curls; nothing about her beautified, neither the rings under her eyes nor the pallor of her cheeks hidden beneath rose-hip cream. Only the handkerchief that she constantly held in her hand had lace trim.

"It must smell like jasmine. Dona Dadama sends me the jasmine oil from Rio, and I panic if there is only one more bottle of it left in the house. The jasmine blossoms are silvery white or yellow-orange-red, and the clusters are so large that you can't encompass them with two hands. Those trees stand in the garden and in the avenues along the streets like parasol pines. At home, over there, in Brazil, in Rio, young girls often crept out into the woods. One night spent sleeping naked under a jasmine tree and nobody can resist her," she had told Fernando.

Bertrand looked at her for a long time. Then he said, as ingenuously as only Bertrand could: "Dona Maria, even if you hold a part of yourself, an earlier one, tightly in your hand with your handkerchief, you should not be frightened about it when obedience and fulfillment of duty slip away from you on occasion. We also have to be able to let go; we have to learn that as well."

"Senhor Bertrand, it is so difficult for me to reconcile myself to the fact that our Maria died. Children are born to live. You feel them for months and talk to them. I had already told her about *Mamãe* and about my sisters. I'm looking for an answer to the question of why we must suffer that - a punishment? For what? A test? For what? Did I give birth to my first two children too easily and therefore demonstrate too little gratitude?"

Bertrand could not say anything. There were tears in his eyes. He shrugged his shoulders helplessly.

"It really has to be enough sometime," she said, tugging at her handkerchief. "For how many thousands of hours they pounded the catechism into me, and now I don't find an answer in a single line of it. Bertrand, you remember, when Augusto died, I swore to myself to live only truthfully anymore, not to avoid the truth any more. I imagined it would be easier. I must sometimes lie away the pains that are inflicted upon me, with the scent of jasmine, with this lace. I tell my children stories of the tropics, and in all my stories there are only good fairies, animals full of beauty and confidence, flowers and trees that embrace and do not oppress each other, stones that glitter, and a sky in which every star has good intentions with regard to the others."

Bertrand understood: "We have all become people who flee, Dona Maria. I leave the room when a few officials argue with each other. Who snaps a position away from someone else more quickly? Who knows better how to defame the other person? I can't stand that anymore. Then I ride out to Vila Flora and sit under an olive tree until my soul has cleansed itself of everything. Olive trees are ancient. I believe that only good stories are hidden within them."

She listened attentively to him: "So that doesn't change. The desire to flee is given to a person like eye color. It's not a trait that can be cured."

Bertrand nodded. He kissed her hand and smelled the handkerchief. "I think they were white jasmine blossoms," he said with a smile.

Finally she began to describe his new assignment to him. The merchants from England would transact their business in a provoking manner. "Bertrand, I know of nobody but you, who can influence the Englishmen. In Belem, there is a magnificent sign attached to the front of the Taylor firm's building. The English flag waves from the roof. None of the English company's scribes speak Portuguese. Some speak Spanish with our farmers and merchants! It can be summed up this way: Our people are being exploited the way the Brazilians were exploited by their colonial masters!" She shook herself. "Senhor Bertrand, will you accept the assignment and organize proper management of trade between England and Portugal?"

Bertrand tried to stand straighter, more erect. "Yes, I'll begin with that immediately!"

In less than a year the English trade firms and the freight offices could actually no longer be distinguished from the Portuguese firms. The name placards resembled each other. Portuguese were employed as scribes and secretaries. The corrupt officials of the advisory and translation offices had to close their offices. There were even associations founded between English and Portuguese firms, "Matos & Miller."

In October of 1842 Clementine wrote: "How good that you succeeded in ending that miserable situation without getting into difficult discussions with England. Never forget - the poisonous snakes in Spain will rack their brains about how to destroy peace with England for you. As long as that Isabella has no children, she will not stop plotting - Portugal must be incorporated into Spain. Dearest Maria Glória, it is unfortunately the case that with your pacific character, with your straight dealing, you breed for yourself all kinds of enemies. The date for my wedding has now been established, March of 1843, so there is still plenty of time for embroidering the rose garlands. The picture that you sent me of tiny João is dearest of all. You write: '...although born in the autumn!' But dearest Maria Glória, you were once again in Rio with your thoughts! Your youngest was born in March and is thus a spring child!"

Clementine Orléans married August Coburg, an additional brother of Fernando.

When the newlyweds came to Lisbon at the end of April of 1843, trees and bushes were in full bloom in all the gardens. The roses were already wilting the first time, and from the Tejo blew the scent of sea animals, water, and the resin from the wharves.

Maria Glória spent weeks preparing the rooms for Clementine and August; with dried roses everywhere, the bed moved around until they could look into the sky from it, the bed curtains perfumed and the screen newly decorated. She did everything the way she would have liked to have had it for her own honeymoon. But when she had married Augusto she was in the mourning year for her father, and when she married Fernando everything was oriented toward the duty to enter into marriage. The romantic and playful elements had been missing each time.

The rooms decorated for Clementine, and in her own rooms calm and order prevailed. Clementine in the muslin dress, who ran laughing to the tearoom to let herself be caught by August; embraces, kisses, caresses - everything with the lightness that Clementine had brought along from her other world. Clementine had oils and essences infused into her bath water. Soon every corner of the living quarters smelled like those two nuptial visitors. The servants ran startled after the smells and the laughter. Did Paris consist only of joyfulness and perfume? How dully life went on in Lisbon. But they had not noticed it at all until Clementine's visit. Each person in *Necessidade* believed nevertheless that he or she had gotten the best of it. To be in the service of Dona Maria meant less hardship and fairer pay than in other households, where the reward was often only food remnants, worn-out clothes, every few weeks a few coins, and as evidence that one served in a good house a seat in the first ten rows in the church.

When Clementine and August had departed again in May, *Necessidade*, the entire castle, and the walls needed several days to find their way back to quietness again.

The year 1843 was the sixth in the circle of twelve. She had begun counting in the year 1838. She saw that year of 1838 as her best year, and the next one, with the beginning of the construction, the renovation of Pena, and the following year, 1840, that brought her a new friend, Victoria; also the year in which she had to learn about letting go in her family, with the death of little Maria; her brother in Rio was no longer Loirinho, Pedrinho - Pedro was Emperor of Brazil; then the year 1841, the fourth year, which was devoted to putting things in order, the decorating of the children's rooms with curtains on which paradise flowers floated, and with a ceiling painting, a jasmine tree in which butterflies, dragonflies, and hummingbirds buzzed. When her children lie awake they should see only beautiful things above them. Her children should not become fearful about monsters that creep out of a room's whitewashed ceiling.

The next year of 1842, in which everything was exuberance, in March the birth of João Fernando, "What a sweet child, the blond

hair of his father and the glowing eyes of his mother." Excursions to Sintra and climbing up scaffolding with Fernando; an additional tower was built, a room in which she could look in all directions, "I need only one, the one toward the ocean, in my, in the southern direction."
That fifth year with embraces and lover's oaths at the waterfall, "I had it reproduced in exact conformity with your stories."
"Yes, that is the Tijuca Waterfall of Rio. A large fern goes there yet. Pedrinho will send it. He promised."

The sixth year, the year 1843, was to become a year of work, and she caught up on things, driving the scent of Clementine from the last corner of her room. She began working with Garrett on the schoolbook: "...the Spanish kings ruled in Portugal until 1640. On Epiphany of the year 1641 António Vieira raved from the pulpit: '*If a man settles and knows nothing of the language and culture of the country, then I say to him: Take your bed and go*' - and that encouraged the Portuguese. They insisted upon independence and soon afterward Portugal was again an independent realm."

In July of 1843 Maria Anna came into the world.

"Didn't you want to name her Leopoldina?" asked Fernando.

Later, she just did not want to provoke Heaven. *Mamãe* was surely not in agreement with everything she did.

Maria Anna, a child that was begotten without any thought of duty. Had *Mamãe*, Dona Leopoldina, ever surrendered her body to desire? For Maria Glória the distance to her mother remained insurmountable. The daughter talked to her mother, but she never conversed with her mother at the same eye level. Maria Glória was unable to imagine her mother as a woman.

Maria Anna was healthy; so the sixth year was a harvest year. Had she subdued fate now? Had it finally become quiet and were distress and action no longer to be feared from anywhere? One day resembled the next. She had the drapes removed from her room. Let daytime and nighttime fall into that room in conformity with the hours.

In that sixth year she also began riding to the Menino Deus

Church. "It's too dangerous, Maria Glória. You have no idea how many hotheads there are in the city, who will lie in wait for you in the end and pull a knife on you," Eulalia said, wanting to hold her back. "Dom Fernando will never permit that," Eulalia almost threatened. "We're not in the jungle here. The queen rides to the church, perhaps even without a companion - a scandal!"

Everything about Fernando remained kind, tender, and concerned, in everything, every day to the same degree. During the initial years of their marriage she felt gratitude about that. She also hoped that Fernando would drive away the Furies that were after her on many days and in many nights. The images of her dying mother, the room in which the coffin stood; the weeping of Loirinho, "She wanted to take me with her; she is an evil woman," when Domitila wanted to abduct her little brother; the endless voyage from Rio to Brest, "I want to cry myself to death." It had been no use; she had survived the voyage.

Her months in Paris, where she sometimes saw only darkness in the middle of the glistening ballroom. "Maria Glória, I must reprimand you. For the entire evening you had a look in your eye, gloomy and distant. That's ungrateful of you! Everyone is trying so hard. Now they are even sending a new dancing instructor." Leonora was horrified by her bad behavior.

Back then she had begun to remain silent. Should she tell Leonora that when her mind, or was it her soul, was unoccupied for a few moments, when she was not occupied with a test of Latin conjugations or a conversation exercise, the Furies grabbed at her? Were they men or women who threw dark things at her from tubs and baskets with their many hands? And they reached her, everywhere.

At the dinner for her thirteenth birthday she had seen her face in the silver bowls. The little curly headed girl laughed, and suddenly the Furies had thrown their shadows at her. Her father would travel to the Azores in the near future, and he would soon die - left alone, with everything dark around her; the glitter is only for others. Sometimes Maria Glória considered, perhaps she could conciliate the Furies with a wound, a cut on her cheek. It would have to be deep enough for the flesh to thrive wildly over it, and with that one wound she would become insensitive to all subsequent ones.

Leonora sometime looked at her reproachfully when the heaviness and darkness clouded her face and wiped away her smile. "Everyone is waiting for your smile, Dona Maria. Your smile heals. A few sentences from you and all trouble is blown away," is what most people say about her. They say, "Dona Maria is always cheerful."

Fernando knows nothing of those Furies. She has never told him about them. Fernando can enumerate all the dates that were decisive for her life: "When you were three years old, your mother had to flee from the revolutionaries, and four years later your father went to war, and during his absence your mother died..."

Dates, those events are nothing more than dates for Fernando. In Fernando's childhood, in the years of his youth there were no dramatic turning points. A good child is well treated by fate. He travels for a few days and is at home in Coburg. His brothers write to him every month. His mother sends him addresses of the best master builders, and his father has him explain the Portuguese language to him by mail. Marrying his way to Portugal and living in Lisbon - those things make him interesting for his friends in Coburg, Brussels, and Vienna. There are so many around him who would handle things for him, intercede for him, and defend him, teachers, educators, comrades, and friends, who have not been removed by intrigue and replaced, but are always present, in letters or in person. Fernando has no dark realm, no dark figures to drag around with him.

In May of the seventh year, in the year of confrontation, Maria Glória drove out to Sintra. She wanted to steal away from Lisbon for a day.

She was also drawn to Lorenzio de Melo. He has his estate on the fork in the road that leads up to the Pena castle. Lorenzio is an Azores emigrant, and she had too little contact with those people.

She wanted to visualize and work out for herself more about the fate of the Azores emigrants, because the restrained rage and disappointment of the refugees from Miguel, the Azores emigrants, threw the country from one crisis into the next. Perhaps sometimes she could feel out and come to a solution as to how she could lead the two groups to reconciliation.

Before the dictatorship of Dom Miguel, Lorenzio had been a respected judge. When they sentenced him, his wife, and his sons to forced labor on the construction of the Evora fortress and his sons died as a result - "There nobody survived longer than three or four months. There were as many dead to bury as there were stones that Miguel had dragged up there" - he fled with his wife to Terceira. Land was already in sight when the weather turned. The ship capsized and only Lorenzio was able to swim ashore and save himself.

On Terceira he worked with the fishermen and acted as sexton in the church. When Dom Pedro finally landed in March of 1832, Lorenzio ran into the church and swung from the bell pull. He wanted the entire island to know that the exile was over. They had all run together; they had driven in carts over the stony roads to the harbor to greet Dom Pedro. They were so intoxicated with joy that it was two or three hours before they noticed that the ringing of the bell did not stop - Lorencio probably means it too well with his welcoming bell ringing. In the evening a few men went into the church. Lorenzio had gotten himself caught in the bell ropes. He was unable to free himself from them, and with his enveloped body he struck the clapper of the bell without interruption. The clangs of the bell, their force had upset the man. He laughed and screamed when the men brought him down. They cared for him for weeks, and his spirit, his soul almost became tranquil again, but he had lost his hearing.

Eulalia had told Maria Glória about Lorenzio and had also asked for the dilapidated farmstead for him. "Lorenzio could set up a horse rental business there. He would perhaps find peace there. He needs an occupation. He will not be installed as a judge again."

Maria Glória climbed out of the carriage at Lorenzio's farm.

"Just for a few hours, Leonora, and don't tell anyone." She spoke French, then loudly added in Portuguese: "Dona Leonora, send Xavier with the coach in the evening. I would like to drive back in the night."

Until Rodolfo, the coachman, passed along this bit of news, "She's having herself brought back in the night," until then nobody would notice her absence.

She wanted to ride the rest of the way to the castle, and Lorenzio got a horse. "My most docile one," he said with a smile. "I have fresh olive bread. It's still warm. May I? Do you want some?" He pointed to a bench and a table below a clump of narcissus.

The May sun warmed as it did in the summer; the narcissus flowers glittered in yellow and orange. Maria Glória remained sitting with Lorenzio, full of anticipation. She would surprise Fernando, stroll with him in the park, inspect the renovated rooms, and admire the pictures on the Dutch tiles. Was the marble table in the little inner courtyard in front of the bedroom finished?

Suddenly a coach turned into the street, Fernando's coach! He himself held the reins; Margarita sat cuddled up to him laughing. Fernando stopped next to a lilac bush and broke off some of the overhanging, fragrant clusters. With kisses he handed the flower sprays to the singer, and then he was already sweeping onward, up toward Pena.

Maria Glória sat motionless for a few seconds.

Eulalia had already often tried to tell her about Margarita Löwenberg-Hensler: "Dom Fernando is also supporting singers of late, I mean that female singer. Her name is Margarita."

Maria Glória had shrugged her shoulders at that. She had not even thought about it.

Lorenzio stroked her hand. He refilled her wineglass. How could he comfort her?

"Just leave it alone," she said. "She has already been in Lisbon for several months. She comes from Brussels, or from Cologne. She speaks German. I speak only a few words of that language."

She looked down at herself as if she were looking at a stranger: The dress unadorned, everything about her female body formless and stretched, adapted to letting babies grow in it; her breasts heavy from milk that comes and goes, her arms and legs swollen, her neck thick and fleshy, but soft for children's mouths that cuddled up to it; in her hair the first white strands.

"Now I have become twenty-five years old, a short period of time, and it seems so infinitely long to me. Many wish me a doubling of my lifetime. I do not want to imagine that, for, to tell the truth, I do not believe that I have the strength for it. Dearest Clementine, thank you very much for your tinctures, but I shall not use them. The white strands in my hair soothe me, they do not frighten me..." she had written a month earlier, in April of 1844.

She remained sitting with Lorenzio. A piece of her ego had collapsed. She felt as if she were maimed, while nothing about her external appearance had changed. Actually nothing had happened to her.

When it became dark, Maria Glória rode back to Lisbon.

"Dona Maria, impossible, you can't go alone. That road is dangerous, and you would need the entire night for it. It's too far." Lorenzio wanted to place himself in her way, but she did not permit herself to be detained.

"Lorenzio, visit me sometime in *Necessidade*. Someday you should give up your seclusion here," she said to him.

She had planned to tell him that he was needed, that she had assignments for him, and that she wanted to do everything so that he could overcome the humiliations of exile. Above all, she wanted to ask him: How were the two groups, the Miguelists and the refugees from Miguel, supposed to find their way to each other, when people like him, Lorenzio, refused reconciliation?

But she did not say a single word of all that. The image of Fernando and Margarita choked her, and without concerning herself any further with Lorenzio, she rode off.

In that night, as she rode through the avenues and the deciduous forests in the semi-darkness of the moonlight, toward the distant lights of Lisbon, she was grateful to her Furies, for they reserved the inflicting of pain for themselves, and Maria Glória was experienced in taking blows.

"How many lives dwell in each of us? In Fernando, one more than I was aware of before. Margarita will depart in a few weeks," she wrote in her diary the next day.

Beginning in that May, in that seventh year, she had also begun walking alone through Lisbon, driving the boys, Pedro and Luís, to church in the open carriage.

"At some time somebody will shoot them," it was whispered. "The people have a right to know that I am alive, and they can see that for themselves every day. It is not true that my coach is equipped with gold-brocaded cushions and that I have white horses sent to me from Venice. Our children have playmates from every quarter of the city."

She often had to stop four or five times during a single trip to church: "*Mamãe*, Eduardo lives here. He wants to show me his new rabbit." - "*Mamãe*, I want to let Cristina and Alfonso ride with us." - "Let's take Alvaro home with us, *Mamãe*. He's helping me with the geometry assignments."

The year 1844 continued to use itself up. She was expecting a baby again and she was looking forward to it. Even Fernando said that he was happy. She no longer believed him; she no longer believed everything he said. "Why the one part of Fernando, the effusive one, remained closed to me - I often ask myself that when he breathes evenly next to me. And I have worked out as an answer for myself that rapture and exuberance would not be the right second half for me. You see, Clementine, each of us has fled into our own world of ideas. We no longer tell each other everything, and I can say that I am more experienced at that - raised to smile and be quiet, and to live as a refugee among cheerful people, I have been practicing that since my twelfth year. Fernando does not have as good a command of that discipline..."

He told her about the plans for the living quarters in Pena. "Eschwege will panel the entire room with Brazil wood, and bathroom facilities go here. It is the latest thing from London. From a vessel similar to a lampshade it rains on your body. That will do you good..."

Then the year 1845, an eighth one in her life clock: "The four, the eight, and the twelve define the limits for us," Leonora had often explained to her. In February of 1845 she brought Antonia into the world: "This child did not want to be born head first. For that reason, dear friend, after those torments I share your reservations about talking only joyfully about a birth...," she wrote to Victoria in London.

She had not written about her greatest worry: "Dona Maria, on her right leg Antonia has, I mean, her little right leg hangs limp on her little body," Eulalia said in despair, and nobody could overlook it any longer. The three-day-old child had a lame leg.

"I kicked at the doctor," Maria Glória sobbed. "He tugged at the child with his tools, turned and twisted it. It must have happened while he was doing that."

Leonora was able to tell her, "In the Alfandega quarter there is the Fountain of Saint Beatrice. It is said that the water has many powers. But you can't put it into pots or into barrels. The water has to be applied directly to the lame legs or the dislocated arms."

Fernando was carrying the little girl in his arms. He hummed a song to her. "The weather is mild. I'll drive out there with Antoninha yet today," he had decided.

"Impossible, that will mean death for the child," Eulalia almost tore the newborn from his arms.

"Give the baby here," Maria Glória ordered. "We'll go immediately. Leonora will come along."

Circles of all colors danced in front of her eyes. She had lost a lot of blood and she was weary. But the baby could not be permitted to die. She did not want to have to bury a child again. She wrapped a woolen shawl from Eulalia around her head. Fernando slipped into the pants and the jacket of a coachman, and thus disguised, Fernando drove - a coachman with his family - to Alfandega early on the February morning.

At the Beatrice Fountain a cluster of people stood around the stone trough. Each of them wanted to hold his leg, his arm, and some of them their necks under the jet of water for a long and even longer time. In so doing they spoke their prayers aloud and begged saints and gods for help, for relief.

When it was finally their turn, Antonia had fallen asleep. At the first touch of the icy water the baby cried out and broke off in the middle of her scream. Antonia was no longer breathing; a cramp gripped the baby's entire body. A few women had immediately rushed up, and with Leonora and Maria Glória many hands rubbed and massaged the infant that Fernando held in his hands. After a few minutes the women gradually went away. "Nothing more will help her," they murmured. Only Leonora did not stop massaging, tickling, and caressing Antonia. "She's breathing, but just very softly, too little, still much too little," she said, until Antonia suddenly sneezed and screamed and cried and angrily began to kick with both legs.

Antonia was well.

Three weeks later Leonora had died. "Dona Maria, I won't awaken you tomorrow. I shall keep to my bed for a while."

"You're feverish, Leonora. I'll send for Doctor Calvez immediately," Maria Glória reassured her lady in waiting.

When she looked up from her papers at Leonora, she was startled. Could a person grow smaller in a few hours? The gray figure stood in front of her looking as if she had withdrawn into herself. "Come, I'll accompany you to your room, and I'll read a story to you the way you so often did to me. 'The girl looked for gold, for glitter in everything, and since she did not want to see anything else, she found in every gray, in every brown and black, a strip, a thread of the glow. She even saw gold shimmering in the pelt of her dog.'"

Leonora smiled, slept, awakened, and held Maria Glória's hand: "Everything is taken care of, Dona Maria. Little Antonia will become a strong child."

She let herself grow weaker, and a week later Dona Leonora had died.

"We all miss Dona Leonora, and she is missed everywhere. The news that is on the black-bordered paper has not really reached me yet - in the next moment the door will open and she will come to get me. Today we'll inspect the *Necessita Hospital* - that is the way life should go on here, I believe. Clementine, she died as conscientiously as she lived. Her diaries tightly bound with string, the training books for our children Pedro, Luís, João, Maria Anna, and Antonia lying meticulously next to each other on her desk. The last line in the book for Luís is: 'Once again I detected the fact that he cannot refrain from reprimanding his sister Maria Anna.' How carelessly I watch the six-year-old, that I have not yet noticed that misbehavior in him. We will keep everything good that she contributed to life in *Necessidade*, but where will I go now, when I am choked by *saudade*?"

In the year 1845 a civil war threatened, another civil war.

"To give you a clear picture, Dona Maria, in Minho the people feel that they are forgotten. That northern province would like to turn away from us. In Porto, and Porto is a wealthy city, they publish their own newspaper, where it is reported that all the taxes are used only here in the South, only for the people here in the South. The people north of Porto live in a state of melancholy that robs them of all their strength. The fields lie fallow and the storehouses are empty. Perhaps we should resettle people from the South in Minho in the North," António Costa Cabral wrote that in June of 1845. "I am always your defender, your protector."

She carried the letter with her for days. Costa Cabra's handwriting was similar to her father's handwriting, and it was not only in his handwriting that Costa Cabral resembled her father. He also resembled him in his determination to pursue his goals and in his violent fits of temper. "Everyone trembles in the face of his screaming fits. He chases a little scribe out of his office if he shoves a portfolio onto his desk from the front and not from the left side."

Maria Glória did not want to be drawn again into the fury of a revolt. She wanted no interruption of her routine in *Necessidade*, with her children growing up, with the discussions about an additional tower and a larger inner courtyard in Pena. "Eschwege brought plans from Cairo. The pillars of the arcades will be placed so that only the morning sun reaches that place. The morning sunlight is still unused; it has the most powers."

Reflections about an invitation to Belem, to Dona Amelia's summer festival: "Dearest daughter, I shall also organize a fishing contest in which your sons Pedro, Luís, and João can prove their agility..." But then she did not accept the invitation after all.

Isabel of Goias, her half-sister, was twenty-one years old. "Fate has set many things right for Isabel again. She is married to Count Max Treuberg. You have known that for a long time..."

Maria Glória had often formulated letter texts to Isabel, but she never found the right tone. They had the same father and the same country of birth. In the initial years of their lives they had played in the same rooms. They had learned to ride on the same horse and had nonetheless remained strangers to each other. Graça had followed Isabel. Graça had succeeded in getting Isabel moved from Paris to London. Isabel probably wrote to Graça, and with that Maria Glória always pushed any thought of Isabel aside. Perhaps Isabel wrote to her and the letter did not reach Maria Glória.

Nor did she fight anymore against the fact that even reports and letters of the ministers had been opened when they reached her, had already been read umpteen times in advance by secretaries and messengers before the documents reached her desk. It would have been misunderstood. They would have interpreted it against her. Until 1851 they always interpreted everything against her: "Now she is carrying on a secret correspondence with the chancellor of the treasury. In it she is surely begging for money for the Pena Castle."

The political climate came to a boil, once again. Minister António Costa Cabral met with hostility from every side, and if they hit Cabral, they also hit her, Maria II, for they both had the same political attitude, moderately liberal. Everyone knew that.

They wrote in the newspaper, "Costa Cabral was raised in London. He lives completely according to the English lifestyle: In England people shake hands with each other; in England they greet with an open gaze; and he wants to introduce all those freedoms here in our country. With that he wants to divert our attention from the fact that he is not a nobleman. In Lisbon, however, the prime ministers have always been noblemen!"

From the newspaper Maria Glória also knew that António Cabral had carried on a discussion about marriage without a church ceremony with Herculano in the state council.

"In the future the mayor of every village should have the right to declare a man and a woman to be a married couple through consultation in front of witnesses. Both Cabral and Herculano alternately explained that with that the superiority of the priests should be kept in check. We, however, ask: What kind of thinkers are we maintaining, who kill our religiosity?"

How often Maria Glória was addressed by young women in front of the church: "Dona Maria, please help me. Father Umberto doesn't want to marry us. I already have a child from one who didn't marry me, but this one now wants to marry me. We've been living on the street for half a year because they chase us away everywhere. They don't want to tolerate me anywhere with my belly and my child born in sin. I worked in the slaughterhouse, and Jorge, he's the best leather cutter, but the priests are everywhere. They tell a master that he has to kick us out. Otherwise he will be turned in to an official and have to close his business. And the priests can buy any official because they still have jugs full of coins from the Miguel era in their tabernacles. Dona Maria, if we don't get married, we won't find any work or any place to sleep anymore. Please..."

Maria Glória wrote letters to the bishop. The answers repeated themselves: "I shall personally attend to the fate of that poor woman and I assure you, Dona Maria, once again, that none of my priests and fathers influences business matters. Our responsibility is taking care of the soul. However, in our spiritual ministry we have to render strict obedience to the commandments..."

She could not help even those women, for nothing could be achieved against the bishop's smooth answers.

She sent Eulalia regularly to the church squares. Eulalia took baskets with corn pancakes, baked codfish, and fruits. "It's not only too little each time, Dona Maria, the people don't dare take our alms."

Maria Glória did not understand. "Taking bread from the Queen's basket means being against the ultraliberal government, and they lie in wait for each other. 'She took a Bragança pancake,' they hiss, and they again lose work and a hiding place to sleep."
Maria Glória was at a loss: "Perhaps we could take the baskets to the monastery?"
"Dona Maria, then nobody will find out that the alms come from you." Eulalia was completely beside herself: "They all greet you with hostility. You don't deserve that!"
"Eulalia, the people are begging. They have no work and nothing to eat! It doesn't matter from whom help comes. Help has to be given. Let's try it at the monastery. Word will get around that people can get a meal there!"

Franz Liszt's Visit to Lisbon, August 1845
"He conquers sensual pleasure and craving"

In August of that eighth year of her life's circle, in August of 1845, Franz Liszt had come to Lisbon.
"Mama kept her word," Fernando was beside himself with joy. "Liszt grew up in the same town as Mama, in Raiding. She often talked about his grandparents - in the Liszt family there is music for breakfast, for dinner, and for supper, and now that genius is coming to Lisbon!"
"Will you persuade him to give a private concert?" she asked. "Then we can invite Minister Costa Cabral and naturally Garrett and Herculano."
"Liszt will surely do that for us, give a private concert. Mama undoubtedly furnished him with a leather bag full of coins, and if that should not be enough, I'll add a few coins to it," Fernando said excitedly.

Without further advance notice, a coach had stopped one afternoon in front of the main gate of *Necessidade*, and after a fierce exchange of words the guards permitted the coach to drive through the garden to the castle.

"A little dwarf is sitting inside it, and the coachman claims it is Franz Liszt. Who is that?" she heard the doormen tell others.

Maria Glória ran down the stairs.

"Dona Maria, he should wait," cried Eulalia, and Mateu, the majordomo, shook his head. "We received no card about the arrival of Senhor Liszt. Besides that, Dom Fernando is in Sintra. Meanwhile we will house the guest in the north wing. Then an official reception dinner can be arranged in the next few days."

"Mateu," Maria Glória almost yelled at him, "you'll come with me right now to welcome Senhor Liszt on behalf of the entire domestic staff."

Mateu and Maria Glória walked toward the coach. There actually was a slender man standing next to the open carriage door, but his gray eyes stared piercingly at them. Nothing about that slenderness made a frail or weary impression. On the contrary, they both felt the power that radiated from this man in the gray travel suit. Mateu, in dark blue livery, with a freshly ironed collar and his hair tamed with oils, and she, Maria Glória, in her housedress, unbleached linen that laid itself in folds around her body, the leather belt well-worn, and on the dress the traces of João's little mouth. The three-year-old had found fresh cocoa beans and had fled screaming to Maria Glória with a violet mouth, "Bitter, bitter," and had wiped his little mouth off on her dress.

They made a remarkable pair. Franz Liszt thought for a few moments and then said to Mateu: "Dom Fernando, I've arrived a week earlier, but the climate in Barcelona was horrible."

"My husband will be very happy that you are already here, Master Liszt. He's in Sintra today. We bid you a cordial welcome here in *Necessidade*," Maria Glória said to him in greeting.

Liszt attempted a few gestures of apology. What an embarrassing mistake. He had taken the queen for the lady-in-waiting. "On behalf of the entire domestic staff I bid you a hearty welcome. I shall personally attend to whatever can enhance your stay in Lisbon," said Mateu with a bow, visibly flattered that he had been taken for Dom Fernando.

Franz Liszt immediately turned his attention only toward Maria Glória any longer: "You have a magnificently beautiful garden." And he walked a few paces toward the avenue of roses.

"Master Liszt, during the first few hours you'll experience quite a mess," she laughed. "You see it in my outward appearance. We were not yet prepared for you to come already. Nor has a genius ever lived within these walls. Hopefully your nerves are not too easily irritated, because our children will lie in wait for you everywhere and watch you. I've already talked so much about you. Pedro and Luís straightened the desk in your room for hours, just so that you can compose by morning light. Or do you prefer the evening hours for that?" she said and walked along the avenue with Liszt, past the roses to the fig trees and the hydrangeas.

He did not say anything, just listened to her, stopped and looked into the trees, into the blossoms.

"Do you also speak German, Dona Maria?" he suddenly asked, measuring her. He followed every line with his eyes, the crease between her eyes, her eyebrows and her cheeks, her mouth, the corners of her mouth, which pointed more downward than upward. Her face became flushed. As if hypnotized she let this gray-clothed man take her hand, let him kiss it and kiss it again. "Your voice fits your eyes precisely, Dona Maria. Maria, that's the maternal part of you. Don't you have a second name, Glória?"

She tore her hand away from him. "For the Portuguese 'Maria' is enough. The other name is too...it isn't suited for here," she blurted out, as if it were an order. "Master Liszt, I hope that you will feel comfortable with us." With that, she turned around and ran back along the avenue, the endless avenue, to the house.

Maria Glória hastened into her workroom. She wanted to be alone. A sob shook her thoroughly. When had she stopped feeling like a woman and turned into a mother animal? There were those hours in the night when she lay awake and drew Augusto into her bed. He then had to throw his arms around her and peel her out of her corpulent body with his kisses and embraces. He had to make the woman in her glow and moan, and not until then did she let him return to his world apart. But there was nothing left from those dreams for the illuminated days. She remained for everyone, even for herself, the plump, dutiful Dona Maria, and as if she had to take leave of the woman in her more and more, she wept and sobbed - the pain of *saudade* almost tore her soul to pieces, *saudade* for her earlier self.

Liszt had soon brought a state of unrest into the house. Everything seemed to whirr around that man, and nobody was able to escape from his commands. And they were all commands that he sent out with his eyes. At dinner Mateu hastily removed the bowl with the gladiolas from the table. "Those flowers are corpses. They have no place on the food table," Liszt had determined, and when Fernado hummed in front of Master Liszt's room one afternoon, to rock the six-month-old Antonia to sleep, Liszt burst from his room shouting: "Is this a children's home here? I need quiet!"

Eulalia stuck colored combs into her hair and wound white lace into her collar. "A rather special person," she whispered. "He admired my walk, Dona Maria. He said to me that he had never heard that a woman could walk as rhythmically as I can," and she again tried a few of her capering steps.

Master Liszt's official visitation program had quickly unwound. He opened a music school, "the first school for musical education in Lisbon." He gave a lecture at the Academy of Fine Arts and talked about music in the colors. At the behest of the government Maria Glória presented him with a medal. He met with the bishop and with Mario Marereles, the university professor from Coimbra. Marereles approached Liszt in his black university garb and said, "As a representative of the free intellectuals of Coimbra, I bring you the greetings of our movement - freedom, equality, and fraternity."

Then the concerts in the newly erected theater took place. The first evening passed quietly. The people came to experience the famous Liszt. But on the second evening the people, especially the women, went completely wild. They almost trampled each other down. Almost everyone who had experienced him at the lecture, the way he lithely drew every note from the keys with his elegant fingers, the way he formed the most daring musical expressions into perfect harmony with his touch - everyone wanted to see him, to hear and experience him once more. "We stood, for two or three hours, Dona Maria. I have never experienced a Mass that made me tremble the way that man's piano playing did. Will you go again, too," Eulalia wanted to know.

"No, Master Liszt will give a private concert here, and then," she took a deep breath, "then he will hopefully depart."

Eulalia did not understand. Dona Maria had never spoken that way about a guest before.

"Eulalia, for me, for all of us, this guest is too arduous. Besides that, he saw and heard enough in *Necessidade* long ago. He will be able to report much to my mother-in-law, Dona Antonia, about me, about the children, about Dom Fernando, even about you, Eulalia. And for that he will let himself be paid once more, even well. It will soon be over."

On the day of the concert that Liszt gave in the red drawing room of *Necessidade*, Fernando left the house very early in the morning. "I'm meeting with Eschwege and the workmen. We're driving out to Belem. A load of Brazil wood arrived yesterday, and we'll select the lumber together," he responded to her "Today of all days?"

"I'll be back long before the concert, and the farewell dinner is not until tomorrow."

Fernando capered around his desk; he randomly packed papers into his portfolio; he threw letters on top of each other. "Until late this afternoon," a kiss on her forehead, on her neck.

What was her name this time?

She became more and more furious and despondent about his unchanging politeness and his friendliness. When had he become unattainable for her? Was there no object in the entire house that she could throw at him, that would actually reach him? He would embrace her the way you embrace a child and tell her about Sintra, "The façade of the side towers will gleam in red. Perhaps we'll get the red of a hibiscus blossom."

She remained sitting at the breakfast table and spooned up thickly stirred chocolate. She heard Fernando's voice as he urged the coachman. When had that other part of herself, the loud, effervescent one been lost? A weary woman pulled herself up from the breakfast table. Her legs hurt. She could hardly hold her back straight. Antonia screamed. The seven-month-old child wanted to be carried. The little girl was already getting her every wish by screaming and by sheer obstinacy. The other woman that she had been earlier would have jumped up and shoved Lucia, the nursemaid, away, and she, herself, would have marched up and down the halls with the child. She would have carried Antonia into the garden and sung songs to her. She would have bathed Antonia until the little sulky child had finally had enough attention. What enormous powers that other woman had had at her disposal. Nothing had wearied her and nothing had exhausted her. Siesta hours - she did not permit herself such periods of rest. That other woman had never needed hours of recuperation, of dozing.

Maria Glória fled into her writing room. She did not want to carry a screaming child around now. Randomly she reached for papers that she simply stared at.

When Eulalia checked on her from the doorway - no, better not to disturb. Dona Maria is working.

Then an exchange of words between Eulalia and Mateu. "I shall never pass that on. Dona Leonora wouldn't have done it either," Eulalia scolded.

"Go away," snarled Mateu, and in the next moment he stood in Maria Glória's room.

"Dona Maria, a note card was left here, from Dona Amelia," and briskly, without waiting for a word from her, he drew nearer and held the tray out to her.

With regard to the two parties of servants, Mateu sided with those who were loyal to Fernando. He did not feel that he was completely Portuguese. His father was an Englishman, at least he told everyone that. And when Fernando, "the German," came into the house, he said condescendingly to the servants of the "Dona Maria party": "No idea of order and cleanliness, as a German is accustomed to it, as a German expects it."

When Liszt, upon his arrival, mistook Mateu for Fernando for a moment, and her, Dona Maria, for a servant, he not only took that as the greatest honor, but for him it was also evidence that he imitated the attitudes of his lord so perfectly that they already mistook him for the other man.

"When did this note card arrive?" she asked.

"Already yesterday evening," he reported peevishly. "Dona Maria, your lady-in-waiting is obviously not accustomed to carrying out orders immediately. Pardon me, I just found out by chance that this dispatch had not yet been given to you."

"Yes, yes," she answered, and she turned away.

He understood and slipped out the door with a persistent "Pardon me, Dona Maria, your Majesty, I beg your pardon."

The note was only loosely closed. So Eulalia had already read it. "Dearest daughter, how I envy you for having lived under the same roof for so many days with a genius. It is too bad that there was no time to visit me in Belem. I have the joyful news that Margarita Löwenberg-Hensler is in Lisbon again. Next week she will present an evening of songs in my modest home, and I hope..."

"Dona Maria, you should not read that," Eulalia implored Maria Glória. "That singer, what kind of woman is she? She will bring unhappiness into this house. She even followed Master Liszt! He has a letter from her lying between his sheets of music. She writes in a different language, but 'Margarita' was easy to decipher."

Maria Glória could hardly listen to her. "Margarita!" she blurted out. Rage and anger rose within her and choked her. Sweat ran down her neck. She tugged at her hairpins, everything bothered her, her dress was too tight, and her hair was drawn back too tightly. She saw Margarita before her, sitting in the coach, leaning against Fernando. Margarita with her blonde, open hair, with her body wrapped in an airy dress; she saw Margarita as she lowered her face into the lilac cluster. "No," Maria Glória almost screamed, and she stood up.

Eulalia had been watching her. What had happened? "Dona Maria, should I get a glass of water...?"

"No," Maria Glória interrupted her confidante. "It is my wish that you never hold back a message again, whatever it may be, but that you pass everything on to me without delay. Eulalia, there is no place in our house for intriguers and conspirators, nor for women whose illusions take them into a world of appearances."

"Dona Maria," Eulalia let the tears run down her cheeks, "that Margarita will bring unhappiness, and Dona Amelia is also having a bad time again. Why do you punish me?"

"Bring João and Antonia to me. I want to walk in the garden with the little ones," she ordered. She did not want to hear anything more, nor talk any longer about domestic discord.

She walked with the children to the beds with the asters and the zinnias.

"Your grandma, Dona Leopoldina, said that she didn't like asters and zinnias. For, when these flowers bloom autumn is already very near in Europe," she explained.

"Which flowers did Grandma like best in Rio?" Antonia wanted to know.

"Roses," Maria Glória knew very well, "and the orange and purple paradise flowers. One of those enormous blossoms was always on her desk."

"When do zinnias grow in Rio, in March or in April? Or don't they grow there at all?" Antonia continued, and Maria Glória did not answer her again. She helped the children pick the autumn flowers. Her thoughts were with Fernando. At that same time he was assuredly sunk in embraces, in conversation with Margarita. They surely spoke German with each other.

Should she have made a greater effort to become at home in Fernando's native language? "I do not like the music of the German language very well. Just the word *ich* [I], how it scratches. How well *eu* snuggles up to every word," she tried to convince Fernando about Portuguese when he had only been in *Necessidade* for a few weeks.

"My dearly treasured Christina, you succeeded masterfully in your discourse about wandering between the cultures. You are correct in saying that the only one who is able to wander in another culture is the one who masters the language of that culture. We both know that not only the spoken word is meant with that. We can study a language to the point of absolute perfection, but we will never overcome the last foreignness. Our body language remains untranslatable. The language in which we remain silent, in which we conceal, remains a sealed letter for the one who wants to approach our soul. So the last step into another language, into another culture can never be taken. We have to know that and accept it as fact. That, beloved Christina, is where my concern for you begins - the friendship with the proud Roman taxes you greatly, for I read behind your words despondency and insecurity! My dearly beloved, what are they doing to you? You are the language genius, and for that reason they have left the work of overcoming language and culture to you. Christina, you will soon be a stranger to yourself. For that reason I advise you: send the boy traveling. Recuperate and write me one of your threatening letters again. A test for your spiritual recovery could be: either I praise your well-developed figure or you let yourself be shorn. I do praise your figure. I have not forgotten it, but your clear intellect is the dearest thing of all to me - you know that. My beloved, revered Queen of Sweden, threaten me. I want to hear strong words from you again. You are important to me, so that I do not lose myself completely in my cunning defense phrases..."

The political situation had already taken a dangerous direction again weeks earlier. There was talk of revolt, of civil war, and a confidential conversation with António Costa Cabral could not be postponed. However, where could she talk with him without them immediately imputing to her: "Dona Maria is planning something. She surely intends to fight to get back the veto right."

For that reason Cabral suggested: "Dona Maria, can we have a talk right before the beginning of the concert?"

He closed the door. "That's one more scandal again now, but what kind of behavior will they expect of me anyway," he laughed.

"I'm the only commoner at this evening's party."

Maria Glória did not want to lose any time. "António, they tell me the Cabralists, the moderates, are no longer in the majority," she immediately began. "What lies ahead of us? They're keeping news from me."

Costa Cabral went to the window and closed the drapes. "Perhaps the ultraliberals in Coimbra have already begun shooting at each other. Although there are also Cabral loyalists in Coimbra, they are in the minority. Most of them cheer Saldanha. For the people, he's the more liberal one. He also talks about being the better Portuguese."

"But everything that they cast in our teeth is lies, dragged in by the hair." Maria Glória wrung her hands. "Dom Fernando is paying for the construction of Pena from his private funds. Why don't they write that in the newspaper? Why don't they set that right at last?"

António smiled bitterly. "Because it doesn't fit into the plans of the ultraliberals."

"What about the construction of the railroad? I haven't heard any further report about it for a year," she continued.

"They say, up to now shipping from north to south has been sufficient!" Costa Cabral tugged at his hair. "And in the same breath they reproach us for not having built enough schools in Minho. At the same time, no city can develop outside of Porto because the people have no roads to each other. The farmers live completely cut off from the world."

"They reject the railroad because it comes from England," Maria Glória blurted out. "Because I'm related to Victoria, so to speak, through my husband, the anti-Cabral people are even more hostile toward me. Besides that, I made the mistake of talking too loudly about my friendship with Victoria. 'How long will it take until we're a colony of England again?' That's what they're saying. That was reported to me."

Cabral nodded. "They call themselves ultraliberals, and call us, because we want to introduce civil marriage, because we want to put limits on the power of the Church, murderers of religion!"

"It was a great mistake of my father's not to take legal steps to punish the Miguel fanatics and lock them up behind bars. They have therefore remained fanatics! Father even gave Miguel money in addition: 'He is my brother!' Who knows? Maybe Miguel is now supporting his former followers from a safe distance, from Baden-Baden," she said, and she shook herself.

"Which is why I wanted to talk to you, Dona Maria. Before another year has passed, I shall have to leave Portugal," Cabral began.

She could not follow him.

"You know, Dona Maria, in order to make the people tractable for an idea, for a revolution, you need an individual, a figure! A government can never be as hated as despised as a person who lives among us - and I am that one. Cabral is responsible for the Church losing its power. Cabral devotes his personal ambition to making the South, thus Lisbon, into the intellectual center and in so doing to letting Coimbra, the city where the heads of the intellectuals steam, where the Inquisition formulated the most cunning judgments, Coimbra degenerate intellectually into a village! Cabral is hatching out more and more prohibitions against the beggars. Cabral is bringing English engineers into the city. Why does Costa Cabral do all that? Because he is an upstart, because he wants to ingratiate himself with Dona Maria; for that reason Costa Cabral even looks away when the gold for the Pena construction in Sintra is taken from the treasurer's bag."

She listened breathlessly to him; she could not believe it all.

"So if it gets to the point, Dona Maria," Costa Cabral continued, "that this hate and this rage should shift over to you, if I feel that you and your family are threatened, then I shall write to you. No, not a letter, I shall send you a gilded hibiscus leaf. Here, I've already prepared it. When you receive that, release me. Send me out of the country immediately. Don't wait until I've formulated my official letter of resignation. Dona Maria, anything can be expected of misguided people, even execution. Don't forget, in Coimbra the students celebrate the 14th of July for days. Remember your great aunt, Marie Antoinette."

When she did not say anything to that, Cabral inquired: "What does Dom Fernando think about the political situation?"

"He has no idea about any of it, António. He has his construction project in Pena. Fernando is a good-hearted husband. I couldn't wish for a better one. But his goodness is wearisome. António, sometimes I have the feeling that Fernando and I stand on two different continents. We never really reach each other." She was appalled. What was she saying? "Soon *saudade* will confuse my mind entirely," she murmured. And with that murmur she had approached António and he had caught her in his arms. "That you vanish in the calyx of the hibiscus blossom..." How did António know that line? Loving couples whispered those words to each other, over there, in Rio de Janeiro. Her skin vibrated under the muslin. She felt the power that flowed into her from António's arms, from those male hands. What bliss! And slowly and reluctantly she unwound herself from António's arms.

She hardly followed the concert by Franz Liszt. She sat next to Fernando. Her skin burned. All fifty or sixty guests looked at her as she sat in the first row and was only able to suppress the trembling of her body with effort.

Moulinier, Dona Amelia's lady-in-waiting, shook her head without interruption. The peacock feathers on the turban of that poisonous serpent glittered in all colors. She let it be read from her face: "So the hot blood that she inherited from her father has run away with her. She locked herself in with that upstart, that slave of England, for at least two hours. Her body is almost steaming. She doesn't even brush away the wrinkles in her dress."

The atmosphere was so irritating for Master Liszt that he almost interrupted his performance and then suddenly stood up and bowed. He hurried to his room and ordered that his things be packed.

Everyone was relieved when the disturber of the peace, Liszt, left *Necessidade*. And it was a long time, several weeks before his gaze, his walk, and his orders had evaporated from all corners and nooks.

Maria Glória 1845-1849
"Then my bones turned to stone"

At the beginning of October 1845 a letter came, an envelope. "Dona Maria, the envelope is empty," said Eulalia, pointing to the open flap. "The seal has been broken." António Costa Cabral's handwriting. Was it already to that point? She had been waiting for three weeks for a report from him. Had an army *"for* the people and *against* the queen" already formed? Would those soldiers fight against the ones who were loyal to the crown? "Down with the Cabralists who have forgotten us in the North, who have brought only hunger and poverty to us in the North, so that the people in Lisbon can live even better, even more splendidly."

You could read that in the newspaper.

Maria Glória took her riding dress from the cabinet.

"Dona Maria, you shouldn't leave the house. That empty envelope, that's a plot. They want to lead you into a trap." Eulalia ran along behind her, buttoned up her riding habit, and pushed against the wall so that Maria Glória could slip into her boots. "Your legs are swollen. You should have new riding boots made for yourself," Eulalia wailed. "What should I say if they ask for you?"

"Put Maria Anna and Antonia to bed punctually. They need their naps. And remind Pedro and Luís that this evening I'll check to see how far they got weaving the rug. For João, here, give him the handkerchief. He needs a piece of *Mamãe.*"

She ran out of the room and raced down the stairs past the gawking servants, into the forecourt, and down to the stables.

Siesta time everywhere in the city, dozing merchants in front of their covered stands, swarms of flies around half-rotten fruit and above trickles of blood that crept onto the street from the slaughterhouses. She rode past the barracks. The sentries swayed in the sun, and only later did they notice the rider. It was probably someone who rode hastily into the commercial district to get hold of a few sacks of cotton. It would surely be a good deal, a few coins for the sailors, a few for the officials, a few for the owner of the schooner who transported the cotton further and for doing so collected a sugar sack full of coins from the go-between who resold the cotton. Illegal trade - everyone knew about it; they all shrugged their shoulders at it. She flew through the backyards in Estrella; she scattered chickens and pigs that were running around. In front of the Botanical Garden loafed a crowd of beggars. "Dona Maria!" one of them shouted in recognition and tried to run after her. Everywhere in the side streets: garbage, wastewater barrels that were only half-covered with sheets of wood, emaciated cats and dogs that limped their way to the shadow of a wastewater barrel.

From the Botanical Garden floated the fragrance of the autumn-blooming magnolias; the fountains threw their cascades of water across the iron fence onto the street. "It is impossible to open the garden for the people. In a short period of time it would be completely polluted and inhabited only by beggars," they said in rejecting her suggestion that "the City Garden should be opened to everyone."

In SãoVicente, in the *Rua Engracia*, the servants sat in front of the houses. What was a rider doing here without a carriage at this time?

When she dismounted and tied Chili to the almond tree, the entry door opened. António pushed his guards aside. "Dona Maria," he greeted her. "I've felt you coming for two hours. Welcome to my house!"

The glazed tiles were cool; the wood of the furniture was dark and smelled of wood stain, everywhere flowers and books. There was no luggage anywhere, no disturbed servants anywhere. Had she actually mounted up because of an insidious intrigue?

"António, an empty envelope reached me today, with your handwriting. I panicked because of it."

He nodded, took her by the arm, and led her through his writing room onto the terrace.

"Right, I sent you a dispatch. There it says: '...that an army has formed in Coimbra to fight against the current government, against the Cabralists. Dona Maria, the few soldiers who are stationed in Coimbra for the defense of your interests are deserting more and more to the ultraliberals, and it is to be feared that this hostile army will soon start out in the direction of Lisbon...' They will undoubtedly publish that text in the newspaper. Now we know how far the audacity of my, our enemies already goes. They intercept dispatches and do not pass them on."

"So, a put-up job." She gradually comprehended and drank the grape juice greedily. "António, I rode to you in panic. They will also report that. That the cause of all false decisions is rashness - that is what I learned, that is what they drummed into me. But if I can't trust anyone anymore!" she cried in despair.

She should have immediately ridden back to *Necessidade*. But she had remained in the house of Costa Cabral. Maria Glória did not think about anything anymore. She wanted to take a few hours for herself. For a short period of time she wanted to live as the Maria Glória that she had pushed away for so many years. She let herself fall into António's embrace. She took from his body and her body was taken, and finally she became familiar to herself again. It was so easy to bring out the woman in her, and only when she had lived herself out with every fiber of her body did she place herself back on her own path again.

She was still strolling with Costa Cabral through his garden, and she admired the rhododendron bush.

"Did that come from England?" she asked him.

He nodded: "I know what they say about me: If our flowers aren't enough for him, let him go to England. That's the way it goes with the emigrants. They are not liked, anywhere; not in the place to which they fled, nor the one from which they fled and to which they want to return. They don't want them there anymore either. Maria Glória, the people are uncomfortable with us, us emigrants. In England they tolerated us. We were willing workers. Who could afford a judge like me as a clerk? As an emigrant, however, I accepted any work. And how thankful we emigrants were in London for any invitation. We had again become acquainted with one or two people from London. Perhaps by watching and learning, by imitating, we could become Englishmen more quickly. Englishmen! That would never have succeeded; they would never have permitted us to do that. We were emigrants. Sometimes we remained silent too much. Then again we talked too much. We asked too much and too little. Whatever we did, we were constantly measured and observed, in everything. Even our kitchen smells - we prepared fish differently; we ate our evening meal very late. That was all strange. An emigrant has strangeness wrapped around him like a coat that drags him down and that he can no longer take off. For, to return home as an emigrant is not condoned either, and being watched, being measured does not cease anymore. Back to Lisbon with a rhododendron seedling in my basket. Maria Glória, I could finally breathe the air that blows from the Tejo up here to SãoVicente again. Very early in the morning I hurried down to the harbor to sit at breakfast with a few sailors - fried fish dipped in coriander sauce, coffee, diluted fig brandy. Some were celebrating an especially good night's fishing. Others needed a drink of liquor because they were shipping out for an extended voyage. Most of them had a day full of work at nets, masts, and boats ahead of them, and they embraced anyone who sat down with them. In those initial weeks they received us emigrants joyfully. We were the bringers of a new time, a new era. Miguel's reign of terror had been finished off at last. But where was I supposed to take lodgings?"

Costa Cabral paused, and they murmured almost simultaneously the text of a letter from António Vieira and gave each other the key words so that the sentences were formulated correctly. In the year 1670 the Jesuit father wrote: "*Beloved Christina, where can we take lodgings? If we ask that question and receive no answer to it, if they refuse to give us lodgings, we belong to the refugees, to those who are driven through the world. The denial of quarters is the most destructive sentence that they can pass. You, dearly beloved, let yourself in for discussion of this topic. You discuss freedom of lodging for the Jews in Rome. A discussion that has been needed for a long time, one that you must pursue with all relentlessness and firmness. But I send a warning: Employ all of your intelligence to reach your goal. Do not forget, the long arm of the Inquisition reaches easily from Coimbra to Rome, and it would be a special victory for the*

Grand Inquisitor if he could impose a punishment upon the Queen of Sweden! After all, they do not trust you. Your conversion to the Catholic faith was too recent. Your first religious experiences were Protestant, and childhood impressions cannot be erased, as we know. Even the Pope does not trust you. Perhaps you are a spy who intends to examine Catholicism with respect to its flexibility. We know that in Vienna they began driving out the Jews this year - what a catastrophe! Ranting and raving against it does not help. They seal our mouths; you can see that in my example. Because I preached against slavery and lashed out at the sugar hell, because I defended the Indians and denounced the colonial bloodsuckers, I had to leave Brazil, and saudade *ripped my soul open. A severe punishment, but when I spoke before the college in Lisbon and said that Portugal will suffer the greatest damage if the Jews are expelled - 'Then the English will receive both, wealth and intelligence' - the bishop threw his water glass on the ground and they all fled from me, and within hours the black-bordered yellow scroll of the Inquisition reached me, and they closed the dungeon doors behind me and forbade me to preach. Therefore, dearly beloved, I warn you once again: Argue clearly in your cause of freedom of lodging for the Jews, but not rashly, as I did. Otherwise you will not achieve quarters for the one group, and you will lose your own quarters in Rome besides. You also should not talk about your fading beauty. A person who is as filled with intelligence as you can only become more beautiful with the years, of course not for priestly knaves who are seeking for a budding body..."*

"So," António Cabral continued after pausing for breath, "where was I supposed to take quarters? Former Miguel soldiers were living with their families in my house. For them everything had deteriorated with our return, with the new era that Dom Pedro, your father, brought. What intruder would drive them from the house? A house was quickly found, but I wasn't at home any more. Because he lived in London for a few years, he thinks he knows everything better - that's how they talked, or, because he fished in the Azores, he thinks he can tell us. Maria Glória, you know it took months and years before we became accustomed to being alien and to the fact that it will never change. Maria Glória, you've adapted your Portuguese to the language of the people of Lisbon. What whispering there was when they said good-by at the first receptions with '*até logo.*' They changed that immediately, '*adeus,*' and then they looked horrified. In your homeland, in Brazil, that is used only for the ultimate farewell, the final one. No mother who has to bury her son would say good-by to him with '*Adeus.*' We'll see each other, see you soon, '*até logo,*' you wept at your father's coffin. So for those who live and end their lives unchanged in the same place, the wanderers remain foreign, and there are times when that foreignness drives too much fear into the residents. They feel themselves constantly watched and criticized by the emigrants. So nothing that they, the residents, have been doing for decades, for generations, is good enough. They toil, knuckle under, and adapt, and they are supposed to listen to criticism? They do not want, they do not tolerate that."

António pushed the boards over the rhododendron bush somewhat apart. "Now the sun doesn't have very much strength any longer. Now it can no longer harm it," he murmured.

He considered: "They will find a reason to drive me away. Until then, I won't let myself be distracted from my work. With our devotion to work, we wanderers, we refugees, are especially alien to them."

"António, I didn't know that a person could learn to turn a deaf ear. I feel as if I had become a human animal. Sometimes I'm amazed that my handwriting is still the same. No change can be seen in my handwriting. 'She is resolute to the point of heartlessness,' is what Moulinier says about me, and I'm not surprised at that. Many see me that way." She sighed, "It's not important anymore."

She took a twig with two rhododendron buds to *Necessidade*. "They should be kept cool. Perhaps we'll get them to bloom," said Eulalia. And they actually did. Just before Christmas in 1845, the petals opened and the flower clusters glowed a silky violet in the vase.

In November of 1845, there was an increase in the inflammatory articles against the Cabral loyalists, the *Cabrais*, and thus against her, the queen. "There is no medical clinic for the indigent. Souza and Mirous have given back their licenses for transporting garbage because they have not received money for their services for eight months! Soon epidemics will break out, but a piano virtuoso from Austria is playing in *Necessidade*," and, "...when the journalist wanted to ask the supreme commander of our army, Dom Fernando, about the condition of the army, Dom Fernando had no time! He was too busy listening to Dona Margarita's singing rehearsals..."

In addition they wrote: "We want to have clarified at last, where the money for the construction in Pena comes from. The workers have to say: Dom Pedro will pay their wages from his personal monetary resources. Who believes that?"

"We wish our dear Papa all the best," said the eight-year-old Pedro for his four siblings on the last day of October of the year 1845. Gifts were presented: the carpet that had been woven by Pedro and Luís; João, at the age of three, presented a drawing on which Mira, the parrot, was supposed to be visible; Maria Anna held a bouquet of carnations in her hand, with the edges of the blossoms already somewhat brown from initial frosts. Maria Glória surprised Fernando with a framed, original sheet of music by Franz Liszt. "It wasn't easy to snatch a sheet with his writing and his signature away from the strict master."

Again a few weeks of harmonious family life. She was expecting her next child. "Dearest friend, thus the year 1846 is a year for an additional child for each of us. You are hoping for a girl, and I wish for an additional son. We still do not have a Fernando, and I made a deal with Heaven, that a little Fernando should always remind me which part of my husband is for me and our children, the best part. And I never intend to venture too far into his private life again. Do not be horrified at my resignation. I hope and wish for you that you never discover anything foreign in your husband Albert and see him disappear into a land into which you cannot follow him.

But in that case, may my words of today be a comfort to you...," she wrote to Victoria in March of 1846.

In the year 1846 the census was also supposed to be completed at last. "Lisbon, Coimbra, Porto, our country must finally become countable. Every mayor, even the administrator of the smallest village is urged to accompany the officials whom we have sent out to the people, into their houses, to their farms, and to write down the names and dates of birth of all family members..." This appeal was in the newspaper for weeks.

There had never been anything like it before. "Not even when the English lived here and squandered their money did officials snoop around in our families!"

Formerly it had been sufficient if the patron, the head of the household, made known the number of people in his family. The children that he had with the servants were missing, of course. The children that were brought from the mountains in the North - "Workers are lacking in the dye works" - nobody counted them among the people in the family either. Those children that the daughters bore before they were well married were also not on any list. The children that the patron took into his household from the parish house in return for good money - "We'll raise him. Nobody will learn who his father is" - they were also not in any document.

Did that Cabral also intend in the end to create confusion in the entire family system with the newfangled census? Was not the patriarchy the only law, even if it was not written down anywhere, that the people could depend upon, that gave them security in their everyday lives?

In the second week of May in 1846 events got under way: "... is to be reported that the soldiers of the opposing ultraliberals have landed in Belem with three ships. They still remain in the barracks outside the city, but they are determined to bring about a change in the state system by force of arms." That was written by Palmela, the Minister of Trade.

An hour later, Lorenzio drove up in the courtyard. Wildly gesticulating, he shook off all the doormen and lackeys. Maria Glória ran toward him. "Dona Maria, here, I am only permitted to give it to you personally." He pressed the envelope into her hand, and without a bow he had disappeared again.

She felt the hibiscus leaf. It was cold from the morning air and tarnished. There was no writing with it. "For my queen, Dona Maria," was written on the envelope in Costa Cabral's broad handwriting.

Now she had to act, immediately. She wrote to the state council: "A revolt is at hand, and I am determined to do everything to avert a revolution. Therefore the letter of dismissal for Minister President António Costa Cabral is being delivered to you with my express wish that this termination be carried out immediately. As evidence of his complete withdrawal from all influence in public law, he will leave our country in the immediate future. In order to avoid the shedding of blood, I bow to the will of the people and pray that my decision of today will prevent injuries and deaths..."

She had waited for days for news from António. Not a line came. Then she sent out Eulalia: "Try to find out when his ship will sail."

"On the 31st of May," Eulalia whispered. "Dona Maria, you can't ride anymore, not in your condition. In six or seven weeks you'll be having a baby."

"Will you accompany me, Eulalia?"

The lady-in-waiting flinched. "Dona Maria, it's very dangerous. The entire city is full of soldiers, and they are not your soldiers!" Eulalia bit her lips: "If they recognize us..."

"Then it's high treason, and that bears the death penalty. But I want to say good-by to António Costa Cabral. They will soon strike his name from the history books. Soon nobody will know any longer that he was there for our country."

They arrived at the harbor at the break of day, with soldiers and police everywhere. There were drills; conferences were being held in groups. Some turned to look at the very pregnant woman and shook their heads. This cook probably wanted to trade palm reading for a sack of grain or a few handfuls of cotton.

António stood alone. His travel baskets were already stowed in the boat. "Carlos will accompany me, a perfect valet," he said to Maria Glória. "I can't kiss your hand. It would harm you too much. What foolhardiness, Maria Glória!"

"I wish you a good voyage," she managed to say. "And, António, come again, come back!"

Maria Glória felt how tears ran down her cheeks and her neck. "Don't leave, António! They have left so often, the people that I loved, *Mamãe, Papai*, Augusto. I just didn't want to be sent away from Rio. Of Lourinho only a secretly cut lock of hair remains in my diary. Come again, António."

He could not give any answer to that, for the coachman was already standing next to her: "Dona Maria, come. Otherwise they will yet kill us all. Please, come!"

Nobody had recognized her, and if they had, how would they have been supposed to react? The queen says good-by to Costa Cabral. That is a scandal, an affair of state!

Shouldn't she finally be dragged into court? She conspired with that Cabral for years and in so doing plunged the country into ruin, not only financially, she even turned our family order topsy-turvy. She signed the manifesto for carrying out the census, and she also supported the idea of civil marriage!"

Did she have even a single defender among the dozens of men who were at the harbor? No, not a single one.

Maria Glória had herself taken directly from the harbor to the Ajuda government office building. Eulalia wanted to hold her back.

"Eulalia, maybe they will shoot at me. It may also be that they will throw rocks at me, for now all their hate will be vented on me, but I won't lock myself up in *Necessidade* because of it." She shook off Eulalia, her good fairy. "But I don't believe it's to that point for me yet."

Vitor Palmela, the provisional minister president, came running toward her. He was wearing no collar; his jacket hung crookedly across his shoulders. "Dona Maria, what a time for a conversation."

"But Senhor Palmela, you are working too, although it's still pitch black night."

They walked slowly along the corridor to his room. Outside a thunderstorm broke. Rain lashed in through the open windows. "You're sitting in the archive chamber, quite provisionally," she said, shaking her head. "So you give your time in office only a few weeks or months?"

Palmela shrugged his shoulders. What should he say?

Maria Glória started talking. She said what should already have been said so long ago: "Senhor Palmela, nobody knows what's going on anymore. Everyone is fighting against everyone. The one group calls itself *Setembristas*, the other *Cabrais*, and the next the *Saldanhistas*. In reality they want only to take the positions away from each other. One of them has long since wanted to sit in the harbor office of the other; the other wants to have the say in the customs office; the next wants to be the supervisor over the linen weavers. We have many more soldiers than men in the fields and in the tanneries, the weaving mills, and on the wharves. Our fish are being stolen from us because our men no longer have time to work as fishermen. They prefer to be soldiers!" She was almost screaming, and she did not let herself be interrupted by Palmela, who whispered, "Dona Maria, I beg you!"

"There is no money available for so many soldiers. The people will go even more into a rage about that and have an additional reason to stir each other up and finally to revolt. And in the face of hunger their wives and children will move to Lisbon from every part of the country and languish away here, be driven away as beggars. Senhor Palmela, in recent weeks I've begun to drive to church in the carriage again, not because of my pregnancy, but because I can't bear to see the children with their swollen starving bellies, the women with their eyes in the dark sockets. I can help. I do help. We send baskets full of bread and fruit into their sector. We have our milk service. But Senhor Palmela, it's always too little, it will always be too little, and every week a few children will starve to death, and every week a woman will jump into the Tejo out of despair."

"Dona Maria, unfortunately I don't have good news from Torres Vedras," Palmela said, pointing to a packet of papers. "They began shooting at each other there yesterday. There have already been some fatalities." He looked at the floor. "They are putting everyone in prison whom they suspect of being a follower of Cabral."

"That's just the beginning. They will soon be fighting that way in Coimbra and in Santarem and in Lisbon. Senhor Cabral has departed. If I were to do the same thing!"

"Dona Maria," cried Palmela and ran out the door. He shooed away the door guard: "Bring a jug of fresh water!"

Nervously he pulled out a chair for her. "There is nobody else in the vicinity. Nobody is listening to us. Dona Maria, I implore you!"

"Senhor Palmela," she said, impatiently pushing the chair away, "you know that I won't abdicate, that I won't leave."

"No, Dom Fernando would never separate himself from the children. Everyone knows how much he loves Pedro, Luís, João, Maria Anna, and Antonia," Palmela said without thinking. He said that much too loudly, ran to the door again and again, closed it, and opened it again. What kind of situation had he gotten himself into? Would he look like a conspirator in the end, one who had participated in toppling the government? He pushed himself along the bookshelves to his desk. He could not be far enough away from that woman who apparently talked in total confusion about the departure of her friend Cabral - perhaps he actually had been her lover - without thinking about it.

"Senhor Palmela, how frightened you react, just because you are alone in your workroom with me."

Palmela moved. He wanted to contradict, but she did not let herself be interrupted: "So we constantly have to examine our view of the world with respect to the mundane and the particulars. These are the five principles that have to guide us: the individual, the society, the things of tomorrow and the future, the direction for our mind and our soul, and finally our deeds, each of which must be supported by the four previous building blocks. For forty years, the individual in our country has felt forgotten. How could it be otherwise, when my grandfather left the country to the English and fled to Brazil? We have no idea about the meaning of the term *society* - for decades each person had to defend himself, from the English officials, from the Miguelists. For decades they clung to the future, to tomorrow, hoping that it would get better. When the English are no longer governors, when Miguel reigns, when Dona Maria comes - an entire generation has been waiting since 1807 for something better, for forty years! They don't believe in it anymore. They don't believe anyone anymore. They want to take for themselves what they have been entitled to for a long time. How starved their souls and their spirits are for a direction is revealed in the fact that they cheer anyone, follow anyone who professes to give them a direction, no matter how false it is. And because they have only uncertainty and insecurity regarding the first four building blocks, for decades they have not been able to set a capstone: the deeds! They have quit working their fields, and they shake their heads when a road into the North leading to Minho is supposed to be built."

Behind the curtain of rain shimmered the morning sun. A rainbow glowed. She continued: "I wonder if they will ever, in decades, become exhausted by cheating each other, whether they will find their way back to their tasks. One teaches the other the sailing trade; the women teach the children cleanliness, and they teach them to read and write - the word *peace*."

The rainbow had disappeared. Daylight had come. From the corridor the scolding and the laughter of the water bearers could be heard.

Palmela stared at her: "I didn't know," he said, pulling himself together, "that you, Dona Maria, belong to the lodge, that you are a *maçonaria*, a Freemason."

She shook her head. "Senhor Palmela, you know that I can't be a member of the lodge. There is no provision for women there. But they can't cut me off from the knowledge," she said with a smile. "I have only explained to you what I see as my task. I'll read out these, my principles, in the state council, and they will be displayed everywhere, in every office, so that people can read what the guiding principle for my actions is and will be."

"Dona Maria," now, at last, embedded in the mundane noises of a workday, Palmela felt safe again, "arrangements will be made for Saturday to be kept open for your speech." Nervously he pushed the papers on his desk back and forth.

Maria Glória was not finished yet. "In a month, even before my Fernando comes into the world, a bank, a business will be opened in the *Retoria* building, where money matters will be managed. The loan-sharking dens will soon no longer exist. If a farmer needs money so that he can buy seed, or if the tanner needs money so that he can buy more hides, then in the future he will borrow that money from our bank, from the *Banco do Portugal*, and no loan sharks will be sitting there, but bookkeepers who were trained in the House of Rothschild."

"Lisbon will have its first independent bank. I'll have that announced immediately. We will post that everywhere - 'Wait to borrow money' - nobody is dependent on the bloodsuckers anymore," Palmela could hardly talk.

"Then I'll go now," Maria Glória nodded. There was nothing more to say or to do, and without paying any attention to the cries of "Dona Maria" that came from every nook and cranny as she scurried past, she went to the coach.

Totally exhausted by the excitement of recent days, Eulalia had fallen asleep there.

At the end of July in that year of 1846 Fernando came into the world. "He is a very beautiful child and has my husband's thick blond hair and blue eyes," she wrote to Victoria, and to Clementine she confided: "...that I love all our children, of course, but I hope that Heaven will not punish me when it is noticed - and nothing remains unnoticed above, of course - that I feel a tenderness for this little boy that I have withheld from the other children. It cannot simply be my years, twenty-seven. It is all the restrained love and tenderness for my husband Fernando that I find again in this child.

For, as I am sure you already know as a married woman, in many respects you become more foreign to one another, and many sides of the other person become so painfully foreign to us that we become extremely reserved..."

In the following, the tenth year of her life cycle, in the year 1847, the civil war reached Lisbon. For weeks there was fighting, murdering, and pillaging. Then the wounded were cared for until they were halfway healthy and the dead were buried. And hardly had the survivors gathered enough strength, when the fighting began all over again.

Thomas Southern, the English diplomat, sought for an audience for weeks. "He requests an interview with you," said Palmela helplessly. Soon he no longer waited for her answer. "We won't talk to the English about our affairs. There is nothing to discuss," she decided, and she rejected an interview with Southern.

In June of 1847 Palmela came to *Necessidade* during the midday meal.

"Dona Maria, please forgive me," he began.

"No formalities, Senhor Palmela, what is it?"

"Mr. Southern has given the order for the Pecada Prison to be opened. There are not enough food supplies for the prisoners, and Mr. Southern believes that only political prisoners are being held in that prison." Palmela held a paper in his hand. "This is the written order from Mr. Southern, which he has given to both prison directors - to be carried out within forty-eight hours, or..."

"England will declare war on us!" Maria Glória was aghast.

"At least Mr. Southern is threatening to request some troops from London for the establishment of our internal peace," and Palmela finally laid the document on her desk.

"There is something else to report," said Palmela, attempting to maintain as neutral a tone as possible. "In recent days Dom Fernando was seen together with Mr. Southern again and again. They are visiting riding stables and dye works."

"I know that," she interrupted him. "Dom Fernando is pressing to have me call on England for help. He believes that only England could bring an end to this insanity of civil war! For that reason I must even have my husband's correspondence watched! Dom Fernando isn't able to manage in our chaos. That is all too understandable. Every week, when he drives to Sintra, he has to choose a different route because there is fighting, sometimes in one street, sometimes in another."

Palmela nodded and returned to the point of departure for the conversation: "General Saldanha is waiting for an order."

"He will receive it tomorrow. Make arrangements for General Saldanha to be in the state council tomorrow at ten o'clock. My husband and I will also be there. My husband, as commander-in-chief of the army, will give the order to defend Portugal against an invasion by the English and to secure our prisons according to our laws." She had become breathless. "And yet today I shall recall our ambassador, Senhor Morais, from London, and correspondingly Mr. Southern will have to leave the country."

"We must assume that the loans will be declared due," Palmela wanted her to bear in mind.

"Obviously, but if England intends to conquer our country as its next colony, that will happen anyway. We're not going to help them as well."

There was no time to lose. She rushed to her desk almost without saying good-by.

She wrote to Jacob Rothschild: "...for which reason, without a long preamble I present a request, and I can do nothing more than make a request of you and your honorable company. Portugal is in the difficult phase of its development, and inner stability can only be found with great difficulty. But I know the people, and they all have only the one goal. They want to live in peace and quiet. They are just trying to bring that to pass by very different means. Our country was governed by foreign powers for too long. An elevated but foreign culture was imposed upon my Portuguese people for almost two decades. All of that led to a despair that is now erupting to the most horrible extent. We owe the House of Rothschild money, a great deal of money. It was used for road construction and for the expansion of the wharves. With your money we were able to erect the first hospital for the indigent, and to five schools we have affixed marble plaques on which your house is thanked for the material prerequisites that made the construction of those schools possible. It is also true that a large portion of the money that was borrowed from your house is being used to pay the soldiers, for the one party as well as the other. Now I am forced to severely limit diplomatic and political relations with England. There are misunderstandings to be cleared up, and it would be the logical consequence for your house to terminate or encumber economic relations with us. Aware that a strict word from you will suffice to destroy our country economically or to keep it alive economically, I ask you to maintain your confidence in us..." And then she added, "Senhor Jacob, eight years ago you gave me a water lily. For a long time it did not want to bloom, but for three years pink stars have been floating in the small pond behind the row of lilacs..."

Only four weeks later came the answer. In a broadly flourishing hand Jacob Rothschild wrote: "Revered Dona Maria, dear Maria Glória, everything is in order. The times may be changeable, but our house is unchangeable in its principles. When water lilies have taken root, they remain true to their water for generations..."

In the year 1847 her life's rhythm had gone into the tenth year, had risen to the culminating point of the circle of life. Many possibilities had come to her to have her work exert influence, as in no previous year. With the promise of the House of Rothschild, the financial situation was secure. Queen Victoria responded brusquely at first: "...I take note of the decision of the Portuguese government..."

In the English newspapers they sneered: "Portugal rejects the help of England! What kind of men sit in the government of Portugal, who let themselves be influenced by the queen from the jungle?"

But when Maria Glória's three boys wrote a letter to "Her honorable Majesty, Dona Victoria," with samples of their English knowledge, Victoria was moved. Pedro, Luís, and João wrote: "A little wealth, a little health, a little house in freedom, and at the end a little friend and a little cause to need him." Only two months later drawings of Victoria's children, little Victoria, Albert Edward, Alice, and Alfred, arrived, "Little Albert is already making an effort to be a gentleman to his sisters, and I am trying to wring a first word from little Helene. Dearest friend Maria Glória, you should not worry too much about the horrible things that are happening right now. We can no longer influence the course of history..."

With that even England was placated again.

When the news of the renewed outbreak of fighting in Patuleia came in July of 1847, Palmela called on Maria Glória.

"I'm tired of reading reports about new skirmishes every day, Dona Maria. For that reason I request that you accept my resignation."

With Palmela one more man departed from Lisbon, who had believed in Father's constitution.

Again she sat in the state council, alone in the front row, listened, and sanctioned what Palmela read aloud: "...in that my resignation was accepted, I recommend General Gregorio Saldanha as my successor and request approval..."

As if on command, they had all jumped up from their seats to say "Yes," and Palmela was able to continue almost without a break, "...and I ask General Saldanha to step up to the crucifix and to take the oath for the homeland of Portugal..."

Saldanha, who lacked all of the elegance of a Palmela - every bow by Saldanha was awkward and angular, his handshake too firm, his hand kiss too intimate, his gaze shamelessly direct, and in his voice there were only screaming and croaking tones - that man was now number one in the state.

"He is the only right man for this hour," she noted in her diary.

And it was true. Within two months Saldanha's soldiers had put down all the revolts. How many dead, how many wounded there were, she did not ask anymore. Again, once more, she had sworn the oath to a new constitution. Each government laid a new constitution in front of her. "If only the basic rights remain, so that there is never any doubt that the rights of all people are the same, then I shall swear to anything that brings peace."

A few days after Fernando's birthday, his thirty-first, on the 4th of November 1847, she brought Augusto into the world.

"Augusto!" Eulalia held her mouth closed when she cried out that name during a pause in her labor. "Dom Fernando is sitting behind the screen," the good Eulalia said disapprovingly.

"If I at least had a child from him," she had sobbed when Augusto had died three weeks after the wedding. Perhaps she could long for one from him, summon him to her, and then force him to come to her with all her dreams. He had to drive Fernando out of her bed. For Augusto it would be easy. She had been so submissive to him, and in the February night she had devoured him. "You were finally able to tear yourself loose from over there," she scolded him. And in one night, in a dream he was with her again. She would not let him go so quickly. He had to talk, embrace her, and keep his promise, again and again. The first child must be a boy. "The queen gave birth to an additional healthy son. He will receive the name Augusto," Eulalia dictated hastily.

Fernando was briefly puzzled. "The name had not been discussed yet at all."

Augusto is even different in the line of her children. He has blond hair and dark eyes, and his skin is fine and alabaster white. In everything this beautiful baby resembles that Augusto whom Maria Glória fetches for herself in her nights, in her dreams.

The eleventh year of the circle of life was supposed to be devoted to friends. Maria Glória was in search of them, and as had been the case back then, in her first year in Lisbon, she did not find any except for her good fairy Eulalia, and except for Bertrand.

Sometimes she had doubts. Had the political events, the intrigues confused her to the point that she no longer trusted her husband, that she no longer counted Fernando among her friends?

The year 1848 flowed away, revolts in the country again, ultraliberals against monarchy loyalists, in the process always fatalities, wounded, always too little money in the state treasury, soon the threat that Spain would intervene and take the country under its protection.

Maria Glória hardly reacted to those messages. She signed new appointments of ministers, of officials, and she no longer asked: "To which party does he belong?"

When Eulalia rushed into the room in December of 1848, a few days before Christmas, she said, "Dona Maria, in London they have published a pamphlet about you, no, much more, a novel in several installments about you and Costa Cabral - the great love story of the Portuguese queen with her minister! They are talking about it all over the city. Even in front of the church they are telling each other: Cabral strewed the bed with silky soft rhododendron blossoms before you sank down! Your visit, back then, three years ago, in his house. Is this going to be another government crisis?"

"They have one more reason to agitate against me," Maria Glória said, shrugging her shoulders. "Perhaps they will shoot me the next time I drive to church. Eulalia, we won't worry about it any further. I promised the children that we would pour colored wax stars today. Have you obtained a beautiful blue for us that we can melt down, a blue in which there are sky and sea?" With that she pushed Eulalia into the playroom where Maria Anna was drawing the Christ child for her two-year-old sister Antonia. "No, not dark eyes. The Christ child has light eyes, and the hair isn't dark either, but blond, like that of Papa," the four-year-old crowed. "Blond and blue-eyed, that's how Margarita, the singer, is."

Maria Glória staggered back into her room. An hour later an official came to notify her officially that an English journalist had published a love story. "Senhor, I beg you, stop. What did you expect? We don't get beyond the civil wars, and we rejected England's help and in so doing deprived the English of a chance for good business deals! England can't accept a provocation of that kind: Just what do the Portuguese think? Does that little country intend to practice self-determination, without England having a say? I remember well how we were received in London at the court of

King William in 1831. Papa almost had to beg for an appointment, and Queen Adelaide gave me a little casket filled with precious stones! They were precious stones from Brazil that she had acquired at a favorable price from a dealer via Portugal, and she gave them to me - what ignorance!"
No, she did not intend to grapple with that for a minute longer than was absolutely necessary.
Fernando had been in Sintra for two days. "By New Year's Day the spiral staircase into the reading room has to be finished, Maria Glória. The view from that room goes directly into the Brazilian garden. You will hardly get around to reading in that room."
Fernando was probably not in Sintra, but in Belem. "It is surely a mistake, but recently we have often seen a nobleman here who resembles your Fernando, but that is probably impossible. This nobleman goes in and out of the Music Academy building," Amelia had written to her.

"When Dona Amelia is alone for too long, you have to be careful about her poison," the servants gossiped. And it was actually the case that because of the nets of intrigue that she cast, the stepmother was avoided by most of the families of the higher officials and ministers. To talk to that woman, to be seen with that woman was dangerous.

Maria Glória knew, "Never react to insinuations," but she did not want to have uncertainty for even another hour. She went into Fernando's room and routed Mauro, his scribe, from his copying tasks: "Wait outside until I call you!"
What did she care about the stammered: "...Dom Fernando - expressly forbidden to touch anything here." She pulled out drawers, opened doors, and broke open a secret compartment with a letter opener - everywhere letters, notes about the construction in Sintra, building plans, drawings of the children, books; books with bookmarks, books with pieces of paper on which Fernando had translated lines of poetry, and on the desk, quite unhidden, the portfolio "Urgent."

She would not find what she was looking for in that portfolio. She pushed it aside, but then opened it after all. The first sheet of paper empty, then a letter in Fernando's handwriting, a letter, many pages long: "Dearest Margarita, the travel plans that you talked about yesterday sound tempting - Rome, Vienna, Dresden. It was not a lie when I told you there is nothing I would rather do than to board the next travel coach, the next ship with you. However, I shall not undertake such a journey in the next few years. I am bound by a promise to my parents to fulfill unreservedly my responsibilities as a husband and father without any scandal until our son Pedro reaches his majority. So I shall not begin traveling before the year 1856. My beloved Margarita, I do not want to conceal from you the fact that I have deep affection for my wife, Maria Glória. That affection does not diminish the passion that I feel for you. The one thing is friendship and the other sensuality, it seems to me, sometimes a bit too much of it. Maria Glória is a person full of warmheartedness and goodness, but above all, Maria Glória is a Brazilian. And although her mother and father were Europeans, her character, her soul is full of the mystique of the country of Brazil. She tries to be a European, to react like a European, and to the superficial observer she may have become successful at that long ago. But I, who am closest to her, know, Maria Glória will never think and feel like a European. They say that for the country of Brazil the middle ground is missing in everything, both in abundance and in lack - tropical orchids and the desert of Sertão are only an hour's ride distant from each other, and in the same way we are often speechless as we stand facing each other - the two continents, the two cultures seem irreconcilable. Europe is my continent. I grew up and am at home here, and I feel how Maria Glória suffers from having been uprooted. My sympathy for her obliges me to support Maria Glória until our firstborn son reaches his majority, and to ease the pain of her exile.

"Now I hear you ask, my beloved: What remains for us? Much remains for us: letters, memories, brief reunions. By the way, do not be angry with me because of my openness. After all, I must share you with Liszt, at least your artistic spirit..."

Maria Glória read the letter several times. She had sunk down on the armchair and noticed nothing but the letters on the stationery that were strung together into words and sentences, which she gradually, very slowly grasped. In it there were statements about duties, promises, and sympathy, especially about sympathy, even about affection, but that affection also had the color of sympathy. Fernando's correctness was mirrored in every word, the same correctness as when he discussed a roof construction with the master builder Eschwege, as when he checked the bills for the delivered basalt stones with Monteiro - the correctness with which Fernando designated the year 1856 as the beginning for his actual free life.

It says in books that women fainted, broke into screaming fits, and withdrew into insanity about information like that which she had just read - for twelve years, from 1836 to 1848, she had lived with a husband and misunderstood everything. "Jupiter, who symbolizes the finding of meaning for us, stands in his original place again after twelve years, and if it should be that we have misunderstood something during those twelve years, that we have denied ourselves to reality, he provides for clarification and clear-sightedness with suddenness. Then we have to submit and begin anew, and we should never forget that his powers are benevolent..."

She read the letter again and again, and finally she saw that it was a copy. The letter had been written over six months ago, and Fernando had laid this copy in his portfolio in a manner, as if it were supposed to be found and also read.

She leafed further in the portfolio. The next letter was addressed to Alexander Herculano: "...for Dona Maria, giving up her position is unimaginable. Abdication - that word is missing in her vocabulary. Obedience to her father and emulation of her mother in bearing duties and suffering would never permit her such a thought. Now, after more than ten years of civil war, the culture of this magnificently beautiful and rich country is threatening to perish. All the money is spent for the soldiers of the one party as well as the other. All that is being built now is 'roofs over heads,' because nobody has any feeling for aesthetics. The newspaper is devoted almost exclusively to criticism, defamation, and lamentation. Alexander, start publishing soon in *O País* texts about the good things in Portugal. Use your own language to give form to events from the history of the country. You will receive an invitation to New Year's dinner for the 1st of January 1849, and I shall arrange things so that your conversation with Dona Maria arrives at that topic without delay..."

Maria Glória made an effort to summarize the letter for herself: Behind her back Fernando was carrying on conversations about the cultural development of the country. For years Fernando would have preferred for her to abdicate. Whenever Costa Cabral or Palmela had implored her not to leave Lisbon - "Dona Maria, you are the symbol for continuity in the country. If you, if that symbol is missing, a civil war will break out that will destroy us all" - and she had nodded at that - "I know where my place is. I'm responsible for that" - Fernando had stood there leaning against a dresser and had smiled. For him, her answer each time had been only an act of obedience to her father and her mother.

With the two letters in her hand, she staggered out. She pushed Mauro away when he cried: "Dona Maria - deathly pale - water for Dona Maria!" And although everything before her eyes was as if enveloped in fog, she found her way back to her room without stumbling. There she carefully folded the pages of the letters and locked them in her diary. Eulalia was somewhere in the room. "Have you seen a ghost? Has bad news come from Dom Fernando? Did one of the children fall?" Her good companion buzzed around her with questions.
"No, nothing."

Frost patterns on the windows, the smell of half-burnt wood in the room, the cooling hands of Eulalia that smelled like lavender, and Fernando, who dripped jasmine oil onto a cloth and cooled her forehead and cheeks with it.
Fernando is not familiar with the jasmine trees. He does not

know the fragrance and the healing power of those starlike blossoms.

"A nervous fever. I can't detect anything else." Senhor Lobato, the doctor, was in the room. How many days, how many nights had she slept away in her fever? "Is it already the 1st of January 1849? Has the New Year's dinner already taken place?" she uttered with effort.

They were all startled and rushed to her bed. "Thank God, Dona Maria!" stammered Eulalia, and Fernando embraced her and kissed her cheeks. "No, the New Year doesn't begin until day after tomorrow, Maria Glória. You should sleep now. Yes, everything is all right with the children."

Word for word the contents of the two letters reeled off within her. Those sentences did not let themselves be pushed away. Between them the voice of the doctor: "It cannot be determined what the cause of this fever attack was. They say - it sounds a lot like the gossip of the lace makers from the church square - they say that *saudade*, which already oppresses our Portuguese soul very much, can almost confound the Brazilian mind. Dom Fernando, I find no other explanation - *saudade*."

For the New Year's dinner Maria Glória was on her feet again. She was expecting a child, "begotten in all friendship and out of sympathy," she often said half aloud to the unborn baby. "You'll come into the world in May. You'll become a spring child. You see, I no longer confuse the seasons."

When Maria Glória invited the guests into the small drawing room after coffee, Fernando led Alexander Herculano to her.

"Senhor Alexander, which part of our, of Portuguese history, will you use for the first text in the newspaper?" she asked him bluntly. Herculano was astounded and immediately quoted: "It was the Lusitanians who drove back the mounted army of Mohammed..."

When he paused, she said, "Good, we'll adopt those texts into the schoolbooks," and she drew Fernando and Herculano into her room. "The question of your honorarium has not yet been resolved," Maria Glória remembered, and she opened her jewel box. Fernando shook his head. "I actually wanted to do that..."

She did not consider that, but drew Herculano to the window. "Look, I brought a few precious stones with me from Rio de Janeiro. Here are the two that are dearest to me - Bahia topazes. It isn't their size that is important. Look into the blue. Nights and days of the tropical sky, the illuminated and the darkened, are contained in it. Take these two stones, Senhor Alexander, and write," and she laid the precious stones in the hand of the dumbfounded man.

The topazes gleamed in all the shades of blue, and Maria Glória needed several moments to turn her gaze away from those stones.

Maria Glória 1849-1852
*"Just because we accomplish nothing against
deceitful guile with human judgment"*

With the 1st of January 1849, her era was actually over. Everything that came afterward was only a closely packed living out of the weeks, months, and years anymore. "Until 1856, then Fernando will leave the house. He will do it quietly and politely, without a scandal, and he will travel."

In May of 1849 she brought Leopoldo into the world.

"The name of your mother is missing," Fernando reminded her. Only a few hours after the christening, the baby boy was dead.

"Unexplainable," said Senhor Lobato, shaking his head. "The child was healthy."

In February of 1851, little Maria Glória came into the world. "If it is a girl, she must receive your name. You have to be there for us all once more," Fernando decided.

He did not know the Glória church, that little baroque building above the ocean of Rio de Janeiro. "A masterpiece of architecture - baroque architecture adapted to the tropics; the floor plan, the windows, everything planned so that while light penetrates into the nave, rays of sunlight still never pierce into the interior of the church," José Bonifácio had explained to Maria Glória. Before the altar the unpadded prayer stool. "Here your father and I prayed for a healthy child. That is why your name is Maria Glória," *Mamãe*, Dona Leopoldina had often said.

"Dearest Clementine, Fernando is inconsolable about the fact that our little daughter Maria Glória died three days after she was born. She seemed completely healthy and nevertheless passed away so suddenly. Now Fernando wants to have doctors come from Paris to cure me. He does not want to grasp the fact that my time to pass life on has run out. Clementine, how long our dying takes, how many years it drags on. Sometimes I pray that it will not last into the year 1856 for me. You should not comfort me. I have made friends with my melancholy, and I treasure Fernando's friendship very much. He is kind to me in everything. I cannot complain about anything..."

Once, about two months after she had found the letter, she said to Fernando, completely out of the blue, "Send Margarita away." And he answered tersely and briefly, "She has already left Lisbon."

That was too little for her. "Fernando, why must there be this Margarita?" She was no longer able to contain herself.

Fernando looked up: "Maria Glória, my friendship with Margarita has nothing to do with our marriage."

"Friendship? Fernando, it's a love affair. You can't deny that," she said, completely losing her composure.

But Fernando did not respond to that. He became sharp: "She has nothing to do with us." Then he stood up and said, "Maria Glória, with our marriage we entered a commitment that we both fulfill. I like you very much. I couldn't wish for a better wife. That really means that our expectations for this marriage were fulfilled for the most part. We support each other in our work, in our interests, and we have friendship with each other. We could not dream of that when we signed our marriage contract."

She had drawn back from Fernando. Never before had she experienced him so firm and inflexible. In those moments nothing of the soft, pensive Fernando could be detected any longer.

He had not lost his perspective, and she stood before him as a stammering, pleading wife: "But I don't want to share you. I will not tolerate a mistress. You write glowing love letters to her, and you already have exact plans about when you will leave."

She could no longer speak to that polite figure, to that calm face. "Fernando!" she sobbed.

He did not take her into his arms. He considered. "When it is no longer absolutely necessary for the education of our son Pedro, I'll undertake some travels, that's right. Maria Glória, you have never traveled since you have been here. You couldn't even accompany me to the monasteries of Minho. Your duties held you here."

She could not believe it. "Fernando, I don't reach you anymore at all with what I say. Were we always so foreign to each other?"

"Oh, my dear, you need a walk in the Brazilian garden. Do you want to drive out to Sintra?" He smiled at her and hugged her to him, the way you soothe a child.

"No, I have my portfolio full of unfinished correspondence," she almost stuttered. And in walking out of the room she added: "Luís has an oral French examination. Do you want to listen to it?"

"Quite definitely. I think his French is outstanding."

She dragged herself into her room. There she sat for hours with her diary in front of her. She had no other conversational partner, and even for that patient book she did not find a word, not a sentence. She had been turned away, very politely pushed aside.

She could not vent her restrained rage; now that rage choked her: "I feel so deceived, not because of Margarita, no, but I have opened my deepest feelings to Fernando in everything. There is not an emotion, not a fiber that I have kept back from him, and he took those things and kept a part of himself closed off to me, locked away. He denied me entry into his dreams, his passions," she wrote late at night.

"It's not good for you to meddle in the private life of your husband," Leonora would scold her.

"But she came back, every year, and sometimes she stayed for many weeks!"

"Why do you worry about it, Dona Maria? Just how could you nose around on Dom Fernando's papers? He doesn't lie to her. His nature as a husband and father is just as true as the one that this singer knows."

Concerning truth, António Vieira, the truth fanatic, wrote: "*Christina, they report to me that you want to get the Pope to approve me as your personal preacher! You know that António da Silva, the Grand Inquisitor of Coimbra and my most passionate persecutor, has imposed on me a prohibition to preach and to speak. In your last letter you already asked - you wanted to discuss truth. Fine - which truth do you want to hear, yours or mine?*"

The year 1851, her body weakened by the birth of her little daughter - "She looked so alive, *Mamãe*. Have evil spirits that took away our sister moved into our house?" wept Maria Anna. The seven-year-old felt how Maria Glória became foreign, how she withdrew more and more. On some evenings she clung to Maria Glória with all her might. "Stay here," she whispered, and she kissed her mother on her neck and on her cheeks.

The older ones, the thirteen-year-old Pedro and Luís, with his twelve years, and the eleven-year-old João were already too grown up, too occupied with their schedules to notice changes in the expression of their mother's language and caresses.

"Maria Anna is the largest of my four little organ pipes," she always explained with a laugh, when the little ones lined up to greet a visitor. Maria Anna at seven years, Antonia at six years, Fernando, the quiet five-year-old, and Augusto, the four-year-old youngest child - for the four little ones nothing changed in their everyday lives. They had their parents as always for walks, ball games, reading stories aloud, playing theater, and their evening prayers.

Whether the year 1851 was a good year or a bad year, it was no longer important for her. When a new revolution announced itself - ultraliberals against moderate monarchy loyalists - she hardly looked up anymore from her correspondence with Rothschild: "I thank your house for the generous reduction of interest. You can judge best that roads represent the arteries of life for a country, and that accordingly the road to Porto and further into the region of Minho..."

Palmela - he had returned - cleared his throat: "Dona Maria, General Saldanha is placing himself with an army of several thousand soldiers against the moderate constitutionalists, that is, against your army."

Maria Glória interrupted him: "Senhor Palmela, I know. Dom Fernando is leading a ridiculously small army against Saldanha. Besides that, as everyone knows, my husband is no military officer. I have therefore written to him," and without hesitation she read to Palmela: "My Fernando, whom I love more than anything else, do not risk a single wound. It has to be enough! Since 1834, since my father's death, there have been revolts, fights, intrigues, deceptions, and lies, for seventeen years. If they confront each other again, the ultraliberals, the intellectuals of the university city of Coimbra, and the poor incited people from the North - and you, with the few monarchy loyalists, then give the order to retreat! With that in mind, negotiate with Saldanha to have him form a government as quickly as possible. I shall ratify it and swear allegiance to it. I shall do everything so that peace finally prevails..." And without paying any further attention to Palmela, she continued writing to Jacob Rothschild.

"Dom Fernando, the conciliatory negotiator," it was reported in October of 1851 in the newspaper *O País*, and, "Dona Maria, the educator, the founder of peace!" they wrote enthusiastically.

Fernando actually had ordered his soldiers to retreat. He had negotiated instead of fighting. On the open balcony General Saldanha passed the laurel wreath on to Maria Glória: "The true victor in this battle for freedom and unity!" He, her archenemy for almost two decades, kneeled before her in front of the cheering crowd, and she did not ward off that bit of ham acting.

"God protect me from intrigues," she continued to write in her diary, but no longer daily. Sometimes she forgot that sentence for weeks, and when she wrote the words, they formed of their own

accord, like a fleeting greeting, a hasty genuflection.
They would not plot any more intrigues against her - she thought. *Regeneracão*, renewal, they called the new era. The political routine had become more peaceful. In the cadence of a school day plan, raises in tariffs, new roads, and the awarding of ship licenses were debated, and in quick sequence new, supposedly fairer laws were passed. Concerning her, the queen, they read in the newspaper: "Yesterday in the theater Dona Maria wore a dress made of especially choice silk. When she moved, she glittered in green. Is she tormented by *saudade* again, that she prefers the color of the forest, the jungle of her origins?"
The speech on Epiphany of 1852 was made by Almeida Garrett. Maria Glória was able to persuade him to give it. "Senhor Garrett, the articles from your pen are what I always read first in the newspaper."
He spoke first about the importance of art, reminding his listeners that one could learn about turning to God from Dante's *Divine Comedy*, that the skepticism of German culture was found in *Faust*, and that Luís Camões, in his *Os Lusíadas*, expressed the special relationship of the Lusitanians to their homeland.
After that first part of his speech, he became pointed: How much more did they intend to ruin Lisbon? Individual sections of the city were already totally dilapidated, and others, on the other hand, would be transformed into small city gardens with new paving, fountains, and parks! A law should be passed that government officials had to take up residence in a different quarter of the city every six months, for only then would the entire city gradually be cleaned and renovated.

On that Epiphany Dona Amelia had also been present.
She pushed Senhor Mariliem, the French ambassador, over to Maria Glória. "That Garrett, what a waste not to install such a man as a minister," he began, and Maria Glória did not react to it for several sentences.
But Senhor Mariliem stuck to the topic: "Pardon me, Dona Maria, for speaking so directly, but with Senhor Garrett you would

have a foreign minister who would revive the ties to Paris to a great degree. He lived there for some time, before he fled to the Azores. His book about Camões appeared in Paris!"

She was able to have an influence on the filling of the post of foreign minister; that was possible for her. Hardly any importance was ascribed to the office of foreign minister. A foreign minister brought hardly any disquiet into the discussions about new real estate taxes, or in the negotiations with the clergy about the return of Miguel estates held in trust.

Maria Glória spoke with Saldanha: "Besides, Senhor Garrett would cost hardly anything. Even now he works without a salary."

Saldanha nodded. "Yes, he is a very wealthy gentleman. But his private life seems to be somewhat complicated," and the bullnecked man searched her face with his eyes.

"He's a friend of Irene Antaras. She's the daughter of the saltern owner, and she studies violin here at the Academy of Music." Maria Glória did not understand.

Saldanha considered, and then he said: "Dona Maria, it can be arranged. Senhor Garrett would indeed be an excellent foreign minister." With that he took his leave.

A few weeks later Garrett actually was foreign minister. Dona Amelia had also come to the swearing-in ceremony.

"How grateful I am to you," she whispered in Maria Glória's ear.

She jerked back - an uncomfortable situation, Dona Maria and Dona Amelia whispering secrets to each other in public.

"I do not deserve the thanks," she stated after a few seconds. "It is the accomplishment of Senhor Garrett and the decision of the state council."

In the evening, when she brought the cocoa, Eulalia was of the opinion, "Maria Glória, she is plotting something, quite certainly."

"Who? What?" She did not want to hear anything about it.

"Maria Glória, didn't you see? Dona Amelia is wearing a new hairdo, those long, drawn-out curls, just the way you see them in the Paris journals, and she had them tie her bodice at least five centimeters tighter! The last time I attended church, her plain seamstress told me that Dona Amelia ordered whalebone from Genoa, and that it is extremely thin and can hardly be felt in the bodice." Maria Glória had to laugh about that. "And even if that's true, I certainly don't need that whalebone, because I haven't worn a bodice for years."

Eulalia was not to be deterred: "She's hatching something out, Maria Glória. Your stepmother has that green glint in her brown eyes again."

The spring and summer months of the year 1852 were overfilled with pleasant responsibilities. Maria Glória did not want to let herself be interrupted. She sat with Herculano for weeks over the manuscripts for the schoolbooks. Fernando was taken to his first communion. In the garden of Sintra she planted cashew and durian trees. She practiced geometrical drawing with Maria Anna. Her friend Victoria of England sent a bicycle. "It is the latest thing. A few technically adept workmen constructed this vehicle, which is actually used only in the circus, for general use." And the two oldest boys, Pedro and Luís, were enthusiastic about it.

At the end of August Maria Glória received an invitation to the "presentation of the work 'Journeys into the Interior of Our Country' by João Baptiste Garrett, in the theater on *Rossio Square*..."

For almost ten years Garrett had researched the history of Portugal. What a rarity - a foreign minister writes, and during his time in office he presents a book, a critical examination of his country.

The theater was filled to the last bit of standing room. Maria Glória and Fernando had to push their way through a crowd of people to their box.

She sensed a mixed audience. Some turned their backs to her. Others stepped aside, smiled, and greeted her in a friendly manner.

A brief musical piece and then came the two friends.

Garrett, in black university garb, and the eleven-years-younger Herculano in a blue suit, as always. They read; they played the text. One of them reached for the other's hand. They exchanged glances.

"Is there anything new in Lisbon?"

"No, I think there was a revolution yesterday."

"Oh, again."

"Let's start out and travel into the country. Let's listen to the people."

"How near do we want to get to them?"

"Not close. Let's travel to Santarem and seek in the olive grove the house in which Carlos finally encounters Enio. One of them recites poems to the other. They have a passion for black eyes, Carlos for those of Enio, Enio for those of Carlos. They want to swear devotion to each other..."

For some minutes the people were swept away, following what was presented to them. Suddenly, from the crowd sitting in the orchestra an old woman gasped, and beside her another one. It was Moulinier, Dona Amelia's lady-in-waiting, and one of Moulinier's women friends. "The two of them are a pair of lovers! What is being presented to us here? What shamelessness! We want out. We can't stand that any longer - two men - no!" the two women's voices rang out.

In the rows in front of and behind them men and women also stood up. "That Herculano is also against celibacy, you know. Surely he'll present that next."

"And he wants to introduce civil marriage! Perhaps instead of praying we should read those obscenities!"

Maria Glória looked into the crowd. It was already surging toward the stage. Would they begin to shoot, to hit each other next? Would people collapse again, wounded, dead? Those were the things that flashed through her mind, and without reacting to the grip of Fernando, who wanted to hold her back, she stood up: "Ladies and gentlemen, this book is the manifesto for the new, peaceful era of Portugal! We are hearing beautiful literature. Let's let the two gentlemen continue..."

She did not get any further in her remarks. Wads of paper were thrown into her box. The side draperies were torn down and swung at her as ropes. "We have her to thank for this Garrett! She calls him a modern mind! We have a foreign minister who loves women and men, and the other one, the younger one writes the schoolbooks for our children! She truly is the daughter of the *vulgario*. Perhaps Pedro cheated on his mistress with a man," was how the cannonades of insults surged up to the royal box.

With effort Maria Glória and Fernando could be brought through the backstage corridors and a side door to their carriage. Directly next to their carriage stood that of Dona Amelia. With the carriage door open, Amelia swung her foot into the August night and watched the way Maria Glória and Fernando forced their way into their carriage. Amelia even raised her hand and waved.

Fernando wanted to say something. No, she crouched in the other corner, not now. She could not talk now. How often she had experienced it, for weeks and months the uneasiness that something was beginning to move against her, and with all her reflection had come to no conclusion. But when the capstone has been placed, the story is easy to read:

Dona Amelia had taken a liking to Garrett. A wealthy man, he could converse charmingly and intelligently. He was a widower, and with Garrett, Amelia could get very close to Saldanha, very close to those in power, and there she could have an influence. Shouldn't Portugal have been proclaimed a republic long ago? How much longer did Portugal want to afford the decoration of a queen? But Garrett did not react. He read his poems in her drawing room and remained polite. So Amelia engineered things so that he became foreign minister. That would flatter him and obligate him to eternal gratitude and in so doing bring him to Amelia at last. But Garrett continued to remain polite. Worse, when he began to see through the scheme, he avoided Amelia's salon. So had she miscalculated once again? Amelia had prepared for that eventuality. Either she would get Garrett, or she would deal Maria Glória a blow. Both would bring her satisfaction, and she had thought out both in detail, and her lady-in-waiting, that poisonous woman, her lady-in-waiting and the other old woman had been sent out to kick the first brick loose that would start the avalanche rolling.

The next day in the newspaper they read: "New times! Queen Maria II, patroness of Garrett and Herculano! Yesterday's presentation of the Garrett work had to be broken off because of a tumult. Even the fact that Dona Maria sought to defend the work did not pacify the aroused people. On the contrary! It became apparent that important questions of morality have to be answered anew. For years Garrett and Herculano have demanded civil marriage, the abolition of celibacy, and, as we have known since yesterday, the approval of homosexual love..."

Saldanha had been asked and his answers were printed: "I never knew about the private inclinations of Mr. Garrett. How should I? It is generally known that the two gentlemen are regular guests in the house of Dona Maria..."

Maria Glória wanted to prepare a few lines for a journalist, but when she had read the newspaper, she left it alone.

Instead of that she began to formulate the letter of dismissal for Garrett, and she was even relieved of that task.

"My most deeply revered Queen, dear Dona Maria, with this they bring you a copy of my letter of resignation to the state council. It is the fate of many creatively active people to be misunderstood. If one is rejected, it is even more painful, but one also becomes accustomed to that. However, if one is threatened and persecuted, then one has to withdraw. Like António Vieira, I shall impose a prohibition upon myself with regard to speaking and writing in public and move to Setubal with my bride Irene. Maybe we will see each other again in a few years..."

Herculano, too, said good-by: "...that I am going to Coimbra. Consider our work together on the schoolbooks to be completed. Let's show that we are perceptive. Fate has beckoned. Nor do we want to forget that what seems incomplete to us today was probably finished long ago, and we just do not want to let go..."

Of course everything quieted down again. Garrett and Herculano were soon no longer a topic of conversation. And from her, the queen, they wanted to know "whether a prince or a princess might be expected once more. In the period when she is expecting, Dona Maria blossoms each time."

From Amelia came another one of her letters: "Beloved daughter, beloved Maria Glória, I find neither consolation nor words. How could I have suspected that my noble acquaintance with Garrett would become a Garrett affair for you? How responsible I feel, and I cannot relieve you of any of that shame. Just a word, a sign from you, beloved Maria Glória..."

She no longer reacted to it. She did not write a letter. She cut off anyone who mentioned the Garrett affair.

Once more she was thankful that she had Fernando at her side. He was occupied with the renovation of Pena in Sintra. "Just no new civil war. I shall not lead a troop of soldiers again." That was his greatest worry.

"No, there will not be another civil war, not under Queen Maria II," she thought.

It was over, everything.

"God protect me from intrigues." Her prayer had not been granted.

She continued to count the years. 1852, that year was almost past. Then there were only three more years until the year 1856, the year in which Fernando "will travel for a longer period of time for study purposes." The diplomats will agree on such a formulation.

Graça, to November 1853
Maria Glória, to November 1853
"The torch bowed toward the ground and disappeared on the horizon"

Graça listened carefully to her. Sometimes she closed her eyes for minutes at a time in order to catch every nuance:

"And now, this child that you will bring into the world tomorrow, why did you let this child happen?"

She straightens up: "It will soon be noon, Maria Glória. I must go. There are still some things to be done. In two days I must be in Belem. In two days I will board the ship. A ship sails directly to Rio de Janeiro only three times a month. Why don't you come along?

You promised me you would, in Brest, twenty years ago. Maria Glória, don't say that you can't leave, for it would be easy for you. Everything that you say comes from a world that I don't know. Were we really born on the same day? Did we grow up in the same city and come to Europe on the same ship? You know the sermon by António Vieira about vanity. Didn't he also write about humility? Abrão read to me from it."

Maria Glória also remembered: "*My dearly beloved, today I must reproach you severely. They tell me that your palace houses a new scene of squandering every day. You have wine flowing from room fountains, and when their minds are completely intoxicated, you have yourself taken through the secret door, the 'little Christina gate,' into your chambers, well accompanied by some young people of both sexes. You complain to me about money problems, reminding me constantly that you renounced the throne of Sweden. You also complain that Cardinal Azzolino just wants to put you off with his friendship. Vanity rages within you! Wake up! It is almost too late anyway. Purify your body, your soul, and your mind. Fast, and do not write to me again until you have completed two tasks:*

Use your friendship, your precious friendship with Azzolino, to bring the freedom of lodging for the Jews more urgently under discussion with the Pope at last. I shall not stop reproaching you until you are able to report something efficient to me. As a second thing, I assign you to write a tract about the importance of art. These two tasks should introduce you to a quality that I have missed in you all this time - humility, Christina, the act of turning toward duties to devote ourselves to an assignment, to submit ourselves to a mission, to our life's mission. I lack the strength to punish and lead you more fully. It is November! My cell is losing more and more light; my body is becoming empty of blood and would require the summer sun of the Latin continent, the sun of Brazil, the sun of Salvador. Saudade is eating at my powers, and after this letter I shall not write a single word for several weeks. It is time to compose myself and only continue with my defense letter in a few weeks. Very dear one, practice the virtue of humility and do not forget, even my soul needs a prayer, one from you, Christina, the fourth day of November 1671."

Graça softly prays each word along with her, nods, and continues: "You credit your husband with friendship and sympathy. How many people don't receive a spoonful of that during their entire lives? You say you are too weak to give birth to children that survive. Maria Glória, I can't make head or tail of your thoughts, of what you say. We both know that since 1849 you have summoned all your powers to have children grow within you, only to let them, the living children, die with the same power. What a cruel punishment for your husband, for all those who don't comfort you in your sorrow - in what sorrow?"

"Two days ago Fernando attended the theater with me. She sang songs by Franz Schubert, Graça. Margarita is in Lisbon again!"

"It's not important." Graça pushed it aside. She let Maria Glória talk.

"In yesterday's newspaper they wrote that I was very pale in the theater, and they fear that I will not survive this next birth."

"Of course you'll die during that birth. After all, you gave yourself that order. You'll both die, you and the baby. In half an hour Eulalia will pick you up here, and tomorrow, on the 15th of November, on the name day of your mother, Dona Leopoldina, you'll leave here, pass over to the other side."

Graça implores her, takes her hands, and massages the skin of those flabby fingers. "Maria Glória, you must not do that. Let's go back, both of us. Your husband, everyone would agree to that - the Queen abdicates!"

"And your years, Graça, what did you experience in those years?" Maria Glória studies her friend's face. "Please, tell me," she added.

Graça lets the past years parade by. How many years Porto is away from Lisbon!

"In the initial years we, Abrão and I, were respected people. We received a gold name placard on our pew in the church. After all, I was almost related to the queen. For many years Abrão used the royal stationery. That spared us awkward situations with offices and agencies. We obtained the best cargo spaces. The cheapest laborers and maids were procured for us, and we needed many helpers, for in the years 1839, 1840, and until 1843 we had our best cocoon harvests. For years the people believed that when Abrão picked up the packet of mail from the agency at the harbor, there was a letter from Dona Maria, from Maria Glória in it, and when Abrão suggested a second horse agency, criticized the prices for wine and oil, wanted to have the smoke houses for the fish further away from the city, or when he had a new cistern dug because ours was at the point of drying up, everyone always believed that those recommendations came directly from Queen Maria II - she wants to see Porto as the cleanest city in Portugal - and none of the officials dared to reject Abrão's recommendations.

"However, the scribe in the postal agency became more impertinent. At first he remained silent for a few small coins. After a few years he wanted more money. Abrão gave it to him, and four years ago he wanted a share of the earnings from our silk spools. Four years ago it was also true that mail from Dona Maria, from Maria Glória, hardly had a value for us anymore. They gossiped: The Bragas are carrying on correspondence with the queen, but we don't permit Dona Maria to prescribe anything for us. She is spending all the money for the construction in Sintra, and she wants to order us to build a new road to the harbor. We manage our own affairs. Then they found the scribe from the postal agency in the pond. Nobody knew who had pushed him into it. That they would put Luiz of all people, the fifteen-year-old Luiz, in the postal agency, how could I have anticipated that? In the monastery they taught him to read and write, and from the age of thirteen on they did not feed anyone anymore. After I was married to Abrão, I wanted to forget Luiz Arantes and the child, and the fire. I wanted to forget everything and start over.

"After a year of marriage Abrão had become sullen. 'Will the Vieira book be the only thing that remains of us?' Should I tell him that I had already given birth to a child, that his blood was perhaps too thin, or - I didn't even want to think about that - that our two skin colors repelled each other? For many nights I twisted and turned in the bed. Arantes had also been a white man. I wanted to go to Luiz Arantes. He would sire a child for me.

"In what confusion I was. Arantes laughed at me! 'Can't your queen send you a nobleman who will lay a foundling in Braga's nest?'

I stood there as if somebody had dumped a wastewater tub over me.

"'Not so loud,' I uttered, but Arantes didn't stop. 'You have a son. He looks just like me. Nobody sees a resemblance to your Indian face in him. Should I talk to Braga when I have a chance?'

"I almost fainted when he said that, and just to keep him quiet, I dug the two emeralds out of my bag and gave them to him. "Not a word, please," I begged and ran away.

"'The respectable Senhora Braga,' I heard him laugh.

"Arranging for Luiz to work in the postal agency was a smart idea on the part of Arantes. Some neighbors and friends already doubted the letters from the queen, and Luiz, my son Luiz, would make sure that the truth came to light. It had already been years since there had been any mail contact with Dona Maria.

"They began to show hostility toward us. Suddenly there was no cargo space available for us. Our nameplate was removed from the church pew. They put some beehives in our mulberry tree plantation and the silkworms stopped eating and fell off before they were mature enough for the cocoons. That was in the year 1851. Two years ago, after that General Saldanha formed a new government, it was actually forbidden in Porto to be loyal to the monarchy.

"Abrão remained in London for several months. In London he has a family, a wife who can read and write. I found letters. Abrão didn't hide them. He was convinced that I couldn't read them anyway. But I took a packet of those letters and went to Ines, to the nun in the convent. Mother Ines read - what Elisabeth wrote to Abrão: 'You say you cannot send Graça away because she is your best worker. Sometimes I believe that you like Graça very much. Would you praise her patience so much otherwise?'

"What was I supposed to think about that? Mother Ines was quiet for a long time, then she explained to me: the Braga farm would continue to be my home, and there was no point in brooding about the distant future.

"A simple piece of advice. On some days I could follow it easily, but on other days tears ran down my cheeks for hours, and slowly I grasped the fact that I was alone. With my hands, my feet, and my obedience I earned for myself the name of *Braga*. Nobody was interested in what was going on in my head. That had no value for anyone. I lived well, much better than I had ever lived in Rio de Janeiro. The Braga estate was my home, and my tears came from *saudade*. I recited those lines to myself. Sometimes they comforted, sometimes they hurt, for no matter how I twisted the words, I was alone with those words, alone."

"When Abrão went to London again in October of last year, I begged: 'Come back before New Year's.' I wanted to be together with him in our house on the first day of the year 1853. The first day repeats itself for the entire year, and I had been afraid for months that Abrão would go away, stay away. I often got up in the middle of the night and ran to the cabinet where the wooden box with the Vieira book was kept. Abrão would never leave the farm without that book. It always lay in the same place.

"We celebrated the beginning of the year 1853 together. We drank mulberry brandy, and Abrão read the fish sermon aloud to me: '*We know that the fish are the only ones among the animals who do not let themselves be tamed and taught. At the time of Noah, the Flood occurred, and which of the animals saved themselves most easily? The fish. They not only all escaped, but they even had more living space than before. The fish avoid human beings and remain out of reach of the politeness and compliments that come from human beings. By that we should recognize that even the human being must avoid human beings in those phases of his life in which he deliberates and thinks...*'

"The next day the first letter came from the mayor. We had to pay for the cistern that had been especially constructed for us Bragas. In each of the following weeks letters arrived. We had to pay for the road and for the land where the mulberry trees stood. They demanded taxes for our house, the one in which we lived, and soon for the barns and the drying sheds. In the beginning I didn't understand why. After all, Abrão had sent me punctually to the city hall every year with a bag of coins: 'I'm bringing the tax money for Braga.' Finally Abrão explained to me: 'They say, that monarchist should pay for what he got surreptitiously through his friendship with the queen, and only when everything is paid for will we accept him into our Party of Liberal Saldinists, and there is no other party in our city any longer. We only keep our queen for show anymore!'"

"We paid. We met the demands, even when they became more and more brazen. Abrão attended meetings in the city hall. We finally had to borrow money. Abrão smoothed out the certificates of indebtedness and laid them in the wooden box with the Vieira book. And in the first week of October, five weeks ago, Luiz Arantes came into our house with his son, with my son.

"We were eating codfish and the yellow corn pancakes. Suddenly the two men were standing in the room. Arantes threw a leather bag on the table: 'Here, Braga, count it. That is what I'm paying you for all your property," and he looked at me. "We'll carry on everything well, my son and I.'

"Luiz had become the spitting image of his father, with the same honey-brown hair, the piercing blue eyes, and his entire body tense, as if ready to jump.

"While I stared at Luiz, at my son, more and more people pushed their way into the house, the helpers, the oil pressers, the fishermen, the laborers and maids of Menezes and of Fegueira, of those business associates with whom we had gotten together on Sunday afternoons for years. I recognized most of them only by the colors of their work uniforms.

"A mass of screaming mouths and waving hands moved toward Abrão. He tried to persuade the infuriated people, but he was shouted down.

"'Arantes, don't spend a long time talking to him. Take over the silk farm. We decided that in yesterday's meeting! He, Braga, is a monarchist," and Jorge, who could read and write even fewer words than I could, pulled a piece of paper out of his shirt. 'In Porto there are no longer any subjects. We are free! We are free people, and we won't wait any longer for what is slipped into our hands or pushed over to us. We have to receive our share of the profits from this silk farm.'

"'Today a new era begins in Porto. What interest do we have in the monarchists in Lisbon or those from Coimbra, where they distribute wisdom with ladles?' That was one of Menezes's oil pressers.

"Their voices became shriller and shriller. They lifted Jorge onto their shoulders. Nothing more could be seen of Abrão, who was surrounded and had disappeared into the howling crowd that harried him.

"I just wanted to get out of that room. How enormous that dining room was. Step by step I worked my way past the bodies of the men and women. Their bodies jerked from bawling and laughing. Behind me, many steps behind me a few of them were fighting over Arantes's moneybag. They began to hit each other. I felt the shoving of their bodies all the way to the door.

"Outside in the courtyard it was quiet, but I immediately heard the crackling and breaking, and at the moment when I grasped it, our kitchen maid cried: 'Fire!'"

"They set fire to the Braga farm. Who did it was and is no longer important. Like back then, in January of 1835, it took them a long time before they grasped the fact that it was burning, before they stopped beating, cursing, and cheering each other. The barns and sheds were ablaze. The flames swung upward into the sky. The wood was dry from a long summer. The cocoons, which lay in the drying huts by the thousands, burst noisily.

"From all sides they jostled and bumped against me. I shouted for Abrão. The people ran in the direction of the cistern, but they had to make a detour. The heat was too intense. One of them suddenly pushed me out of the way. He struck out at me, so that I fell down, and as I lay there for a few moments, unable to get up, I saw how a breath of wind, a very light gust of wind, carried a tongue of flame to the residence. Almost cautiously the orange-red feather settled on the roof, and within the next few moments even our residence was in flames."

"Whether I slept, whether I was numb, I don't know. In the middle of the terrible heat I felt how two male arms picked me up and carried me away. He ran with me and gasped. I could hardly hold onto his leather jacket. It was not Abrão. It was a foreign smell. Next to an olive tree he let me slide down onto the grass.

"'You'll be safe here,' said Luiz, my son Luiz. Then he nudged me with his foot: 'I'll come and get you later.'

"For the entire next day and an additional night I remained lying there next to the olive tree. There was buzzing and pounding in my head, but I could move my arms and my legs. On the second day I crawled in the direction of our house, in the direction of the Braga farm. Threads of smoke curled into the air. Fine ashes lay everywhere, ashes that were still warm. Everything was destroyed, even the residence. Timbers jutted half burned into the air. Individual pieces of furniture, our bed and the chest of drawers in Abrão's writing room were in their places as always, but now partially under the open sky.

"Coachmen and stable workers pushed litters past me. People who didn't move were laid on those litters. Finally I saw the cabinet with the inlaid roses. It stood a few steps away from me. There, in that cabinet, the wooden box with the book by António Vieira was kept, and without paying any attention to the shouts, 'Don't! You'll break through! The ashes are hot!' I ran and stumbled toward the cabinet.

"The leather of my shoes hissed. I tore at the cabinet. The drawers were already open, the doors, too. But my screaming into the dark spaces in the cabinet was of no use. The wooden box with the Vieira book was no longer there! The silverware and the onyx inkbottle were also missing. All that was not important.

"The book with the sermons of António Vieira had disappeared, burned, or someone had taken it with him. *Saudade* is written on the first page of the book. Many hundreds of pages are filled with writing in blood-red ink. António Vieira, that priest who languished in Rome in 1670, almost two hundred years ago, and almost died of *saudade*, had written that book, the letters, and the sermons. At the age of seventy-eight he had sailed from Europe back to Brazil, to Salvador. 'When this book is no longer in our family, the Bragas will cease to be, the Braga family will cease to exist.'"

Graça pauses. "The book disappeared," she murmurs.

She opens her hands, stares at the half-scarred palms and fingers: "I wanted to find it. I dug in the ashes, in the coals, and I didn't find it."

When she notices Maria Glória's gaze focused on her wounds, she smiles: "No, these wounds don't hurt. Later perhaps, when tears flow, then these bulges will become soft and break open, and that will hurt. Everything is seared and hardened, so many years, and it seems to me that I said good-by to you yesterday in Brest."

She continues to talk: "In the residence, many of those who had stormed our dining room perished. The beams had broken, walls had collapsed, and the people were trapped inside. Even Abrão and Luiz, my son Luiz, they couldn't escape into the open. All dead.

"For me there was nothing more to do. I stowed my possessions in Leão's bag. Then I went to Mother Ines in the convent. I stayed there for a few weeks, and when I became calmer inside, I had the letter written to you.

"Maria Glória, I wanted to see you, to hear your voice. What it sounds like when you tell about your last nineteen years."

They are both exhausted. They have entrusted their years to each other and will now, separately, go their ways.

"...*because our soul will never be quite hardened enough for a good-by. We could not stand that. We do not want to think about that. Good-by, never! Until by and by, see you soon...*"

With her embrace Graça passes on all her warmth and softness. She has an overabundance of them, and Maria Glória partakes of them - the child, the woman, and the sister, the friend Maria Glória. Graça had always been the stronger one. She is also the stronger one now. She puts Maria Glória back on her trail, reaches for her travel bag, and goes. She clears the way, the view.

Now everything has been cleaned up, the characters distributed, each character led to the right continent, Maria and Glória. Eulalia comes toward the stone bench: "Dona Maria, you should come back to *Necessidade*. You must not leave the house anymore. The shaking in the coach will harm you," she says, trying to persuade the woman in the linen dress. Eulalia helps Dona Maria up, supports her, and leads her to the coach.

Everything is ready. The one woman, the one who is pursued by the Furies, confides in Eulalia. She has not permitted herself to omit anything. She has organized the letters, does not owe any minister, any official an answer, a signature. The currency and the certificates of indebtedness have been pressed smooth, the servants taken care of. For the children, for Pedro, Luís, João, Maria Anna, Antonia, Fernando, and Augusto, the principles for their education have been written down: "All areas of knowledge are to be studied, but the science of subtle hypocrisy is to be rejected and despised. They have to practice and examine themselves constantly in their respect for their neighbor, in the fulfillment of their duties."

The other woman follows behind Graça, runs ahead of her. The dress made of organzine silk, which she has not felt on her body for two decades, brushes across the dried-out November grass. Hand in hand with the two children, Leopoldo and little Maria Glória, she walks past giant ferns and waterfalls, down the winding path. These children are recorded in the baptismal book as dead, and yet they have just waited for her here. Quickly down to the harbor. There the third child is waiting, with whom she will entrust herself to the ocean in two days. "*In order to arrive at love, each person must go through his own hell,*" and she has gone the entire way. Her hair curls again into little curls, and the ribbon in her hair is green and yellow, jungle and gold. The blue of the Bahia topazes, the blue of her ocean, she will let herself be borne with the children across those waves, with Belem, Lisbon long ago behind her. This ocean knows her direction, and she will reach springtime before Graça. In November the jasmine blossoms open, and the hummingbirds dip deeply into the paradise flowers and buzz around hibiscus blossoms. Walk through the avenue with the cashew trees and draw in the fragrance of the orange-golden fruits. Break a white and yellow blossom from a mango tree, run up the red and dusty road to the house at *Boa Vista*. Briefly stop for the time that it takes to take a few breaths and draw in the sweetness and heaviness of the air. The parrots cry. Finally to throw herself toward the tropical light and to make herself at home and settle there: "I have come back. I have finally come back."

The quotes are taken from the "Lusiaden" — "Os Lusíadas" by Luís Camões (1524-1580).

AFTERWORD

If we tell the story of Maria II of Portugal, it seems to be an easy, worry-free venture, for only a little was written about her. There is no multiplicity of biographies that lure the researcher into a thicket of enthusiasm or into undergrowth of accusation and indictment and there divert his gaze from correspondence, diplomatic reports, and diary entries.

So wasn't this life interesting enough to be told? Did it lack the internal tension that is necessary to form a special character? Did it murmur tepidly and in an average way so that one could summarize: born, lived, died, baptismal candle, bridal wreath, funeral flowers?

Nothing like that.

However, the special things in this story cannot be read from two or three prominent vantage points between which the entire drama of life lined up, for the era of Maria II was not shaken politically by *one*, by *the* revolution that changed the spiritual life of all of Europe. Politically, the two decades of Maria II were characterized by almost uninterrupted revolts and revolutions. Fighting, suffering, protesting, and enduring were daily life for the Portuguese and the daily life of Maria II, and those decades of political disruption had to be overcome without help or attention and consideration from the rest of Europe - which perhaps carries more weight.

Even in the private life of Maria II, big events, scandals are missing, but there were many little, evil intrigues and tricks against which she was not able to protect herself, even with her plea to Heaven: "God protect me from intrigues." Her life was not ended by the executioner's hand or through the coincidence of tragic circumstances - Maria II died in bed.

As if fate wanted to counterpoint the adult life of Maria Glória clearly and blatantly, she is initially placed on her path quite lovingly. In December of 1826 Dona Leopoldina dies. Maria Glória is not quite eight years old and with the death of her mother she is forcibly evicted from the realm of childhood. The years of pampering are past, and after the eight childhood years she is drawn with all vigor through eight years of difficulty. In those eight years snapshots will already reveal what Maria Glória has to live out and endure after her sixteenth year of life, in all its nuances and chords: At the age of seventeen, her stepmother, Dona Amelia, is too immature for her task and develops into a schemer; her father, Dom Pedro, has to abdicate and leave Brazil in 1831. For the twelve-year-old Maria Glória that means having to tear herself away from her siblings, having to leave her Brazilian homeland, and embarking with her father on the voyage into exile. For her new homeland, Portugal, is still closed to them; the Braganças are not wanted in England; they have to be thankful that they are tolerated in France. After two years of waiting in Paris, Maria Glória is finally able to enter Portugal, and after the end of Miguel's terrorism she stands for the new beginning in Portugal. But the wave of enthusiasm that breaks against her is soon followed by skepticism and mistrust. In addition, even during the first encounter with the citizens of Portugal a shadow flares up, a warning sign, as a small delegation of the Azores refugees welcomes Maria Glória separately in a brief, serious gesture. In reality, the conflict with the Azores refugees became a lifelong, difficult task for Maria Glória.

When the death day of her first husband comes, seven days before her sixteenth birthday, her eight years of difficulty are finished. All the veils of minimizations, palliations, and dreams are pulled away, and she is placed on her path, and there she stands alone in a country that she hardly knows.

As reconstructors we do not believe that we can trust the pictures. We guess that there are decades between the one picture with the somewhat sweet face framed in curls and the one with the hair that is tightly pulled back. We look into serious eyes, where the dress is not decorated with any piece of jewelry or any medal. In the first picture Maria Glória is fourteen years old, and in the second, seventeen.

With the corset of fulfillment of duty and discipline tightly laced, Maria Glória lives out the following nineteen years. A queen has to give birth to children in order to make the dynasty, and with it the continuity of the monarchical system, secure, and she has deeds to do that can be read in the history books.

Maria Glória gave birth to eleven children. Four of them died in infancy. As queen she introduced mandatory education in Portugal; she is called Maria II, the Educator, in the history books. She was the founder of the Academy of Fine Arts and the national library. On her initiative colleges for chemistry, pharmacy, and astronomy were established. She supported the building of railroads and the construction of roads. Through the establishment of traffic arteries the remote northern regions were supposed to be connected to Porto, Coimbra, and Lisbon.

Aside from those identifiable deeds, however, above all Maria II stayed the course. Amid the constant back and forth of the political powers she did not abandon her place, and when the pendulum swung from ultraliberal to liberal, to conservative-reactionary, and back to ultraliberal, for the sake of peace she swore to uphold each new constitution. She successfully resisted the interference of Spain, and two years before her death, when civil war again threatened to tear the country apart, she advised her husband, the artistically minded Ferdinand von Sachsen-Coburg-Gotha, who had to march against the ultraliberals as the supreme commander of the Royal Army, to negotiate instead of to fight! With that she avoided bloodshed, and with the accord of September 1851, the phase of renewal, the *Regeneracão*, could begin for Portugal.

We know that a political system can never be as hated as an individual human being. The distress, the poverty, the injustice, and the disappointment need a name, a guilty party - Maria II.

In order to undermine the political system - the constitutional monarchy was too liberal for some, too conservative for the others - the queen had to be attacked. For that reason she was deprived of the veto right and she was soon only a decoration.

When that was not sufficient for the rebels, the human being in Maria II was attacked. They published a pamphlet about a purported love affair of Maria II with a minister. And when all that was still not enough to devalue her impact, her efforts, her opponents had one more trump up their sleeve, with which they could stab, degrade everything: "Maria II is, after all, a foreigner, a Brazilian. How can she hope to understand Portugal and its people?"

Can we call Maria Glória an average character? No, she demonstrated strength; it just did not occur in great actions. But she opposed the sale of the valley bottoms of Lezirias and for that reason, as a fifteen-year-old, insisted almost recklessly on her veto right. She did not flee during the first or during all the subsequent revolutions. She did not tolerate the interference of the English and thereby at least kept the economic dependency within limits. She held her own - and that must be emphasized especially - in the net of intrigues that was woven around her, went her way, and made her decisions without regard to opinions, to suggestions.

Everything happened to Maria Glória ahead of time - she was a half-orphan too soon; she was responsible for her siblings too soon; she had to be separated from her family too soon; her father died too soon; she was proclaimed queen too soon; she was a widow too soon.

Her true self, the deeply hidden one, can be read from the dialogue with the letters of António Vieira and Christina of Sweden. She would surely have liked to decide her own fate as independently and self-confidently as Christina did, but after the years of difficulty she lacked the courage for it.

The inner conflict of wanting to be Portuguese, European, and yet constantly feeling her Brazilian roots, of suffering from *saudade*, ground Maria Glória down. She demanded too much composure of herself; she lived constantly aware of a higher duty and in so doing overlooked the point in time after which everything that she had held back, everything that she had swallowed became too much pressure for her.

People who keep a part of themselves locked away, who constantly command themselves to play the role of the duty-conscious, the smiling person, can gather a reservoir of strength from that disproportion of the visible and the invisible. Those people are exercised in giving orders to themselves; their bodies, their minds are drilled to carry out every command - and when they prepare for the last command, to let go of this life, then that order is usually obeyed by an exhausted spirit, by a weary soul, by a washed-out body.

Maria Glória ordered herself to leave. The life that had been assigned to her finally seemed finished. She also selected for that a very specific day, the name day of her mother, Dona Leopoldina, and died on the 15th of November 1853, five months before completing the thirty-fifth year of her life, during the birth of her eleventh child.

Now all that is left to report is what became of the children and how her husband continued his life.

Fernando, in accordance with Maria Glória's wish and in conformance with the constitution, assumed the regency as titular king of Portugal for two years, until 1855, until the firstborn son Pedro reached his majority. In educating the children he followed the wish of Maria Glória: "The state form of the monarchy is not hostile to the people by nature. Our behavior must be characterized by honesty, conciliatoriness, and benevolence." During the short period of his regency, the son Pedro actually did acquire for himself the appellation of a Citizen King.

Fernando remained the "Artist King" all his life. His patronage encompassed all artistic domains. He endowed scholarships for painters and musicians and gave hundreds of volumes from his private library to the national library. He made his private art collection available for exhibits and he continued to devote himself to his passion, architecture. Through his efforts many old buildings, castles, and monasteries were revitalized, and thereby treasures of Portuguese architecture were saved from ruin. Pena Castle in Sintra is only one example of that.

As a father Fernando had to suffer a series of vicissitudes. In the year 1859, the typhoid fever epidemic first snatched away his daughter-in-law, the wife of his firstborn son Pedro, Stefanie von Hohenzollern, at the age of twenty-two years. Two years later, his son Pedro, the twenty-four-year-old king of Portugal, died of typhoid fever. A few months later in that year of 1861, the nineteen-year-old João and the fifteen-year-old Fernando also died of typhoid fever.

After the deaths of these three of his seven children, after this catastrophe in his life, Fernando withdrew more and more into private life. The relationship with the singer Margarita Löwenberg-Hensler was surely a comfort to him. It gave comfort and certainly support to him as well, when they offered him, the humanist, the moderate, art-minded German, the crown of Greece in 1862. Fernando declined.

In the year 1868 he was offered the crown of Spain, and Fernando also declined that offer. The Spanish diplomats did not want to accept that refusal. They reacted angrily to his inflexibility, especially to the fact that in an official letter he bluntly discussed Spain's intentions, which he had obviously seen through: "That could mean preparation for the union of the two peoples, of Portugal and Spain, to form a single nation! I, however, shall never perform an act that could bring that idea to realization!"

The speculating and urging on Spain's part did not stop until Fernando married Margarita in 1869. Although the title of Countess of Edla had been conferred upon her even before the wedding, the fact of the morganatic marriage still existed, and with that Fernando was no longer eligible to be the king of Spain.

After the wedding Fernando devoted himself entirely and finally to the arts, to his passion for collecting, and to traveling.

The four remaining children maintained cordial contact with him. Luís, the second-born son, who was married to Maria Pia of Savoy, reigned as King of Portugal until 1889. The daughter Maria Anna married Friedrich August von Sachsen and Antonia married Leopold von Hohenzollern. She had inherited the artistic nature of her father. She painted watercolors, played the piano with the maturity of a concert pianist, and she, too, promoted artists. The youngest son, Augusto, remained unmarried, lived as a private scholar, and wrote scientific works on botany and ornithology.

When Fernando died in Lisbon in December of 1885, they wrote in the newspaper: "A foreigner by birth, he was able to identify with the interests of Portugal like the best Portuguese."

The monarchy was ended violently in Portugal in 1908 by the shooting assassination of the grandson Carlos. In 1912 the republic was proclaimed, and with that all hope was placed in a new Portugal once again.

Half Portuguese, half Austrian, completely Brazilian, *saudade* formed Maria Glória into a special person. She lived the qualities of fulfillment of duty and constancy, as well as tenacity. She lived *saudade*, love for the past, love and pain about what has been lost, about being uprooted. She lived with it without complaining, without appealing for help from the public for her inner sorrow; and with those qualities she shines out far above the crowd of honorable daughters of her century.

TRANSLATOR'S AFTERWORD

Although only the most recent of Gloria Kaiser's historical novels about the imperial family of Brazil bears the title *Saudade*, a rigorous comparison of the three works reveals that the Portuguese term, with all of its implications of longing, fond remembrance, melancholy, intense sorrow, and unfulfilled desire, might well provide a point of departure for interpreting and understanding not only the story of Maria Glória, Queen Maria II of Portugal, but also the stories of her brother, Pedro II of Brazil, and her mother, Dona Leopoldina, the Habsburg Empress of Brazil. In the prologue to her account of the life of Maria Glória, Kaiser imbues *saudade* with characteristics of yearning "for contact, for congeniality of temperament, [...] for that spot of earth from which we have grown, for our homeland," or for "the lost paradise," and also describes it as "the wish to regain something, to see something again, and the pain caused by what is absent, the unattainable, the pain caused by want." (p. 6) With respect to these factors and the other ideas that the author associates with the word in the course of the novel, *saudade* is obviously an important key to Maria Glória's view of and interaction with her adopted Portuguese world. But it also concretely ties her inner experiences to those of a mother whose fate removed her from the land of her childhood and cut her off from parents, siblings, and former friends, and to those of a brother who was ultimately forced by the circumstances of the times to go into exile and leave behind everything that formed his life.

As developed within the novel about Maria Glória's life, the theme of *saudade* is employed by the author in an interesting way to emphasize the duality of the central character's nature. According to the narrator, the figures who discuss the concept within the context of the story, and the writings of António Vieira, whose repeated voice constantly brings the account back into focus, *saudade* is an emotion that is peculiarly Portuguese, albeit related to less powerful feelings that are made manifest in other cultures. By presenting *saudade* as a key force in the development of Maria Glória's inner life,

Kaiser emphasizes almost ironically the Portuguese dimension of her character, while simultaneously projecting the image of the queen against a world that rejects her as an outsider who cannot understand the Portuguese people. On the other hand, the clear narrative revelation that the young woman's *saudade* is focused upon the truly meaningful things that she has lost in leaving the world of her origins highlights with even greater force the eternally Brazilian part of her being.

The duality of her nature is further underscored by the juxtaposition of the memories of her experiences with the account given by the Brazilian servant Graça of a life lived parallel to but largely apart from that of the queen. Like Maria Glória, Graça lives a life in Portugal that is informed by the experience of *saudade*. Thus she also struggles with problems of isolation, distance from the world of her childhood, the necessity to adapt to a foreign culture with which she remains in conflict, and intense longing for people, places, and relationships that belong to a past that can never be reclaimed. And like Maria Glória, she is motivated and enabled to endure the separation from her native origins only by a sense of duty that binds her to the reality into which she has entered, without hope of being released to return to that other world until every demand of her duty has been satisfied. For Graça, as for Maria Glória, *saudade* is the very essence of the tension that exists between her Portuguese persona - embodied for the Indian woman in her role as Senhora Braga, the wife of the Portuguese silk farmer - and her identity as a Brazilian who remains a product of her origins. By intertwining the stories of the two women, Kaiser successfully reinforces the notion that *saudade* is the key to a duality that cannot be dissolved for either Maria Glória or Graça until harmony between them and their external world is restored. In Graça's case that restoration occurs with her physical return to Brazil; for Maria Glória it happens only in the author's portrayal of a spiritual return to Brazil that is triggered by and follows her death.

It is interesting to note that in a more general sense, Kaiser's employment of the *saudade* motif enables her to reclaim and refurbish for a literary work of the 21st century a major focus of German literature from an earlier movement. By consciously associating the "word that crosses only Lusitanian lips" with profound longing for "the lost paradise" in the prologue to the novel (p. 6), the author establishes a clear literary connection between the experiences of her characters and the yearning for a lost idyllic world, a lost golden age, a realm of forgotten natural harmony, which is an important hallmark in the writings of the German Romantics. In that respect, it is especially significant that for the two women, Maria Glória and Graça, the beckoning memories of the Brazilian homeland do not focus most readily upon scenes from urban life in Rio de Janeiro, but upon images of deeply felt ties to nature, upon the diversity of vibrant shades of green in the primeval forest, upon the richness of color found in the native flowers, plants, and red earth, upon hummingbirds, cashew trees, topazes, and coffee beans. And taken within the context of the description of new lives experienced in the foreign European context, these images of memory become a significant part of a powerful contemporary treatment of the dynamic existential tension between nature and culture, an important theme in not only German Romantic literature, but also European literature as a whole.

It is not only the relationship between Kaiser's treatment of *saudade* and typical 19th-century literary explorations of Romantic longing, however, that ties her most recent novel to the historical mainstream of literature written in German. Although it is clearly a historical novel, *Saudade* also exhibits characteristics of the *Bildungsroman*, the novel of educational development that became a staple of German narrative literature with the appearance of Johann Wolfgang von Goethe's *Wilhelm Meister* novels and remained a key literary form for the Romantics, the Realists, and many significant German language writers of the 20th century.

The process of educational development that is presented in the *Wilhelm Meister* narratives - which can be regarded as models for the German *Bildungsroman* - has two major aspects. On one level, it is a seemingly random process of self-education, in which the title figure sets out to realize his personal development goals by learning essential lessons through experience gained from his encounters with the world. On another level, however, his education is influenced by outside forces - the mysterious Society of the Tower in *Wilhelm Meisters Lehrjahre* and the Community of Renunciation in *Wilhelm Meisters Wanderjahre* - whose contributions to his development derive from the application of specific educational principles.

To a greater or lesser degree, this same duality of educational process is present in all three of Gloria Kaiser's historical novels about members of the Brazilian imperial family. Like Wilhelm Meister, the title figures of *Dona Leopoldina* and *Pedro II of Brazil* and the central character of *Saudade* are moved by their personalities and circumstances to embark on educational journeys in which individual and often seemingly random and unanticipated experience becomes a singularly important teacher. One significant lesson, for example, that Kaiser's female protagonists learn through personal encounters with their respective realities is what it actually means to be a woman in a traditionally patriarchal world. At least equally important, however, for each of Kaiser's main characters is the role played by outside forces in their education. The training that is imposed upon them is also dual in nature. Important general elements are a product of established traditions pertaining to social role and are mediated by somewhat interchangeable governesses, ladies-in-waiting, teachers, and tutors. At the same time, specific principles that have the potential to separate the three prospective rulers from the traditional pattern and cause them to become more enlightened than others of similar station are given to them by special individuals whose impact is greater in many respects than that of their tradition-oriented educators. For Dona Leopoldina and her son Pedro II, that figure is José Bonifácio de Andrada; for Maria Glória it is the Brazilian priest from an earlier century, António Vieira, whose writings influence not only her decisions and her view of the world, but those of her equally Brazilian counterpart within the tumultuous Portuguese society, Graça.

One thing that is particularly interesting about the manner in which the two-fold educational process contributes to the development of Kaiser's characters is the ultimate result. It makes of them educators in their own right. It causes Dona Leopoldina to record maxims and rules of behavior that are to be applied in the training of her children. It makes of Pedro II a man who would rather be a teacher or a librarian than Emperor of Brazil. It causes Maria Glória, like her mother, to write prescriptions for her children's education, as well as to promote compulsory public education and to establish institutions of higher learning. In that sense, Maria Glória becomes a culminating symbol for the educational process as the basis for enlightenment and progress - Maria II, the Educator.

The process of educational development as a central theme is only one of many elements in the novel *Saudade* that enable it to transcend normal expectations for historical fiction and assume a measure of the timelessness that is characteristic of enduring literature. What educated reader, for example, does not recognize in the black and gray "uniforms" worn by the brutal and opportunistic followers of the tyrant Miguel a reflection of the 20th-century German experience? And who cannot equate the relationship between Maria Glória and her scheming stepmother Amelia or the young girl's dream of marrying her own "Prince Charming" Augusto with situations portrayed in the fairytales of the Brothers Grimm? Such connections underscore, if nothing else, the eternally powerful ties between true literature and the world of our own lives.

Does that mean that we should regard *Saudade* as a novel that employs historical figures and situations from another culture and century to come to grips with realities of the Nazi era in Europe, or as a new, but somewhat tragic version of a fairytale like *Cinderella*?

No, but once upon a time...

Lowell A. Bangerter

CHRONOLOGY

Maria Glória (Maria II, The Educator)

April 4, 1819	Birth of Maria Glória Joana Leopoldina Gabriela Rafaela in Rio de Janeiro, *Boa Vista Castle*; she is the first child of Dona Leopoldina, Habsburg Princess (1797-1826) and Pedro of Bragança (1798-1834).
Sept. 7, 1822	Brazil's declaration of independence.
May 26, 1824	Birth of Isabel, Duchess of Goias, in Rio de Janeiro, (child of Pedro's mistress).
Dec. 11, 1826	Death of Dona Leopoldina in Rio de Janeiro.
October 1829	Arrival of Amelia von Leuchtenberg-Beauharnais (1812-1873) in Rio de Janeiro, second wife of Pedro I, stepmother of Maria Glória.
April 7, 1831	Pedro I must abdicate as Emperor of Brazil; he travels into exile in Europe with his wife Amelia and Maria Glória.
July 1831	Arrival of the Bragança family in Brest; they journey on to Paris.
January 1832	Pedro Bragança travels to the Azores and together with the Azores emigrants forms an army to overthrow the Miguel dictatorship in Portugal.
June 1833	Pedro liberates Portugal from the Miguel regime; Miguel is placed in Evora under house arrest.
August 1833	Maria Glória travels from Paris to Lisbon.
May 25, 1834	Miguel is banished from Portugal and withdraws to Germany.
Sept. 9, 1834	Duke Pedro of Bragança (Pedro I) dies in Lisbon; Maria Glória is named Queen Maria II of Portugal.
March 6, 1835	Marriage to Duke August (Augusto) Eugen Napoleon of Leuchtenberg-Beauharnais (1810-1835).
March 28, 1835	Husband Augusto dies.
September 1835	Maria Glória exercises her veto in the state council against the sale of the Lezirias river bottoms.
October 1835	First newspaper, *O País*, appears.
November 1835	First public compulsory school.

January 1, 1836	Marriage by proxy to Ferdinand (Fernando) August Franz Sachsen-Coburg-Gotha (1816-1885).
September 1836	First revolt against the moderate *Carta Constitutional*, Maria Glória loses her veto right.
Sept. 16, 1837	Birth of the first son, Pedro Rafael Gabriel.
October 1837	Opening of the Royal Library, the Academy of Fine Arts, the Institutes of Chemistry, Pharmacy, and the observatory in Lisbon.
October 1838	Dom Fernando purchases the *Convent of Our Lady of Pena* in Sintra; beginning of the remodeling into a castle.
Oct. 31, 1838	Birth of the son Luís Filippe.
April 4, 1840	Birth of the daughter Maria; she dies three days later.
March 16, 1842	Birth of the son João Gregorio.
July 27, 1843	Birth of the daughter Maria Anna.
Feb. 17, 1845	Birth of the daughter Antonia Michaela.
August 1845	Franz Liszt's visit to Lisbon.
July 23, 1846	Birth of the son Fernando Francisco.
June 1847	Conflict with England (England's involvement to end the permanent civil wars and revolts in Portugal).
Nov. 4, 1847	Birth of the son Augusto Carlos.
June 1848	Publication in London of the pamphlet about the purported love affair of Maria Glória (Queen Maria II) and Minister António Costa Cabral.
May 10, 1849	Birth of the son Leopoldo; he dies after birth.
Feb. 19, 1851	Birth of the daughter little Maria Glória; she dies after the birth.
October 1851	End of the revolts and revolutionary battles through negotiations between Dom Fernando and General Saldanha - beginning of the *Regeneracão* - renewal in Portugal.
Nov. 15, 1853	Birth of the daughter Eugénie; the child dies immediately; Maria Glória - Queen Maria II, The Educator (*Maria II a Educadora*) dies at the birth of this child.